Wickett's Remedy

ALSO BY MYLA GOLDBERG

Bee Season
Time's Magpie

Wickett's Remedy

A NOVEL

MYLA GOLDBERG

DOUBLEDAY

New York London Toronto
Sydney Auckland

PUBLISHED BY DOUBLEDAY
a division of Random House, Inc.

DOUBLEDAY and the portrayal of an anchor with a dolphin are registered
trademarks of Random House, Inc.

Book design by rlf design

Library of Congress Cataloging-in-Publication Data
Goldberg, Myla.
  Wickett's remedy / Myla Goldberg.—1st ed.
    p.   cm.
1. Irish American women—Fiction. 2. Influenza epidemic, 1918–1919—
Fiction. 3. Patent medicines—Fiction. 4. Boston (Mass.)—Fiction.
5. Widows—Fiction. I. Title.
  PS3557.O35819W53 2004
  813'.54—dc22

                                        2005048103

ISBN 0-385-51324-0

PRINTED IN THE UNITED STATES OF AMERICA
October 2005
First Edition
10 9 8 7 6 5 4 3 2 1

For Jason

Wickett's Remedy

On D Street there was no need for alarm clocks: the drays, ever punctual, were an army storming the gates of sleep. The wooden wagons were heavy and low-riding with loud rattling wheels, their broad planks too battered and begrimed to recall distant origins as trees. Each dray was pulled by horses—two, four, or sometimes six per wagon—pounding down nearby Third Street. Windows rattled and floors shook; the sound was a giant hand shaking Lydia Kilkenny's sleeping shoulders. Each morning she did not awaken to the sound, but inside it. In winter the drays came when the sky was still dark, their pounding hooves sharp reports against the frozen cobblestones. In summer, perhaps because the sky was already pale with light, the sound of the horses seemed kinder.

When her daughter was still a wee thing, Cora Kilkenny recalls Liddie crediting the sound to God waking up all the good Catholics of D Street.

She knew the clattering wagons were bound for Boston proper, but the vague tangle of streets across the Broadway bridge surfaced in her mind with the sound of the horses and resubmerged with its diminishment. As the flow of drays subsided—the wagons no longer traveling two by two but single file—pounding hooves gave way to the creak of floorboards and the muffled voices of neighbors. Factory whistles blew.

Church bells rang. The vegetable man made his way down D Street shouting, "Fresh tomatoes," even if there were no tomatoes, because those words distinguished him from the other vegetable men who plied their carts through Southie.

As Lydia stirred, her mother put up water for cocoa and oatmeal. By the time Lydia had the little ones dressed, Michael and their father had finished their morning ablutions and the washbasin was hers alone. By the time she had brushed and pinned her hair, the drays were gone. Indeterminate Boston had once again been vanquished by the certainty of Southie.

South Boston belonged to Lydia as profoundly and wordlessly as her thimble finger. Her knowledge of its streets was more complete than any atlas, her mental maps reflecting changes that occurred from season to season, day to day, and hour to hour. Each time she left 28 D Street—one among a row of identical triple-decker tenements lining the street like so many stained teeth—her route reflected this internal almanac. If on a Tuesday afternoon her mother wanted flour and jam from Hennessy's, Lydia would avoid the more direct route along Fifth Street due to her dislike of the soap grease man and his fleshy block of laundry soap. No matter what the errand, Third Street was best avoided in early evening when the flood tide of drays returning to their stables posed a threat to both body and nose.

In deep winter, when ice and hard-packed snow made walking treacherous, West Broadway was the place to catch a ride on the tailboard of a snow dray delivering milk, groceries, or beer, but sledding was best saved for Dorchester Heights. If a good enough sled could be found, and if the streets were not too crowded, it was possible to start at G Street and traverse almost a quarter of the alphabet—all the way to L Street. Whether because he was luckier or a year older, Michael was the superior sledder; at her best Lydia could only make J Street before her sled or her resolve gave out.

Jamie remembers the warm press of his sister's hands as she lifted him from bed and set him down beside the clothes she had waiting for him, the sound of the horses rattling inside his head like loose marbles.

Because Dan Kilkenny was an iceman, the whole D Street gang was in thrall to Lydia and Michael in summer. In the thick of that season there were few things more magical than ice—the blocks that emerged, impossibly, from the back of the wagon, steaming not with heat but with cold, the unmistakable stomp of the iceman conquering the stairwell, gleaming blocks of ice piled on his broad back like enormous melting diamonds. Contrary to Father O'Brian's Sunday descriptions of a place streaming with light and angel song, Lydia was certain Heaven resembled the interior of her father's ice wagon: a dark place, cool and quiet. There the salt hay, sawdust, and straw effaced the airborne tang of leather and glue from the nearby shoe factory and muted the call of the ragman.

On very hot days there was no need to confer in advance. The lot of them would be playing ball in Commonwealth Park, or ambling toward the beach at City Point, or playing marbles or Kick the Wicket on the street. Without a word Michael would turn to Lydia, or she toward him, and with a whoop they would preempt the day's pursuit and set out for ice. At the sight of Dan Kilkenny's brood, the iceman would toss out an extra block, the surplus ice arcing toward the street in a dream of captured light before exploding into frozen bliss on the cobbles. Decorum was traded for the fleeting comfort of ice pressed into the perfect place. Frozen shatterings found their way into mouths, inside shirts and dresses, under chins, and atop closed eyes. Ice was nestled into the hollows of throats and hammocked by the webbing between fingers and toes. Ice bent the iron rule of summer for a few precious moments before the heat clamped down again.

For ten years, this was enough. Then in fifth grade, Lydia saw a city map and realized her entire world was the smallest finger of Boston's broad hand. The hazy destination of the morning drays acquired focus. Across the bridge lay Boston

Had Margaret Kelly, of 32 D Street, claimed an iceman for her da, she would not have been so lordly about it. Liddie and Mick always waited until the worst of the heat and then made them line up for Indian knuckle burns before bringing them down the right street.

[3]

Common and the swan boats of the Public Garden. Across the bridge lay Washington Street—the longest street in all New England—which began like any other but then continued south, a single, determined thread of cobblestone that wove itself through every town from Boston to Providence. Once Lydia saw Washington Street she knew she could not allow it to exist without her.

She had imagined Washington wide like West Broadway but instead it was narrower, its buildings taller. On Washington, men in blazers and boaters strutted three and four abreast and bustled women drifted cloudlike between shop-windows. The air on Washington smelled neither of factories nor piers but of occasional cigar smoke and wafting perfume. The buildings—with their marble façades and grand entranceways and their seemingly endless layers of arched windows—resembled fancy wedding cakes. On Washington Street there was not a clothesline in sight, not a single vegetable or fish man. Striped awnings stretched proudly above showcases containing objects Southie had never seen: a silk opera gown with black glass buttons, a set of tortoiseshell combs, a rocking horse with a mane of real hair. Lydia turned toward Michael—whose trolley fare she had provided from a cache of saved pennies, their passage across the Broadway bridge her eleventh birthday present to herself—and announced that this was her future.

Mick recalls only his disappointment. Before Liddie went gaga over Washington Street, they had always pooled their copper for penny fudge.

On graduating eighth grade, when her girlfriends found jobs behind sewing machines, Lydia rode to Washington Street alone and procured a position in the stockroom of Gilchrist's department store. Now every morning she had to wake before the drays in order to make the streetcar. During dreary hours of inventory and reshelving, her resolve to work on the far side of the bridge would falter, but her doubts vanished whenever she was called onto the gleaming sales floor.

[4]

Walking among the wonders of the display rooms, she would calculate the weeks of salary required to purchase a beaded French chapeau or the impossible amount of roast ham that could be eaten in lieu of one opal earring. Rather than discouraging her, these extreme calculations bred optimism. Once she was promoted to sales, she hoped eventually to save enough so that she too could point to one of those fantastical objects and have it delivered into her outstretched hand.

Michael joked that his sister rode the streetcar every day to make up for never having outdistanced him on a sled. Though he was as immune as the rest of the family to the forces that drew her to Washington Street, he formulated a theory to explain the aberration.

"I don't know how it came to be," he informed her once it became clear she would not be abandoning her streetcar commute, "but it looks like you turned out the migrating bird in a family of pigeons." Lydia treasured his gift, picturing herself as she rode the streetcar as one of the long-necked geese whose silhouettes she observed angling south in late autumn.

On the other side of the bridge, Lydia learned the difference between a heavy tub silk and a crepe de chine shirt and the relative merits of a Norfolk versus a sacque suit. She learned that the best suit jackets were nipped in at the waist and slope-shouldered. When a counter girl was fired for tardiness, Lydia was ready. She claimed the sales floor for herself.

For four years she worked behind a lustrous wood counter on the store's ground level, amid polished marble floors and hanging crystal lamps. Gilchrist's Tiffany rotunda gazed down from three levels above like an emerald eye. Inside her starched, white shirtwaist, her hair piled into a careful bun, she felt as if her best self lurked just beneath her skin, a shimmery fish that might breach the surface at any moment. Standing before a selection of men's shirts in a dazzling array of

Maisie French, in Collars, insists the Tiffany rotunda was blue, not green.

colored fabric, she could eye a man's collar size, budget, and tastes in a glance and knew, just by looking, the thread count of a cotton shirt or the origins of a piece of silk.

Even after four years, she thrilled at sealing a customer's payment into a pneumatic capsule and sending it to the cashier for change. Miles and miles of pneumatic tubing crisscrossed Gilchrist's walls and ceilings. Capsules left Men's Furnishings on a current of compressed air to travel over Silks and Velvets, over Embroideries and Trimmings, past Veilings, and past Black and Colored Dress Goods. Lydia pictured her customers' sales slips speeding past counter girls whispering among themselves in Millinery, past the solitary salesgirl at Umbrellas who every day prayed for rain.

Lydia once visited the Cashier's Office just to see the veritable pipe organ of commerce where each capsule arrived with a thunk, its contents scrutinized by a woman whose hands were bound to smell like money. Lydia wondered if the woman scrubbed the scent from her fingers each night, or if her dreams wafted with visions of wealth. Whenever Lydia retrieved a returning capsule containing a customer's correct change, she felt the cold, dry breath of the tube tickle the back of her hand. On slow days she hearkened to Gilchrist's pneumatic exhalations. After four years, she still marveled at the notion that money pumped through the store no less fervently than the blood in her veins.

The morning of Lydia's first lunch with a customer, she had been standing with her back to the sales floor straightening stock when her attention was redirected by a neighboring counter girl, who whispered Lydia's name once the gentleman had been standing a few moments unattended. The fellow was impressively dressed for someone so clearly uncomfortable in his own skin. His clothing seemed to subsume rather than enhance his form, as if his legs were no match for worsted wool, his chest unequal to the task of imported linen. Though he was a striking man, Lydia was reminded of a child dressed with care by his mother.

"How may I help you?" she asked, having already determined his measurements. She intended to skip straight to silk unless cotton was specifically requested, and then only cambric would do; Fridays were slow and the hardest days in which to meet her sales quota.

"Oh, but you see, you already have helped me," the man stammered. "I wanted to thank you. The shirt you sold me? My mother liked it very much."

"Of course!" Lydia lied with professional zeal. She racked her brain for a memory of the sale; normally she was good with faces. "I suppose you've come for another shirt," she offered. "I've just the thing. We received the shipment this week from Italy—they're brand new for the season. I'm sure you'll appreciate the quality." She hoped to convince him to buy two.

The gentleman shook his head and looked at Lydia with such regret she wondered if she had insulted him, though she could not imagine anyone taking offense at an Italian shirt.

"Ah no," he replied with a quavering sigh. "Thanks all the same, but I don't intend to make any purchase today." He was blushing with unusual violence. "I was hoping I might accompany you to lunch. To thank you. You see, my mother really did like the shirt and she is so often hard to please. You were very kind and patient, and I thought it was the least I could do."

"You want to take me to lunch?" Lydia echoed.

"To thank you," the fellow repeated. Though he appeared to be in his twenties, he had the demeanor of a much older man. "For your assistance. That is, if you're permitted?" With her silence, his blush returned. "I've never done anything like this before," he mumbled. "I'm sorry. I haven't even introduced myself. My name is Henry Wickett. You can be certain of my good intentions, and if my motives prove unseemly you

Maisie does not blame Lydia for forgetting her name, as they were not particular friends—but she thinks Lydia's memory has been awfully kind to Henry Wickett. If the fellow had been a looker, Maisie would have helped him herself.

Henry had not intended to speak at all. Recalling the young woman in Shirts, he had hoped only to observe her from afar. Finding her unengaged, he had approached without thinking.

And here the gentle lie of Lydia's memory is revealed, for had Henry's features been distinctive she would not have forgotten them. Vision is memory at its most fickle. It is practically impossible to retain the homeliness of unfamiliar features once they have grown dear.

Henry credits his uncharacteristic boldness to the obvious pleasure the young woman in Shirts took in even the smallest aspects of her work. Such élan could not be purchased, even at Gilchrist's.

could easily wallop me yourself." By this time the fellow's voice had grown so soft Lydia could barely hear him above the bustle of the store.

Lydia scanned the floor for the manager, but Miss Palantine so seldom left her desk that she had been dubbed "Her Royal Boulder." There were rumors Miss Palantine had been barred from sales after an incident in which she had tearfully but with some force thrown a ladies shoe at the head of a male customer after a heated exchange in Neckties. It was difficult for Lydia to imagine the drab, officious Palantine involved in passionate discourse of any sort, but then she had also been shocked to learn that Her Royal Boulder was not a spinster in her thirties, but merely twenty-three.

Invitations from customers were uncommon but not unheard of; it was not technically improper to take lunch elsewhere so long as one did not return late. Until now Lydia's curiosity had been tempered by her refusal to be an object of pity or lust. Such intent was absent in Henry Wickett who, true to his own appraisal, looked far easier to fend off than the Southie boys she had, on occasion, needed to put in their place.

"I haven't got time for a proper lunch," she replied, "but I won't say no if you don't mind being quick about it." Never had consent garnered her so sweet a smile.

As well as she knew Washington Street, she was a stranger to its early afternoon habits: Gilchrist's was a creature that inhaled its personnel in the morning and held its breath until evening. Among the businessmen and lady shoppers Lydia was revisited by the feeling, birthed by her girlhood visits, that she had arrived at the center of things. After years of close observation she had perfected her bearing. She walked with the ideal combination of confidence and propriety, and held her chin at just the right angle. The appeal of this lunch invitation, she realized, lay in walking in such a fashion and in such com-

Walking beside Lydia, Henry felt as if he were on parade. She moved like a living, breathing portent of Spring.

[8]

pany. Having studied the world of Washington Street for so long, she could now display her erudition.

Timeliness demanded she elect Monty's, a salaryman's lunchroom convenient to the store, but once inside she wished that she and her lunch date might have promenaded longer. Monty's was a noisy place that smelled of boiled beef. Its counter was overhung with stooped diners abridging as much as possible the distance between mouth and plate. A harried plug of a man in a stained apron served as cook, waiter, and cashier and was adept at none. At the sight of Lydia Kilkenny and Henry Wickett he gestured dismissively at the restaurant's few tables. Lydia selected one in the front corner that offered a view of the street. With her back to the restaurant she could imagine she was dining in more genteel circumstances.

"It's not much to look at," she apologized, "but I hear the food's decent. Anything fancier and I'd risk being late."

"Please order anything you like," Henry Wickett urged. As they waited to place their orders he concentrated on his flatware, displaying the absorption of a child immersed in a private game. She waited for him to speak; she was uncertain what sort of topics gentlemen discussed over lunch and feared sounding common. At unexpected intervals Henry Wickett darted his head upward—a swimmer gasping for air—and she leaned forward in anticipation of conversation but each time was disappointed: his intention was merely to look at her before blushing and returning his gaze to the table, as if she were some brightly burning thing that could only be glimpsed at intervals.

Henry feared grinning like an idiot if he stared at her any longer.

"It was kind of you to ask me to lunch," she offered. "It's nice to get a bit of air."

"Please don't thank me," he demurred. "I'm afraid you'll find I'm not very good at conversation."

"No?"

"No," he confirmed, and returned his gaze to his fork.

[9]

"Are you a student?" she attempted. Henry Wickett had small, uncallused, unscarred hands marred only by habitual nail-biting. In Southie such unused hands would be cause for embarrassment but here, across the bridge, Lydia viewed them as she might an exotic zoo specimen.

"Yes," he affirmed, his head darting once again upward as if for a lungful of air. "I study medicine. I'm meant to be a doctor. This table is really quite interesting."

"What?" she stammered. The table was filmed with grease and scarred from top to bottom with the names and initials of former diners, details that had previously escaped her notice. Before she could speak, the waiter arrived to take their orders. Her dismay over the state of the table was compounded when, after ordering the daily special for herself, her companion requested only a bowl of chicken broth. "I'm sorry," she sighed. "I suppose this isn't the sort of place you're accustomed to."

"No need for apology!" Henry Wickett exclaimed. His startled hands winged upward and upended his water glass, revealing the surface of the table to be sloped in his direction. One hand enlisted an oversized handkerchief to stop the flow while the other righted the glass. Lydia watched, powerless as a small rivulet escaped blotting and dropped onto Henry Wickett's imported wool trousers.

Henry remembers Lydia spilling the water.

"Oh dear!" she cried, and started up from her chair with her napkin.

"Please don't!" he urged. The water was sopped, the glass righted. Henry Wickett darted a glance in Lydia's direction while his hand furtively blotted his pant leg. "Since childhood I have been allergic to most foods," he explained. He reached for his water glass and brought it to his lips: it was empty. "My stomach is quite sensitive and so in unfamiliar restaurants I order only calming liquids. And as for the table, it reminds me of an oak."

"An oak—" she echoed. She observed her reflection in the

restaurant window for the first time since leaving the store. The starch had left her collar, and the bodice of her shirtwaist was deeply creased from a morning of refolding stock. Her hair had become mussed and dark shadows ringed her eyes. She was grateful her back faced the other diners. The restaurant had become strangely silent since she had risen from her seat.

"Yes!" Henry affirmed, seemingly unconcerned or unaware of their impression on their fellow diners. "The venerable trunk of an oak, carved by generations of courtship beneath its branches—" His eyes widened. "That isn't to say—I didn't mean to imply—" But words failed him. He dabbed vehemently at the water stain on his pant leg.

Their food arrived. According to the restaurant clock she had fifteen minutes in which to eat her meal and return to her counter to avoid being fined for lateness, precluding the possibility of further conversation. By the time she finished her lunch, her companion had taken barely three spoonfuls of soup but insisted he was satisfied. After escorting her to the store's employee entrance he scurried toward the bustle of Washington Street with the single-mindedness of a mouse seeking its mousehole and Lydia assumed that was the last she would see of Henry Wickett.

But in the days that followed, while Lydia rode the trolley or tallied receipts, Henry Wickett's image surfaced in her mind. His unexpected observation—initially forgotten in her embarrassment over spilt water and inelegant dining—now echoed in her memory. "It reminds me of an oak," she would think to herself, and the smaller details of the world would sharpen.

When Henry Wickett reappeared the following Friday and asked her to lunch a second time, she was taken completely by surprise. "Are you sure?" she asked. Though pleased at the chance to refine her first impression, she feared for Henry Wickett's digestion, as well as for his trousers. "We'd have to go to Monty's again."

Memory's egoism is often a kindness. None of Monty's regulars recall this incident.

Henry was too busy watching Lydia eat. This, too, reminded him of a parade. Her every gesture expressed refinement and vivacity.

Once he had lost himself in the crowd, Henry allowed himself to skip, briefly, before becoming winded.

"I've come prepared this time," he replied, and pulled three handkerchiefs from his pocket. Lydia had never laughed inside Gilchrist's before; until now, that pleasure had been relegated to the other side of the bridge. Henry's smile at the sound reminded Lydia how guarded most faces were. Even once the smile passed, she could see its stamp on his face in the small, light lines around the skin of his mouth and eyes, faint ripples that only graced a face that smiled often.

The man behind the grease-stained apron pretended not to recognize them as they reclaimed the same window table. Though Henry's shyness and Lydia's limited time made conversation difficult, she learned her companion was the only son of a Roxbury businessman, his medical school career the family's first chance at claiming a doctor. Henry had few friends, as his studies and uncertain health occupied most of his time. His mother had despaired of his eligibility as a bachelor and hoped his becoming a doctor would compensate for his other failings. Though Henry Wickett tended to keep his eyes downcast, when he spoke he gazed at her with a forthrightness much more common to children than to adults. His openness and gentleness—qualities she was unaccustomed to seeing in young men—convinced her that his motives for seeking her company, while mysterious, were almost certainly not dishonorable. Perhaps Henry Wickett wanted to improve his conversational skills preparatory to whatever future courtship he planned to undertake; perhaps he simply did not like to eat alone. Whatever the reason, she was happy to oblige him. In poignant tones she described to her brothers the poor fellow she had begun accompanying to lunch each Friday, her depiction so woeful that all save Michael assumed an act of charity for a man greatly advanced in age.

The first letter arrived by courier on a Wednesday afternoon. She was certain some mistake had been made, but the messenger's docket read: "To Miss Lydia Kilkenny, Who Works Behind the Shirt Counter in the Gilchrist Department Store." On D Street very occasional letters arrived from a distant cousin in County Cork and Michael had once written to Babe Ruth for an autographed photo, but never in her life had Lydia received an envelope bearing her name. Before an audience of gawking counter girls, she signed for the post with a pale, trembling hand; she was certain only bad news traveled with such pomp. From his pouch the courier withdrew an elegant envelope of cream-colored linen, embossed with a wax seal depicting the silhouette of a bird in flight. The nearest thing to it that Lydia had ever seen was the certificate she had received confirming her successful graduation from the eighth grade. To avoid breaking the wax seal, which seemed too fine a thing to corrupt, she slit the side of the envelope with a hatpin. The words were penned in a clear, elegant hand, in even lines of dark blue ink across a single, powder blue page:

Dearest Lydia,

I am certain you did not expect to hear from me so soon after yet another lunch in which you valiantly carried the day while I sat frozen like some awkward creature made of sticks. Oh Lydia, forgive me, but I have always felt so much more myself on paper. I have ceased to seek reasons for this odd truth: I accept I am a man of letters, my heart filled with ink. If I am to hold any hope of winning you, this is something you must know.

Lydia, I am changed from the poor wretch you took in hand in the Gilchrist's Men's Department six short weeks ago. That man was a trembling creature too overwhelmed by the world to think he might ever carve his own bit of happiness from it, a man resigned to a solitary life lit only by the

Fond repetition is amnesia's adversary. To this day each word of Henry's letter retains its savor.

[13]

lamp of his studies. His desire to help others did not extend to the belief he could help himself—but Lydia, you have changed that. You have revealed a world in which some measure of shared happiness is reserved even for life's humblest creatures, so long as they have the courage to lay claim to it when it comes.

You are my happiness, Lydia. The joy with which you move through the world is infectious, reminding me of the pleasure to be found in even life's smallest facets. Please know as I sit mute and uncompanionable by your side I am silently praising your person and all its fine attributes: even as I write this I am gathering strength for a day when I might speak aloud the thoughts and feelings presently prisoned by the narrow chamber of my pen.

Yours in heart and mind,

Henry Wickett

Her hand began to tremble, forcing her to place the letter on the counter in order to read it again. In demeanor Henry was unchanged from the fellow who had, with such difficulty, first requested her company. And yet the idea of a courtship filled her with a sense of imminence, as if she housed an embryonic chick pecking with its egg tooth against the inner surface of its shell. Henry was different from the D Street boys who took her to the Imperial for the Sunday matinee, or to Castle Island for doughnuts and fried clams—boys with rough hands and loud voices for whom a table was only ever a table and never a tree.

Only now did she admit to herself that for several weeks, unexpected thoughts of Henry Wickett had been finding her. In the middle of a sale, her mind would recall his hopeful smile, or the quiet sincerity with which he spoke, or the mind-

Seeing as she was the cause for the couple's acquaintance, Maisie thinks it stingy of Lydia not once to have read the letter out loud.

For all the good it did him, Liam Dougherty took Liddie on a Sunday picnic where they ate off an actual tree stump.

fulness with which he attended her voice. With Henry's letter, she acknowledged that her thoughts of him had become a melody in the back of her mind, present even when too soft to hear.

The next evening she took extra care with her Friday shirt-waist, pressing it a second time.

"Getting ready for tomorrow's lunch?" Michael teased as she stood over the ironing board.

"He's different from you or any of the other boys here in Southie," she replied. She had not spoken this thought aloud before and the words, leaving her throat, felt like the beginning of a new season.

Friday morning, wanting to look fresh for her suitor, she conducted herself as if she were coated in a thin layer of slow-drying varnish. When five minutes past his customary arrival time he had yet to appear, she was seized by an odd constriction of her throat, and went so far as to risk a dress code violation by unbuttoning her collar. He had never been late before. Then, just as she stepped from behind her counter to join the other girls in the lunchroom, she looked down the center aisle to see him walking toward her with an odd, clipped pace, his face downturned and his neck thrust inside his collar like a sheltering turtle. On reaching her counter he froze, the cords of his neck standing out from his skin as if lifting his head had become a monumental task, achievable only with the aid of ropes and pulleys. Slowly, his face rose to meet hers. The heat of his blush was almost tangible. His eyes were small moons.

"Will you come to lunch?" he whispered, his lips trembling.

"I will," she answered with a shy smile and then Henry blossomed: his spine unfurled, his shoulders broadened, and his smile burst into happy bloom.

In the letters that now arrived each Wednesday, Henry

Henry was not late, only terror stricken: he was at that moment hyperventilating behind a mannequin.

By this point anxiety had struck Henry deaf. He intuited Lydia's consent only by that redemptive smile.

proved an effusive and poetic correspondent. She came to know of the lonely childhood spent in sickbeds, the time taken up by reading; of Henry's hope to curry his father's favor by his successful study of medicine; and of his desire to prove to his mother he could succeed in the world. Lydia was uncertain she knew her own heart as well as she came to know Henry's. His letters were the equivalent of personal maps, lovingly rendered and lush in detail. In her experience, self-reflection was not a quality widely cultivated, requiring as it did such dear resources of time. Her self-knowledge was a wordless creature of light and contour, whose movements she knew but could not always explain. Henry's letters accomplished an act of transubstantiation, transforming Henry's soul from an elusive chimera into a creature Lydia could know and feel. She collected his letters in a small purse she kept near her at all times to protect against their becoming misplaced. During her daily shifts she carried the most recent missive in her shirtwaist pocket so that she could, at any moment, brush her fingers against the smooth paper.

As conversation became easier, Henry graduated from chicken broth to chicken itself, and then to the daily special. His cheeks gained a discernible color, he stopped coughing so often, and a scarf he was inclined to wear both indoors and out disappeared. An entire week passed without Henry once feeling faint or feverish. To celebrate he engaged in the unprecedented act of ordering dessert.

Chocolate pudding, to be precise. Henry recalls the rich brown, the smoothness of the pudding on his tongue and—most prized of all, as taste fades so quickly among Us—the piquancy of cocoa.

Henry's letters imbued even the banal particulars of Lydia's day with magic. Passages would come to her at odd moments: while eating in the lunchroom, or while combing her hair. She would hear these words in a stronger, more assured version of Henry's voice, as if a second Henry, just as real, had taken residence inside her. This second Henry accompanied her to Southie: he was with her as she met her girlfriends for a soda, as she bantered with her brothers, and even as she sat at the Imperial beside the D Street boys, who were no longer permitted to hold her hand. Henry's letters, now sometimes as long as ten pages, necessitated the purchase, on credit, of a larger purse from Handbags. On evenings when she verged on bursting with his admiration, she would quit the streetcar early and stand at the Channel's western edge. "Lips like plums!" she would declaim to a gull pecking at a piece of detritus along the bank. "Sympathy and intelligence in rare proportion!" she would sing to the blurred, anonymous faces inside a passing train car. The constant hum of factories and the rattle and whistle of the northbound line provided Lydia rare shelter for her curious tryst—for here and only here did she allow herself to lend breath to her lover's words, reciting from his letters as loudly as her proud, hopeful voice would allow.

. . .

FADS OF FASHION

In colors for suits this season grays and browns predominate; antelope gray is much in demand, and all browns, from cream to deep chestnut, are favored.

One of the smart new touches is to match the taffeta dress with a hat faced with the same material, trimming the top of the hat with a contrasting color.

Very attractive are the taffeta-waist models, both in dressy and in semi-tailored finish. The changeable are stronger, but fancy stripes and checks also appear.

The small hat is a mass of budding blooms. The crown is usually dome or bowl shaped, and entirely covered with flowers, half-blown, or buds mingled with foliage.

The popular taffeta suits are elaborately trimmed with ruchings, pleatings, shirrings, or puffings. The skirts show fullness, and the jackets are short and invariably cutaway.

. . .

THE QD SODA WALKING TOUR

Welcome to Boston!

Hello! If you're reading this you know that Boston is more than just the home of Paul Revere and the Boston Tea Party. You also know that it's the birthplace of QD Soda! As you read this guide, whether it's while sitting in your armchair or walking the streets of Boston, why don't you open up a chilled QD? Because, as we all know, QD Makes It Better!™

First Stop: Washington Street

As you step onto Washington Street, you may notice that it is narrower than many modern streets. That's because it is so old! Just as QD Soda is one of Boston's original soft drinks, Washington is one of Boston's original streets. When it was named for George Washington after the Revolutionary War, it was already a great place to go shopping! Today, a standout among Washington Street's fine stores is historic Filene's Department Store where, if you mention the QD Soda Walking Tour with your purchase of $10 or more, you will receive a free 75th Anniversary QD Soda Makes It Better!™ T-Shirt!*

Washington is a street of firsts. Across from Filene's is the Gilchrist Building, which originally housed Boston's first department store. But most importantly, Washington Street was the first place in the world to offer QD Soda! Continue two blocks past Filene's and cross the street. In this very spot once stood the first restaurant to sell QD Soda. There's a different restaurant there now, but if you mention the QD Soda Walking Tour when you purchase any sandwich, you can buy a QD Soda for five cents,† the same price people paid in 1918.

---

*Offer limited to Washington Street location, while supply lasts, no rain checks.

†Limited time only, offer subject to product availability, different purchase requirements may apply, offer subject to individual manager discretion.

B y the time they announced their engagement, Henry had visited 28 D Street often enough to have acquired a nickname, and Lydia's visits to Roxbury no longer ended with Mrs. Wickett presenting her with parcels of cast-off clothing to take back to Southie. To demonstrate the seriousness of his intent, Henry began arriving to Southie early enough to attend Sunday Mass, where he sat between Lydia and her mother and intently studied the hymnal.

Henry took to "Professor" so fast that Mick did not have the heart to admit he had first meant it in a left-handed sort of way.

As the Wicketts were not practicing Protestants, Lydia's Catholicism was less troubling than her social station. Having been schooled by Henry in advance of her first visit to Roxbury, Lydia had known where to place her teaspoon when she finished stirring in the milk and when to murmur appreciatively during the elaborate genealogical recitation that linked Henry's family to several Founding Fathers. When Ernestine Wickett requested that, "in the interest of social intercourse," Lydia chose to hail from "some other place—perhaps Winchester or Milton," she knew she had been paid the highest compliment she could ever expect from her future mother-in-law. The ladies to whom Lydia was presented in Ernestine Wickett's damask parlor were Southie gossips with nicer clothes and an inexplicable fondness for English muffins, which—even with the addition of butter and jam—absorbed all the moisture from Lydia's mouth. In the interest of social intercourse, Lydia settled on a respectable Winchester address. Though she was certain Roxbury's ladies suspected her family seat was located elsewhere, none suggested so while sitting in Ernestine Wickett's parlor. Because it was their best option, Lydia and Henry chose to find humor in the fact that her side of the bridge thought her strange and his side thought him seduced.

On marrying, Mr. and Mrs. Henry Wickett rented a furnished five-room flat in the West end, an area that neighbored Beacon Hill. Though the West end had ceased to be a fashionable address several decades previous, it evinced its former pedigree in its architecture, which far surpassed Southie's. From its start Southie had been a repository for factories and the immigrant fodder that kept them running. Accordingly, Southie's buildings were functional and simplistic, and only inadvertently charming when these traits combined to best advantage. By contrast, the West end address where the newly-weds took up residence not only possessed its own name—the Somerset—but also a curved façade replete with terra-cotta, full-length windows, and a peaked roof. Lydia and Henry let the smartest of the top-floor flats, situating them a floor above a married German couple roughly the age of Lydia's parents, and down the corridor from a grouping of lesser flats inhabited by an international assortment of bachelors—two Italians, a Swede, and one Pole who was possibly a Jew. A few times Lydia observed an Irishman in the downstairs lobby, but uncertain a married woman ought to be seen talking with an unfamiliar man, she refrained from introducing herself.

Her first night in the flat, wearing the taffeta-waisted dress and matching hat that Henry had bought her as a wedding

The building was not named for the street but for its original owner, Hubert Somerset, who spends his time among Us muttering that he has been forgotten. We mention him here in the hope that Our consideration will inspire him to pause, however briefly, from his complaint.

present, she traveled from room to room touching each piece of rented furniture with the giddiness of a child who has received everything on her Christmas list. "This is our settee," she declared, stroking its faded chintz. "This is our armoire." The next morning, beside the sink, she smiled to think of the Gilchrist girls straightening their stock while she, a married woman, cleaned the plate of her husband, who every passing minute was closer to becoming a doctor.

She began to feel strange directly after putting away the breakfast things, once there was no longer the distraction of running water or the clink of plates and cups. The strangeness manifested as a nervous feeling in her stomach. She speculated, hopefully, that she might already be pregnant; but when she sat at the table, ceasing even the sound of her footsteps, she realized its origins were external. Previously in her life she might have chanced, fleetingly, to occupy an otherwise empty room but there had always been her mother through the kitchen doorway or her brothers nearby. Never before had silence filled her mouth and ears the way it did now, silence so absolute it was tangible. Lydia sat gape-mouthed at the table: for the first time in her life she was truly alone.

Slowly, she rose from her chair. She crept from the kitchen to the hallway on the balls of her feet. She blushed to think of the previous night's giddy waltz among the flat's furniture and the gross misunderstanding such an action represented. It was now clear to her, as she stood alone in the flat, that this silence—and not a divan or an armoire—was truly the finest object she had ever owned. Stealthily she crept down the hall, peering into each quiet room in turn, but when she reached the parlor she could no longer contain herself: she made a small sound. The sound liberated her; she realized she was no slave to this silence but its master, free to destroy or create it at whim. After glancing about the room, as though to make certain there was no one to stop her, she sat on the settee. Speaking with the bearing of a queen she intoned her name aloud:

"Lydia."

Almost as soon as the word was spoken it was absorbed by the surrounding silence.

Hubert is quite proud of the Somerset's construction, in which he spared no expense, believing—however foolishly—that his wife would be grateful. Accordingly, its walls were thick, its floors and ceilings solid.

"Lydia Claire Kilkenny," she proclaimed a little louder, then clapped a surprised hand over her mouth.

"Lydia Claire Wickett!" she corrected. She strode from the parlor to the hallway. She felt giddy with the knowledge she was completely unobserved. Henry would not be home for hours; her family lived two streetcars and one bridge away. She stood on one leg and hopped several times. In the dining room she held her skirt above her head and loudly hummed, "I'm Afraid to Go Home in the Dark," before, blushing, she returned to the kitchen and attempted to resume her housework—but there the fierce silence of the flat seemed to intensify, gripping her with a strength of will independent from her own. Lydia froze, imprisoned by the relentless quiet. She strained her ears for anything—a footstep, the creak of a stair, a distant voice. She began to feel as if she were dead. The longer she remained motionless, the stronger this sensation became. Surely this was what it was like to be dead: the stillness, the quiet. Worse, this was what it was like to be buried alive. The only slight sounds—coming and going like sputtering matches in an airless room—were the rasp of her own breath and the frantic beating of her heart. With a shriek she ran to the nearest window and threw it open. From the street below came the soothing sounds of motorcars and the welcome screech of the trolley. From that day forward, no matter what the weather, one window was left ajar.

Had Hubert consulted her in advance rather than surprising her with the most cumbersome building she had ever seen, Wilmette Somerset might have been happier with her husband's labors.

Lydia's notion is charmingly backward. The whispering undercurrent in which We reside does not abide a moment's hush.

Her first bout of homesickness arrived with the realization that even simple errands had been made arduous by her new surroundings. After a lifetime in Southie she so took for granted her ability to locate fresh groceries that her first day in her new home she waltzed onto the streets of the West end already hearing her accustomed "Good morning, dearie" from Mr. Leary at the vegetable stand. But when her feet guilelessly traced the path that in Southie would have led to Mr. Leary's green awning, she found herself instead at the corner of Hawkins and Chardon, feeling disoriented to the point of tears. When finally she located a stand where the produce met with her satisfaction, it was so strange to have her purchases weighed and tallied by a colored man that she found herself wiping the palm into which he delivered her change. The potpourri of Italians and Poles and Jews and coloreds she passed on her way back to the flat left her convinced that the cabbage and potatoes in her grocery sack would differ from the sort sold across the bridge. Her discovery that these foods tasted the same in the Somerset as on D Street engendered such gratitude that she swore allegiance to the colored produce man, a promise she kept even after discovering a more convenient stand on Bullfinch.

Her acclimation to her new church was equally difficult. Prior to its reconsecration, Saint Joseph's had been a Unitarian meetinghouse, and as such lacked steeples and—even more egregious—stained glass windows. With its stately columns and marble pediment it more closely resembled the county courthouse than a cathedral. Lydia attempted to put aside these differences during the service, but the familiarity of the psalms was undercut by their delivery in Father Gianino's weighty bass and not Father O'Brian's bright tenor. Sitting among the Irish parishioners she could transport herself across the bridge to the Church of Our Lady of the Rosary. The voices surrounding her sounded enough like Southie voices that when she closed her eyes she could hear her former neighbors and friends and even hints of her mother's shy soprano. These fleeting moments became as essential to Lydia's nourishment as her mother's recipe for colcannon, which she found herself making with a frequency that would have engendered culinary despair had she still lived on D Street.

During her tenure at Gilchrist's, Lydia's Southie friendships had been sustained by the notion of a shared fate. For four years she had neither reason nor desire to rebut Southie's claim on her future; then Henry expanded her heart's terrain. As Mrs. Henry Wickett, Lydia mourned Southie's daily absence, but among old friends and old places she became impatient to return to her new life across the bridge.

The differences in her spurred differences in others. Inside the Somerset flat, Lydia's Southie girlfriends became formal. They moved as though they feared breaking something and invented reasons to leave after one cup of tea. None visited more than twice before the invitation itself and not the second cup of tea was met with an excuse, most often the lack of trolley fare. When Lydia offered to pay their way, always smiling and easy about it—it was really no different than one fellow standing another to a pint—her girlfriends colored and cast their eyes downward. They explained that they really ought not to, nickels did not grow on trees, and besides it was the time as much as anything else; they were none of them girls anymore. Just the trip there and back took ninety minutes, and there were husbands to feed and errands to run and clothes to mend.

Margaret Kelly is sure she made the trip not less than four times.

When Lydia visited Southie, aspects of people she had known all her life were tucked away as matter-of-factly as a flat tidied in anticipation of an infrequent guest. That these shifts were affected without malice did not assuage Lydia's deepening loneliness. Every other month, when her family piled into the streetcar to visit, her mother made everyone wear church clothes. Cora Kilkenny insisted it was nothing to do with Lydia or Henry—she just wanted Southie shown at its best advantage to the rest of Boston. When Henry's mother visited, Lydia exhausted herself examining Ernestine Wickett's every word and gesture for assurance that the dress she had chosen to wear conveyed the proper respect without suggesting she was spending too much of her father-in-law's money.

Michael was the only guest who seemed to feel at home at the Somerset flat. Like any Southie bachelor, Michael acknowledged the city across the bridge only on weekends, when he visited Scollay Square or Fenway. Initially Lydia and Henry's had been the first stop on Scollay evenings for Michael and his friends, many of whom Lydia had known since first grade, but the visits had struck Henry as improper. Whether they were improper or not Lydia could not say, but it was certainly true that Henry did not know what to do during these social calls. Though the fellows were polite and Henry and Michael shared a certain rapport, her husband not being Southie-born precluded his joining most conversations. After a time Lydia would realize that her husband was no longer in the sitting room. And when it came out that Lydia, before becoming Mrs. Wickett, had accompanied a few of Michael's friends to matinees at the Imperial, that was the end of that.

Occasionally Michael still came to the West end alone. Lydia loved that he draped himself across the divan just like it was the sofa at 28 D Street, and that he drank his beer straight from the bottle. Because she never knew when to expect him, she always finished her Saturday errands early, just in case. She would wait a few moments before answering Michael's knock, hiding the extent of her gratitude for his arrival, afraid it might scare him off.

At least once a week, but never on Saturday—because Lydia hated to think that she might miss one of her brother's visits—Henry would grasp her hand after dinner and lead her

Henry remembers objecting not to the matinees but to the liquid appetites of Michael's Southie chums, who by evening's end would grow too garrulous for the modest parlor.

Mick knew just how badly his sister wanted for visitors, which is why he came every month—even when there was nothing doing at Scollay or Fenway.

to the bedroom. According to *Marriage and Parenthood: The Catholic Ideal,* with which Father O'Brian had equipped Lydia the week prior to her wedding, intercourse was to be completed as quickly as possible in order to preserve its power and to keep it from becoming disgusting. But even *The Catholic Ideal*—which Lydia found fusty and which told her nothing she and Margaret Kelly had not deduced by the time they were fourteen—did not call it a sin for a husband and wife to enjoy each other's bodies while engaging in their Catholic duty. Having grown up within the confines of three thin-walled rooms, Lydia knew what that enjoyment sounded like, but neither she nor Henry made the sounds she thought they ought to make. Henry's passionate—but in retrospect vague—letters had implied a certain level of worldliness that he refuted with shy pride their first night together, explaining that as a surrogate he had carefully studied the relevant portions of his medical texts. On their wedding night, as if to prove his diligence, he whispered the Latin names of their respective anatomies as they lay together, a tutorial that ended when Lydia confessed that the words reminded her of Sunday Mass. The ensuing silence was briefly interrupted when Lydia attempted to imitate sounds she remembered emanating from her parents' bed, but her performance so startled Henry that he shrieked like a girl. The brisk performance that followed removed any lingering doubts regarding Henry's naiveté. This left Lydia secretly disappointed. Among her girlfriends it had been agreed that while it was fine for a husband to claim inexperience, it was best if he had also learned a few lessons at Scollay.

Under the command of her old heart, Lydia would have known whom to approach with questions of conjugation, but her new station in life left her stymied. She feared her mother's acceptance of her non-Catholic son-in-law was too fragile to support queries on such an intimate topic, and she could not

To Henry the terms seemed neither religious nor didactic. To his mind, nothing rendered the body more beautiful than Latin.

[26]

imagine asking her father or brother. She supposed she could have sought counsel among her married girlfriends, but even between her and Margaret Kelly—who had once run three blocks to announce to Lydia the arrival of her first monthlies—there had grown an undercurrent of reserve that now confined them to discussions of fashion, movies, and the price of ground hamburger. Lacking an alternative, Lydia resigned herself to the notion that diligent repetition would allow her and Henry to improve on their own.

They had not been married long before she learned that, Latin vocabulary aside, her husband's enthusiasm for his medical studies was limited. On evenings following surgeries or dissections Henry would leave his dinner untouched and retire to bed early, complaining of headache. Even on days in which he avoided the operating theater he complained of dull classes and overdemanding instructors. Far more interesting to him was the news from Europe. Henry's journalistic aspirations had been stanched by his mother, who did not think newspapers a proper occupation for a Wickett, and so he had made his passion an avocation instead. When not decrying the latest development in European affairs, he was attacking the newsprint itself with a pen, reworking sentences and sometimes whole paragraphs he found lacking in flair, and then sharing with his wife the results of his labors. While Lydia enjoyed a newspaper as much as the next person, she did not see why Henry should take such pains to rewrite something that had already been printed. Nor did she share her husband's passion for news from somewhere so distant as Austro-Hungary: she had certainly never heard of the Archduke Ferdinand before he was shot. She looked forward to the end of Henry's medical studies. Once he was a doctor they would be freed from Mr. and Mrs. Wickett's purse strings and he could focus on an aspect of medicine that he liked, perhaps one that did not involve too much blood.

Franz Ferdinand is far more popular among Us than he was in Sarajevo: his memories of his wife, Sophie, remain delectably keen. For this We are thankful. On average, erotic memory possesses a woefully short half-life.

In Southie, Lydia would have thought nothing of taking a break from housework to visit a neighbor's kitchen for tea and conversation, but the Somerset did not offer that comfort. Though she supposed somewhere within the Somerset lurked another young married couple, the building had not yet yielded such a treasure. Short of wandering the halls and crouching before closed doors with her ears perked for sounds of another young wife, Lydia reasoned she would just have to wait until she met such a person by chance—in the lobby, perhaps, or in the stairwell. In the meantime she did her best to banish the small troubles that dogged her thoughts through the long afternoons. When the silence of the empty flat grew oppressive, she reminded herself that in a year such quiet would likely seem precious. She hoped they would have a girl first: though Michael had been of some use, Mrs. Kilkenny often exclaimed that she did not know how she would have managed her brood without a daughter. As Lydia dusted and swept, ironed and folded, she shuffled her features with her husband's to create a girl with her light freckles and Henry's long fingers, and a boy with Henry's green eyes and her up-turned mouth.

She was thus engaged one afternoon when Henry burst into the flat with such exuberance that she thought the door had been staved in. She rushed to the hallway armed with the metal pot she had been preparing to put on the stove. Break-ins were rare in Southie, but Southie offered little to steal. Before she realized the intruder was her husband, she had steeled herself to defend every last stick of rented furniture in their rented flat.

"I've done it!" Henry announced on seeing his wife. He circled her waist with his arm and drew her to him, painting her neck with kisses.

"Darling!" she squealed. Her neck grew progressively

damp. "What did you do?" She could not imagine what would inspire such high spirits, unless Henry had somehow graduated medical school early or convinced his father to raise his allowance.

"I'm done with the whole business," he murmured to her left earlobe.

"Done with what?" She enjoyed standing in the hallway being kissed by her husband, even if his kisses were a little too wet.

He held her at arm's length in order to gaze into her face. "All of it," he proclaimed. "The tedious lectures, the revolting dissections and surgeries. I feel like an immense weight has been lifted."

"I don't know what you mean." She examined her husband's face for clues.

"But of course you do!" he giggled. "After all, I was only taking your lead."

"I'm sorry, dear, but really I don't understand." She turned from her husband and entered the parlor. "Has something happened?" She felt the need to sit. Henry followed her in; he kneeled beside her as she rested on the settee.

"Really, I don't know how you tolerated me for as long as you did." He beamed. "Sometimes I think I don't deserve you—you were criminally patient with me, listening to my complaints night after night, month after month, but I suppose you knew all along if you let me wander long enough in the desert, finally I'd come home."

"Henry," she began carefully, trying to keep her voice calm in direct opposition to her fluttery stomach. "I think you ought to tell me exactly what you've done."

"You want to hear it from my own lips, don't you?" He nodded as though she had answered him. "Well, I finally did it, my darling. I've resigned from medical school."

Unlike Ferdinand's superb conjugal recall, Lydia's sensory impressions of Henry have been effaced. Sadly, his kisses here are purely semantic.

She smiled. "Tell me really."

"I just did, my love."

According to Henry, his wife embraced him at this moment. He has no memory of an argument and is certain of Lydia's unstinting support for his new career.

Her smile froze along with the rest of her. While she felt pinned to the divan, her thoughts flew at such a speed that the room might have been filled with other voices. "You didn't," she amended, her voice practically inaudible above the din inside her head. "You wouldn't actually do that, not actually."

"But darling," he countered, "it was you who showed me that this was what I was meant to do."

He was too skinny. Southie men were never as skinny as Henry, and if they were they found jobs as streetcar conductors or soda jerks or store managers, but she did not think he was suited for any of these. He certainly could not be an iceman or a factory hand. Lydia realized that she was still holding the pot she had grabbed from the kitchen. She wished the door *had* been broken in. She could have given the burglar a solid knock to the head and sent him on his way.

"I did nothing of the sort," she insisted.

"But you did," he averred. He sat beside her on the settee and reached for her hand, but she would not give it. When he spoke again his voice had softened. "You accomplished this feat by healing me in mind and body. Lydia, when I met you I was unwell. I had no strength, no stamina! My childhood was wasted on expensive doctors who achieved nothing at all. Then I met you. You believed in me; you appreciated me for who I was. You cured me, Lydia, and for the first time in my life I'm healthy. No fevers, no coughing, no weakness. Today, after I did what I ought to have done months ago, I actually *skipped* home. Can you imagine? Before you cured me I would have exhausted myself just walking from the trolley to the front door. Darling, you've shown me that medicine is bunkum!"

She could certainly work until they had children, but after

that he would need to bring home a salary. She supposed he could work at Wickett Imports, Ltd., but he hated his father's business. She felt strangely exhausted. She needed to lie down.

Henry's voice grew more certain. In his excitement he launched himself from the settee to pace the room. "And so now, instead of doing what others expect, I'm going to follow my destiny," he declared.

If she went immediately to sleep, there was a chance her husband would arrive home at the expected hour. She would apologize for not having dinner ready and tell him about her strange midafternoon dream.

But instead he continued. "Today is the beginning of a new life for us, Lydia. We are going to be the sole proprietors of—you're going to like this—Wickett's Remedy!" He stood tall and proud before the window, the light behind him transforming his face into a silhouette of the sort found inside anonymous, abandoned cameo brooches.

"You're not making any sense," she insisted from the couch, a veritable wax statue save for her moving lips. Then, as though the pin holding her to the divan had been spontaneously withdrawn, she started up in a burst of movement and began to pace the path her husband had abandoned. It still seemed possible he would reveal his announcement to be a terrible joke.

"No, my dear, for the first time in my life I *am* making sense," he rallied. "I finally know what I am meant to do. You can't imagine how stultifying it is to spend life so uncertain of what path to take, going through motions someone else prescribed simply due to an inability to choose a different course. When I look back on my boyhood I can't help but despair at how much time spent in sickbeds might have been avoided."

In his renewed excitement he resumed his pacing, matching his steps with his wife's. "I ask you: how much sickness is caused by loneliness? By lack of sympathy? These are the people I intend to reach, darling. These are the people Wickett's Remedy is meant to cure."

She hated the whisper of her house slippers against the floor. Her steps sounding like a curtain being pushed aside. She would have gladly traded her nicest pumps for a pair of her brother's work boots in order to fill the room with sound.

"Henry Wickett," she cried, "if I'd wanted to marry a man who thought loneliness could be cured by something from inside a bottle I would have stayed in Southie."

Henry smiled. "You're exactly right, darling, you can't cure loneliness or provide sympathy with a bottle. But you can with a letter."

She stood at the far corner of the room and stared at her husband as if he were speaking Chinese.

"If I hadn't written you," Henry explained in the patient, tender voice she had adored in every circumstance until now, "you would either still be working at Gilchrist's or you would be a Southie wife. And I—I would still be sickly and devoting myself to something I despised."

Though it was petty, she would have liked to remind Henry that she had not received a single letter since becoming his wife. She did not know why she had expected Henry's letters to continue once the days no longer kept them apart, but for months Wednesday had felt hollow when it brought no blue envelope bearing her name.

Henry's voice swelled. "If letters could bring us so much good, then what's to stop them from helping others? Sufferers of hypochondriacal illnesses will never find lasting relief from a bottle, but if my letters can offer them some pale happiness or companionship, then perhaps they will feel a small degree of the rejuvenation that has blessed me, through you."

"But Henry," she cried, "I didn't write you any letters! And while it's true your letters brought us together, if I hadn't been inclined toward you already, your letters wouldn't have made a bit of difference!"

"Exactly!" Henry exclaimed, and it was all she could do not to shriek. "And the people who buy remedies *want* to get well! Just as my letters coaxed a latent feeling from within you, they will foster an inclination already present within my customers! What does it matter if someone buys a bottle of Wickett's looking for a cure inside it and instead finds one in the letter that comes with it? The important thing is that they are cured! People will not accept being cured by words alone. They want something they can hold in their hand, something they can point to and say, 'This did the trick.' This is my calling, Lydia. This is why I have left medical school behind. So that I can help those whom medicine cannot."

He stared triumphant from the opposite corner, his arms crossed, looking like he expected her to applaud.

She leaned against the wall for support. She closed her eyes and swallowed. She had worked so hard to make the flat feel new. Just yesterday she had found an old stain on the settee, one that had preceded their arrival, and though it had taken thirty minutes of vigorous scrubbing she had managed to remove it completely from the upholstery. She did not want to have to leave. Henry's parents certainly would not take them in. They would have to return to Southie.

Angelina Fratelli is positive Lydia is referring to the pomodoro stain left by a misfired plate of spaghetti thrown by her cross-eyed husband. As long as Angelina lived in the flat, she looked at that couch with fondness.

"It was a dissection today, wasn't it?" she began, proud of the evenness of her voice. "I know how hard those can be for you. I'm sure if you returned right now and apologized for whatever it was you said, they'd take you back. You're the son of a prominent family; I'm sure they'd be happy to do it."

"Lydia," he began.

"I'm certain it's not too late," she continued.

"Lydia—"

"You can tell them you weren't yourself," she assured him. "Something came over you, but now you're fine."

Henry is certain his wife never caused him to speak in anger.

"LYDIA," he shouted. It was the first time she had ever heard him raise his voice. "You're the one who's not yourself!" The way he was shaking his finger reminded her of Father O'Brian. "I have finally realized my destiny, the very destiny *you* prepared me for. You can't possibly be displeased. I remind you that you are my *wife*."

He left the parlor. His steps moved down the hallway and into the bedroom. She observed the stillness of the room he had left behind: the settee from which she had once proclaimed her name as if she were royalty; the side table on which she had imagined Henry's medical school friends would rest their drinks during parties they would now never throw; the broad, smooth floorboards of pumpkin pine on which she had imagined hosting dances once they could afford a phonograph. Lydia felt like she was attending a funeral for the room, the various aspects of its stillborn future laid out before her. She thrust her head out the parlor window and sucked in draughts of tepid West end air.

According to Angelina, the room was much too small for dancing.

Before the Somerset was divided into flats, Paolo di Franzio points out that it housed a dance academy. He prefers to think Lydia's thoughts at this moment were influenced by his memory of having waltzed across that once spacious floor. His hope is Our shared desire: that at an unguarded moment, Our whisperings will broach a living ear.

. . .

You need an extra man behind the counter today, Mr. Thornly?

Hello there, Quentin. I wasn't expecting to see you until Saturday.

I know, but I figured the news might make it more like a Saturday in here than usual. You heard about what happened?

I did. Absolutely terrible. I hate the water, can't imagine a worse way to die. Gives me a sick feeling every time I think about it. I had to fix myself a bromide and then was too shook up to drink it standing, so I had to sit on one of my own stools.

One thousand innocent people.

One hundred twenty-eight of them American! I don't see how Wilson can keep us out of it now.

The Huns are lower than a dog's belly. They all deserve to be sunk. I figure people'll be wanting to talk.

Well, so far it's just a regular Tuesday in here, Quent. I suppose you could check back later if you wanted, but if you want my opinion I think you're getting too old for this sort of thing.

What's your meaning, Mr. Thornly?

It's time you started up with something of your own instead of selling sodas for me. You ought to be selling something for yourself.

One day I will, Mr. Thornly. You just watch. One day I'll have a store of my own.

Sure, but how are you gonna go about getting yourself that store, Quentin? When I was your age, I had already been selling headache powder for five years.

Headache powder?

It was a good product. I started when I was sixteen, first door to door, and then to the drugstores, and eventually I expanded into stomach pills and hair tonics and by the time I was twenty-eight, I had saved enough to rent a storefront.

You're not trying to fire me, are you?

Hell no, Quentin! But if you're serious about running a store of your own, you'd be doing yourself a favor to take up with a product. It'll round out the education you're getting here with me.

I don't think headache powder's my line, though. In today's modern world, you need something that stands out.

Now you're talking sharp. If you keep an eye to the world and an ear to the ground, I'm sure you'll find the perfect thing. In the meantime, have a lemon soda and don't let this *Lusitania* business drag you down.

Thanks, Mr. Thornly.

That'll be a nickel.

All right, but so long as you're charging me, make it the way I make it—in a nice glass with lots of syrup.

. . .

THE QDISPATCH

VOLUME 9, ISSUE 2   SPRING 1991

The Coin-Op Show

Those of us who were able to make it this year were not disappointed. Stan Apotts won the prize for farthest traveled, having flown in from Wisconsin, as Cathy Beauregard, our usual long-distance spoiler, stayed in California this year to help look after her newest grandchild, who she's already turning into a QD fan!

There were several handsome QD ads picked up by yours truly, including an almost mint condition metal sign featuring Delores Opple, my favorite QD Cutie. But the real gem of the show was found by Francis Greely, who was lucky enough to discover a 24-jag crown cap of the sort that was discontinued after the bottling facility was upgraded in 1925! And if anyone out there has thoughts of a swap, believe me, we've all already tried and she's not trading!

Of course, the best part of the weekend was catching up with old friends. In our usual suite at the Days Inn we stayed up past our bedtimes listening to tapes of the old radio programs and swapping remembrances. To those of our regulars unable to join the fun this year due to poor health: I wish you a speedy recovery and hope to see you next year!

An Unexpected Call

I was sitting at home one night a few weeks ago when the phone rang. When I picked up, the voice on the other end said, "Hello, Lorena, this is Ralph Finnister." Of course at first I thought it was one of you QDevils out there up to your usual good-natured hijinks, but the voice at the other end of the line assured me that this was no trick. I asked him to prove it. When he asked me how he might do that, I suggested that he tell me the secret recipe for QD. He laughed and said that he was afraid he couldn't do that and then it was like we were old friends. Of course the President of QD Soda has been on the *QDispatch* mailing list for as long as the *QDispatch* has been in existence, but I certainly never expected that he would call yours truly! Or that he'd ask to submit something for an upcoming issue!! But friends, that's exactly what happened, and so, starting with the next issue, the *QDispatch* will be appearing bi-monthly in order to run a multi-part series by the President of QD Soda himself entitled "QD and Me," which Mr. Finnister hopes some day to turn into a book. I'm of course honored that we'll be printing it first and I'm sure you're looking forward to the first exclusive installment as much as I am!

In This Issue

Henry's transformation on quitting medical school was dramatic. Traits Lydia previously had assumed integral to her husband's character instead were revealed to be manifestations of his former unhappiness, while habits she would never before have associated with her husband emerged like butterflies from latent cocoons. Henry metamorphosed into an early riser, often preceding her out of bed and preparing their morning tea. He had been an absentminded medical student at best, but now he kept ordered notebooks and had transformed the small room off the parlor into an immaculate office. The first time she heard him whistle she thought she had left the kettle on, though she thought it strange that the teapot had managed the first few bars of "Hello My Baby"; then she discovered the sound was coming from her husband, who had arrived home with a new selection of business titles. Henry no longer resembled an old man inhabiting a young man's body. His belief in Wickett's Remedy had remade him, and while this had not made a believer out of Lydia, she thought her husband's new happiness might.

Henry hoped to persuade his father to make him a loan for

the Remedy's starting costs, and toward that end he procured a book entitled *Business Finance Made Easy.* He drew up, in his elegant hand, a chart listing the Remedy's expenses and projected earnings and prepared a small speech, which he practiced in front of Lydia so often she memorized it as well. Saturday evening, she pressed Henry's shirt and trousers and pretended not to notice he could not fall asleep.

Her offer to accompany him to Roxbury that Sunday was politely rejected—he thought it best he face his parents alone. Lydia was chagrined by her relief at being spared the visit, but the prospect of witnessing Mr. and Mrs. Wickett's reaction was even more unpleasant. Her only uncertainty concerning her husband's fate in Roxbury was whether his parents would dissuade him by reason or by force. When she visited D Street alone that Sunday she kept silent on the topic of Henry's absence, preferring her family to think she and Henry had quarreled rather than cause him future embarrassment. She told herself she was performing a kindness, but her silence felt disloyal, as if she was abetting the return of her husband's lifelong discontent. And because that made her feel terrible, she tried—as she went through the motions of her weekly visit home—not to think of Roxbury at all.

Lydia had no cause for shame. Henry was just as relieved to stay his wife from the scene of his almost-certain failure.

She returned to the West end with a cold portion of the Kilkenny Sunday ham wrapped in wax paper. She found Henry at his desk, his silent figure offering no sign of his parents' verdict.

"Henry?" she began softly, not wanting to startle him.

"Don't *do* that!" he gasped.

"I'm sorry." She placed a tentative hand on her husband's narrow shoulder. "Did it go well?"

He smiled, but looked tired. "Yes, very well." He hesitated, scanning her face. "Not at first, of course. They weren't very pleased to hear that I'd left school."

"No," she confirmed. "I didn't think they would be."

[39]

The silence of the flat engulfed them. Henry turned to face her, but his gaze sought other moorings. She felt as if time had reversed, returning them to Monty's lunchroom. She waited for her husband to continue but each potential recommencement dissolved, an uplifted eyebrow or an intake of breath instead presaging more silence.

"What did your mother say?" she prompted once she could not bear to wait any longer.

"She didn't like it," he replied. "But this was a business proposition, which is my father's arena."

Lydia could not fathom how Henry had gained his father's ear within Ernestine Wickett's domain. Her mother-in-law was not a woman who deferred to anyone in any matter, business-related or otherwise. Henry's cheeks were perhaps more flushed than usual, but his appearance was otherwise unchanged. There was no outward sign of her husband's new-forged mettle.

"So you took up the matter with him," she confirmed, as though such a thing were not wholly revolutionary.

Henry hesitated. When he did speak his words came quickly. "We had a bit of an argument then and things became rather unpleasant—but it all worked out in the end."

Lydia waited. "And?"

"And," Henry confirmed. "And—" He looked toward her and then away again. "Starting tomorrow, and until the Remedy is on its feet, I'm to clerk at Father's office."

"But you hate your father's business!" she protested. "You've told me countless times of the tedium of the import industry!"

"It's only temporary, only until the Remedy gets on its feet." He smiled weakly, and she realized that no revolution—whether conducted from a battlefield or a chaise lounge—came without casualties. "It will provide us an income in the

Henry admits to being deliberately vague. In fact, his father threatened to cut off his allowance in six months if he had not returned to medical school—an ultimatum Henry thought best to keep to himself.

This was the only time Henry was untruthful to his beloved. He reported uninvited to Wickett Imports, Ltd., hoping his father's aversion to public scenes would secure him a position. Because his ploy worked, his wife was spared knowledge of his bluff.

interim, and some of what I do at the office I'll be able to apply to our work with the Remedy."

"I can work," she offered quietly, avoiding her husband's face as she spoke. In the afterglow of their wedding she had shared Henry's view that she had been spared a weary life of gainful employment, but a household was tedious in its agreeability: a rug required no persuasion to be beaten, a dish did not need coaxing to try on a coat of soap. Lately she had been assigning to her housework the names of Gilchrist customers, so that waxing the floor turned into a dialogue with Mr. Tanner on the relative merits of British and French tailoring, and cleaning the stove became an exercise in selling a shirt to Mr. Ludlow. "It would be easy to find a store that would take me," she shrugged in an attempt to counter the excitement that had crept into her voice. She would enjoy working again, at least part-time; at least until a baby came.

Henry shook his head. She could not tell if his disappointment lay with her or with their new circumstance. "I knew you would offer to find employment." He sighed. "But if you do return to work, it ought not to be with any store."

For one horrifying instant, she pictured herself installed in the Wickett household, imprisoned within a black dress and a white apron.

"You may have grave reservations about the Remedy's prospects," Henry continued, "but you spent four years on a sales floor. Nothing I could read in a book would equal that experience."

"But Henry," she objected, "what would you have me do? I'm a counter girl, not a doctor or a pharmacist."

"That doesn't matter," he insisted. "You know how to make something appeal to a customer; you know the little tricks that make a product catch a person's eye."

"I sold shirts," she reminded him.

"And you were brilliant at it," he pressed. "Lydia, I need you to invent Wickett's Remedy. The bottle, the label, the liquid inside. If people aren't attracted to Wickett's to begin with, then my letters haven't got a chance. I need you to convince customers to try their first bottle."

She could feel her pulse in her neck. He was right; this was something she could do. Her mind began assembling a list of elements to consider, her memory recalling the various bottles that had, at one time or another, claimed her family's allegiance.

"I suppose I could manage a label pretty well," she conceded, "but Henry, you can't ask me to invent a medicine."

"No," he agreed. "You'll do nothing of the sort. Wickett's Remedy will not purport to cure yellow fever, or pneumonia, or even a simple headache, because the illnesses I propose to treat have no foothold in the body. Your tonic is to be an accompaniment to the true medicine of my letters, without any power of its own save for the power of suggestion. What you concoct I leave completely up to you. If you wish, it can be a simple sugar syrup."

When he paused, she could tell he wanted her assent, or at least an encouraging smile, but she had been a salesgirl, not an actress. If she opened her mouth now it would only be to say that he was asking too much. Henry jerked his chin up and down. It was the sort of quick, sharp nod given in response to bad news. She turned toward the door. There was housework to do and supper to cook.

"Lydia," he called. His voice was softer now. "Whether or not Wickett's succeeds may be beyond our control," he conceded, "but without you I know it is absolutely certain to fail." She turned to face her husband. Henry was standing beside his chair, one hand resting on his desk as if for support. "Please. Will you help me?"

He had asked for her companionship and he had asked for her hand, but never before had he asked for her help. In the silence she examined him with a scrutiny previously only accorded her in his sleep. She was shocked by how well she knew his face. There was his nose, narrow and slightly off center, its subtle curve to the right only noticeable when observed straight on. There were his eyelashes, longer than she had ever seen on a man, which tempted her to brush her fingertips along their tips as one would against the wing of a captive butterfly. A year ago this face had belonged to a stranger, and now it beheld her as though she were all that mattered in the world. She was struck by the ease with which she could wound the man. She could already taste the strange, sharp sweetness of such an effortless victory. Then the feeling passed. The face of the man sitting at the desk once again became the face of her husband. His vulnerability became hers; his features became her own.

"Of course I will help you," she said.

. . .

NEWTONVILLE MAN PLANS TORPEDO-CARRYING BATTLESHIP WITH GUNS BEARING ANAESTHETICS WHICH HE THINKS WILL BRING PEACE

A new scheme of war—or, rather of war against war—has been developed by Carl M. Wheaton of Newtonville, Mass., several of whose inventions along other lines are at the present time in successful use. Mr. Wheaton feels confident of his plan for a torpedo-carrying battleship: it will fire a powerful anaesthetic and render the crews of hostile ships unconscious and also release a "smudge" which, enveloping their ships, will prevent the gunners on board from seeing their opponents, consequently causing their fire to be totally ineffective.

"I have offered the navy department to make perfect drawings of all my devices, if they pay me a reasonable salary for the time required," Mr. Wheaton said. "I will now offer to furnish the same information to any nation on earth which has the price to pay for it."

. . .

THE QD SODA WALKING TOUR

Second Stop: The West End

For the next stop on our tour, walk to the northwestern edge of City Hall Plaza, at the corner of Cambridge and Sudbury streets. Imagine a bustling intersection, with an impressive theater on the right and stores on all sides. Until 1960, you wouldn't have had to use your imagination to see Bowdoin Square, once part of Boston's old West End, which in 1894 witnessed the birth of one of its favorite sons, Quentin Driscoll. It was here where he first worked behind a soda counter—and here where he dreamed of a new soft drink.

There is not even a plaque where Quentin Driscoll's childhood home once stood. In the name of urban renewal, this entire neighborhood of historic buildings and winding streets was demolished to make room for high-rise luxury apartment buildings. When the West End was destroyed, a crucial part of QD history was destroyed along with it.

The following words appeared in the newspaper two weeks after Henry reported for work at his father's office:

Try WICKETT'S REMEDY for a new lease on life!
Find your spirits lifted, your outlook improved!
All queries answered personally.
Send 25¢ and an accompanying letter to:
Post Office Square, Box 27, Boston.

The printed word is our most reliable benchmark of memory. We collectively recall entire libraries.

The authority of crisp newsprint bestowed on the venture the aura of imminent success. Seeing the notice, Lydia could not help but feel that Henry would not be consigned to his father's office for long.

In becoming a clerk Henry became a man divided, Monday through Friday manifesting the melancholy that had marred his medical school career but on Saturday emerging from the chrysalis of his unhappiness to engage in his work with the Remedy. The difference was striking enough that Lydia felt married to two men; and she privately vowed to do all she could to enable the timely replacement of the former with the latter.

By the time of the advertisement's appearance in the paper, she had—per Henry's request—invented both a Remedy recipe and a label. Of the two, only the recipe gave her trouble. She had wanted Wickett's to taste different: interesting but not unpleasant, not too sweet but also not bitter. As a girl she had been subject to her mother's faith in Jenson's Indian Cure, which was administered for everything from headaches to bunions. She hated the taste and smell of Jenson's which contained—in addition to other undiscernible unpleasantries—sage and not a small bit of alcohol, two ingredients she was determined not to include in her own creation.

After a week in which she experimented variously with salt, pepper, parsley, onion, lemon, and hickory root to no avail, the Remedy's recipe came to her in a dream of her Granny K, whom Lydia had only ever known from the faded tintype her father had carried with him across the Atlantic. In Lydia's dream, Granny K stood before the sod house where Lydia's father had been born and patiently explained to her granddaughter what flavorings she ought to add and in what proportion. Lydia, who did not generally remember her dreams, was struck by her grandmother's hands: their broad palms and strong fingers resembled her own. On waking, Lydia jotted down her grandmother's instructions and purchased the proper ingredients, along with a pot large enough to cook ten bottles' worth of Remedy at a time. That afternoon—feeling as though her own hands were being guided by her grandmother's—she boiled up the first batch of Wickett's.

From the moment Henry invested her with the task of designing the Wickett's label, Lydia had known it would be a pale blue shield depicting a girl with dark plaits clutching a flower blossom, topped by the words WICKETT'S REMEDY in bold, dark letters. She had assumed an artist would be needed for its execution, but to her surprise Henry not only lettered

Maureen Kilkenny takes no credit for the recipe, but she would like to think she engineered her appearance in her American granddaughter's dream. Our whisperings are most often heard in life's interstices: in dreams, in sickness, and in the moments preceding sleep or waking.

In the tintype to which her granddaughter refers, Maureen's hands are hidden by her dress, but they were just as her granddaughter describes.

the label but drew the requisite portrait, emerging from his office only a few hours after she had submitted her design.

The picture came as a shock. In her mind, the girl on the Wickett's label was one of those generic, soft-haired cherubs who graced cookie tins and cough syrup. Henry's creation had Lydia's rounded nose and his gentle eyes. Though her daydreams were filled with children who shared her and Henry's features, seeing an actual picture caused her chest to ache. Her first instinct was to hide the girl's portrait in her top dresser drawer with her letters from the worldly suitor who also had not succeeded from paper to flesh and blood.

The face Henry drew had quietly graced his imagination since his wedding night. It belonged to a daughter whose name—Lucy—he had also intended to share with Lydia until he observed the portrait's unintended effect.

After the first months of marriage, their shared silence on the topic of childlessness seemed to stem from the mutual sense that discussion would grant the subject unwanted substance. The appearance of such a picture after a year of fruitless, wordless efforts breached this tacit agreement. A different portrait would be better, one that did not take as its model their unrealized hopes. But when Lydia turned toward Henry to explain this, the yearning she saw there revealed the cruelty of such a request. He had created a child. And so, because she had to say something, she exclaimed that she had no idea she had married an artist. In answer, he explained that he had been embarrassed by his doodling until medical school, where to avoid wielding a scalpel he had diagrammed dissections for his lab mates and, in so doing, improved his technique. Thus was the unspeakable topic opened and closed without either of them ever saying a word.

With the appearance of the first Wickett's advertisement Lydia adopted the twice-daily habit of walking to the post office to collect incoming Remedy correspondence. When the first morning yielded an empty letter box she followed a different path to Post Office Square to avoid encountering the same bad luck along the way. Though the afternoon letter box was just as empty, she retained this custom, and cast about for additional measures to help their luck. The next day she chanted a Hail Mary just before climbing the post office stairs. The third day she wore one of her better dresses, and on the fourth she decided to change her dress between morning and afternoon outings. When, on the afternoon of the fourth day, she arrived at the letter box to discover a letter waiting, the hopeful practices she had adopted became codified; and from that moment forward she observed all of them with the same fastidiousness with which certain older Southie women attended obscure Masses.

Their first customer was a middle-aged North end woman named Carlotta Agnozzi, whose complaints included fatigue and dyspepsia. After an hour spent cloistered in his office Henry emerged waving his inaugural letter with the pride of a boy who has caught a pop fly. On seeing the once-familiar sheet of pale blue stationery, Lydia understood the origins of the color of her Wickett's label. But while the blue hue of the labels exerted a pleasant, fluttery effect on her heart, that same shade on a letter intended for someone else caused her ears to buzz and her throat to tighten. Henry, oblivious to his wife's distress, strode to the middle of the sitting room and began to read what he had written.

Carlotta Agnozzi lived to be 103—but she credits leeks, not Wickett's Remedy.

"The dyspeptic stomach is like a child, longing for Mama's comfort," he intoned, a pair of reading glasses perched on his nose, the hair on the left side of his head standing up in odd tufts from repeated tugs and smoothings by his excitable non-writing hand. "Be kind and patient and feed it wholesome foods. Try dining in new places: a riverside picnic can do wonders for the morale and the digestion, and fresh air is a known enemy of fatigue."

Mrs. Agnozzi doubts Dr. Wickett had allowed for the stink from the Boston Gas Company Wharf.

As Henry read on, Lydia was forced to acknowledge that neither the words nor the sentiments were familiar: only the stationery belonged to her former beau. She had not suspected that a person's paper face could be any more changeable than its flesh counterpart. The notion that her husband contained such diverse men replaced Lydia's jealousy with a melancholy strain of consolation: for though she did not have to share her paper lover, Henry's letter to the North end dyspeptic confirmed that her passionate, impetuous suitor was forever confined to the aging bundle of letters in her top bureau drawer.

Mrs. Agnozzi's letter marked the beginning of a regular trickle of correspondence into the Remedy's post office box. Most first-time customers were short and to the point, but occasionally Lydia found herself listening to detailed lists of woes ranging from rheumatism to an ungrateful spouse to a cat who shed out of season. In reply to these complaints Henry penned letters ranging from two to five pages, written in his beautiful, almost feminine hand, sending warmth, encouragement, and confidence. They soon became accustomed to letters that began, "I am a friend of Mrs. So-and-So, who just showed me the extraordinary letter she received from you, and I was hoping you would send me hope of a similar kind along with your Restorative." To Henry, it marked the beginning of a medical revolution.

But while a growing number of people perceived the good contained in Henry's letters, no one appreciated that medicine not issuing from a bottle still ought to be paid for. Rather than reorders, envelopes bearing familiar return addresses yielded letters that opened, "Dear Dr. Wickett, As soon as I read your words I realized that I had met a kindred soul," or "Dear Dr. Wickett, Though I myself am a man of position, I will ask that you call me Fred, for we are clearly two men meant to walk in the land of friendship, not commerce." None of these repeat correspondents enclosed payment: they had exhausted the letter's content, not the bottle's.

Henry was no more immune from the effect of a friendly letter than his erstwhile customers. The replies he received were so warm, appreciative, and genuine in their desire for a continuing correspondence that he—despite Lydia's efforts to convince him otherwise—could not bring himself to demand payment for what was, in his mind, a reciprocal act. According to Henry it would have been rude to withhold the courtesy of a response and mercenary to insist on payment for one. And so, the Wickett's advertisement garnered Henry a middling but steady number of new inquiries and very few repeat customers, but several pen pals.

Henry's clerkship stretched for six months, and then twelve months, and then eighteen. His unhappiness could be measured by the frequency of the evening headaches that banished him to the bedroom and the difficulty Lydia had in rousing him the following morning. She proposed that if she found work, the additional income provided by a part-time position would at least allow him to clerk part time, but her offer was again refused. Henry saw no point in leaving his father's office when he would have to return as soon as his wife became pregnant. Though Lydia had ceased to believe in this possibility, she viewed Henry's abiding faith in their procreative potential as too precious a thing to squander. In lieu of part-time store work, he taught her to keep up the Remedy ledger. This was more involved than the account book she had been required to keep as a Gilchrist girl, and therefore more interesting. She liked the neat, straight columns of the Wickett notebooks and the feeling of importance granted by Henry's desk, an oversized slab of mahogany of which he was quite protective but that she was now permitted to employ whenever conducting Remedy business.

As events in Europe accelerated, Henry's dedication to the daily newspaper intensified. By evening, the orderly printed columns of the morning edition were transformed by his pencil into a dense thicket of corrections. Sometimes an entire ar-

Henry had no more faith in this matter than Lydia, but he feared she would be devastated by mutual acknowledgment of their infertility.

Here is a rare fragment of Henry's visual memory flash-frozen: Lydia's pale hand resting against the dark-hued wood.

ticle would be crossed out, with Henry's rewritten version squeezed into the newspaper's white gutters. By that March, talk of entering the war was rampant and so it came as no surprise in early April when President Wilson announced that America would be joining the fight against the Germans. The weekend following the President's declaration, Henry exhibited high spirits the likes of which Lydia had never seen. On Saturday, they took lunch out and walked along the Charlesbank, then rode a swan boat in the Public Garden. On Sunday they caught a matinee and dined at Scollay. While riding the streetcar Henry grabbed her hand and murmured endearments into her ear, and while watching the feature he kissed her neck with an ardency that made her feel like she was a Southie girl of eighteen again. With the arrival of Sunday evening, she did not feel her usual dread. Her memories of that weekend would easily carry her through the five days preceding the next. Henry seemed to share this feeling. That evening he neither complained of headache nor went to bed early. Instead he invited her to sit beside him at his desk while he penned letters to customers, and as she balanced the accounts he occasionally paused in his writing to stroke her head or squeeze her hand.

When Lydia awoke on Monday morning, Henry's absence beside her brought a grateful flush to her cheeks. She donned her dressing gown and went quickly to the kitchen, but he was not there; she supposed he was working at his desk. She would surprise him by bringing him breakfast. Pouring his tea, she smiled to think of a new era in which the afterglow of each weekend would lighten the week to follow.

She strode into the parlor with a tray. "Henry," she called, "there's tea." But when she reached the study it was empty.

"Henry?" she asked the cold room. She left the tray and proceeded to the washroom, then returned to the bedroom, thinking he must be dressing, and only then did she see the letter pinned to her husband's pillow.

"My dearest Wife," it began:

Now that Wilson has declared war, History has presented me an opportunity that I can't resist. As a soldier I will be able to write about everything that is going on over there. By the time I return, I'll be a first-class journalist. If I had told you, you would have tried to stop me and there would have been an argument, and you look so peaceful sleeping that I can't stand to wake you. Don't worry. I will write you every day. Thinking of you will keep me strong. I know you'll understand.

Love,

Henry

She stared at the note as if she could unwrite it with her gaze, the delicate loops and curves of the letters unspooling into inconsequential blue lines; but the note remained stubbornly intact.

"Henry?" she called, her voice reflecting off the bedroom walls. She had not been paying attention before, or she would have noticed the flat's emptiness from the character of the surrounding silence; with Henry in his study, the quiet was less lonely, as if the flat could sense within it the beating of a second heart. She did not unpin the note from his pillow. She would not touch it—touching it would lend the words more credence. She returned to the parlor and sat down to her tea, not noticing until her cup was half empty that she had neglected to add milk or sugar. She ate her toast, then fixed her tea, and then drank Henry's tea and ate his toast because she could not bear it going to waste. Buffered by the familiarity of

[52]

two empty plates, she returned to the bedroom to dress where—so long as she avoided the sight of their bed—she could pretend that Henry, having finished his breakfast, had run for the streetcar. Once dressed, however, her imagination faltered. Unable to bear the note's presence, she fled the flat as though the air had turned sour.

On reaching the ground floor Lydia sank gratefully into one of the couches that dotted the lobby's interior. She had left the flat without a clear idea of where she would go, but the sight of the street through the front entrance was a comfort. In the lobby, immersed in the Somerset's usual morning bustle, she found it far easier to pretend at the note's nonexistence. The pretense of normalcy lasted until Mrs. Lieben appeared. Usually the two women merely nodded politely in greeting but today her downstairs neighbor called out, "Good morning!" in a cheery voice that did not reach her eyes.

Mrs. Liebnitz wonders if Mrs. Wickett never knew her proper name or if she forgot. When Mrs. Wickett moved in, Mrs. Liebnitz brought her a strudel, which she thinks Mrs. Wickett also forgot.

"It is such wonderful news, yes?" Mrs. Lieben asked, her smile anxious.

In Lydia's current state it seemed Mrs. Lieben could only be talking of one thing.

"Did you see him on his way out?" she asked, trying to keep her voice even.

"Who do you speak of?" Mrs. Lieben asked in return, then smiled again. "Ah, it is your husband, the doctor."

"Yes," Lydia answered, starting up from the couch. "Please, what did he tell you?"

"I have not seen him," Mrs. Lieben answered, placing her hand on Lydia's shoulder. She was talking too loudly now, as though she feared Lydia had gone deaf. "But I would like very much to tell him how too wonderful it is for our great President to declare the war. You will tell him for me, yes? You will tell him," she confirmed, and nodding and smiling made her exit.

Mrs. Liebnitz remembers the fear inside her heart. Her husband laughed, but it was not for nothing she was afraid. Two months later their rent was raised with no warning, and she and Wolfgang had to find a building with kindness for Germans.

In the wake of Mrs. Lieben's departure Lydia found it impossible to perpetuate her charade; in the Somerset's lobby Henry's note had become as palpable a presence as it had been upstairs, and so she ventured outside. More people were on the street than usual and American flags hung from several buildings where there had been none before. Because she had not considered where she would go, her feet started by default toward her twice-daily destination. On her way to the post office, a boy in Scollay Square cried, "War at Last! Five cents! War at Last! Five cents!" When she quickened her pace to escape the newspaper boy she inadvertently crossed before an oncoming streetcar. Normally this would have caused a minor commotion but today the city was distracted by another matter. All around Lydia voices murmured; people stood on corners talking excitedly and making grand gestures with their hands.

She sighed with relief on reaching the post office lobby. She turned her gaze toward the familiar wall of letter boxes as one looks homeward at the conclusion of a long journey—but the boxes were empty. Only then did she think to check the time. She was early: the morning mail had not yet been delivered. She found a bench along the wall, one that neither faced the letter boxes nor a clock. Her first thought was to wait for the morning delivery, but the initial comfort of this instinct faltered as soon as she realized that any incoming letters would require responses, which forced her mind to return to Henry's note and its significance. Her husband had enlisted.

She remained on the post office bench, observing the various comings and goings of strangers until the fact of her husband's absence was no longer paralyzing. Then she retreated outside, mechanically retracing her steps. Intent on returning home, she became blind to the flags and newspaper boys, but when she reached the Somerset the prospect of the empty flat offered no comfort. She continued to walk.

On Blossom Street she entered a small, strange bakery that smelled comfortingly of dough. Because there was no tea she ordered coffee and received a tiny ceramic cup with no handle, which contained the darkest, most bitter coffee she had ever tasted. The bakery was occupied by older women dressed in black, their gray-streaked hair wound into bulky buns behind their heads. The flesh of their faces and arms had gone soft. Fingers swollen with age immobilized rings planted by long-dead husbands. These women called and gestured to one another like children in a playground, their voices commanding the room. Lydia did not recognize the language but she was certain they spoke of the war—today the entire city was engaged in the same simultaneous conversation.

Lydia finished her coffee. She would need a glass of water to drive the taste from her mouth, but rather than approach the counter she found herself tapping a neighboring shoulder. The woman who turned wore an expression more curious than friendly, as if Lydia were a stray cat with unusual markings who might or might not scratch when stroked.

"My husband has joined the army," she confessed, surprising herself. It seemed unlikely she would be understood and even if she was, she did not know what comfort a stranger could offer.

The woman's face spread into a broad, wide grin, revealing a gold tooth. "That is good," she laughed, clapping her hands. The other women turned to look. "Very good," the woman continued, nodding. "Army need strong men."

The other women began to nod as well, a chorus of moving heads.

"Good!" one repeated.

"Very good!" echoed another.

"Strong men!" cackled a third, causing the entire room to burst into laughter.

The café was not strange, only Italian; and Vincent Iannacone thinks the young lady ungrateful for not remembering that her espresso that day was free.

Lucia Petronelli does not remember what she and her friends were discussing the day the young *sconoscuita* came to their café, but she knows they were not discussing the war. Ignoring men's foolishness was one great pleasure of widowhood.

"But you don't understand," Lydia protested, her eyes filling with tears. "My husband isn't strong at all; he's small and frail." She did not know which was more absurd: that Henry had joined the army or that this had become a topic of discussion among the widows of this odd café. She wished she had not spoken. She ought to have left as soon as she learned there was no tea.

"Army make him strong," the smiling woman pronounced. When she turned from Lydia the other women turned away as well, resuming their previous conversation as though they had never been interrupted. When Lydia staggered up from her table and stumbled outside, no one noticed. When she looked back through the window, her coffee cup had already been cleared away. There was no sign she had been there at all.

Because she was crying the streets blurred, but she knew she could trust her feet to lead her to Saint Joseph's. She felt strange passing over the church threshold: she had always pitied women who frequented churches when there was no scheduled service. She knelt uncertainly in a back pew, head bowed and eyes closed. She did not know if there was a saint of war. She seemed to remember a saint for soldiers but could not remember his name. She scanned the church interior until her eyes fell on a small statue of Sebastian. She remembered Father O'Brian once describing Saint Sebastian's days as a soldier. The thought that Sebastian, like Henry, had been neither large nor powerfully built was only briefly heartening. Sebastian, after all, had been pierced to death by arrows. Doing her best to overlook the saint's dire end, Lydia tendered a brief prayer to Sebastian in her husband's name.

It was a cold day but clear. On quitting the church she walked east to the Charles. A group of girls in modest uniforms walked the path along the river's edge, led by a nun encouraging them to take in the brisk air. Lydia watched the progress of a pleasure boat filled with women and chil-

If the young lady had ever returned she would have thought differently. Soon after her visit, tea graced Signore Iannacone's menu.

Father O'Brian recalls that saints were never Liddie Kilkenny's strong suit. The primary patron saint of soldiers is Saint George.

dren, many of whom waved as they passed. Behind the ferry, a scull stroked its way southward. Before coming to the West end she had never seen such boats. The harbor was too rough for them. She did not like sculls—they reminded her of D Street waterbugs, which laid claim to the washbasin each morning.

To further postpone her return home she decided to visit the Bowdoin. As she hopped the Cambridge trolley she smiled bitterly to think of the money she was wasting—a nickel for coffee, a nickel for the streetcar, and now a nickel for the matinee—all weekend luxuries and it was only Monday. She had never attended a picture on a weekday afternoon. She blushed to think of the breakfast things she had left in the parlor. One of the worst things her mother could say about a woman was that she kept an unclean home.

Lydia liked the Bowdoin because it reminded her of the Imperial: both had high, gold ceilings illuminated with electric stars; both commanded luxurious red curtains fringed with gold tassel, which whisked away with an impressive whoosh as the lights dimmed; and both were redolent of roasted peanuts. Accustomed as she was to weekend crowds, Lydia felt a flush of excitement at finding the theater only partially filled. She could choose practically any seat she liked. This freedom was magnified by Henry's absence. He favored the balcony: any closer and the looming shapes of the screen actors gave him headaches. Without even a glance to the balcony stairs, she strode to the theater's front rows. A few seats were occupied by women with young children, old ladies— Lydia had never thought to wonder where they went after Mass—and a smattering of men of various ages. Lydia doubted that any proper sort of man would allow himself to be seen inside a movie theater in the middle of the day and made sure to give these loafers a wide berth.

A large flag, which hung down the center of the curtain, re-

As manager of the Bowdoin for forty years, Mr. Chester Crowley cannot imagine how anyone could conflate the Imperial's vulgar red curtain with the Bowdoin's regal violet one.

mained in place once the curtains had been pulled aside, and Lydia wondered if she would be expected to watch the movie against a background of stars and stripes. When the piano man asked them to rise for "The Star-Spangled Banner," the theater stood like this was the most customary thing in the world, as though flags in theaters were commonplace and movies had always begun with a recitation of patriotic tunes and not with songs like "Me and My Girl," or "Dancing on a Cloud." The flag remained in place for "My Country 'Tis of Thee" and "America the Beautiful," making it difficult for Lydia to read the projected lyrics, and so she hummed, hoping no one would think less of her for it. It ought to have been perfectly acceptable to sit back down, but no one reclaimed their seat. It felt silly to remain standing, but Lydia was not sure whether her embarrassment stemmed from being influenced by the others or because it seemed that only she had not known that the rules had changed. Thankfully the flag rose high into the rafters after the songs finished, and people resumed their seats, allowing her an uncompromised view of the first two-reeler and the feature that followed.

The feature turned out to be a war picture. Lydia could not watch the screen soldiers for more than a few seconds before each one changed into Henry. Soon the screen became filled with drably uniformed Henrys clutching guns and staring into the distance, and when even Douglas Fairbanks himself acquired her husband's pale features she knew she had to leave. From the lobby she could hear the muted strains of the piano, which now sounded like it was being played by a ghost.

Back on the street she remembered that she had not returned for the morning delivery. In her prolonged absence the afternoon correspondence had certainly arrived as well. This was the first time since Wickett's beginning that she had not

As war had just been declared, Mr. Crowley is certain the Bowdoin's feature that day was of some other type.

Mr. Fairbanks adds that he did not appear in any war pictures in 1917. He suspects the young woman is remembering a comedy called *A Modern Musketeer.*

[58]

collected the mail promptly, a realization that transformed the day's distress into panic. She began to run.

At the sight of the Somerset, she pictured the flat with utter clarity: the dirty breakfast dishes in the parlor, the unswept floors, the unmade bed with Henry's note still pinned to the pillow. She would walk straight to the bedroom to pack whatever bare essentials would be necessary for a night's stay on D Street. Afterward she could return to the flat with her mother or Michael to collect any additional things. When Henry returned from the war—if Henry returned from the war—he would have to come across the bridge to get her.

To avoid facing the darkness, she reached her arm along the wall just inside the front door until she found the switch and with a relieved sigh depressed it. Though she had meant to go straight to the bedroom, she realized she could not quit an apartment that contained dirty dishes. To combat the surrounding silence she began to hum. This, at least, would do until she reached the kitchen, where the business of dishwashing would allay her panic long enough to allow her to finish the job.

Nearing the parlor and humming "America the Beautiful" under her breath—the song had been repeating mercilessly inside her head ever since she had quit the Bowdoin—she felt that something was not quite right. Then she saw it: a dark shape on the divan. Her stomach leapt into her throat. She thrust her arm into the sitting room and began fumbling for the light, but before she could manage the switch, the shape rose from its chair. She shrieked and fell backward. The shape rushed at her into the light.

"Liddie—" the shape snuffled. "Liddie." It fell to its knees and buried its head in her dress. "They wouldn't take me," Henry sobbed into her skirt, his shoulders quaking. "They took one look and sent me home."

. . .

TELLS OF MORAL PERIL TO SOLDIERS

Capt. Ralph M. Harrison, marshal of the provost guard, with headquarters in the South armory, called the attention of the Twentieth Century Club yesterday to the large number of young girls who accost soldiers and sailors in Boston, indicating the corner of Tremont and Boylston streets as "the worst place" and "between 11 and 12 p.m." as "the worst time."

"I have referred before to this place," he added, "as 'the happy hunting ground' because everybody seems to be so industrious down there."

The speaker told of being himself accosted, and cited experiences of the same kind by officers and men of the guard.

"I was appalled," he went on to say, "at the huge number of young girls for whom the uniform seems to have a particular attraction. I have seen in Tremont and Boylston street and on the Common soldiers and sailors passing a couple of these little girls and have heard the girls say, 'Hello! Why in such a hurry?'

"I have given orders to immediately arrest any soldier or sailor who addresses or endeavors to approach any girl in the street, but it is impossible for the guard to do the same with the young girls and women who accost the soldiers and sailors. As far as the men from Boston are concerned I think it is of primary importance for the people of Boston to correct this."

. . .

Ladies and gentlemen, we live in miraculous times. Thanks to advances in modern medicine, we no longer live in fear of typhus, smallpox, or yellow fever, diseases which only a generation ago wielded deadly power over young and old. A generation ago, one of every four children died before their second birthday. Now, with the help of such innovations as pasteurization, our children are thriving in numbers as never before.

But ladies and gentlemen, we find ourselves faced with a new and even deadlier scourge, a scourge that threatens not only our lives but our country, and that is the scourge of War. As typhus is a disease of the body, so War is a disease of nations. Like any disease, it is spread by a germ. It is no accident that those same four letters spell the name of our enemy, ladies and gentlemen. *Germ*any. Mile by mile, the *Germ*-man line has been snaking its way westward, an infection of continental proportions. Many a noble soldier has fallen and many still fight in their attempt to keep this infection at bay.

The good men and women of Europe have turned to us for help in defeating this deadly scourge and we have answered their call. We have done so not only because it is right, but because it is crucial. This disease is not limited to Europe, ladies and gentlemen. This disease could easily cast its shadow across the Atlantic to reach our very shores. But sending our soldiers is not enough. It is up to you, ladies and gentlemen, to provide the force for an American vaccine against *Germ*any. Only by putting our national wealth in the service of this great cause can we make it strong.

It is vital that you support the Liberty Loan. It is our duty as a healthy, modern nation to hurry to the War Front with every resource that our two hundred and fifty billion in national wealth can command. We need every cent of these billions not only to stave off further infection, but to reclaim the health of Europe and to defeat the *Germ*-man Kaiser, once and for all. Only if we do our duty, ladies and gentlemen, and support the Liberty Loan, can the disease of War be banished forever into the history books. Buy bonds now so that in the future you can say that you did your part to render the dread disease of War obsolete.

. . .

Third Stop: Scollay Square

Now turn your attention to City Hall Plaza and Government Center. As you walk the stately brick plaza, try to imagine you are walking instead on a brightly lit stage, surrounded by beautiful young performers. It's not as big a stretch as you might think: what is now City Hall Plaza was once part of Scollay Square, an area chockablock with theaters featuring everything from vaudeville to movies to burlesque shows to boxing. And prime among these entertainments was the *QD Follies.*

QD Soda became a national sensation thanks, in large part, to the first "QD Cutie," Sara Lampe, who also became the first Mrs. Quentin Driscoll and whose beautiful voice turned "I'm Just a QD Cutie" into a national hit. In 1926, with Sara pregnant, Quentin picked for his next "Cutie" a young singer from Newton named—Cara Blaine. It is often forgotten that one of our most beloved Hollywood stars got her start as the spokesmodel for one of our most beloved soft drinks!

In 1931—the year of the tragic boating accident that killed Sara and the couple's young son, Ralph—a heartbroken Quentin Driscoll lowered the curtain on the *QD Follies.* Though this spelled the sad end of the QD Cutie, it marked the beginning of a new era in entertainment. Stars from Clyde Hanley to George Kent got their start on *QD Comedy Hour,* one of the nation's most popular and long-running radio variety programs. In 1949 the *QD Comedy Hour* made a brief foray into television, but when the show's longtime host, Preston "Hewey" Hughes, died of a sudden heart attack during a live broadcast, the show was unable to survive him.

By the 1960s, the Scollay's heyday was long past and the area was rife with drugs and crime. In a sweeping attempt to revitalize the area, the Boston Redevelopment Authority razed Scollay Square to make way for the very complex in which you now stand. Though the *QD Follies* is just a memory, the soda it celebrated lives on.

. . .

Ralph Finnister
QD Soda Headquarters
162 B Street
Boston, MA 02127

March 2, 1993

The Honorable Mayor Raymond Flynn
Mayor's Office
1 City Hall Plaza
Boston, MA 02201

Dear Mayor Flynn:

Boston's history represents a substantial asset for its tourists as well as its citizenry. This year marks the 75th Anniversary of QD Soda, which was invented in Boston by a Boston native in 1918 and is still manufactured on South Boston's B Street, in a historic building that has remained practically unchanged since it was first built. In this Jubilee year, we strive to honor seventy-five years of faithful service by renaming B Street in its honor. "QD Street" would join the esteemed honor guard of corporate thoroughfares named for native products of Beantown.

We will be celebrating our 75th Anniversary this summer.

May we count on you to lead a street renaming ceremony to be added to QD Soda's exciting roster of Jubilee events? Thank you in advance for your consideration. Please enjoy this free case of QD Soda compliments of myself.

Sincerely,
Ralph Finnister
President and CEO
QD Soda

ours would pass with no sign Lydia lived in a country at war. War had not altered the clang of the alarm clock, nor the difficulty of brushing out her hair, nor the way the stove burner burst into blue flame beneath the tea kettle. There were still dishes to clean and floors to mop and dusting to be done. After a year of war it seemed the air ought to have grown thicker or acquired a different smell; water ought to have taken longer to boil and made dirt and dust more difficult to banish from beneath furniture or inside corners. She was grateful for Wheatless Mondays, Meatless Tuesdays, and Porkless Saturdays: these, at least, affirmed the change in the world.

Outside the flat, the war's progress was more readily apparent. With her Liberty Bond button affixed to her coat she felt that the city was filled with friends—strangers would nod and smile, pointing meaningfully to their own buttons as they passed. Billboards reminded her to conserve electricity and coal; street corner paperboys hawked the news as though they were making and not just reading the headlines. She was most fond of the changes the war had wrought on Scollay Square, where the profusion of flags adorning the theaters and streetcars lent the place a carnival atmosphere even in midday. Beginning in the afternoon and carrying into the evening, Scollay would fill with uniformed men, their crisp haircuts and brass voices jumping the wattage of the marquee lights. Scollay embraced these men with the smell of its roasted peanuts and the bravado of its vaudeville hucksters, with cobbles worn flat and with posters promising never-before-seen wonders. These men would crowd before the stage door to the Old Howard to catch a glimpse of one of Billy Watson's Orientals. They would fidget in line at Joe and Nemo's where a quarter and their uniform would buy them two victory dogs, a coffee, and a slice of apple pie. While Lydia would never have allowed herself to accompany these bright-eyed boys who smelled of sweat and shoe polish and cheap cologne, her stomach fluttered at their proffered invitations; the Sunday roto and the newsreels teemed with pictures of soldiers in training and boarding ships and marching in formation. Being addressed by such men was the closest she had come to meeting movie stars. Some girls asked for autographs but Lydia thought this common. She was content merely to smile in their direction.

Having been denied his own trip overseas, Henry purchased a four-foot-by-three-foot map of the war zones, upon which he charted troop movements with colored pushpins. Black pushpins represented the German soldiers, red the French and English, white the Belgian, and blue the American Expeditionary Forces. Until beholding Henry's map, Lydia's conception of the war had been provincial. She had not appreciated the war's breadth and scope, the brute numbers of men involved—men fighting not only in Europe, but in Arabia and Palestine, places as seemingly distant as the moon itself!

In the evening Lydia would read aloud the pertinent arti-

Though she is correct on every other count, Henry interjects that his white pushpins represented the British, not the Belgians. He was never able to disabuse his wife of the notion that Belgium possessed an army.

cles from the afternoon edition while Henry adjusted his pushpins accordingly, moving his troops east or west, north or south, to reflect the changing military landscape. Within weeks of its purchase the map became so riddled with holes that its pockmarked terrain seemed to her a fair approximation of the battlefields she and Henry projected on it nightly. Sitting with Henry, her voice enunciating the strange place names of European towns while her husband's hands took in the width and breadth of a continent, the newspaper stories no longer felt distant or irrelevant. The war felt thrillingly close.

War had little effect on sales of Wickett's Remedy, which continued to provide a meager income and a rich supply of pen pals. When one of Henry's newest correspondents proposed himself as a business partner, Lydia assumed Henry would rid himself of at least one epistolary freeloader, but to her shock he expressed interest in the notion. Apparently this Quentin Driscoll fellow was taken with the flavor of Wickett's and thought it would hold its own on pharmacy shelves. In exchange for permission to be Wickett's exclusive store representative, he would share half his profits.

Lydia was against it. Wickett's, she reminded Henry, was not a medicine. But Henry countered that if Wickett's was sold in pharmacies, a purchaser needed only to send him their receipt in order to receive a letter. If the fellow was right about Wickett's chances in the pharmacy, he coaxed, this might be the opportunity they had been waiting for. Lydia was skeptical, but she could not bring herself to oppose the prospect of Henry's liberation from the import trade. She agreed they could give Quentin Driscoll a try.

Meanwhile, Henry continued to work for his father and, in lieu of frontline reporting, funneled his thwarted ambition into his Wickett's correspondence. "Stay Healthy for the Boys" became his motto, which he penned in red ink across the back of each sealed envelope. He attributed April's marked increase in business to his new approach, but Lydia reasoned the more likely cause was the appearance in Boston of an unseasonable flu. She was loathe to confess her suspicion to Henry as she did not wish to dampen his fire: since he had been refused a uniform, his letters and their subsequent recitations had taken on a fierce energy whose spirit recalled the long-lost author of her love letters.

Henry's renewed pride in his missives was evinced by his reading manner. Calling Lydia to the settee, he would mount a straight-backed chair and declaim to her as if she were a crowd of hundreds. His body would sway, his free arm would gesticulate as though conducting an orchestra—but at the eye of this oratorical storm, the hand holding the letter would remain perfectly still. Lydia found her husband's speeches as rousing as the ones she heard in Adams Square and began dressing for his performances, each evening after dinner changing into his favorite blue tea gown. Henry, in kind, adopted a naval cap he had found in an empty seat at the Olympia after a screening of *Shoulder Arms*. Lydia assured Henry the hat became him when in truth it was slightly large for his head and occasionally flew off when his recitations became fervent—but while the hat remained in place Lydia enjoyed the illusion she was being addressed by a sailor.

We can almost feel the quickening of Henry's heart as he waited for his wife to appear. In all his memories of Lydia, including that of their wedding day, she only ever appears in the blue linen dress that so perfectly matched her eyes.

"We each one of us embody our own vital American Expeditionary Force!" Henry declaimed. "An Army resides in our muscles, a Navy in our blood, and an Air Service in our lungs. As the health of Europe depends upon the efforts of the national A.E.F., so too does the health of our country depend upon the efforts of our internal A.E.F. We must make it our personal duty to rally this force to action with no less strength and courage than if we were each General Pershing himself!"

He spoke with such passion that Lydia could practically feel the power of the country pounding through her blood, as if miniature American soldiers were fighting inside her on her behalf; so when Henry caught a cold, Lydia felt as violated as though the Hun had invaded Boston itself.

It seemed at first that the cold would be defeated by no stronger salvos than a ready handkerchief, copious amounts of honeyed tea, and regular doses of Remedy, which Lydia insisted on administering for the sake of good form. When the cold lingered and Henry acquired a wet, deep cough she suggested a day of bed rest, which he rejected out of hand, explaining he had already spent far too much of his life in bed. By the next day his pallor had increased and it was clear he had a fever, but he insisted on going to work. Only when her husband returned early that afternoon, shivering like it was winter and not spring, did he agree to return to bed. Henry had told her once—in a voice so casual it was clear he thought it commonplace—that as a boy he had slept alone. A childhood in which bedrooms were not shared seemed dreadful—never in Lydia's life had she been forced to endure a night shut away from the rhythm of another's breathing. That afternoon she brought a chair into their bedroom: there was no reason not to keep Henry company as she balanced the books.

The next morning his cough was worse and he provided no resistance to staying in bed, though he asked Lydia to fetch a few letters from his desk so that he might do some small bit of work. She spent the morning ferrying pots of steaming water down the long, narrow hallway from the kitchen to the bedroom so that he could inhale the vapors, as overnight his chest had become worse. She asked if she ought to fetch a doctor but he demurred.

"I'm enough of a doctor to know I have the flu," he diagnosed. "A doctor would merely feel my pulse, prescribe bed rest, and charge some ungodly sum for the privilege of his prescription." He smiled at her. "You are taking excellent care of me. I already sense I shall be improved by supper."

That evening his fever rose. Chills caused his hand to shake too much to handle a spoon and so she fed him soup as he lay propped in bed. Never before had a mouth seemed so vulnerable. Henry's lips were thin and delicate, the pale pink hue found along the inner curve of a seashell. Holding the spoon to his mouth Lydia became shy. The gesture was as intimate as anything they had done together in the dark.

Henry yearned to tell Lydia of his love, but feared he sounded and looked too frightful to do justice to the sentiment. His whispers among Us seek belated release for his ardor.

"Thank you," he wheezed as she fed him, his eyes gazing into her own. "Thank you." She felt compelled to make him stop—he was thanking her after every spoonful of broth. When he could eat no more she returned to the kitchen to prepare a poultice of onion and black pepper. Fetching onions from the larder summoned the sharp, intrusive smell of the poultice from the stores of her memory. She associated the scent with darkness and the sound of her mother's humming. She would have to keep the windows open for a day to erase its pungence.

When she sat beside Henry with the poultice she thought at first he had turned his head to ward off the odor. Then she saw he was blushing. She often had helped James and John with their clothes when their fingers had been too small to manage buttons, but until now she had never undressed her husband. She averted her eyes as she undid the buttons of his pajamas. His chest was not as broad as Da's or Michael's, but it was a man's chest all the same.

"This will help clear your lungs," she stammered. To calm her mind she recalled all the poultices her mother had applied through the years. Her mind quieted and Henry turned toward her.

"What's that you're humming?" he whispered.

"Am I humming?" she asked.

He nodded and hummed a few notes back to her.

She smiled. "It's something my mother used to hum when one of us had taken ill. It helped to cancel out the smell."

Cora Kilkenny has no recollection of this tune. She suspects it was her daughter's own.

"What's it called?" he asked.

She hummed a few more notes. "I'm not truly sure. Ma's always singing or humming something. I suppose it's called 'The Poultice Song.' "

"The Poultice Song," he whispered, smiling, and closed his eyes. His breathing eased. She wanted to sleep pressed against him but he was too hot, so she settled for her hand resting on his shoulder.

Very early the next morning she was awakened by a terrible rasping sound. Henry's eyes were wide with exertion as he tried to breathe, his mouth gaping, his lips tinged blue.

"Henry, darling, I'm calling an ambulance!" she shrieked, to which he nodded, blinking back tears. She kissed his forehead and rushed downstairs to the Somerset's telephone. The lobby was deserted save for the night deskman. Though he stared rudely, he assured her he would send up the ambulance men as soon as they arrived.

Mrs. Wickett was wearing only a nightgown and no bra of any sort! It was all Walter Darrow could do to keep his eyes on her face.

Silence had wrapped the building in a thick, choking gauze; Lydia wanted to cry out but the still air had drawn the moisture from her throat. As she returned upstairs, the sound of her feet inside the stairwell was as loud as an alarm, but when she regained the fourth floor, the hallway remained quiet, its every door closed except her own. She felt as if she and Henry were the only living creatures in Boston.

When she entered their bedroom, she was grateful to see he had returned to sleep. She whispered that an ambulance was on its way and thought she saw him nod. She held his hand while they waited, and stroked his fingers. She whispered of the Carney clinic, where she had once been taken after step-

Henry recalls a soft voice, but not the words it spoke. At first the voice sounded like his wife's, but it soon became a chorus of whispers.

ping barefoot on a broken bottle at Castle Island. The nuns had whispered soothingly as the doctor lifted the dark emerald glass from the pale pillow of her instep, which was then stitched up like a sock in need of darning. She promised to show him the scar as soon as he was better—he had never seen the bottoms of her feet.

Years seemed to pass in the time they waited for help to come, Lydia gazing at Henry's hand and stroking his fingers as she hummed something else of her mother's, not the Poultice Song but a tune for when bad dreams had sent her scrambling awake. Her husband's hand was beautiful, with a wide palm and long, tapering fingers. She remembered his palms being unshaped by any sort of work but this was no longer the case: on his writing hand—just beside the top knuckle of the left middle finger—was a single callus. She traced the callus with her fingertips, then pressed it softly to her lips. She gently rubbed her face against the top part of his hand, allowing the thin, dark hairs there to stroke her cheek. By pressing only slightly harder she could feel the delicate lattice of his bones against her skin. She admired his fingernails with their well-formed half-moons. She held Henry's hand like he was a child she did not want to lose in a crowd. She clutched his hand until the ambulance men arrived with their white canvas stretcher and informed her that her husband was dead.

. . .

THE AMERICAN EAGLE'S SCREAMING DEFY TO POTSDAM

Just what every red-blooded American feels in the depths of his or her heart; what we know has happened and what we fervently hope the future holds out for the Kaiser and his lust-mad legions, has been vigorously produced in what has already been pronounced the greatest photoplay sensation ever offered America's legions.

Let's not bother with the streetcar; we're better off walking, leastways 'til we get to Hanover.

Boy it's packed! I never seen it so crowded, excepting maybe the last time we was here. It's a wonder anyone gets anywhere with all these people.

Y'know Lester actually met his girl here.

The brunette?

The streetcar she was sittin' in was stopped in traffic, so he just walked beside it and introduced himself. Once he showed what a nice fella he was, she stepped right off the car and went with him.

That's a neat trick.

Course he was wearing his uniform at the time.

Lucky son of a gun. If they don't call me up soon I'm gonna go down to Lafayette Mall myself no matter what my ma says.

Is that yours?

No, mine had lighter hair.

You sure?

I think so. It's so hard to tell. They all look alike in those uniforms.

He said to meet him here?

By the statue.

And he's bringing a friend?

I told you already.

He wasn't too fresh? I can't stand a fellow who's too fresh.

He was nice. He was from Ohio.

Ohio! Well then.

He wants me to write when he ships out.

Will you?

Oh I'd write just about any fellow who asked. I wouldn't even have to like him that much.

Hello fellas!

Bentley? Jeez, Frankie, what the devil are you doin' here? Fitzy'll have your hide!

Not if he don't know—I waited until he started out himself before I quit the deck. As long as I get back in time he won't be the wiser. I wasn't about to let him rob me of my last night!

Who'd you get to cover for you, Frankie?

I told Culver I'd give him half a week's pay if he'd take my sentry duty. He's not shipping out yet so he don't care so much about losing a night on the town.

You ain't gonna actually pay him, are you?

Sure I am! Way I see it, it's a fair price for one last breath of freedom.

Well for that kind of dough we'd better make sure you have a real time of it!

It's a very special show tonight, ladies and gents! The delightful Miss Mary Blake with her red, white, and blue accordion will be singing a medley of popular favorites including "My Belgian Rose," "My Baby Boy," and "Minnie Shimmie for Me," followed by Mr. Hubie Lowe, Scollay's favorite comedian, and then, of course, the enchanting Lonna Bay, who will astound and inspire you with her grace and beauty. Step right in, gents. This is what you came for!

Belgian Rose, my drooping Belgian Rose
For ev'ry hour of sorrow you've had,
You'll have a year in which to be glad,
You were not born in vain,
For you will bloom again,
And tho' they've taken all your sunshine and dew,
We'll make an American Beauty of you,
And you will find repose over here, my Belgian Rose!

What time is it?
Time fer another round!
I dunno if that's such a good idea, Frankie.
Aw, don't be such a wet blanket. We got th' whole night ahead of us!
Bentley's right. Another round! To tonight!
Looks more like morning to me.
Would you can it already, Neddo? We got serious drinkin' to do.

Poor Johnny's heart went pitty pitty pat,
Somewhere in sunny France.
He met a girl by chance with ze naughty naughty glance,
She looked just like a kitty kitty cat,
She loved to dance and play,
Tho' he learned no French when he left the trench,
He knew well enough to say:
Oui Oui Marie, will you do zis for me,

Oui Oui Marie, then I'll do zat for you,
Oui Oui Marie,
Oui Oui Marie!

Where'd those girls go?

There's some right there.

Not that kind. The ones that was with us before.

Aw, they went home hours ago, don't ya remember? You had the one promisin' to write.

Did she kiss me?

Naw, she weren't like that. If yer wantin' that yer better off with those girls over there.

I don't got enough scratch left fer that kind of girl.

Maybe between us we got enough.

Forget it. We don't got time anyhow. We better get some coffee, we gotta be goin' soon.

But I wanna piece of somethin' sweet.

Then put some sugar in yer joe, cause that's the closest yer gettin' tonight.

Hasten son, fling the window wide,
Let me kiss the staff our flag hangs from
And salute the Stars and Stripes with pride,
For God be praised "The Americans come!"

Bentley, wake up!

'Sno use. He's out.

How're we gonna git him back?

Could carry 'im.

Us carry Frankie? What are ya, drunk? He's too heavy!

But we ain't got enough dough for a cab.

I say leave 'im. Lean 'im 'gainst this statue.

But if Frankie don't show, that's derilision of duty. Fitzy'll kill 'im fer sure.

Aw, he'll make it back. Bentley kin take care 'f himself.

I don't know, fellas—

C'mon! Bentley's bein' a real pain in the neck passin' out like this. We tole 'im t' take it easy but did 'e listen? Nope. He did not.

'Sides, if we tried t' carry 'im back we'd get in plenny trouble ourselves, either bein' late or gettin' seen with 'im. 'Ts our patrialic duty t' ship out tomorrow no madder wha'. Otherwise we're all of us in derilision, and what's th' good o' that?

Well, Joey, you put it like that I s'pose I can't argue.

Easy now. There.

Don' 'e look sweet?

Y'sure Bentley'll be okay?

Look, he's sleepin' it off unner the protection of—whoozzat? I can't see straight.

Says here, "John Winthrop, Guvnor Massachusetts, 1629."

See? Frankie'll be fine. He's got the guvnor hisself lookin' after him.

· · ·

THE QDISPATCH

VOLUME 9, ISSUE 3   MAY 1991

QD and Me:
A Sodaman's Journey
By Ralph Finnister

Chapter 1
Water Meets Flavor

We never know what the day holds. On one day, we are created—on another, we expire. In between, we flow or we float according to our natures—and if we are lucky, we mix with something that changes us for the better. I am a Sodaman. I see the world through a Sodaman's eyes.

I was sixteen when I started working at QD Soda. Few boys know what they want out of life at that age, and if someone had asked me I would have said I wanted to be Hewey Hughes, the host of the *QD Radio Comedy Hour.* I only came to QD Headquarters on account of that show, but after I was hired I learned it was broadcast from somewhere else. By then, of course, it was too late. I was already a mailroom clerk.

To see me then was not to see the future president of QD Soda. By the time Quentin Driscoll was sixteen, he was an apprentice at a soda counter and well on his way to fulfilling his life's ambition—but as for me, I was content to sort envelopes and daydream.

The future began with a simple errand. One day the regular delivery boy was out sick, so the manager asked me to take the mail up to Three. I was standing at the secretary's desk when a voice asked me to bring it in myself. And that voice was none other than Quentin Driscoll's.

Over the years I have been asked many times about that moment. Was I excited? Was I nervous? Always I ask in return: Is a star excited before it streaks across the night sky? Is a bird excited before it takes wing? No. Star and bird are only doing what they are meant to do. At that moment, I was just a boy delivering the mail. But I will say this—it was a powerful voice that called from behind that door, the kind of voice you don't refuse.

My first memory of Quentin Driscoll is not a memory of him at all. It is a memory of his desk, the likes of which I have never seen elsewhere. It was seven feet wide and made of polished wood. It had curved sides and the letters "Q.D." across its front in gold. Like everything else in that man's life, his desk had a story behind it. But I did not know that sad story, at least not yet.

Only after Quentin Driscoll said, "You are not the usual boy," did I turn my attention to his face. Once I did, I knew I was in the presence of greatness. The square jaw, the dark, intelligent eyes, and the broad, expressive brow all bespoke intelligence, savvy, and ambition. Though I had seen pictures of great men in history books I had never met one before, and I have not met one since.

"Tell me your name," he asked.

"My name is Ralph," I replied.

Imagine my shock when that noble visage blanched!

"I had a son named Ralph," the Sodaman said softly. "He

would have been seven this year."

I was old enough to observe more than sadness filling Quentin Driscoll's face, but too young to give those other emotions names.

"I'm sorry," I replied.

"Why?" he said in return. "It's not your fault that my son is dead, or that you have his name."

I did not know what to say. A moment ago I had been a boy content to daydream by the radio. Now, more than anything in life, I wanted to impress this man—but I was torn between wanting to appear humble and wiser than my years.

"I don't know if Ralph is the name of a great man," I said, "but I think it is the name of a good one. I feel sorry because it's sad to think that the world lost someone good."

"Is it better to be great or to be good?" Quentin Driscoll asked quietly, with a sad smile.

I had wanted to sound noble. Instead, I felt foolish.

"It's best to be both," I answered, hoping to make up for what I had said before, "but if a man can only be one, perhaps it would be better for him to be good and not great instead of great and not good."

I did not know it then, but with those words my Sodaman's journey had begun.

In This Issue

At first day and night were meaningless. Lydia slept; and when sleep disowned her she stared at the cracked ceiling and the faded walls, wishing sleep would take her back. Sometimes the familiarity of the room persuaded her that she was Lydia Kilkenny of 28 D Street, who worked at Gilchrist's and had always slept on the pallet beside her parents' bed. But then she would remember the sheet being stretched over Henry's corpse, or the soiled onion poultice that had slipped to the floor unnoticed until she was alone with it in the room. These memories sent the rest rushing back, a crush that left her gasping for breath.

Sometimes she emerged from the gray blur of her mourning to find Michael sitting beside her, his broad hand stroking her forehead as if trying to smooth away a fever. Later, she was told no one else could soothe her during that first week, shards of days she recalled only in narrow slivers of memory.

Henry's funeral took place during those first shattered days. She was unsure how many people attended, or in what church the service was held. She remembered standing across the open grave from Henry's parents. She remembered gripping

Grief has obliterated Lydia's memory of her departure from the West end. We can only surmise she rode the streetcar back over the bridge. We know she telephoned Roxbury because the call reverberates like a scream in the memories of Mr. and Mrs. Wickett.

Liddie clutched Mick's hand for hours at a time. That first week he slept on the floor beside her so that she could hold his hand through the night.

someone's arm so tightly that her nails cut through the fabric of her gloves. The lowering coffin seemed much larger than her husband and her mind flashed to an image of Henry's body rolling back and forth inside the box. To keep from shrieking, she pictured herself inside there with him, her arms wrapped around his body to hold him in place.

Eventually time regained its form. She stopped hoarding sleep, and the bowls of soup her mother delivered to her bedside no longer grew cold. Meals in bed progressed to meals at the table—at first in bedclothes and then in proper clothes—and from there to assisting her mother in the kitchen. Soon she found herself undertaking short trips to the corner grocery for an essential item somehow "forgotten" by her mother; and in this way Lydia gradually reentered the world.

She would have preferred a world that no longer contained the Somerset. It seemed only fair the building that embodied her life with Henry should disappear along with him. Both Michael and her mother offered to pack up the flat, but she did not wish to cede that task; she was simply furious that the building was still standing when the decent thing would have been for it to sink into the earth. Her wrath was so acute that it overshadowed her dread of being pitied. On the day she returned, anger propelled her through the lobby and up the stairs to the fourth floor, heedless of those she passed on her way.

The fourth floor hallway was as indifferent to her as it had always been. Nothing about the door to the flat indicated that a man had died on the other side of it. She had unlocked that door countless times when Henry had been alive. As she unlocked it now she could have just as easily been returning from errands—her wrist rotated the same way; the lock gave its small but resolute click. The idea that anything in this building should feel as it had before was intolerable. Lydia clamped

It was Mick's arm. The Roxbury funeral was mostly attended by friends and associates of the Wicketts, but several Southie neighbors made the long trip out by streetcar.

Walter Darrow supposes his condolence card escaped Mrs. Wickett's notice. Once he figured he had been giving the glad eye to a new widow, he traded the Somerset for a men-only building to spare himself any more compromising situations.

the tip of her tongue between her jaws and held it there, pinioned by her teeth. There was not pain, only a growing pressure that would safeguard against familiarity. Biting her tongue, she opened the door and stepped into the flat.

It smelled the same. She had never attributed a particular smell to the flat before, but having been away from it she recognized it in an instant. It was cooking and clothes, bodies and housework; it was a compendium of little smells that embodied the scent of her and Henry. Standing inside the doorway, she inhaled the air in greedy draughts, trying to memorize the scent of her marriage before it disappeared.

According to Michael, at the funeral she had accepted her mother-in-law's offer to help pack Henry's things. Without Michael's reminder she would not have known what to make of the cartons she found neatly lining the hall. In the bedroom, the bed had already been stripped. It was possible Lydia had done this herself but she did not think so. A faint pulse beat in the tip of her tongue. She could feel the edges of her front teeth pressing in. She sat on the mattress and dared herself to look at the floor. The onion poultice was gone. Some angel had removed it. Her hands had been clenched fists, but now her fingers unfurled.

Packing did not take long. Her clothes fit into one large suitcase. A second suitcase held odd things: toiletries; a wooden oatmeal spoon brought from D Street; the Remedy ledger, labels, and correspondence. She placed Henry's love letters in the same handbag that had held them before. Even in her visions of the Somerset's destruction, she had spared these letters, imagining them resting unscathed on the blighted lot, awaiting her return. The tip of her tongue ached as a fingertip aches when tied too tightly with string. A faint coppery taste filled her mouth.

In the entryway, Henry's life had been reduced to four boxes. Placed end to end, they would have made a narrow cot

Ernestine Wickett felt physically ill unmaking her son's marriage bed, but it allowed her to cry for him rather than for herself—which in turn allowed her, on seeing the onion poultice, to cry for her daughter-in-law.

just long enough for Lydia to lie on and just shorter than the man whose effects they contained. She could too easily picture the boxes stacked in a corner of a disused room somewhere above the damask parlor, or their contents dispersed among Ernestine Wickett's manifold charitable causes. In Lydia's desire to save the boxes from such a fate, she imagined a room wallpapered with pages from Henry's letters and notebooks and carpeted with his clothes. She would be the only one permitted to enter this room, and inside it she would do whatever she liked—cry or scream, laugh or sleep. But since no amount of wishing would bring this room into being, she would select for herself one article of Henry's clothing and that was all.

After the first year—when even the clothes Ernestine had refrained from handling no longer smelled like Henry—she allowed his father to donate all but her favorites to a South Boston church. Save for several framed illustrations from her son's notebooks, she kept his bedroom as it had always been.

The letter was fastened to the top of the first box of clothes. When she saw it, her mouth opened in surprise and the blood trapped in the tip of her tongue by her clenched teeth surged back into her body on its way to the heart.

"Dear Lydia," the letter read in penmanship that looked just like Henry's:

When he was alive, it was easier to be angry at you than at him. Now I am only angry at myself. Forgive me, if you can. Even if you can't, please know that I wish you well.

Beside the letter was a fifty-dollar bill. Even when she had worked at Gilchrist's Lydia had never seen anything larger than a twenty. The bill was crisp and unlined. It felt heavy in her hand and smelled slightly bitter. Fronting the fifty was a portrait of Ulysses S. Grant. On its back, rising from the middle of the ocean, was a picture of a woman named Panama.

Lydia opened the box and removed Henry's favorite white collarless shirt, the one with a tea stain on the right sleeve. On top of the box, Lydia left the fifty-dollar bill and several pieces of Remedy correspondence. "Dear Mrs. Wickett," she wrote in reply, "I am angry too, but at everyone and no one all at once. I am leaving some letters for you. They were written by people your son made happy. Maybe they can give you some happiness in return."

The two suitcases and the handbag were not too much to carry. After she locked the flat she slipped the key under the door. The hallway did not smell like the flat. The hallway smelled like strangers.

She had been in Southie six weeks when, by a stroke of good fortune, the need for a part-time counter girl arose at Gorin's and a neighbor's cousin's brother-in-law was persuaded to offer her the position. Though Lydia was not ungrateful, the opportunity seemed simply another of her mother's bowls of soup that she knew she ought to eat while it was still warm. With the job's commencement it seemed possible time had reversed. Once again she found herself rising with the sound of the drays to assume the starched, white shirtwaist of the shopgirl; once again she took breakfast at her mother's table, careful not to spill jelly on her sleeve—but this was an illusion impossible to sustain. With its airy rooms, ample dimensions, and up-to-date furnishings the Somerset had permanently altered Lydia's sense of comfort. Now the small rooms and sturdy furniture of her childhood were suffocating. The space created by Michael boarding at Mrs. Flynn's had been more than taken up by Tom, James, and John—all of whom had grown far too much in her absence still to be considered little brothers. On her return to D Street, a sheet was hung between the front room and kitchen to allow Thomas, James, and John privacy as they dressed. The addition left Lydia feeling like she had devolved from the sister who had once bathed them to a spinster aunt. In retrospect she realized

Neither good fortune nor good neighbors were at work. Mrs. Kilkenny importuned Father O'Brian to help her find Lydia a job before her daughter strayed across the bridge again.

her underestimation, among all the Somerset flat's amenities, of its hallway. Nowhere in Southie was a room permitted the sole, luxurious purpose of leading to other rooms.

Outside the D Street flat every aspect of Lydia's person proclaimed her a stranger. Liddie Kilkenny had been a D Street girl but Lydia Wickett just as certainly had been born across the bridge. Lydia Wickett pinned her hair in far too elaborate a style for a Southie girl; Lydia Wickett did not put her elbows on the table at employee lunch; and Lydia Wickett's accent was certainly not Irish. When she attempted to resume the Southie inflections after so many years of assiduous correction, she felt as if a stranger's tongue had been sewn into her mouth. Shopkeepers called her Madam instead of Dearie; conversations ceased when she neared; children froze as she walked through their midst, their games resuming only once she had passed; and at Gorin's the shopgirls took her for a stool pigeon and remained guarded. Liddie Kilkenny had known this brand of distrust. She had felt it toward the society women who were driven down West Broadway for a taste of "local color," as well as toward the occasional Harvard boys who ventured across the bridge for an evening's diversion. Liddie had rolled her eyes at these interlopers. She had spoken with a brogue so exaggerated she knew she would not be understood and pointed them opposite their desired direction. Then, once they had gone, she had laughed at their receding backs while secretly longing to follow them across the Channel.

Mornings, on her way to work, she half expected to encounter this younger self, a girl with thick braids down her back wearing a carefully mended yellow dress, who would dash past as though Lydia were invisible. At times she thought she spied this girl in the afternoon gaggle of unfamiliar children who now laid claim to Southie's stoops and curbs, but every girl who caught Lydia's eye invariably revealed a face as

Lizzy Cavanaugh from Notions thought Liddie was more of a snoot than a stool pigeon.

Mary Williams in Overcoats would no sooner have let a young widow cross her path than a black cat.

strange as any other. In each instance Lydia was grateful to have been spared a meeting: she would have felt duty-bound to offer advice but was not sure whether to warn Liddie Kilkenny never to leave Southie or never to return.

In the wake of her own return, Southie's prodigal daughter quickly learned that she was expected to be mourning a soldier. A country at war anticipated losses from battlefields, not sickbeds. Correcting the impressions of the well-intentioned became so tiresome Lydia abridged her period of public mourning, deciding she could mourn Henry better without the black armband that elicited constant requests for her husband's rank and regiment. People were not so much unsympathetic as disappointed at her answer. It was far more fashionable to die in a trench than of the flu, and it was tempting to lie. If she became a war widow, then Henry became a hero. Heroism and journalism had been alike enough in Henry's mind that a soldier's death overseas was a postmortem gift she was tempted to give him. Instead she replaced her black armband with a personal disregard for the Armed Forces, which she privately held responsible for Henry's demise—for had her husband been permitted to enlist, he would have been across the ocean from the flu that struck Boston that spring. In observance of her antipathy, Lydia refrained from discussions on the progress of the American Expeditionary Force and refused to take sides in her brothers' ongoing debate as to the relative superiority of the Navy or Air Service.

Southie did all it could to foil her boycott. Little boys played soldier, their sparrow chests thrust out in single file as they pounded the soles of their hand-me-down shoes into the sidewalks. Every woman and girl occupied her idle moments with the knitting of sweaters, mufflers, or socks in khaki or gray four-ply Number Ten wool for donation to the Red Cross. Newspapers were particular enemies. Lydia was so accustomed to Henry's editorial revisions that the sight of an unmarked broadsheet was a provocation to grief. She hated being at the mercy of such a commonplace object—she deserved to mourn when and where she pleased. She began avoiding street corners commandeered by newspaper boys and asked her father not to leave his copy of the afternoon edition in the front room.

Newspapers had the added detriment of reminding her of the Remedy. At Henry's death, the Wickett's advertisement had been paid through the end of the month. Once it lapsed, the face of the girl with Lydia's nose and Henry's eyes disappeared from the pages of the *Herald*. In spite of her original misgivings, Lydia had grown fond of that small face. Given a choice, she would have preferred to prolong its worldly life, but the best she could hope for was to provide it a dignified end.

The beginning of that end did not commence until her dread of a post office box clotted with letters was overshadowed by visions of a box whose contents had been repossessed by the postmaster. Lydia used one of her days off from Gorin's to return to Post Office Square. She donned an old dress plainer than her West end wardrobe and waited until mid-afternoon to catch the streetcar, in order to arrive when she would be least likely to encounter familiar faces. Approaching the building, she refused her lips their accustomed Hail Mary. Despite these attempts to exorcise her old ways, her habitual excitement shadowed her up the post office stairs. Even now, the familiar sensation of pushing open the heavy wooden door fired one last dumb yellow flare of reflexive anticipation through her limbs. This unhappy trip was her most fruitful, yielding up almost twenty envelopes bearing her husband's name.

Alone in her mother's kitchen, Lydia drafted twenty identical notes on the backs of twenty unused Remedy labels. After the fifth note her hand no longer shook; after the tenth she

was no longer crying; and by the eighteenth she was not thinking of the words at all. Each unopened letter was sealed with
one of Lydia's notes into a new envelope addressed to its original sender. As she worked, she trained her eyes on the return
addresses in the upper left-hand corners to spare herself the
recurrent shock of seeing Henry's name.

She had utterly forgotten about Henry's business partner
until she spotted an envelope from Mr. Driscoll. Though she
would have preferred to treat Mr. Driscoll's letter no differently than the others, she slit the envelope open. She generally
opened an envelope along its length, but she found herself
opening this one along its width. Only as she withdrew the letter from this smaller opening did she recognize it as Henry's
habit. Mr. Driscoll's writing was compact and clear, reminding
her of a department store circular. Henry had missed their
monthly meeting. Mr. Driscoll hoped all was well and suggested that Henry propose an alternate date.

She looked back over the letter. On the day of his scheduled meeting with Mr. Driscoll, Henry had been almost three
weeks dead. Lydia wondered if such a dire possibility had entered Mr. Driscoll's thoughts as he had waited. She wondered
if Mr. Driscoll had been outdoors or indoors, if he had read to
pass the time, how long he had waited before giving up, and
if aggravation or worry had won the day. She could not toler-
ate the notion that Henry might have been a cause for annoy-
ance after death had robbed him of the ability to defend or
redeem himself. She wrote to Mr. Driscoll and proposed a
meeting.

She arranged to meet him at a restaurant she knew from
her Gilchrist days but had never patronized, which was therefore safe from old memories. She did not know if arriving
early would give her the chance to collect herself or if anticipation might cause her undoing, but because the thought of

Mr. Driscoll being kept waiting a second time was unbearable, she arrived at the restaurant thirty minutes in advance of the agreed-upon time.

Of her nice dresses, only two were not linked to specific memories of Henry. Of those, only one was appropriate for spring, which simplified the issue of her costume, a convenience that felt like a godsend.

Having only ever admired its elegant, if aging, exterior in her Gilchrist days, Lydia was surprised to discover the restaurant she had chosen was a favorite of clerks. They sat on short-legged stools aligned before a narrow counter and at small, close-set tables beneath ceiling fans that wobbled on disreputable axes. They wore interchangeable dark suits several seasons old, their collars softened by sweat. Their ties, having loosened over the course of the morning, had not been reknotted and now hung broken below the knobs of their Adam's apples. Despite the novelty of her gender and the misplaced prosperity of her West end dress, not one gave Lydia a second glance. This caused her to wonder, not for the first time, if grief exuded an odor as undetectable to its sufferer as the tang of one's own body, a smell that whether acrid or cloying kept others away.

Seemingly unnoticed, Lydia selected a table in the far corner—the only one not within range of a fan's erratic trajectory. She turned her chair to face the door. Henry had only ever described his business partner as a youngish "go-getter," and she worried she would not recognize him, but at precisely the scheduled time, a man entered the restaurant's door wearing the prearranged yellow carnation in his lapel and projecting an air of confidence absent from the hunched men hurriedly ingesting the daily special.

Of Henry's age, though taller and more robust, Mr. Driscoll's features connoted a specifically nonpatrician strain of good breeding. In his pressed suit and starched collar, Mr. Driscoll looked every inch the young businessman, but he had the broad hands and handsome brow of a foreman or trades- man. Something about Driscoll's face was distinctly and uniquely American—a melding of features suggestive of far- flung forebears, united through the auspices of immigration. Lydia did not need to speak to Mr. Driscoll to understand why Henry had accepted him as his business partner: optimism was as natural to him as breath.

"Mrs. Wickett," he said, extending his hand. "I was shocked by the news. Please accept my condolences. I knew that some- thing had to be wrong when Henry missed our meeting, but I never suspected—" Mr. Driscoll shook his head.

"Thank you," she answered as she stood to shake his hand. She was impressed by the firmness of his grip. In her experi- ence a fellow's handshake underwent a marked dilution when its recipient was wearing a dress. "I'm sorry not to have in- formed you earlier or invited you to the funeral," she apolo- gized. "My husband's death was completely unexpected and to be honest, I'd forgotten your existence until I saw your name on that letter."

Mr. Driscoll sat opposite her. She was gratified the clerks had taken no more notice of his entrance than her own: it meant that grief was not to blame. "There's no need to apolo- gize," Mr. Driscoll assured her. "I'm just glad my letter reached the post office before you did. I hope it doesn't sound too strange, but I'm pleased to meet you. Henry said he was the voice of Wickett's but that you were its body and soul. I'd hoped we'd meet one day—but not like this."

She offered Mr. Driscoll a conciliatory smile. "I don't know if Henry told you, but I was against the idea of him taking you on. I came up with the Remedy to go with my husband's let- ters, not to sell alone."

"Oh, I know, Mrs. Wickett," Mr. Driscoll answered.

Lydia's memory is Our sole benchmark of this event. Like many who join Us after a long old age, Mr. Driscoll's recol- lections are clouded be- yond comprehension.

"Henry said the same thing. I'm awfully grateful to the two of you for taking me on. If you don't mind me saying so, it's a real humdinger of a tonic, a real stand-out product. I used to think I wanted to own my own drugstore, but one taste of Wickett's changed all that. I'm just certain it's destined for greatness. One day Wickett's Remedy will be in drugstores all across New England!"

Mr. Driscoll's conviction was contagious. Lydia found herself picturing shelves filled with familiar blue labels.

"And how is the Remedy doing so far, Mr. Driscoll?" she asked. Residual electricity from Driscoll's enthusiasm charged the air around their table. Lydia could sense their waiter trying to place its source as he took their orders. She wondered if the waiter supposed that she and Driscoll were lovers, and immediately felt terrible for the thought.

"Mrs. Wickett," Mr. Driscoll continued once the waiter had left. "I wish I had a fistful of greenbacks to hand over, but I'm afraid I don't. At least, not yet." He handed her an envelope of assorted change. "As you may know, the agreement is that in exchange for having been licensed the recipe I give fifty percent of everything I sell, after expenses. Right now I've got Wickett's Remedy in three pharmacies. I'm hoping that once people develop a taste for it, they'll start coming back."

"If you're going to sell something just because it tastes good," Lydia mused aloud, "I wonder if you ought to carbonate it and call it a soda instead."

Save for one man obstinately sopping every last drop of beef broth with the butt end of his bread, theirs was the only table still occupied. At the counter, the cook consulted with a man studying a racing form. Above the grill, a flecked strip of flypaper pulsed in time with the irregular draughts from the ceiling fans.

"Mrs. Wickett," Driscoll began, his voice more tentative. "You've had a terrible blow and I imagine there's all sorts of

The simultaneous specificity and opacity of memory is Our constant taunt. Lydia recalls Mr. Driscoll's manner, his words, and even a piece of flypaper, but not the name of the restaurant in which this pivotal event took place.

things you need to consider right now. But if it's all right with you I'd like to continue with our arrangement. I don't expect you to give me an answer right away. You can mail me your decision whenever you're ready."

Though the prospect of the Remedy being sold without Henry's letters still gnawed at her, Lydia enjoyed the notion of a certain small portrait preserving a foothold in the world. "Mr. Driscoll," she answered. "Before meeting you, I was prepared to curb my own inclinations in favor of whatever I thought my husband would have wanted, so it's a happy surprise to realize that my wishes aren't any different from what I think Henry's would have been. I see no reason to cancel our arrangement. Now that I've met you, I'm pleased to think that Wickett's might have a chance to live on."

Mr. Driscoll grinned. "Gee, Mrs. Wickett, I'm awfully grateful. I've got big plans for the Remedy—just you wait and see!" She suspected that if Henry could see them at that moment, he too would be smiling.

Alas, Henry was unaware of this meeting until Lydia joined Us. Our knowledge is confined to Our collective memory, the conflux of Our whisperings.

They shook hands once more. For a few months, Lydia received accountings from her business partner by mail, his envelopes weighted with a few coins and accompanied by friendly notes detailing modest sales. When the letters stopped she hoped that Wickett's final advocate had found a more profitable use of his time. Whatever it was, she wished him well.

· · ·

GERMAN HELD AS ALLEGED SECRET AGENT

The proprietor of a West end pawnshop Thursday telephoned the department of justice that a young German had pawned a suitcase for $1.50 and that inside he had found German papers, a checkbook showing large expenditures and several timetables. Deputy Marshals Bradley and McGrath, armed with a warrant, hastened to the shop and there arrested D.H.G. Speckermann, a farmhand, of 21 Pine Street, Waltham.

Speckermann explained that after he had returned to Boston from a visit to his aunt in Napoleon, Ohio, he did not have money enough to get to Waltham. Therefore, he said, he pawned his suitcase.

He explained the checkbook—from which none of the checks had been detached—by saying that while he was in Ohio his 13-year-old cousin had found the book, and making believe they were wealthy, had written the checks for the joy of economical extravagance. One was for $110 in payment for an alleged mythical taxicab bill.

He was also questioned regarding a small note-book, in which were found such Biblical phrases as, "Friends of Jesus," "Service of God," "Precious Ointment," "Example of Love," "Divine Anointing," and "The Great Commandment." It was thought at first that these were code words.

. . .

THE QD SODA WALKING TOUR

Fourth Stop: B Street

For the last and most exciting stop on our tour, take the red line to South Boston's Broadway station. It's no coincidence that this T line is the same color as the QD label: it used to be known as the QD line!

Once you arrive, walk down West 2nd Street. Turn left on B Street and walk to number 169. You are now standing before the home of QD Soda! At its heyday, the plant was open daily and accommodated thousands of visitors each year. Though daily tours ended in 1956, QD Soda Headquarters has remained a popular destination for QD Soda aficionados from around the country, who come to "see the source," and to stock up on their favorite soda! Tours are now conducted every other Sunday or by special appointment. See the machine that filled the very first bottle of QD Soda, and learn how QD Soda is made today. This tour will tell you everything you ever wanted to know about QD . . . except the secret recipe! Mention this walking tour at the Gift Shop and enjoy a 20% discount on all purchases!*

We hope you've enjoyed this unique glimpse into our soda's—and our city's—history. Don't forget to tell a friend!

---

*Antique items excluded. Only soda purchases of 6 or more 16 oz. bottles qualify for discount.

Two months after registering for the draft Michael received his letter of induction. For eight weeks they had all been waiting—Michael and his brothers impatient, Lydia and her mother anxious, and her father often alternating between excitement and trepidation in the course of a day. Then one evening Michael came early to dinner waving the letter in his hand like it was a winning lottery ticket, and the wait was over. Thomas, James, and John danced around him giddy as puppies, while Lydia stared from her place at the kitchen table. The longer she remained motionless and silent, the longer she could postpone the onset of a moment she had, through sheer force of will, convinced herself might never arrive. This gained her five additional seconds in a world in which her brother was not navy-bound. Then Michael was standing before her and she had no choice but to put her arms around him, his excitement not contagious but tangible, a runnel of charged air that enveloped her as they embraced. Even as she told herself it was better for her brother to welcome a circumstance over which he had no control, she could not help but take his enthusiasm personally. Her reaction was selfish and childish and completely beyond her ability to temper.

When she imagined him gone her tongue turned to ash in her mouth.

For the going-away party she baked a rectangular cake with black-market sugar, using rose water and violet water icings to create a flag. The result was paler than she had hoped but she was proud to have fit in all forty-eight stars. She had not worn one of her West end dresses since meeting with Mr. Driscoll. Of the three, she preferred Henry's favorite. When she removed the blue linen dress from its suitcase, it smelled of the West end flat, but after an overnight airing the fabric absorbed the smells of D Street to become a dress again and not a ghost.

The afternoon of the party was sunny and pleasantly warm for early March. Even once everything was in order—the flat tidy, the cake and other delicacies removed from the icebox, the borrowed plates and utensils marked so that they could be returned to their owners once the well-wishers had been fed and sent home—she delayed getting dressed. As long as the blue dress hung from the bedroom door, the party remained in the looming but still measurably distant future. Once she put the dress on, her brother's departure would be reduced to a matter of hours, and then minutes, and then breaths.

The boys decorated the stoop and stairwell in red, white, and blue bunting. Mrs. Feeney moved her phonograph from her sitting room to the second-floor hallway, which while too narrow for set dancing would permit pairings so long as everyone watched their elbows. Jennie Feeney's daughter Alice was Lydia's age and had married the same Malachy O'Toole who as a boy had teased them as they walked to school. Now Alice, Malachy, and their three children occupied the second-floor flat across the hall from the elder Feeneys. Well aware of her mother's fondness for reels—and uncertain the hallway would withstand more than waltzes

Malachy did not much notice Alice until Liddie went out of his league by becoming a Gilchrist girl.

and two-steps—Alice appointed herself the day's musical custodian.

Michael's brethren from the icehouse arrived with a barrel of beer from O'Reilly's, which they had ferried through the neighborhood on a dray wagon decked in red, white, and blue ribbons. Within moments of the wagon's arrival to 28 D Street the party had begun. In addition to Lydia's cake there were cookies baked by Alice and decorated with miniature paper flags from Gorin's; a bunch of bananas brought over from Mr. Leary's by Mr. Leary himself; several mince pies, which their mother had baked because they were Michael's favorite; and savory toasts made by Mrs. Feeney, which were only eaten once the rest of the food was gone.

Patrick Lucas and the boys arrived with a few flasks of whiskey as well, but they kept those to themselves.

Jennie Feeney is sure her toasts went as quickly as anything else.

The kitchen collected women while the front room drew men, but from the moment the music started Michael could be found only on the second floor, where it was said he was dancing with all comers. The party was young enough that Mrs. Feeney's phonograph could be heard over the kitchen's hubbub. The kitchen table and its chairs had been pushed against the far wall to create a small rectangular clearing the approximate size of Lydia's sleeping pallet. She had positioned herself by the table in order to cut slices of cake, while her mother stood by the sink mixing pitchers of lemonade, a drink that while not seasonal matched the afternoon's temperate weather. With every new song Cora Kilkenny paused in trading gossip with Mrs. Kirkpatrick and Mrs. Tierney to look toward her daughter, a conversational break that served each time to redirect the room's eyes.

"You go, Ma," Lydia finally offered when she could no longer withstand the room's collective gaze. "I bet it's been ages since you and Da took a spin."

"But Liddie, you love to dance," her mother protested.

Once a month Lydia and Henry had plied the Scollay

Square dance halls. Henry was a more careful dancer than Lydia was used to, but she grew to enjoy the courtly manner with which he waltzed her about the room. She shook her head. "I'd rather stay here and look after things."

Her mother shrugged. "Well then I think I will go. Your da and I are overdue for a proper go-round. But I'll expect to see you up there later on. A bit of prancing will do you good."

Without the diversion of her mother, Lydia realized what a curiosity she had become. Since her return to Southie she had only ventured from the flat to go to work or to run errands, so Michael's party functioned as her inadvertent debut. She realized too late the mistake of reviving her West end wardrobe. The blue dress was the costume of a visitor for whom Southie was only a Sunday destination, causing the guests who entered her family's kitchen to treat her as a guest herself. Well-intentioned friends with whom she was no longer intimate made polite queries, while people Lydia knew only third-hand—their restraint likely loosened by a few pints—so often repeated the same unflinchingly direct questions that she was tempted to hang a sign around her neck: yes, her late husband's family was wealthy but her late husband was not; yes, it was true she had no children; no, she did not mind being back in Southie; no, she did not dress like this every day.

Michael saved her from her inquisitors when he burst into the front room, his hair tousled from dancing and the top two buttons of his shirt undone. Her brother pretended not to know he was good-looking, just as he pretended not to care about how he dressed—when in truth he had made the most of having a sister who, for four years, had dressed men for a living. The shirt and trousers he was wearing that day had been Christmas presents from Lydia's Gilchrist period but they still looked new due to the care he had taken with them. Her brother was the only fellow Lydia knew who was as adept with an iron as any housewife.

Mary Riordan points out that she was wearing a dress every bit as nice as Liddie's.

This was the first time Margaret Kelly had seen Liddie since Henry's funeral. When eventually Margaret became a widow herself she wished she had been friendlier—but at the time Liddie seemed too different from the friend she had once known.

Liddie can think what she likes, but Fiona Purley knows firsthand it was more than dancing that disarranged Mick that day.

And Sinead McPherson knows that Fiona was not the only one doing the disarranging.

"Where's Liddie?" he bellowed as he made for the kitchen.

On hearing his voice, Lydia cursed her earlier reluctance to go upstairs. An entire hour had been wasted when she could have been watching her brother. Now he was sixty minutes closer to being gone.

"You're too pretty to be stuck in the kitchen," he pronounced on finding her. "That's a dancing dress." Grasping her shoulders, he propelled her into the front room. The particular clasp of his fingers on her clavicle recalled barreling with him through City Point when nothing in life had been more urgent than securing a seat for the Punch and Judy show.

As they made their way through the crowd, Michael stopped for every bit of advice or congratulations offered him by young husbands, who were variously regretful or relieved that their wives and children had earned them service exemptions. All agreed that with American soldiers smashing through the German line and Babe Ruth bringing home the pennant, now was an auspicious time to be called up. Men too old for the draft pounded Michael's back with a vigor meant to prove their own fitness for combat, while boys too young looked at him with a wistfulness generally reserved for first love. To each well-wisher Michael sensed just what to offer in return, whether a few confiding words or a handshake, a clap on the back or a bear hug. At his side, Lydia realized what her brother had clearly known from the outset: a going-away party was as much for those being left as it was for the one who was leaving.

The second-floor hallway was filled with dancing bodies, the dancers spinning in place to avoid collision with the walls or each other and forming a frantic centipede with gartered legs. The air was thick with beery sweat. The smell of dancing caused Lydia to realize how keenly she had missed it. With a whoop Michael maneuvered her into the chain of

Colin Kehoe saw too many draft parties to keep them all straight, but the dancing at Mick's was especially fine.

Stephen Cavanaugh's hands were allowed

[99]

more liberty at Mick's party than on any other day of his bachelor life.

dancers, which through some magic of synchronicity was moving up and back along the hallway without mishap, as though the dancers truly had become a single creature. At times the stomping feet overpowered the sound of the phonograph or caused the record to skip, but this only spurred the dancers on. Lydia's face grew shiny. She immersed herself in the scent of her brother's cologne and the solidity of his arm.

Meaghan O'Leary will wager it was perfume and not cologne that Liddie was smelling.

It felt good to stomp her feet and swing her hips. As if she were a rug receiving a needed airing, each collision with a neighbor brought out the accumulated grief of the past six months, bursting from her in invisible clouds. Then she remembered that tomorrow her brother would board a train and she wished she was not dancing but downstairs, the seven of them seated around the kitchen table like this was any ordinary Sunday.

"You're already practically gone." She murmured beneath the strains of "St. Margaret's Waltz." If she started crying she was not sure she would be able to stop.

Her brother grinned. "I go back and forth between feeling like a kid on Christmas Eve and feeling like I'm back in Miss Donnegal's class not having studied for a test. Try to be happy for me, Liddie. I'm going to France!"

As the song came to an end, Alice rushed from Malachy's side, threading her way between frozen couples to change the record.

Alice knew all about her husband's old eyes for her downstairs neighbor and wanted to finish the job before Malachy thought to ask Liddie to dance.

"Aren't you frightened?" Lydia asked in the pause before the next song began. She was not sure if Michael had not heard her or did not wish to answer, but then he turned his face toward hers.

"Do you remember the time Mr. Riordan caught me sneaking you into the Imperial?" he asked. "I'd told you it was foolproof and there you were waiting for me by the side door in your Saturday dress just as he came out of his office?"

She smiled. "I thought I was going to faint."

"Right," Michael agreed, "but then, when Mr. Riordan saw you all dolled up, he let you in himself? Well, I feel like that, Liddie—like I'm being allowed to get away with something that's too good to be true."

The music had started up again but they were not dancing. "Promise me that you'll be very, very careful," she demanded, as though he were twelve again and they were standing at the top of Sixth Street, their sleds in their hands.

"Liddie, you know I'll be as careful as I can. How about if I promise to keep my head on straight and my wits about me? That's a promise I can make for sure."

She shook her head. It was not nearly enough. "Will you write at least every Sunday?"

Michael nodded. "If I didn't Ma would come across the ocean after me! But you gotta promise me to start getting out more. Henry wouldn't want you keeping yourself to yourself the way you have been." He kissed her on her forehead. "I love you, Lydia Claire. Now stop your snuffles and go find yourself a nice fella to dance with; I'm going to sit a spell with Da." Within moments she had lost sight of him.

Without her brother, she felt unequal to the hallway's bustle and sought refuge in a doorway. Her brothers—who had been biding their time in Alice's flat with the other children—scrambled past her, determined not to let their brother leave their sight. She decided to join them, but it was far more difficult to make her way downstairs without Michael clearing her path. She was flushed from dancing. She would have liked to explain to every woman she passed that she had only been with her brother but the mere thought of doing so exhausted her. She focused on returning to the kitchen as quickly as possible.

In a previous lifetime the fathers and sons who filled the front room had patted Lydia on the head and called her "Mickey's kid sister." Today their formality as they stood aside

Angela Landry cannot see how anyone else would have wanted a widow for a dancing partner, seeing as it was such bad luck.

Sean Kelly would have been happy to give Liddie a spin, but she left too quickly to give him the chance.

more aptly befit an old maid, but she was grateful for anything that eased her passage to the relative obscurity of the neighboring room.

"Oh good," her mother exclaimed on her reappearance. "You're just in time. Himself's building up to a speech."

In the sitting room Dan Kilkenny had risen from the couch to stand beside his son. It was strange to see them together. Age had begun to diminish her father, making her brother seem like the original from which their father's lesser copy had been fashioned. Even slightly diminished, however, Dan Kilkenny needed only to raise his arm to bring a silence to the room that most men could have achieved only with a shrill whistle.

"I'd like to toast me boy," her father announced. The cadence of his voice carried out the door and up the stairs, quieting the people there as effectively as if he'd been standing beside them.

"Mick," he began, "I'm proud of you two times over: first for your wanting to sign up as soon as Mr. Wilson declared war and second for agreeing for your ma's sake not to go until you was called. These things attest that you're brave but not foolhardy, for though it takes a brave man to fight for his country only a fool would try to go against the wishes of Mrs. Kilkenny!"

Mick recollects a pretty fierce argument before "agreeing" not to enlist.

Once the laughter subsided her father continued, his voice all the more compelling for being softer. "I know that if you're even half the man in France that you are here, you'll make a world of difference in this war. Once you get on that train tomorrow morning, whether you be at Devens or across the ocean, I want you always to remember, Son, that my love and the love of your ma and your sister and your brothers is going right along with you." As he ended, someone in the room began to sing.

Seamus Delancey started up a version of this song at every draft party.

"MICKEY get your gun, get your gun, get your gun, Take

it on the run, on the run, on the run, Hear them calling you and me, Ev'-ry son of SOUTH-IE, Hurry right away, no de-lay, go to-day, Make KILKENNY glad to have had such a lad, Tell your mother not to pine, To be proud MICKEY'S in line.

"O-ver there—o-ver there—Send the word, send the word o-ver there—"

The strains of the song swelled through the ceiling. Soon every voice was joining in, the singers upstairs a few words behind the singers downstairs to create an echo, as though the cluster of people in the front room were standing at the edge of a great divide:

"So prepare ('pare)—say a pray'r (pray'r)—Send the word, send the word to beware ('ware)—We'll be over, MICKEY'S coming over, And he won't be back 'til it's over over there! ('ver there!)"

Once the beer ran dry Michael's pals carried him off to Scollay and the party, having lost its center, dissipated. Mrs. Feeney retired her gramophone. Men called loud farewells as if these were long good-byes, preferring for the moment not to remember that they would be seeing one another tomorrow at the factory or in the shipyard. Several of the older women stayed behind to help Cora and Lydia clean up before heading home to get supper. When Lydia changed out of her dress, she noticed that a small, oblong stain spotted the left sleeve and the collar had lost its starch. The skirt pleats would need to be repressed and both the bodice and skirt needed ironing, but she was in no rush. She preferred the dress to hold her brother's memory.

The next morning the family met Michael at the train to say their final good-byes. The platform was so overrun that Lydia feared they would miss him completely, which caused her to transform every passing figure into her brother until she spotted him shouldering his way through the sea of well-

At this point, there were always enough voices for Seamus—whose voice was not nearly so flat as his feet—to insert his own name without anyone being the wiser.

wishers, debarkees, and duffel bags. Michael smiled through his hangover and promised once again to write every Sunday. Lydia managed not to cry until her mother started. She apologized for the wet spot she left on her brother's chest at the end of their embrace, but Michael only laughed and hugged her tighter. After he boarded, they found his car and stood shouting last-minute instructions and endearments through his open window until the train began to move. As he waved, he leaned out the window, allowing her to watch him long after she could no longer see his face. She waved back until her brother was not even a discernible shape on the horizon.

Michael's absence reversed Lydia's relationship to the daily newspaper. She became avid for news from Europe, scrutinizing the morning and evening editions so that by the time her brother shipped out from Camp Devens, she would be thoroughly versed in the situation overseas. She glossed over the photographic subjects of the Sunday *Herald*'s roto section in favor of the photographic backgrounds. She was not as interested in soldiers-at-arms as she was in the roads, trees, buildings, and tents that would in a matter of weeks compose her brother's new surroundings.

At first it was impossible to read a newspaper article without hearing Henry's voice or spotting an untidy sentence that would have aroused his editorial ire, but then the newspaper became a newspaper again and not a harbinger of fresh grief. One day she realized that she no longer heard her husband as she read. At some point Henry's voice had fallen silent. Several emotions clashed at this simple proof of time's passage. Guilt and relief, anger and resignation were easy enough to distinguish, but others faded too quickly after their fierce combustion to be named.

When Michael's first letter from Devens arrived it was

The mnemonic brevity of this leave-taking causes Us to wonder if Lydia might have been slightly hungover herself.

passed around 28 D Street with as much ceremony as a strap from Saint Patrick's sandal. Lydia's mother was quick to point out the steady penmanship and proper spelling—and if she was disappointed by the missive's brevity she did not let on. According to his letter Michael was working very hard, the food was lousy, and the fellows were first-rate. As there was no more room in the barracks, his regiment was sleeping in tents; but once the next company shipped out they would be moved inside. He sent his love and dearly missed his mother's cooking. He hoped the grub would be better in France. Once the letter had completed its tour of the building it was tacked beside Cora's picture of the Sacred Heart in the front room, where all visitors were enjoined to read it even if they had read it before.

Michael's second letter from Devens arrived exactly a week after his first. Its resemblance to its forebear did not stanch anyone's enthusiasm for the knowledge that he was still working very hard, and that neither had the quality of the food improved nor the quality of his comrades declined. There seemed to be a nasty flu going around, Michael's tent mate had finally begun brushing his teeth, and Michael had impressed the lieutenant with how much he could carry on his back.

Between the two letters' arrivals there was a parade. This in itself was not unusual. Since Wilson had declared war there were often parades for Liberty Bonds or the Red Cross or new enlistees. The Win-the-War-for-Freedom parade was different, however, because it was a sailors' parade. Lydia hoped that observing men in naval uniform would more easily allow her to picture her brother in his.

The morning of the parade James and John washed behind their ears without being told, Thomas arose early in order to shine his shoes, and Lydia braided a red, white, and blue ribbon through her hair. Upstairs similar pains were taken, as the

Mick hated the sleeping arrangements. The strange noises of Devens kept him awake and his tent buddy smelled like onions.

According to William Curly, Mick Kilkenny was no prize tent mate either, being a terrible snorer.

shipyard workers from the pier—Malachy included—would be marching in solidarity with the naval recruits. All Southie, it seemed, was headed west across the bridge. The streetcar was so crowded that Lydia placed John, who was too old for such things, on her lap. The streetcar was filled with Sunday suits and dresses adorned with Liberty Bond pins. It was rumored the parade was to be filmed in order to boost morale overseas, and on the crowded streetcar people sat with handmade signs between their legs, which read HELLO JIMMY FROM YOUR B STREET PALS and OLLIE YOUR MOTHER LOVES YOU.

In his entire life John was never so embarrassed as when he grew a hard-on sitting right there on his sister's lap. He was sure it meant he was going to Hell.

Lydia's favorite part of any parade was the marching band. Marches on the Victrola had no flash or strut: the drums did not electrify, the trumpets did not exalt, and the tubas did not pull the strings of her legs in time to the music's promise of good news just out of reach. She loved the erect carriage of the marchers in their impeccable uniforms and the proud way they held their instruments, as though each trumpet and flute and drum were incontrovertible evidence of all that had gone right with the world. As strong as her love of marching bands was her conviction that she was as indispensable to a parade's success as the marchers themselves. Without people spilling over the sidewalks and onto the street, without the crush of elbows and peanut breath and frantically waving flags, a parade was merely a contrived walk.

The air was crisp and cool from a recent rain, which had washed clean the streets and sidewalks and store awnings so that the city, like its citizenry, was wearing its best clothes. No one was certain of the exact parade route, so her father decided they would disembark at Hawley Street and walk. This proved wise as the crowds overflowing the sidewalks soon reduced the streetcars to stationary viewing platforms.

Vendors hawked peanuts and flags and patriotic buttons;

there were penny candies and victory dogs. James and John had a nickel between them and bought a flag they vowed to share, agreeing to alternate possession at ten-minute intervals. This proved highly contentious as neither owned a watch. Thomas walked slightly ahead, his proud shoulders thrown back, his head erect, and his draft card at the ready. To his delight, the draft age had been lowered to eighteen the week before.

Against a street clock leaned a veteran of uncertain vintage, clad in a faded uniform from the Spanish-American War. At unpredictable intervals the antique soldier placed a weathered bugle to his faded lips and produced sounds of astonishing vigor, startling Lydia, who had not at first noticed him. At the sound of the horn she recalled a scene from a war picture, in which a bugler summons his regiment. The theater accompanist had played reveille on the piano but there was no comparison to the sounds emanating from the old man's battered instrument. She had never heard a live bugle before. If at that moment the bugler had beckoned to her, she would have followed without question.

Zachariah Obedy remembers this particular young lady no better than she remembers her history. He was a Civil War veteran.

Her family slowly made their way toward State Street until, reaching the corner of State and Congress, they could progress no further—the crowd had grown too thick. At first John squatted, hoping to peer at the parade through the legs of the crowd—but when this provided only glimpses of shoes and pant cuffs, he resigned himself to receiving the parade in the irregular interstices offered by the constantly shifting crowd. Lydia bragged to fellow spectators that her neighbor was in the parade, but her thoughts were with her brother. Today's parade was necessary preparation for his eventual appearance on a street like this one, on his way to a ship that would carry him to Europe.

. . .

BANISHES HER PET FLOWER
TO PROVE HER PATRIOTISM

Hears Kaiser Likes Them

Mrs. Charles A. Abbot, wife of the engineer of the webbing mill, had planted a garden beside her home for many years, and particularly loved bachelor's buttons. But now her hollyhocks and the spicy little pinks bloom alone. For last Tuesday night when Mrs. Abbot unfolded her evening paper she could scarcely believe her eyes when she read that the inoffensive blue blossoms in her garden were the favorites of Kaiserism, associated with our enemy's domain, in a word, the official flower of Germany. Mrs. Abbot's fighting mood was aroused immediately. She hustled out to her garden and with a hoe and a rake removed all traces of the alien blossoms.

"To think," she exclaimed indignantly, "that people have been driving past my house all summer thinking maybe I was a sympathizer with the Kaiser. You would never believe how many bachelor's buttons I had."

Perhaps, as Mrs. Abbot says, the summer may come soon when the blue bachelor's buttons can grow again unmolested.

In the meantime, hats off to Mrs. Abbot's staunch patriotism that forced her to sacrifice something she loved out of loyalty to America.

. . .

Well, Quentin, I must admit that when you first took up with that tonic, I wasn't sure it was the stand-out product you were looking for. There was something just slightly off about it.

Gee, Mr. Thornly, why didn't you tell me?

I didn't want to quench your fire! You reminded me too much of myself when I was your age and, besides, I'm an old man. It was possible I was missing something.

You wouldn't hold back on me now, though, would you? That is, if you've still got doubts?

Quentin, I'll be straight with you: you've definitely got something. What made you think of it?

Well, it was partly the widow. She reminded me how Dr. Wickett had never thought of the Remedy as a medicine—

You tried to explain this to me before. Some cockamamy thing having to do with letters?

I never quite followed it either, but I didn't let it bother me on account of the tonic's taste. And then it hit me—I wasn't any more interested in medicine than they were: I was interested in flavor! And what do people drink when they're after something that tastes good? *Soda!*

What does the widow think?

I haven't told her yet. You see, if no one likes it, I don't want to risk upsetting her over nothing. I figure if I can come to her with guaranteed money from proven sales, it'll help my case.

Well if it keeps selling like it has been, then you've got nothing to worry about.

. . .

THE QDISPATCH

VOLUME 9, ISSUE 6   NOVEMBER 1991

QD and Me:
A Sodaman's Journey
By Ralph Finnister

Chapter 4
The Promise

That night I could barely sleep. Why did Quentin Driscoll want to see me? For two years I had been moved from department to department like a bottle on a conveyor belt. At every stop I had worked my hardest, only to feel the belt lurch beneath me and move me on. Was Quentin Driscoll's hand on the lever? Sometimes this seemed the only answer and sometimes this seemed a boy's folly.

The next morning I reported to the third floor just as I had two years before, but this time with nothing to deliver except myself. The crazy conveyor belt that had carried me for so long was reaching its end. But would my little bottle pass inspection?

Quentin Driscoll was just as I remembered him. When I entered his office, those dark eyes stared at me with such intensity that I trembled.

"Let me look at you," he offered as I stood before him. Though he was unchanged, in the course of my two-year journey, I had grown from a boy into a man. My arms and legs had lengthened, and my voice had deepened. I had even begun to grow a moustache like one I had first seen two years ago—on Quentin Driscoll's face.

"When you came to me before, had you ever traveled?" the Sodaman asked me.

"Traveled?" I replied. "No, Sir."

"And what do you think of the trip you have just completed?" he asked with a knowing smile.

I was as still as flat soda. After two years of uncertainty, it seemed my fondest wish might be true.

"For two years, my boy, you have been traveling the world of QD Soda. I have been pleased to learn that you learn fast and travel well."

"Thank you, Sir," I replied. Those words of praise would have been enough, but there was more.

"I've been keeping an eye on you, my dear boy. I wanted to see if the instinct I had wasn't merely a sad man's fancy. If there was more to you than just a name. I am pleased to say I have not been disappointed."

And now, though I could still feel my inspector's eyes on me, I did not feel fear, but happiness.

"Ralph," the Sodaman murmured, his voice becoming softer. "I have great plans for you."

I had not returned to Quentin Driscoll as an empty vessel. My bottle had been filled at each stop with some new and valuable ingredient, all according to the recipe of a master craftsman. I was not ready to be capped off yet—no, I still had much to learn—but I was well on my way.

"I won't let you down, Sir!" I replied.

Quentin Driscoll rose from his desk and strode toward me. He placed his broad hand on my shoulder.

"Ralph," he declared. Though I had been called that name all my life, I felt I was being christened anew. "It is a fine, fine name!"

In This Issue

The parade was not a week past when Malachy came back ill from the shipyard. Alice sickened a day later and Mrs. Feeney removed the children to her flat hoping to subdue the contagion, but each in turn took ill and was returned across the hall to what had become the family sickroom. News of the second floor's fate spread through 28 D Street. The second-floor hallway was pronounced off-limits for indoor games and breaths were held while climbing the stair. A doctor was reluctantly summoned: according to him a virulent flu had started at the pier. His prescription of bed rest, food, salts of quinine, and aspirin cost Mrs. Feeney one dollar. Ever since Lydia could remember, her mother and Jennie Feeney had nursed one another's families whenever sickness blazed through Southie, so when Lydia returned from Gorin's to find no sign of her mother in the kitchen, she knew for certain Alice and her brood had grown worse.

In happier times the doors to the second-floor flats stood open, Alice's children dashing between their apartment and their Gran's as supper smells wafted from both kitchens. Now the doors were shut. A note written in Jennie Feeney's careful hand was fastened to her daughter's door, and read: "QUAR-

Jennie Feeney wonders if things might have gone differently had she taken the children sooner.

INTEEN! DO NOT GO IN!!" It was strange to think that only a few weeks prior, the same hallway had been used for dancing.

After a perfunctory knock, Lydia opened the door. The front room was dark and quiet, but toward the back she discerned low voices.

"Alice? Mrs. Feeney?" she called. "It's me, Liddie, come to see if you're needing anything."

Alice's flat was a testament to the life that would have been Lydia's had Southie triumphed over life across the bridge: there was the couch and end table purchased on credit from McCormick's Slightly Used Furnishings; there was the picture of the Virgin given Alice by the church Sisterhood on her marriage; there was the heirloom rocking chair, resembling almost exactly the one in which Lydia's mother hoped to rock her own grandchildren. When the unfairness of Henry's death still knocked the wind out of her, Lydia had sought comfort envisioning this version of life, which would have been hers had she laughed on receiving Henry's first letter. But as she faced the trappings of this unchosen path, Lydia felt protective love for her handbag filled with letters, her suitcase of dresses, and all the memories that would not be hers if Alice's flat was her own.

The air was stale and smelled of fitful sleep, reminding Lydia of long Southie winters when the windows were closed against the cold for weeks and the stove tinged everything gray. Opening the windows helped. As the cool outside air wafted in, she could practically hear the stifled apartment exhale. She thought she heard barking. Small packs of abandoned dogs haunted the alleys behind butcher shops and trailed the water truck in summer. These strays were adopted by children, who surreptitiously left scraps on stoops. This dog was likely expecting one of Alice's brood to feed it.

"Alice? Mrs. Feeney?" she repeated. "I hope you don't mind—I've opened a few windows."

"Liddie?" came her mother's voice from the bedroom. "Be a dear and go fetch Jennie from across the hall."

Her mother's cheerful urgency was even more unsettling than the flat's fetid air. Lydia dashed into the hallway and through the door to Jennie's flat without bothering to knock. Mrs. Feeney was deep asleep, the circles under her eyes attesting to a string of wakeful nights, but at the touch of Lydia's hand she snapped awake.

"My ma says to come," Lydia explained. Jennie Feeney bolted from her bed and rushed to her daughter's flat across the hall.

Alice and Malachy occupied the bed by the window. Patty, Meagan, and Brian shared the pallet on the floor. The bed frame was made of the same poor wood as the Kilkennys', its blocky design perforated by knotholes. On the wall above Alice's and Malachy's heads hung the same Sacred Heart to which Lydia had directed her nightly prayers as a girl. That she had never entered this room before did not temper its familiarity: only the curtains, which were green gingham rather than white with lace trim, distinguished it from the one below.

The bedroom was even danker than the rest of the apartment. The air was dense with the smells of fever sweat, phlegm, and unwashed sheets and seemed, by its very thickness, responsible for the prostration of its inhabitants. Whether sickness alone or a combination of poor health and poor light contributed to the family's complexions, their skin reminded Lydia of potato broth, save for Brian's lips—which were tinged blue, as though it were possible to be chilled in that stifling room. When Brian coughed, Lydia realized the barking she had heard earlier had not come from any stray dog.

Alice lay on her side, her brown hair pasted across her pallid neck. Malachy was barely distinguishable in his stillness from the bedding in which he lay, but when he coughed Lydia

Sick as he was, Malachy was still highly embarrassed to be seen by Liddie in such a state.

was able to discern his head facing the wall. Surely Alice's original intention in lying on her side had been to watch over her children, but fever had reduced her gaze to a glazed stare. Occasionally during the fever epidemics of Lydia's childhood, entire families had sickened. As a girl, her dread of purgatory and damnation had been matched by the fear of her mother falling ill.

On seeing her mother with Alice, Lydia became momentarily disembodied, moving back in time to observe herself in a different room, beside a different sickbed. In the dim light her mother could have been a younger woman, while Alice's pallor and slim limbs could have been Henry's. Then the woman before her once again became her mother, who was gently stroking her neighbor's head.

"Jennie, she's only gotten worse. We ought to send her and the little one to Carney," Cora murmured like she was crooning a lullaby.

"Ooh, my poor Alice," Jennie moaned, bending over her daughter.

"Get away, devil," Alice croaked. What had initially looked like shivering was Alice's crippled attempt to wrest her head from her neighbor's hand.

"Alice," Lydia whispered. "What are you saying?"

Cora shook her head. "It's no use," she continued. "She's burning up." She turned toward Jennie. "It's only my talking calm this way that keeps her still, otherwise she'd be ranting and raving and scaring the children half to death. I don't think Meagan and Patty are quite so bad off but I'm worried for Brian."

The truth of Cora's appraisal was self-evident. The girls were as pale as their brother but their lips were pink, not blue.

Jennie Feeney nodded and directed herself to her granddaughters. "It's all right, dearies," she cooed, adopting the same soothing tone as her neighbor. "Your ma's not well on account of fever, but now Gran's here. If I were to fetch some nice broth do you think you might drink it?"

The girls—their eyes wide and glassy, their hands tightly intertwined—nodded as one.

"Brian, dearie, shall I fix you some broth as well?" Jennie offered.

Brian coughed. His coughs were thick and deep, his eyes imploring those around him to make them stop.

Malachy's voice came soft from beside the window. "It's no use, Jennie. He's too sick. Take him, Cora. You won't get Alice to go, but take Brian."

"No." Alice rolled her head in protest, the word bubbling thick from the back of her throat. Mrs. Feeney knelt beside her daughter's bed. Malachy heaved himself away from the window to place a hand on his wife's side.

"Alice," he whispered hoarsely. "Angel, we got to let him go."

Alice reached toward her children. Her arm shuddered before exhausting itself, arcing toward the bed frame, and striking the knotty wood. The sound of the collision was unexpectedly substantial, as though more than a hand had fallen—but if it had hurt, Alice's face betrayed nothing. Sickness had turned her into a spectator of her own body.

Malachy lifted his head just high enough to see his children. "Brian," he croaked. "Son, there's nothing for it but to go. Be a soldier, son. Be brave and go with your auntie Cora." He turned. "Please excuse my Alice," he pleaded, his body trembling with the effort of remaining even partially upright. "I'm afraid she ain't herself."

"Don't we know it, dearie!" Cora cried.

Malachy eased himself back onto the bed. Jennie put her mouth to her daughter's ear. Her hand trembled as she stroked her daughter's face, which seemed finally to relax, but as Cora

Meagan does not remember seeing or hearing anyone except the Virgin Mary, who asked her if she and her sister were good girls.

Patricia only recalls a nightmare in which her mother turned into a witch.

Malachy's fever was so high that he could not see anything, but he kept this to himself. Sending his son away when he could not see him go was a torment he would not wish on anyone.

moved toward Brian, Alice's hand shot forward and latched on to the fabric of her neighbor's dress.

"Keep away!" Alice hissed. Her voice bore little resemblance to the voice Lydia knew, and she could not fathom where Alice found the strength to speak.

"Ma, I'll take him," Lydia offered as calmly as she could. "You stay with Malachy and the girls." But nothing would placate Alice now.

"Stay AWAY, devil, stay away, DEVIL, leave him BE!" Alice's thick, labored speech rose in intensity to become the voice of sickness itself. It was as if a large, phantom hand was squeezing her chest from inside to expel the cobwebby air that powered her words. To Lydia, the prospect of removing Brian to Carney Hospital was no longer an act of desperation; it was an exorcism.

Alice remembers only feeling awfully tired and deciding to lie down.

Lydia lifted Brian from the mattress. His head rolled back as if he were an infant too young to manage his neck. Alice howled like she had been struck. Lydia adjusted her arm to hold the boy, pretending he was a newborn and not a child six years old.

"Brian," she murmured into his ear. "I'm taking you to Carney where they can help you to get better. Auntie Cora and your gran will take great care of your ma and da and sisters while you're gone."

If the boy struggled, she told herself, she would simply clasp him tightly to her chest and make the best of it. Instead, he whispered, "Hurry."

She needed no further encouragement. Making sure to give Alice's bed as wide a berth as she could, she started toward the door.

"NOO, put 'im back, put 'im back, put—" but Alice's voice collapsed on itself.

"Fetch the doctor while you're gone," Cora called, all pre-

Auntie Liddie did not hear right. Brian said, "Sorry." He knows he was being punished for scaring his sisters with his bad breathing noises. Usually he liked to scare them, but only when he wasn't scared himself.

tense of calm abandoned. Lydia was already in the kitchen, Brian easily mistakable for a bundle of bedclothes in her arms. "Tell him they're much, much worse."

Somehow Alice found the strength to scream.

. . .

AN APPEAL BY AMERICAN BREWERS
TO THE AMERICAN PEOPLE

In many publications the word "German" is applied to the word "brewer" and there is continued and persistent effort to create in the minds of readers the impression that brewers are of a class unpatriotic. This is a malicious and cowardly lie!

Since the beginning of the war brewers have been among the largest purchasers of every Liberty Bond issue. They have contributed in large amounts to the Red Cross and other war activities. Brewers themselves are wearing the uniform of service, and the sons and grandsons of brewers are fighting under the Stars and Stripes.

In the many acts of disloyalty discovered by the Department of Justice prior to and during the war, there is not one single instance where any brewer, directly or indirectly, has in any way been found guilty of an act which could be considered disloyal.

WE ARE APPEALING TO YOU AS CITIZENS
TO HELP PROTECT THE GOOD NAME
OF OURSELVES AND OUR FAMILIES.

. . .

But I heard it started on the pier.

Nah, nah, I'm tellin' you it was the cruisin' ships what brought it. See, first they got to pass through the Arctic and then they got to pass through the Gulf Stream—so first they're catchin' colds and then they're gettin' fevers. It's the perfect recipe. Beats me, though, why anyone would be takin' a cruise at a time like this, what with the war. If you ask me, it's disrespectful.

If you could afford it you'd be singin' a different tune.

You're both of you wrong. Don't you read the papers? It's Fritz. It's a known fact a Gerry submarine was spotted in the Harbor releasing gas into the air. Spanish influenza gas.

You're pullin' my leg.

Honest! I read it with my own eyes.

Now that's low.

The Hun'll stop at nothing. When I read that it made me want to sign myself up, even if it would be helping the English.

Molly would kill you.

That's why I didn't.

. . .

Ralph Finnister
QD Soda Headquarters
162 B Street
Boston, MA 02127

May 27, 1993

The Honorable Mayor Raymond Flynn
Mayor's Office
1 City Hall Plaza
Boston, MA 02201

Dear Mayor Flynn:

You suggested in your letter that it would neither be practical nor appropriate to rename B Street—which exceeds twenty blocks in length—in QD Soda's honor. Prior to your response, the repercussions of such a name change for letter carriers and mapmakers had not been considered, nor that sizable urban thoroughfares are generally reserved for figures such as notable clergy and slain civil rights leaders.

In light of those pertinent facts, we submit an alternate proposal: that only the 160 block of B Street—upon which QD Soda Headquarters has been in continuous operation since its construction—be renamed. Given the quarter mile of South Boston roadways honoring the former location of the New England Confectionery Company—by which we refer to Necco Court, Necco Place, and Necco Street—this proposal both falls within existing parameters of corporate signage and poses a negligible burden to signage industries and their related affiliates. Additionally, the renaming of a single block of roadway would honor QD Soda's founder, Quentin Driscoll, without challenging the primacy of thoroughfares such as Cardinal O'Connor Way and Martin Luther King Jr. Boulevard.

Mr. Mayor, thank you for your reconsideration of this revised request. For your edification and enjoyment I have enclosed *The QD Soda Walking Tour,* a limited-edition pamphlet that highlights over seven decades of QD Soda history. I am also enclosing a limited edition QD Soda lapel pin and a framed and numbered reprint of a vintage QD Soda magazine advertisement, all of which I hope will illustrate, in decor-enhancing and collectible ways, the import and value of QD Soda.

I look forward to hearing from you.

Very Sincerely,
Ralph Finnister
President and CEO
QD Soda

Running, intrinsic to childhood, becomes in adulthood an act of last resort. The sharpness of the cobbles beneath Lydia's thin soles recalled the slap of each stair as she raced to the Somerset lobby to summon an ambulance. Just as then, the world dimmed save for the path before her. The only sounds were hers and those made by the boy she held in her arms.

Brian's breathing eased on his exposure to the open air and his coughs lessened but his body had not unclenched since his mother's scream. Banishing thoughts of Henry from her mind, Lydia attempted to comfort the boy as she ran, holding him against her body to dampen the jostling.

"Wee little chick," she murmured, "wee little kitten, it will be all right." By the time Henry's ambulance had arrived, it had been too late. "Wee lamb, littlest mouse." The moment she had returned to the bedroom, she had known something was wrong. She had gone to the bed and held Henry's hand and talked to him as if he were still living, but she had known. She pressed her lips together, pursing her mouth against further thought.

Brian whimpered. She wondered if there was a better way to carry him. The last time she had held a child she had been

When Auntie Liddie took him from his bed, Brian was sure he was going to be spanked. He did not want to go out—he wanted to go back to bed—but Auntie Liddie was holding him too tightly for him to say so.

fourteen. She was out of practice. Finally she felt Brian's body relax as something warm and wet seeped into her shirt. It was good if he cried a little—in the bedroom he had been too frightened even for tears. "That's right, let it out," she panted. Barely discernible beneath the smell of Brian's sickness was the sweet scent of a child's skin.

By the time she caught sight of the hospital building at the base of Telegraph Hill, her chest and throat burned, her arms ached, and her breath came in jagged bursts from her mouth. Sweat had soaked the fabric of her shirtwaist and she worried it would soak into Brian's clothes and give him a chill. She ignored her body's plea to walk. She would rest later, when Brian was safe. She was convinced the boy's breathing was much improved. The air had certainly done him good—perhaps the doctor would examine him and send him home.

Carney Hospital was half a mile from the flat. We strongly doubt Lydia ran this distance, especially with a child in her arms.

She avoided the grand stone archway at the hospital's main entrance, opting for the smaller clinic door to the left. The registering nurse took one look at Brian and directed Lydia past the few waiting patients to the far end of the room, to the doorway that led to the hospital itself. With no choice but to obey, Lydia focused on that door to the exclusion of all else, knowing better than to look at the clinic patients, who would be staring with a mixture of dread and relief at witnessing a circumstance worse than their own. To combat her own uneasiness Lydia forced a smile, but when she passed over the threshold even this shred of optimism faltered.

The hospital corridor loomed before her, thick with the sound of coughs and the smell of stale breath. A Sister of Mercy led Lydia up a flight of stairs, the wings of her wimple fluttering with each upward step. What Lydia remembered most clearly from her girlhood visits to the Carney clinic were those broad white wimples, which had looked to Lydia like angel wings hovering about the nuns' heads. When she had needed the glass removed from her foot, this vision had simul-

[122]

taneously assured her and intensified her fear—for while the extraordinary sight of angelic nuns had drawn her attention away from the doctor's efforts, the Sisters' cherubic appearance seemed to confirm her belief that the hospital served as Heaven's antechamber.

The children's ward was a narrow, white room with a row of ten metal beds running along each of the two longest walls, the space between them forming a wide aisle. Some of the beds were concealed by screens, but beside each visible bed was a small nightstand on which rested a single water glass and a white enamel pitcher. Lydia, who had never been beyond the clinic door, was disquieted by the ward's simplicity. Each of its children ought to have been taking medicine or receiving an examination. The hospital of Lydia's imagination housed one doctor for every bedside, but here there was not a doctor in sight. The nun who had led Lydia up the stairs seemed unalarmed by the ward's dearth of personnel and instructed her to place Brian in a bed midway down the row. A nurse followed immediately with a screen to partition the bed as Lydia set Brian down.

"I'm just putting you into a bed of your own," Lydia explained when Brian began to whimper, tightening his grip on the fabric of her dress. "You'll need your own bed if you're going to get better."

She suspected the ease with which she bedded the boy was due more to his fatigue than to her powers of reassurance.

"How long has he been ill?" the nurse asked. Her mask made it difficult to tell her age.

"He fell sick only yesterday or the day before," Lydia explained. "The whole family's stricken. The doctor said it was the flu but that was before it grew so dire."

The nurse turned toward the boy. "You poor dear," she murmured as she applied a compress and then a plaster. "You poor, poor dear." Neither action impressed Lydia as effica-

Cora Kilkenny is sure it was Mick who stepped on the glass and Liddie who only watched it happen. As for Liddie's scar, Cora suspects it came from her daughter once holding her foot too close to the stove in winter.

Brian was not tired but embarrassed: he had just peed his pants.

Brian is sure the mean nursie was rough with him and never said a word.

[123]

cious—both were too reminiscent of her ministrations for Henry. Had Brian remained at D Street he would have received no better care but at least it would have come sooner.

"Was I right to bring him here?" she asked.

"You were," the nurse confirmed. "It's a terrible flu that's going round and it's been bringing a pneumonia with it even worse. We'll be able to keep an eye on him here and of course the doctor will see him. Now as soon as you get home, remove your clothing, rub yourself dry, and take a laxative for protection. Otherwise it's just as likely you'll be back yourself." She patted Brian on the head. "I know it smells awful, dearie, but you've got to leave that plaster on your chest. It's going to help you breathe. I'll be back to check on you soon." With a smile, she slipped through the break in the screen. Lydia began to button her coat.

"Don't go," Brian wheezed. The sound startled Lydia. This was the first time he had spoken since D Street. His words were wet and thick, as if the syllables were coated in phlegm.

"I can only stay a little while longer," she answered. "The nice nurse is going to take good care of you while I go back home to check on your ma and da and sisters. Before you know it, it'll be morning and you'll have visitors again."

Brian shook his head, his eyes filling with tears. "Please—" he whispered.

"Brian, love—" she sighed, her smile faltering. "You've got to be brave like your da said. You know, I came here once when I was a girl and as you can see for yourself they fixed me up just grand. They'll do the same for you, you'll see."

Brian nodded, she the precipice to which he clung.

"That's a good, brave boy," she whispered. "Your da is going to be so proud." She kissed his forehead. "Now close your eyes and try to sleep." She stayed beside him until he drifted off, his chest rising and falling with the frantic breaths of a small bird. The screen around his bed reflected the sound, but

He was not asleep. He heard Auntie Liddie's footsteps disappear and felt scared at being all alone.

on the other side of the screen, the sound was barely audible. Brian's bed became indistinguishable from the other screened beds lining the aisle. Lydia waited until the nurse of indeterminate age reappeared.

"Is he going to be all right?" she asked.

The nurse was evasive. "It was good you brought him when you did." Likely, nurses were schooled not to answer that sort of question.

"But Brian's not the only one sick," Lydia continued. "His mother's just as bad."

The nurse shook her head. "If his mother's as sick as that, she ought to come in too."

"She won't," Lydia said. "Isn't there someone you could send?"

"We're too short-staffed to send nurses into the field, not to mention doctors," the nurse apologized. "I'm afraid the best way to help her is to convince her to come."

She could not return to D Street with so little to offer. "Isn't there anything else I can do?" Lydia demanded. "It's a desperate situation."

"You can go home," the nurse replied gently. "You can do what I told you to do and you can pray to stay healthy. They're saying that down at the pier—" The nurse's features shifted. "But you're hurt!" she exclaimed. She swabbed Lydia's shoulder and brought back blood.

Lydia touched her shoulder. The pressure of her hand recalled her recent cargo. "I'm fine," she answered dully, nodding toward the white screen that shut Brian off from the rest of the world. She would have much preferred the blood to be her own. "That was where he lay as I carried him."

The nurse wiped what she could, then moved down the aisle. Lydia did as she had been told, quietly leaving the ward and descending the stairs, but she would have preferred to pull Brian back into her arms and run with him all the way home.

Back at 28 D Street she was met by a silence that would have driven away anyone who did not live there. When Lydia stepped into the front hall, the door to her flat opened.

"Ma's upstairs," Thomas whispered into the stillness of the stairwell. The door opened wider and Da appeared beside Tom.

"Brian's in hospital?" Da asked. She nodded. "It was good you took him when you did."

"That's not what his ma thought," Lydia replied. "Alice was sure I was the devil himself."

"Well she's in a better place now," Da offered, his words lending incontrovertible shape to the quiet. Lydia turned and took the stairs two at a time until she reached the Feeneys' landing.

"Who's there?" came her mother's voice.

"It's me, Ma."

"There's none of them with you?"

"All downstairs."

Mrs. Kilkenny sighed. "Then you may as well come in."

Alice's corpse lay across the front room sofa. Beside the sofa knelt Alice's mother, who was motionless save for the steady activity of her hands, which neither ceased nor slowed at Lydia's arrival. Jennie Feeney was carefully unbraiding her daughter's hair.

"When it's done, she braids it up again," Cora explained in a cautious whisper. Mrs. Feeney gave neither indication that she had heard Cora nor that she knew she was not alone. "She was wailing like a banshee before but Mr. Feeney quieted her for the sake of the girls. He's with them now. Malachy told them that their ma's in hospital but I don't fancy they believe him."

Meagan knew her ma was in Heaven because the Virgin told her so.

Cora turned toward her neighbor. "Jennie darling?" Even as Jennie turned toward the sound, her fingers continued their dogged work. "Dearie, look who's here. Liddie's back." Cora gently stilled Mrs. Feeney's hands. One half of one braid remained.

"Where's my grandson?" Jennie Feeney asked, her eyes searching Lydia's face.

"I left him in good hands," Lydia answered with more assurance than she felt.

"She—oughter've gone too," Mrs. Feeney whispered, her sobs interspersing themselves between her words. "I oughter've—made her go." She rocked back and forth, the floor creaking as she shifted.

"Alice wanted to stay," Cora countered, her voice tired from repeated, fruitless consolation. "You did everything you could."

Jennie turned to her daughter's corpse and stroked its face. "Such a lovely—girl," she whispered.

There had been no extra sheet in which to wind the body. Alice's right arm—the hand curled into a claw at the collar of her nightdress, the arm bent at the elbow—rested on her chest like a dislocated wing, while her left arm pressed at her side straight as a soldier's. Alice's mouth was frozen in a grimace, her eyebrows raised in astonishment. She looked neither asleep, nor at peace. The body, which had begun to stiffen, lay rigid on the couch, its loose, limp hair adding incongruous color to the faded, threadbare sofa. Mrs. Feeney gathered the leftmost strands of her daughter's hair and resumed the braid.

Jennie Feeney is certain her daughter looked beautiful.

"Mrs. Feeney," Lydia ventured softly. As girls she and Alice occasionally had played jacks, a pastime at which Alice had excelled. Jennie Feeney's hands recalled with eerie clarity the deftness with which Alice had scooped five and six jacks at a time while Lydia languished on threesies. "Mrs. Feeney," she repeated, turning her gaze from those hands, "is there anything I can do for you?"

Jennie shook her head, though whether in response to Lydia or to some internal query it was at first impossible to tell. "She were a wife and a mother," Mrs. Feeney murmured. "A wife and—a mother." Lydia thought her question had not been heard until Jeannie turned toward her and exclaimed, *"She* were a wife *and* a mother!"

Jennie Feeney remembers blessed little of that terrible day, but she never would have said something so unkind.

"I'm so sorry," Lydia whispered. "I'll leave you now." She was shaking so violently that her hand could not at first turn the knob of the door.

· · ·

TWO HITS

FROM SONG HEADQUARTERS

Songs win wars! Kaiser Bill—Beware! America is singing! We sing in camp—we sing on ships—we sing at home—"community sings"—morning, noon, and night. Keep it up, America—it's the road to Berlin.

Here are two new hits. Learn 'em, play 'em, sing 'em! Get the cheero, fun-loving, full-of-pep Yankee spirit woven into every note and every word.

"K-K-K-Katy"—Stammering Song

Fun is the doughboy's pal—that's why he wrote and sings "K-K-K-Katy"—the song of songs, with a zippy, catchy melody and those beautifully simple words stammered by Katy's tongue-tied beau. "K-K-K-Katy" is the song of the boys—why shouldn't it make a tremendous hit in every theater, eat-palace, and home in Yankeeland! Try it out now!

"If He Can Fight Like He Can Love,
Good Night, Germany!"

A rollicking, happy Yankee melody and clever, honest-to-goodness words—no wonder it's sweeping the land! Only a deaf man could keep his feet and lips quiet when the band plays and the singer sings this great hit.

These two song hits are published in our new approved Patriotic-War-size that is more convenient for you and saves paper for Uncle Sam.

· · ·

I don't see how they're gonna do it.

Leave the sick ones behind.

But that's everybody.

Not nearly. Not if you only count the really sick ones.

Like Riley?

Like Riley. Leave Riley behind. But take Piker, for instance.

He don't look so hot.

Sure, but he'll have plenty of time to get better on board.

I suppose.

Or maybe you think we oughter send a telegram to France: Sorry boys. Stop. Can't help with those Gerries. Stop. Feeling under the weather.

Course not.

Well then?

I'm just saying we're not exactly in top form.

But Sergeant Husker'll straighten all that out. He can tell a faker for sure. Some of those fellas ain't nearly as sick as they let on—What? What'd I say that's so funny?

Sergeant Husker checked into infirmary this morning.

That's a bunch of hokey! I saw him just last night!

Well, visit him yourself if you don't believe me. When I saw him this morning he was pale as a sheet and shaking like a shaved dog.

Of all the rotten luck. What're we gonna do?

Sprinkle sulfur in your shoes.

Honest?

It's kept me pretty near out of it so far.

I'll be darned. Sulfur, huh?

It's a natural repellent. Goes back to Indian times.

Wish you'd've told that to Sergeant Husker.

I did. I guess he just didn't use enough.

. . .

LAWNVIEW SENIOR COMPLEX LETS YOU BE "RIGHT IN THE THICK OF IT!!"™

In the heart of historic South Boston beside Telegraph Hill, Lawnview Senior Complex offers today's Seniors an ideal blend of autonomy and assisted living. A range of apartment sizes and styles, along with attractive financing packages and a spectrum of meal plans ensures that Lawnview will meet the needs of many of today's fixed incomes. Complimentary amenities include: a 24-hour doorman, regular cleaning service,* emergency call buttons† in bedrooms and bathrooms, round-the-clock access to a home health aide,‡ and reduced prices on door-to-door delivery of groceries, meals, sundries, prescription drugs, and spirits.§

Our cafeteria and social rooms on the ground floor provide our Seniors with places to mix and mingle, creating the kind of unique community that can make the "golden years" so special. Lawnview's staff goes that extra mile to provide our Seniors with unique and memorable events such as Sunday Sing-Along, Arts and Crafts, Sadie Hawkins Day, and much much more!

Don't Delay! Visit Lawnview Today and See How You Too Can Be "Right in the Thick of It!!"™

---

*Service provided once monthly. More frequent service available at additional charge.

†Does not include cost of ambulance transport.

‡Inquire for rates of service.

§From participating businesses only.

. . .

THE QDISPATCH

VOLUME 10, ISSUE 6   NOVEMBER 1993

QD and Me:
A Sodaman's Journey
By Ralph Finnister

Chapter 10
Women

None of Quentin Driscoll's marriages lasted as long as his marriage to Sara. Because I did not know him then, I shall not talk about that time or that tragedy. But I am certain that if

Sara had known what was in her true love's heart she would not have done what she did.

It would be an understatement to say that he never forgave himself. Every visitor to his office noticed and admired his desk—as I did on that first day—but only a nautical man would be able to tell it had been made from the stern of a boat. Quentin Driscoll spent every day of his working life behind that desk, his hands resting where their clothes were discovered, neatly folded, when the boat was found adrift.

He did not share matters of the heart with me as he did matters of business, but I could sense the loneliness that time and time again led him down the matrimonial aisle. A Sodaman's life is solitary and all-consuming, and soda a harsh and demanding mistress. That Quentin Driscoll had once known happiness in the arms of Sara Lampe perhaps made that loneliness all the more difficult to bear.

I will not write the names of his ex-wives here. They do not deserve mention. All I will say is that in each case the woman to whom Quentin Driscoll pledged his troth rewarded his affection—and his faithfulness—with treachery and avarice.

At this writing, the great Sodaman is living out the end of his long and extraordinary life confident that when he leaves this world behind, he will be returned to his true love's arms.

In This Issue

They all awoke feeling under the weather, but none of them were sick enough to stay home. Lydia wondered if the first day of Alice's illness had begun so modestly. She donned her shirtwaist and brushed her hair, acutely aware of the silence above her. Absent were the heavy footsteps that signaled Malachy's departure for the dock; there were no light, staccato footfalls describing the children's preparations for school. Brian was likely awake in his bed at Carney Hospital, the loneliness of strange surroundings deepened by the screen that shut him off from the ward, but at least he had gained an extra night in which his mother was still alive.

Though Thomas, James, and John had slept in the front room as always, on waking they tried to avoid it as much as their morning routines would allow. Lydia knew without asking that her brothers were thinking of the body on the couch inside the room one floor above. Lydia was struck—as she had been the day she returned to the Somerset—by the treachery of appearances. Familiar walls and furnishings fostered the illusion that each day would resemble the one before. Certainly Alice Feeney O'Toole had never looked at her sofa and imagined her corpse there. As Lydia made her way toward Gorin's, the familiar streetscape became a backdrop for an unknown and potentially ominous future.

Gorin's occupied the first floor of a narrow brick building, the name of its proprietor painted on the window in large, red capitals below a sun-faded canopy. Its interior was long and plain. Walking toward the back of the store felt like entering a messy closet. The walls were lined with floor-to-ceiling shelves crammed with stock, some in labeled boxes and some in open view, a sight that at Gilchrist's was consigned to the back rooms. In front of these, leaving just enough space for a girl to stand, were simple glass counters in which each department's fanciest goods were displayed, though from the perspective of Washington Street these were strictly middlebrow, representing the shoddier imports or the better ready-made items. What might have been a generous center aisle was bisected by tables of sale merchandise, which made it impossible for two people to walk abreast. Instead of pneumatics, ropes and pulleys conveyed overhead baskets to the back of the store, where Mr. Gorin himself made change at the register. To Lydia the persistent squeak of the pulleys was the sound of all things second-rate. She missed the soft suck of air that had accompanied the release of a capsule into a pneumatic dispatch tube, the decisive plunk of a capsule's return, filled with change.

The store owned by Nell Gorin's husband was the best of its type on West Broadway, and was decorated with several paintings by her husband's own hand, not to mention the window display she personally redesigned monthly.

Several of the girls were out that day, leaving Lydia responsible for more counters than usual, but there were fewer customers as well. Since everyone seemed to be suffering from a cold, Mr. Gorin ran a sale on handkerchiefs and instructed his girls to inform customers that silk handkerchiefs—which cost twice as much—were the most hygienic, though Lydia observed that Mr. Gorin used plain cotton.

The rules at Gorin's were more relaxed than at Gilchrist's. During slow stretches the girls were permitted to talk among themselves but today they did not. To fill the dull silence,

Lydia envisioned a giant conveyance that could move her back in time with the speed and elegance of a pneumatic capsule. The previous twenty-four hours would unknit. If the world could be as it had been yesterday, perhaps events could manifest differently: somehow they would persuade Alice to enter the hospital; somehow Brian's mother would be saved. But instead—perhaps while Lydia was handing a customer a card of faux-pearl buttons or while she was writing a receipt—the undertaker would come for Alice's body. Lydia's mother would take up a collection for a wreath. Lydia felt as if only half of her had left 28 D Street, her other half remaining to post invisible vigil at the second-floor landing.

Lydia's thoughts were interrupted by the sound of something large colliding with the floor. Her gaze sought the fallen object, and instead encountered a customer backing away from Ladies Neckwares. At first Lydia was confused. Everything about that counter seemed in order—except there was no longer a girl standing behind it.

"Kelly!" cried one of the counter girls as she rushed toward Neckwares. Mr. Gorin pushed his way past several customers who had frozen in place as he made his way down the aisle.

"Is she hurt?" Mr. Gorin called as he reached the counter, kneeling out of view.

The customer who had backed away from the counter rushed toward it again.

"She were just about to fetch me a collar from the case when she looked all of a sudden pale and before I could ask what were the matter, she fell over!"

The store burst into sound. Several customers ran toward Neckwares, craning to get a look at the stricken girl; others remained frozen. Voices issued from all corners.

"She's so pale!"

"Poor thing."

"What's wrong with her?"

At first Norah Flaugherty thought that Kelly was shamming. They had a mutual pact to help one another to leave early and it was Kelly's turn, Norah having "fainted" the week before.

"She's burning up!"

"Fetch a doctor!"

"Give her some air."

"Give her a drink."

Occasionally girls fainted: tight girdles or stingy breakfasts were two possible causes. Normally such an event was cause for nothing more than momentary excitement but today was different. Mr. Gorin appeared above the counter, the color drained from his face.

"When she came in this morning she only said she were feeling a little poorly," he began quietly, as if talking to himself. "It didn't seem no different from how I felt, otherwise I would've told her to go home, get some rest. My own daughter's at home in bed, you know, and she were feeling fine just yesterday. It don't come on the way you'd think; it sneaks up from behind."

He paused, as if thinking something over. He looked at the girl on the floor, then returned his gaze to the assembled.

"Ladies and gentlemen," he announced, scanning the faces before him. "I'm closing early. I've had a bad feelin' all day and this clinches it. There's something strange going around. Please take a handkerchief from the front table on your way out, any one you like, compliments of myself; and I'd like to recommend that every one of you go straight home and check on your families, because that's certainly what I'll be doing as soon as I get this young lady home."

A few customers quit the store without their complimentary handkerchiefs. Others grabbed blindly from the pile on their way out. A minority rooted through the bin, in case prolonged inspection would yield one square of cheap cotton superior to the rest. Along with the other girls Lydia began closing down her counter. Her hands trembled as she refolded her stock. She thought Mr. Gorin was wrong to close early when only a few hours remained in the workday. The other

Kelly Dooley blames Mr. Gorin. She had already asked permission to leave only to be told no.

If Kelly and Norah were not forever trying to leave work early, perhaps that day Tom might have let her, but there was no trusting those two.

girls' faces confirmed her opinion. Kelly's sudden illness had startled them, but it had taken Mr. Gorin's announcement to make them scared.

The last of the customers watched along with the counter girls as Kelly—who had revived but was too weak to walk unassisted—was led to a hansom cab by Mr. Gorin, who paid the driver with money from his own pocket.

"Help her to the door and wait until someone from the family takes her from you," Mr. Gorin instructed the driver. At Gilchrist's, a counter girl would have never received such kind treatment, and Lydia felt a wave of tenderness for Mr. Gorin and his narrow, cluttered store with its overhead baskets.

The fellow did not give him enough, but Gregory Finn took the girl to the address anyhow, which kindness he credits to God seeing fit to spare his own family.

With the hansom gone, the last of the customers dispersed quickly. As Mr. Gorin shut off the lights, Lydia and the other girls huddled together at the front of the store.

"Look after yourselves, girls," Mr. Gorin advised as they stood before the doors, the store interior dark. To each of them Mr. Gorin solemnly presented two of the penny handkerchiefs he had offered his customers. The fabric would have to be laundered before it would soften. "Don't come in tomorrow if you're feeling poorly; it's bad for a business to have girls fainting." The store, standing empty in the late afternoon, resembled a stage on which the curtain had failed to descend at the end of a play.

Lydia started down West Broadway with the rest of the girls. A few stores she passed along the way were also shuttered, leading her to wonder if similar scenes had played out there. As they walked, the girls whispered of brothers or friends or neighbors who had fallen ill, and speculated on the condition of Mr. Gorin's daughter. The other girls were the age Lydia had been when she worked at Gilchrist's, and all still unmarried. Among them she felt old.

As her counterparts turned onto the lettered streets that led to their families' crowded flats, Lydia followed West Broadway to Dorchester and turned toward Telegraph Hill. She would not tell Brian about his mother if he did not already know, but whether he had been informed or not, she was sure he could use company.

The traffic on Dorchester was heavier than West Broadway but not until she reached Old Harbor Street did she realize why. The approach to Carney was so thick with ambulances, private cars, and cabs that many had given up the prospect of reaching the hospital entrance and had debarked their passengers a block or more distant. The afflicted who could no longer walk were carried on backs or held upright by abler bodies.

Something beyond the street traffic struck Lydia as odd, but before she could determine what it was a woman in front of her stumbled. Lydia helped the woman to her feet and placed an arm around her waist, joining the strange tableau. At the top of the hill, she began leading the woman to the hospital entrance but the woman shook her head.

"No," she whispered. "Clinic."

The morbid scene on the street had failed to prepare Lydia for the clinic's transformation. A day seemed somehow both too long and too short a period to have passed since she had carried Brian through the same door. The ill could not be contained by the clinic's benches. People covered every available space, some sitting, others lying on the floor or propped up against the wall. Open windows and camphor failed to mask the stink of sickness—a moist, mucosal smell that hung, dank and bitter, over everything. Lydia realized with a shock that she was surrounded by people her age. The usual victims of Southie's flus and fevers—the very young and the very old— were absent. In their place were young men and women in numbers one would expect to see at a dance—only in place of movement there was stillness. Walking carefully to avoid crushing a prone leg or hand, Lydia maneuvered into the room with the sick woman.

"Where shall I take you?" she asked into the woman's ear, hoping to spot an unclaimed patch of bench or floor.

The woman shook her head, her face panicked. "It's no good here," she croaked. She stumbled toward the clinic door, turning to look one last time at those who had preceded her before lurching outside.

One of the Sisters appeared from behind the curtained examination area. The nun's habit was stained and creased and the wings of her wimple drooped, a sight so startling that Lydia averted her face as if the woman were naked. The Sister wove her way between the supine and the seated with practiced steps.

"If you wish to be seen by a nurse, you may give me your name," she began. The weariness of her face was matched by her voice. "Only the most dire cases will be accepted for treatment as we are suffering from a shortage of beds. If you are not afflicted with a perilously high fever we suggest you return home, take to your bed, and drink clear liquids. If you wish to remain you'll need to be patient. A nurse will see you as soon as she can. Raise your hand to give me your name." Pale hands appeared around the room's edges like a fairy ring.

Lydia inched her way toward the hospital door, careful to avoid trampling feet or fingers. She never would have imagined Brian lucky in his illness, but its early onset had at least afforded him prompt attention. On the opposite side of the door, benches and cots had been added along the walls, a narrow aisle left between them to permit passage. The only observable difference between the patients lining the hospital hall and those in the clinic was that these people had been waiting even longer.

An extra row of beds had been added down the middle aisle of the second floor children's ward. Partitions stood between as many beds as possible, turning the ward into a labyrinth that foiled Lydia's attempt to find Brian by memory. She discovered several unfamiliar faces before deciding to work her way down the row, screen by screen, until she found him.

The majority of beds were now filled with patients closer to Lydia's age than Brian's. Those who were not sleeping either looked through her with fevered eyes, or gazed with such intensity that she felt criminal for replacing their screen and moving on. She was mid row when she was yanked into the aisle.

"What do you think you're doing?" a nurse cried through a gauze mask. When the nurse spoke, the material across her mouth billowed like a sheet on a clothesline. "You're spreading germs, going from one bed to another like that. You think these screens are for decoration? Who gave you permission to be here?"

"I'm sorry," Lydia apologized. "I'm looking for a boy called Brian O'Toole. I brought him last night, but I suppose he's been moved, or his Gran took him home."

"You'll have to ask Head Nurse," the woman answered, pointing toward the opposite end of the room. "The way they're coming in it's more than I can do just to find them beds." Behind one of the far curtains came the sound of choking. "Excuse me," the nurse cried and rushed off.

Nurse Christine Wilson was too upset and exhausted to admit knowing the boy to whom the visitor referred.

The sounds of the ward were made more ominous by the screens that blocked their sources from view. It was difficult not to attribute each cough to Brian. When Lydia reached the other end of the ward there was still no other nurse in sight, and it seemed cruel to allow his solitude to continue.

"Brian!" she called. She was being true to the nurse's request—she was not peering inside the curtains. "Brian, it's Auntie Liddie from D Street. Just make a little sound so I know how to find you."

The noises of the room seemed to intensify. Lydia perked

Sally Nichols, in Bed Twelve, took the voice for an angel's and was comforted by the notion that her name might also soon be called.

her ears for a moan or a cough that sounded more familiar than the rest, or a small voice whispering her name.

Then the Head Nurse emerged from behind one of the curtains. "Miss, I must ask you to restrain yourself," she ordered. "We can't have that here." The hollows shadowing her eyes extended below the upper edge of the mask stretching across her nose and mouth.

"Please, I'm looking for a boy called Brian O'Toole."

"O'Toole," the nurse echoed. "He was brought in yesterday?"

"That's right," Lydia replied. "Yesterday afternoon, going on evening."

The nurse gave a quick nod. "Are you a relation?" she asked.

"A friend of the family. I brought him here myself. He's six but small for his age—"

"I'm very sorry to tell you," the nurse replied quietly, "but he passed late last night. The grandmother was here this morning. She has made provisions."

The air rushed out of Lydia's lungs. "Are you quite sure?" she asked, the words almost inaudible. "He was very ill but the nurse said they'd look after him. She said the doctor would see to him."

"I'm sorry," the nurse repeated. "Once they become that ill there is very little we can do."

"Were you with him?" Lydia asked. "When he died, were you there?" She did not mean to sound angry, but in the space of a day the world had become a place where shops closed early and children disappeared overnight.

"No," the nurse answered. "It happened during the night shift. We lost four. Not since yellow fever have we lost that many at a time. When the duty nurse realized the graveness of the situation she woke one of the Sisters and they took turns sitting at the beds." The nurse's voice remained steady, and be-

At the beginning of the epidemic, Henrietta Pauling was still able to tally the number of times she had been called upon to inform a visitor of a death.

cause of the mask it was impossible for Lydia to know the set of her features as she spoke. "I'm certain that one of them was with Brian when his time came."

The walk back to D Street was longer than Lydia remembered. The few children playing on stoops or along streets, regardless of their age or appearance, reminded her of Brian. At the sight of a small boy with auburn hair she stopped in her tracks, certain the nurse had erred. Then the boy turned toward her, and the nurse's news reasserted itself. Lydia felt strangely relieved for Alice, who was at least spared such unwelcome knowledge.

As she reached her block, Lydia found herself studying objects that had for years evaded her notice: a streetlamp, a tree, a hydrant, the small pebbles that collected between cobblestones. She could not describe what she was looking for, only the imperative of the search. If the rules had changed, then she would learn them. If this was some new and dire season, then she would come to know its name.

Lydia expected the same heavy silence that had greeted her on her first return from the hospital. She was not prepared for shrieks, and her throat clenched at the intensity of the sound. Anguish verged on overwhelming the very medium that carried it, perhaps causing the air to bleed black ash or gray dust. It was a sound that only ever meant one thing, conveying that meaning to all who heard it even if they had never heard it before.

The cries were so sense scrambling that they were at first difficult to pinpoint. Lydia assumed they emanated from the upstairs apartment until she opened the door to her family's flat. Her next thought was that Mrs. Feeney was downstairs, but instead there was her mother bent over the couch, raw sound pouring from her open mouth and from the mouths of her brothers and her father. None were standing or sitting;

Brian remembers a lady with bird wings on either side of her head. He thought she was an angel, but once he could not breathe anymore he realized she was nothing at all.

Alice, having joined Us previously, was of course the first in her family to know.

they were crouching like animals. And as much as Lydia wished it could be true, she knew it was impossible that they would cry like this for poor Brian.

. . .

INFLUENZA NO MATCH FOR THE ARMY

New influenza cases are falling off at Fort Devens where Major General Henry P. McCain, commander of the Twelfth Infantry Division, asserts that despite the massive influenza outbreak, his men will be ready to disembark to France on the schedule called for by Generals Grant and Pershing.

Though over 10,000 men have thus far been stricken, and 66 have died, numbers of new influenza cases are falling off due to the "tireless efforts of our doctors and nurses, who have been working day and night to bring the epidemic under control."

"I made a promise that I would have the Twelfth Infantry Division ready to face Gerry by the month's end and I don't intend to back out on that promise now," McCain told officials. "It will take more than influenza to stop our fighting men."

. . .

What do you call it again?

QD Soda, sir.

But last week you said it was a tonic.

Oh no, sir, that was something else. This you can sell right along with your lemon-lime and your orange and your rickey, something with a new taste all its own. A soda, not a remedy.

In case you didn't notice, we're standing at a counter here. I don't sell soda in bottles.

I'll sell you the syrup, then.

I don't know.

Honest to Abe, sir, you'll be letting your customers down if you don't. They'll start going over to Klyborn's on Revere or Pinkney's on Allen.

Are you telling me those fellows are carrying your syrup?

Here, taste a bottle for yourself.

Hmm . . . you know, you might have something here. What did you put in there—chicory? A little anise maybe?

It's a taste that people will come back for.

Give me a half-gallon and we'll see how it goes.

I only sell it by the gallon, sir.

Well, if you want my business you'll sell me half a gallon and check back with me next week.

You won't be sorry, sir. If you like, I can give you a sign for your front window, absolutely free of cost, of course.

Young man, it's a little early to be talking windows. Come back next week and I'll let you know whether or not you're wasting my time.

. . .

My Dear Boy—

Though you have been gone awhile now there are mornings I forget. By the time I am putting up the coffee I have remembered and I am embarrassed that I forgot to begin with. You might think that being alone is protection against embarrassment, but it is not. Solitude is the biggest embarrassment of all.

I could name a few girls here who have made it clear they would be happy to bear the burden of my company, but you will be happy to know I have given up on all that. I have come to realize that I am no longer the sort of man a good woman comes to. I have not been that sort of man for some time now, not since your mother. I used to think that if you and she had lived I would have turned out differently, but I have given up on that as well. All my life I have prided myself on being a self-made man and a self-made man has no right to blame anyone but himself for the way he turns out.

And just how has your old dad turned out? Though I

never ranked longevity among my ambitions, I seem to have achieved it anyway. I am not proud of being old. I do not feel that I have had much to do with it, considering how much trouble I made over the years for my gut and my liver and the rest of the scrapple I am carrying around inside my skin. I suppose I would be grateful if I were not so goddamn bored.

Forgive me for talking to you this way, but it is time I stopped thinking of you as a little boy. You have not been a little boy for a very long time. Not a day goes by when I do not think of you.

Love,

Your Father

The drays were clattering down Third Street as if nothing was different. Lydia had forgotten what it was to be hauled from oblivion into a world she had disowned, but now her skin weighed on her body like the pelt of a lifeless animal, and she remembered. For a moment she was confused: in the early days of mourning Henry she had often garbled time and so for one sharp inhalation of breath she thought she was still a new widow. Then came the exhale and her realization that this was something else, something that defied description. There was no word for a sister whose brother had died. This simple, callous fact of language extinguished her desire to speak.

Michael's last letter had mentioned a flu, but in spite of all that had been happening, she had not recalled that remark until she was told he was dead. This lapse lodged itself alongside her failure to call an ambulance in time for Henry, and became its twin—indictments too tenuous to survive exposure to air, but incontrovertible within the confine of her body.

Her mother was the first to rise when the sound of the drays subsided. Mrs. Kilkenney pulled a dressing gown over her shoulders and shuffled from the bedroom to the kitchen.

From her pallet Lydia heard the icebox door open and close. A pan clattered against the stove. Then came the sizzle and aroma of cooking fat, a scent that this morning turned her stomach. To distract herself she stared at the window, but the blueness of the sky made her angry. She turned her head toward the wall.

"Morning," her father said. He was looking out the window also, the word not a greeting but an accusation directed toward the sun.

Cooking smells thickened the air. "Breakfast," her mother said.

"I'm not hungry, Ma," rasped Thomas from the front room.

"Me neither," echoed James.

"You'll eat whether you're hungry or not," her mother explained. "We all of us need our strength."

Moving like an old man, her da eased his legs to the floor. "You'll do what your ma says," he ordered. Overnight, his voice had been reduced from a bellow to something small and tinny. There was movement from the front room into the kitchen, then a sharp intake of breath.

"Ma?" she heard Thomas say, his voice tearing the last remaining barrier between Lydia and the beginning of the first full day without Michael. Henry had been hers alone and she had owned her grief for him, but Michael had belonged to all of them.

While her mother stood over the stove, intent on the simmering tea kettle, the eyes of her brothers and father were fixed on a kitchen table choked with food. There were three pots at the table's center, one filled with oatmeal, one with gravy, and one with cocoa. The table's six plates were weighted with double portions of biscuits. A week's supply of rationed eggs had been fried and divided between them, each plate subjugated by the dumb cheer of runny yellow yolks.

Her mother emerged from behind the stove with the

steaming tea kettle. "He always teased me about being stingy with food," she whispered. "He said the food at Devens was no good. I was fixing to send him a package, only I hadn't quite gotten around to it." She sat down. "It might have saved him, that package." She winced. "It might have helped to keep his strength up."

"I was going to write him back," Thomas whimpered. "I had started a letter, but it wasn't done yet." His eyes widened. "He was probably lying sick in hospital, just hoping for a letter to raise his spirits, and I hadn't even written!"

"There was nothing any of us could've done," her father said. "Now let's all sit. We'll bring whatever's left over to Malachy and the girls upstairs."

Once they were seated, her father bowed his head. He usually only recited grace over dinner. Today, over breakfast, he bowed his head but did not speak. Lydia could not imagine words to fill the space. Yesterday she had pondered portents in streetlamps, as though the world's transformation were a subtle thing. Today she needed to look no farther than the kitchen table.

Father O'Brian was the first person Lydia heard use the word epidemic. He arrived to the flat late that afternoon. In a haggard voice he explained that he had been at Carney, where the need for doctors was matched only by the need for clergy; nuns could offer solace but they could not perform Extreme Unction. Father O'Brian had been forced to cancel morning mass: all the altar boys were sick and there was too much other work to be done. Today there were three funerals to perform, all of them young people. He did not want to think about tomorrow. He felt unwell himself but there was too much work to consider resting.

According to the telegram, they could visit the grave or arrange a transfer once the camp received a clean bill of health. Father O'Brian appeared visibly relieved to learn that Michael

Dan Kilkenny does not remember this. He wonders if Liddie is recalling the time they got the letter telling of Granny K's death, which was troubling sad for everyone.

had been buried at Devens. He led them in the Lord's Prayer and assured them that once the epidemic had passed, Michael would receive a funeral far grander than the truncated services the current circumstances permitted.

That night, she and her brother danced, his hand large and comforting at the small of her back. Saturated with their combined sweat, the fabric of her dress formed a second skin beneath his palm. As they moved she could smell her brother's aftershave and the pomade he used in his hair. She had forgotten these scents and was overwhelmed with gratitude for their return. The other dancers were unfamiliar save for Alice Feeney O'Toole. Her hair was woven into two neat braids that lifted as she twirled.

"Mick, I knew it wasn't true!" she murmured, leaning toward her brother's ear. "I knew you weren't really dead!" Her brother was smiling his usual crooked smile.

"Oh I'm dead all right, Liddie," his voice whispered in her ear, so low it was more a vibration than words. She opened her eyes to a dark figure standing in the doorway. The sight almost made her scream.

Michael may or may not have contributed to his sister's nightmare. We are powerless over all aspects of Our whisperings save their ceaseless production.

"There's something wrong with Tom," came James's voice from the darkness. She heard the springs of her parents' bed creak. Before she managed to pull back her blankets her mother already had leapt from bed. For a moment Lydia was able to convince herself she was still dreaming but the trick did not last. Soon her mother's voice called from the other room. The vibration of the floor as her father jumped from bed was too small and telling a detail to belong to a nightmare. She had just managed to stand when her father returned with Thomas in his arms—a large, awkward bundle that caused him to stagger with each step.

"Get out!" her mother shrieked, appearing in the doorway behind him. "Get out!" She squeezed around her husband, grasped her daughter by the arms and pulled her from the room.

Lydia found herself standing barefoot in the kitchen with James, the cold floor sending darts of alertness up through her legs.

"What happened?" she asked, her voice still thick with sleep.

"He got sicker," James whispered. "I woke up feeling like I was stuck inside an oven and realized it was on account of Tom. When we went to bed he was feeling lousy but he made me promise not to tell. But I had to do it. Didn't I have to do it, Liddie?"

She put her hand on James's shoulder but this reminded her too much of the banished dream. She removed her hand. "You did right," she promised.

"He's sure to hate me," James squeaked. "And now he's the only older brother I've got."

Jamie was awful scared. When he first learned about Mick, he and Tom had been fighting and he wished it had been Tom instead.

John had managed to sleep through the commotion of Thomas's removal, but woke up on hearing his brother.

"Jamie, what's wrong?" he called from the other room. "Where's Tom?" John sat half upright on the mattress in the front room, too sleep-muddled to progress any further.

"Tom's sick," Lydia called to him. "Ma's got him now."

"But I thought we weren't going to worry her," John said. "He said it were just a small fever."

"It got bigger," James replied.

"I dreamed I were floating on the sun," John whispered.

Their father appeared from the bedroom. "We're all to go to the front room. Liddie, you're to sleep on the couch and I'm to sleep with the boys. On no account are you to go into the bedroom or your ma's sure to kill me. You're not even to go to the kitchen unless there's nothing for it and tomorrow you're to stay clear of the flat 'til supper." He knelt on the floor so quickly Lydia thought he had fallen. "Oh Heavenly Father," he whispered, "please look over your child Thomas this night and see that his fever lessens. Please keep your children Lydia, James, and John from slipping into illness. And please tell Mick, who is with you in Heaven, that we miss him—" He began to cry, the sound of the earth cracking open.

Dan Kilkenny remembers Tom falling ill, but he is sure as taxes that Mick outlived him.

When her husband's memory began to slip in his later years, he often assumed Michael still lived, a mistake Cora eventually stopped trying to correct.

. . .

BOARD ADJUDGES FLU NOT
OF SPANISH VARIETY
SUGGESTS SIMPLE STEPS
TO AVOID THE DISEASE

The Department of Health assured the public last night that Boston has no reason to fear an epidemic of Spanish influenza. "While there have been reports of a limited outbreak of some virulence," officials said, "our findings, pending further investigation, suggest that pneumonia may be the culprit, accompanied by a flu of the normal and not Spanish type."

To avoid infection health officials advised against kissing "except through a handkerchief." Citizens are further advised to take the following simple steps to protect themselves:

Spray nose and throat daily with di-chloramine.

Get plenty of rest in bed.

Keep windows wide open.

Eat meals regularly and do not curtail on quantity.

Beware of persons shaking their handkerchiefs.

Don't use common towels, cups, or other articles which come into contact with face.

Don't spit in public places.

. . .

How're you holding up?

Pretty rough. They turned E Deck into another sick bay and so now I'm in H-8.

Christ! All the way down there?

It's not very good. I feel lousy but I ain't about to see the doctor.

I'm kinda shabby myself but I think it's seasickness. Least-ways that's what I tell myself.

What's the idea sending us out like this? We're not even halfway to France!

It's lousy, but we gotta make it.

It's the ship that's making it so bad. We're all crammed to-gether.

Do like I do and stay on deck. At least that way you get air. I been sleeping up there too.

Nobody stopped you?

Who's gonna stop me? It's all too big a mess.

It'll be better once we hit Brest. As long as we're on board we ain't soldiers, we're fish in a lousy barrel.

Tell me a story.

Nurse!

Water, can someone bring me water?

Oh God.

Please, any kind of story. Tell me about your girl.

Don't got a girl.

Nurse!

It's so hot.

Tell me about her. Is she pretty?

Ain't there any water?

Can't—breathe.

She's pretty.

Does she have a nice smile?

She has a nice smile.

Where's a nurse?

We're all alone here! We're gonna die here!

Shut up, you!

Does she sing to you at night?

Nurse!

She sings.

What does she sing?

Can't—breathe.

I'll do the cookin', I'll pay the rent—baby—I know I done you wrong.

Water!

You're lucky, having a girl like that.

So hot.

Go to sleep.

Nurse!

Can't. I'm afraid to close my eyes.

Harmon, Lewis, Cahill, Mahoney, take E Deck, Sections Three through Five, port side. You heard me! Move it!

No sir.

What did you just say?

I said, "No sir."

Harmon, go down to E Deck and clean those compartments and bring up anyone you find down there. That's a direct order.

Sir, if I go down there I'll end up like them.

This is not open for discussion, Harmon.

Sir, it's terrible down there. The bodies are beginning to smell and there's blood and piss all over the floor.

Harmon, if those compartments aren't cleaned every day they are only going to get worse. We are still three days from France and I won't have this ship turning into a floating shit pile.

It's already worse than that, sir.

Harmon, I expected better from you.

It's a floating coffin.

I'm not going, sir.

Me neither, sir.

Court-martial us if you want, but we ain't going down there. Sir.

. . .

My Dear Boy—

I am sure your mother would not have liked being old, especially not here, where they do not leave you alone and there is always somebody checking on you. Either the maid, or the fellow who comes to make sure I have taken my pills, or the girl who just comes to "chat." She is the worst of them. She wants to ferret out if I am still up to the task of looking after myself in this little apartment that your mother would have hated. This girl can tell I am not my regular self lately, but the only answer she will get from me is that I have a lot on my mind.

The truth of the matter is that I am having trouble sleeping. The only bright side to this is that it gives us something in common. You never did sleep through the night. We tried everything—leaving a light on, not leaving a light on, feeding you extra, feeding you less. The doctor said you would outgrow it eventually, but you showed him. Sometimes you had to pee. You would wander into our room, your little eyes half closed and your little feet vanishing into the carpet your mother had special-ordered from Brussels. Then you would stand beside our bed, more asleep than awake, and let loose all over that nice, expensive, imported carpet. That was when we decided to stop giving you warm milk. I have started taking the same precautions. No liquids after six p.m. or I cannot be held responsible for the consequences. I am never so grateful to be living alone as when I wake up to find I have wet the bed.

What did you do when a bad dream woke you up? I suppose your mother would know the answer. I will add it to the mile-long list of questions I would like to ask her. I have never been the sort to remember my dreams, so when one shoves me awake in the middle of the night, I am not prepared. Mostly I just stare at the ceiling and invite whatever cockamamy thought that wants a piece of me to help themselves. I cannot recommend it as a pastime, but it is better than the pills the doctor here gave me when I told him about it. Taking those things is like pouring syrup into my head. The next morning I feel like someone traded my tongue for a chunk of tire rubber.

Love,
Your Father

A sound pounded in Lydia's ears. On first waking, she was confused by the narrowness of her bed. Then the tide of drays subsided and she opened her eyes. At the sight of Michael's two letters still tacked beside the faded picture of the Sacred Heart, the previous day's events emerged from sleep's temporary blind. Today was the first day of Thomas's illness and the second day without Michael. Lydia's father and brothers sat motionless at the front room's threshold as if staring hard enough would permit them to see through the dividing curtain that separated them from the kitchen and Tom's sickroom.

"It's so quiet," John whispered.

If their mother had not barred them from the kitchen, Lydia could have put breakfast on. She was not hungry—she doubted any of them were—but she needed to do something. She did not think she could bear to wait there, useless as a severed limb.

They heard their mother before she saw her. Not more than a few seconds elapsed between the sound of her step on the floorboards and her appearance in the front room, but in those interminable moments, steps too slow or too fast would have foretold unwelcome news.

"Is he all right?" they asked as one when Cora appeared.

"He's asleep," she replied, "but it were a strange night. Maybe two hours after I had got him settled down, we were both of us resting when Tom on a sudden sat up and asked did I recall Sally, the oldest Connelly girl? I told him sure, and then he says in a voice that weren't like him at all: 'Well, she just passed on.' Then he lay back down, calm as can be, and drifted off to sleep." Cora's mouth tightened. "I kept my eye on him after that; his fever climbed awful high, and I kept a cold cloth on him 'til it went down. Every time he opened his eyes I got a dreadful feeling, wondering what he'd say next."

"Is Sally all right?" Lydia asked. She remembered the Connelly girl from Michael's send-off. She was a few years younger and had spent the party dancing.

"I don't know one way or the other," her mother replied. "And neither does Tom. When I asked him this morning he had no memory of such a thing."

James rose from the mattress. "Then he's awake? Can I see him, just for a minute?" he pleaded. "If you like, I'll hold my breath. I won't say a word and I won't touch him. I'll just see him, is all, and I'll wave."

Their mother shook her head. "None of you are to go into that room until he's improved. I know it's a hard thing to ask, but the very best thing is for you to go about your business same as always. At the very least I can't have you staying here. I won't have you setting in a sickhouse all day long."

Lydia thought back to the fainting girl and the way Mr. Gorin's voice shook as he told them he was closing the store. Her mother's request seemed pointless. All of Southie was a sickhouse.

"Your ma's got a point," her father agreed. "We'd not be doing a thing to honor Mick's memory if we fell ill."

"But Ma, you'll need someone," Lydia reasoned. "At least let me spell you while you rest up from last night." Michael had died miles distant, but Tom was right here, where she could do something to help before it was too late.

"Stupid girl!" Cora scolded. "Do you think I'll let you knit your own shroud? It wants the young!"

"I'm sorry, Ma," Lydia breathed. She no longer felt twenty-three, but thirteen.

"Good Lord," her mother whispered, "I didn't mean to yell." She enclosed Lydia in her arms, surrounding her in the scents of soap and rose water.

"I couldn't stand to lose you," she spoke into her daughter's hair. "It would kill me for sure. And that's why you'll obey along with your brothers and leave me to care for Tom."

"I'll do whatever you ask," Lydia promised, her words absorbed by the fragile skin of her mother's neck.

John was sent to school, James to the factory. Lydia's wage could be used for medicines for Thomas, an assurance that did nothing to assuage the futility of reporting for work.

Several people she passed on the way to Gorin's wore gauze masks over their noses and mouths. Others wore pouches around their necks filled with camphor. Southie's streets were silent, as though it had been determined that even trading pleasantries risked contagion. The houses were similarly changed. Funeral wreaths adorned doors in a grim profusion of black, gray, and white. At first Lydia was consoled that she was not alone in her grief, but by the time she reached West Broadway the unceasing displays had crowned Death a conquering hero.

She could not remember when she had seen so few cars and carriages on West Broadway. So many stores were shuttered that she did not realize she had passed Gorin's until she reached the end of the block and was forced to retrace her steps. In Gorin's front window a sign read, CLOSED FOR THE DURATION OF THE WEEK, in handwriting other than Mr. Gorin's. The handwriting affected Lydia more profoundly

According to Katy Donnell, camphor never did a lick of good.

Frances Messinger swears on wormwood.

Jonah Siles cured his wife by placing a shotgun beneath her bed, the magnetism of which drew out her fever.

Though it was not his handwriting, the sign was his: in the days following his daughter's death, Tom Gorin's hands shook uncontrollably.

than the message, for only something terrible would have prevented Mr. Gorin from creating the notice himself.

As she turned to face the deserted street, she made a decision. The notion had occurred to her after her mother had barred her from the house, but Gorin's shuttered window gave her the license and the resolve. She walked the length of West Broadway, all the way to Dorchester, and then on toward Telegraph Hill.

On arriving at Carney Hospital, the sight of white canvas tents filled with patients and stretching in orderly rows across the lawn banished the doubts that had trailed her from West Broadway. Her instinct—informed by her memory of the overcrowded clinic and the hospital hallways lined with beds—was correct: the situation had grown worse. She never would have imagined tents here, but the sight was unexpectedly comforting. Michael had been quartered inside a tent.

Joseph Powers, of the Bolton Street Powers, was sure he had dreamed the lovely lady who entered his tent.

The young man in the first tent she entered was near Michael's age. He had matted brown hair and asked through chapped lips for a glass of water. Exiting the tent, Lydia nearly collided with a passing nurse.

"Can I help you?" the nurse asked, observing Lydia's shirtwaist with confusion. Lydia was not nurse, nor nun, nor patient.

"The man in that tent wants water," Lydia answered, this the first time she had lent breath to the impulse that honored the letter of her mother's mandate while ignoring the spirit. "I'm going to fetch it for him."

"Are you Red Cross?" the nurse asked.

"The tents weren't here when I came yesterday," Lydia replied. "They all have flu, don't they?"

"We erected the field hospital early yesterday evening," the nurse confirmed. "We're waiting on more nurses from the Red Cross. Have you any nursing experience at all?"

"Let me help. There's so many—" Lydia paused. In that instant the tents seemed to stretch for miles. "Surely I can do *something,*" she urged.

If the nurse turned her away she would find another hospital. She did not know where another hospital was. She would walk until she found one.

The nurse's voice softened. "Are you able-bodied?" she asked.

Lydia nodded, expectation weighting her tongue.

"Well," the nurse conceded, "you'd better don a mask before you check with Head Nurse, or she'll think you're completely unfit, but as far as I'm concerned we need all the help we can get." The woman extended her hand, exhaustion inhabiting even her smallest motions. "Welcome to Carney," she said, and vanished into a tent.

Katherine Jennings remembers neither the young volunteer's name nor her face, only the force of her desire to help.

Diverted by the needs of others, Lydia's grief faded to a dull ache and then to merciful numbness. She yielded to the serial refilling of water glasses, their transport from sink to tent, and their delivery to myriad lips—men's lips and women's lips; lips smooth and lips chapped, some with fever blisters; lips wide and narrow, roseate and pale. The effect of this act did not diminish with repetition. It was a ministration necessarily tender and careful, attuned to the tilt of a chin, the vigor of a swallow. Sometimes she accidentally angled the glass too far and water spilled onto necks and chests, or she angled the glass too slightly, requiring a patient to stretch. The gaffe embarrassed her but the patients did not complain. Grateful stares caressed her even as water soaked bedclothes or necks strained for water just out of reach. With Lydia beside them they were not alone.

Lydia stroked fevered heads. Her fingers clasped other fingers. Never in her life had she so often touched and been touched. Beneath the smells of sickness she sometimes caught the musky scent of skin. Pajamas divulged geometries of chest hair, a small flat scar, a constellation of moles. Sickness and

Jack Manley, from Tent Seven, remembers Lydia's hand as pale and cool.

Fiona Keane recalls a hand that was ruddy and warm.

[159]

Terrence Donohue re-
members a woman
who hummed as she
tended him.

Kelly Frame admired
the lady for not
flinching as she
changed her bed-
sheets.

When George Mc-
Clellan recovered, he
vowed to ask the
pretty volunteer to
marry him, but when
he could not find her
he asked his girl-
friend instead.

Sarah Hoolihan was too
sick to argue when the
doctor put her in the
boy's section. She
blames nits, and the
haircut she was made
to get because of them.

Ethan Dougherty did
not mistake Lydia for
his sister—he thought
she was a nun.

need obviated convention and left, in its place, intimacy. Lydia
had perceived this intimacy once before. Because she had been
tending Henry, she had assumed it was conjugal but she now
discovered it was universal—a shared human undercurrent
detectable only when the dictates of name, sex, and social
standing were effaced. Revealed, it became an embrace. Lydia
had not been three hours at Carney before she knew she was
meant to be a nurse.

Hours passed in which she barely recalled her own name, in
which the activity of Carney bestowed its own purpose and belonging. Awareness of the epidemic itself was subsumed by its
particulars—the precarious gravity of a tray of water glasses,
the smell of blankets imbued with camphor, the cavernous
feeling of the sick wards compared to the tents. She preferred
the tents. The air was fresher there, the smells less trenchant.
Open tent flaps permitted sun and wind, healing forces that
could not penetrate Carney's red brick walls.

Her day at Carney furnished her a strange education. She
learned that a few deep inhalations could deaden her nose to
the smell of bile and sputum and blood. She learned to steel
herself against the sight of soiled sheets. Her face grew an invisible callus that held her features in place so she did not
flinch at the gurgling blue-lipped boy; or the bog-chested
woman whose skin was covered in dark blotches and whose
nose dripped thick, black blood; or the delirious young man
who, in his fever, mistook Lydia for his sister, dead days before. But however hard she tried she could not cotton her ears
against the sounds of sickness. Influenza loosed pneumonia
into the lungs, and pneumonia's sounds were those of a body
drowning from within. Pneumonia turned skin and lips the
bruised gray-blue of an evening sky before a storm. She was
informed in hushed voices by the nurses that those with feet
tinged that color seldom lived through the night. Patients un-
fortunate enough to arrive in such a state were partitioned

from the rest. Doctors did not visit these patients, nor nurses. Only the Sisters in their winged wimples passed through, sometimes in the company of a priest. In the rush, the priest performed last rites over unconscious but still-moving forms, their toes already tagged for the undertaker. Passing through this part of the hospital, Lydia heard these patients struggling for breath, a dirge of clotted lungs.

Across the ocean, the enemy had a discernible face and could be fought with something as simple as a gun. Battles in Europe had beginnings and ends. At Carney, no sooner had she brought water or blankets to one patient when she was called by another, only to be sent elsewhere by a nurse. Lydia could not believe she had given so much of herself to a sales counter, her labor meted in collars and shirts. By the end of the day she felt as if she had spent a lifetime at Carney, her memories of other places the products of dreams.

The hospital's frantic pace precluded the possibility of a slower, more peaceful existence elsewhere, and yet not ten blocks away her mother was preparing supper. If Lydia arrived late she would have to explain where she had been. The same nurse whom she had petitioned that morning was still on duty when she reluctantly took her leave. Despite the nurse's assurances that Lydia had far surpassed expectations—that she ought to go home and rest and was welcome to return to-morrow—leaving Carney still felt just short of criminal.

The serenity of the streets beyond Carney was unsettling. Such stillness should not have coexisted beside such tumult without a rift in the paving stones. Lydia's body ought not to have passed from one state to the other without suffering some sort of change, as when one stands up too quickly or is thrust into freezing water; and yet here she was, returned unscathed to a world where people ate sitting down, where masks did not cover mouths, and where the sounds and smells of the sick did not create a separate climate. She had returned to a world

Katherine Jennings loved to tell the story of the woman who appeared from nowhere to bring comfort to the patients during the worst of the epidemic. She dubbed her the "Carney Angel," a figure that came to be credited for any unexpected boon at the hospital, and which future nurses took to be pure invention.

where she served as a conduit for cuffs and fancy buttons, a flesh extension of the baskets that traveled the length of Gorin's delivering receipts and change. Once again she inhabited a world where human intimacy was as fleeting and rarely sighted as an obscure comet.

As she returned home, she considered how to reconcile her newfound vocation with her old life. Once Gorin's reopened, her work schedule would grant her three days a week to give to Carney. It was both not enough and more than she could hope for. In the unlikely event she was permitted to remain once the Red Cross nurses arrived, she doubtless would be relegated to tasks that kept her away from sickbeds. No matter how astute her powers of observation, she would not learn nursing in the hospital laundry or in its kitchen.

Had she been questioned on returning home, she would have admitted that she had avoided Thomas's sickbed by attending countless others. She would have done her best to temper her family's dismay by describing the imperative to volunteer and the nobility and purpose of her labor, but hiding the truth—no matter how distressing—would not have been a possibility. But her arrival was not met with questions. The Lydia who had left that morning appeared no different from the Lydia who returned. Michael might have been able to detect the change, but Michael was gone. With no outward sign of her internal revelation, her family had no cause to ask anything.

Thomas's fever was down and his cough no worse. Though Lydia and her father were still barred from sleeping in the bedroom, the kitchen was no longer a no-man's-land between health and sickness. Thomas's improved condition was the day's only good news. John had arrived at school to learn that class had been canceled due to his teacher falling ill. James was one of four metal punchers who had reported to Gillette healthy enough to work.

Lydia considered mentioning Carney over dinner, but was deterred by the sight of the table's two empty chairs. She remarked only that Gorin's had been closed. She did not describe nurses ferrying aspirin between tents or the small room toward the rear entrance where the bodies lay stacked. Neither did she share the comforting sound the wind made as it whistled through a tent or the warmth that filled her chest when a patient's eyes met hers. She would explain Carney to them tomorrow. And if, by chance, she arrived to Carney tomorrow only to be turned away, she could postpone the topic for less troubled times.

She was leafing through her father's newspaper when she saw the notice. Mr. H. G. Cory of the Public Health Service was seeking experienced nurses to aid in a government test concerning the flu, to be conducted on Gallups Island. Lydia looked up from the newspaper, feeling as if she had been caught reading a dime-store romance, but her mother was tending Thomas in the bedroom, her brothers were talking in low voices on the front stoop, and her father was dozing at the other end of the divan. She carefully tore the ad from the page. She was a more experienced nurse than she had been when she woke up this morning, and this morning her lack of experience at Carney had been counteracted by their need and her ardor. Three times that evening she verged on throwing the notice away. She fell asleep certain that tomorrow morning she would disregard the notice she still held in her hand.

John told James he thought it might be the end of the world. James tried to convince him otherwise, but it was clear he was wondering the same thing.

. . .

When did this one come in?

A few hours ago, Doctor.

Well, there's nothing we can do for him now. Who's next?

Here, Doctor.

Is there any room in the field hospital?

Tent D-4 is vacant.

Wasn't that the young woman?

Yes, Doctor.

Well, put this one in D-4 then.

Does her family know?

They're—waiting out there. I'm supposed to tell them—but it's too much.

How bad is it?

The husband—arrived a few days ago. He was dead—by the time she came in but we told her—he was too weak to see her. In case—it made a difference, but it didn't.

She was bad off?

Couldn't even get enough air—to push properly. The wee thing—had to be pulled out of her and of course he was dead. God I can't—talk to 'em so long—as I'm crying like this.

Then let them wait a little longer. Shh. It's all right. You're doing a kindness letting them wait.

. . .

TO THE PUBLIC:

It is important for the Public to know at this time that the telephone service of this Company is to considerable extent impaired as a result of the prevalence of Grippe among its forces. As a result of a daily absentee list of several hundred employees, the service is necessarily slower than at normal times in spite of the splendid effort of those who are capable of remaining on duty.

The Public can greatly aid the efforts of our operating forces in the following ways:

1. *By eliminating unnecessary calls.*
2. *By refraining, so far as possible, from special appeals to the Chief Operators, whose entire time should in the present emergency be given to the supervision of their Central Offices.*

3. *By showing leniency to those still capable of remaining at work.*

New England Telephone & Telegraph Company
By W. R. Driver, Jr., General Manager

. . .

THE QDISPATCH

VOLUME II, ISSUE 4   JULY 1993

QD and Me:
A Sodaman's Journey
By Ralph Finnister

Chapter 14
Sad Ascension

It seems fitting that 1968, such a tumultuous year for our country, was also a season of change for QD Soda. After those grueling months fending off the soda consortium, the great Sodaman announced his intention to retire. It should not have come as a shock. By that time Quentin Driscoll was in his seventy-second year and the battle against the consortium—though successful—had taken its toll. But still, when Quentin Driscoll called me to his office and told me that the time had come, my first reaction was disbelief. Though the features of the Sodaman's face had softened, a fierce light still shone from his eyes. Quentin Driscoll may have no longer been as proud and tall as he had once been, but I still saw in him a Sodaman strong of figure and fearless in thought and deed.

For thirty-five years I had been groomed to lead QD Soda into the future. Now this future had arrived. The soda Quentin Driscoll had created still looked and tasted the same after fifty years—but he had become an old man.

Many parallels exist between the world of soda and the world of man, and many paradoxes as well. Man, like soda, is well over fifty percent water and yet the differences from soda to soda and man to man are striking. Some sodas are bland and undistinguished. Others are sickly sweet, while others have a flavor that becomes tiresome. The same is true for man who, like soda, is created by a manufacturing process that renders him different from the way he begins.

An empty bottle is filled with plain water, to which carbonation and flavorings are added. Like most men, I began life as something plain, and like most men I might have ended that way, had I not encountered Quentin Driscoll. The great Sodaman flavored the contents of my humble bottle to create something much better than would have otherwise been. And on the eve of his retirement, the full meaning of this truth was revealed.

Soon before he was to hand me the reins to the empire he had single-handedly created, Quentin Driscoll called me into his office. It was very common for the two of us to remain at work long after everyone else had gone home. This evening, the sun had long set and the Sodaman's office was lit by a lamp that graced his desk's broad surface. The gold initials that fronted the desk glowed dimly. In such light, Quentin Driscoll's face looked to have been carved from ancient stone.

"You first came to me at a very dark time," he began. "Life had lost its savor and I felt hopelessly adrift. If you and my dead son had not shared a name, you would have passed from my office that day without leaving so much as a ripple behind you."

How strange it was to hear this truth spoken aloud! This thought had haunted my nights and spurred me to prove—to myself and to the world—that I was worthy of all that chance had bestowed! I had thought of Ralph Driscoll countless times over the years, but not since my first visit to the great Sodaman's office had he mentioned his son. I had been certain I would not hear that name pass those lips again. Never was I so happy to be wrong.

"Though I will continue to miss my son with every breath I take, until I breathe no more," Quentin Driscoll continued, "even had my own son lived I cannot imagine a more loyal and able partner than you. Dear boy, I am proud of you and of the Sodaman you have become."

My own father could not have inspired the joy I felt on hearing those words. "Thank you, Sir," I replied. "That is all I ever wished for."

But while Quentin Driscoll was not a man to deny life's happy moments, neither was he a man who could dwell in them.

"Do you remember what you said the first time you stood

before me thirty-five years ago?" he asked.

I blushed. I remembered it all too well.

"I was young," I apologized, thirty-five years too late. "When I said I wasn't sure if Ralph was the name of a great man, I was speaking of myself, not your son."

"What Ralph Driscoll may or may not have become is a question whose time is long past," Quentin Driscoll said. "Thirty-five years ago I asked you whether it was better to be good or to be great and you answered that it was better to be good."

"But that it was best to be both," I gently reminded him.

"But if only one was possible—" he began.

"I chose goodness over greatness," I agreed. "But only because, of the two, it is the one quality an average man can ever hope to achieve. It has been my great privilege to work with one of the few notable exceptions to that rule."

The great Sodaman shook his head. To my surprise, pride had been replaced by deepest regret.

"There is something I would like to tell you," he said, his voice strangely quiet. "Something I have never told anyone."

For the first time in thirty-five years, I saw something close to fear enter the great Sodaman's face. To imagine Quentin Driscoll might think he had anything to fear from me! I was overwhelmed by the desire to reassure my mentor, my master—my friend.

"You don't need to tell me a thing," I cried as my emotions overtook me. "Nothing you could say would erase my profound regard for you. Sir, you have filled my little bottle with everything that you have, and I am all the richer for it."

Never had I dared to dream that my words—however spontaneous and heartfelt—would bring tears to the great Sodaman's eyes.

"My son!" Quentin Driscoll declared, rising from his desk like a mighty oak. We embraced like soldiers. I can imagine no greater honor than the one bestowed on me that day by those two words.

The next morning, even as Lydia waited for the streetcar, she doubted the cogency of her plan. It was nonsense to think she would be offered the position—and if she was she did not know how she could possibly tell her family. But she was haunted by the timing of her discovery. A day earlier and the newspaper notice would have meant nothing; a day later and she might have been obliged to return to her sales counter. She preferred to present herself and be turned away by Mr. Cory than never to have made the attempt.

The streetcar driver wore a mask. A handwritten sign above his head read: IF YORE FEELING SICK PLEESE DO NOT RIDE. I HAVE A WIFE AND FAMLY. The last time Lydia rode the streetcar into Boston, people had sung as they made their way to the sailors' parade. But the streetcar was no longer a place where people even exchanged greetings. When a man sitting toward the middle of the car coughed, the passengers around him recoiled as if snakes had slithered from his mouth.

All her life Lydia had taken for granted the showmanship of Boston's streetcar conductors. Some intoned each successive stop as one small part of a larger song, while others bellowed like Wrigley Field umpires. Today's driver dispensed the

Gerard Davis holds that sign one part responsible for his abiding good health, the second part being hot whiskey.

names from inside his mask in a muffled monotone. Perhaps even more contagious than the flu germ itself—which may or may not have inhabited that car—was the fear being inhaled and exhaled, spoken and swallowed, invisible yet tangible as it passed from person to person. Lydia knew she ought to have shared this fear; inside the moving streetcar she provided fear a captive audience. Instead she felt resignation. If flu wanted her, it would take her as it had already taken Henry and Michael. If it did not, then riding this streetcar would make no difference.

The trolley made its way over the bridge to reveal a city of empty streets and shuttered stores. Lydia had not counted on the sight of Boston free of traffic. Until now her cognizance of the epidemic's breadth had been as provincial as her first conception of the war. Newspapers had described the flu's effect in Boston and elsewhere, but their full meaning was easily upstaged by daily circumstance. The sight of the city shut down vivified all that newsprint. Boston's shuttered storefronts had their equals in Philadelphia and New York and Washington, D.C. All across New England and the east coast there were hospitals like Carney, overflowing with the desperately ill; and in the past few days, newspapers had reported flu making inroads west. Riding the streetcar, Lydia imagined a United States map like the one Henry had purchased of Europe, but this time she populated it with pushpins of a single color, pushpins that did not represent an army but a disease.

She debarked on Tremont Street. Morning here felt miscued, as if flu had muddled the earth's diurnal rhythm. Such a deserted street ought to have belonged to the dark, anonymous hours of night. She began striding—and then running—toward Boylston. Of all the buildings on the block, her destined address was the liveliest, but its activity was not a blow against the epidemic—it was a marker of it. These were the offices of the Public Health Service.

Inside the front lobby, a sign instructed each visitor to don a gauze mask from a box beside the door. A masked receptionist directed Lydia to a small elevator, which she shared with two masked officials carrying briefcases. At the sight of the briefcases, Lydia realized the extent of her folly. She was riding an elevator to meet a man who did not expect her, in order to apply for a position for which she was not qualified, and which would fill her family with dread. She examined her clothes. She had been too tired to clean her shirtwaist the night before. Several small stains dotted the sleeve and collar, one of which was likely blood. Looking at the two officials, Lydia was frozen by the notion that there were millions of men in the world, and her brother was no longer among them. The elevator door opened.

Jefferson Carver, the Public Health Service's first colored elevator operator and the car's fourth occupant, has become resigned to his omission from the memories of his white passengers.

According to the lobby receptionist, Mr. Cory's office was just beyond the elevator. To the right, an open doorway cast a slanted oblong of light into the darker corridor. Lydia started toward it and then turned around. If she stopped now she could leave without anyone ever knowing she had come.

"Hello?" came a voice from inside the room. She heard a chair scrape against the floor. A head was silhouetted in the hallway. "Hello? Miss?" a man called as Lydia willed the elevator to return. "Is there something I can help you with?"

"I'm sorry. I made a mistake," Lydia apologized. "I had come about the notice—"

"You mean the Gallups Island project?" the man asked.

"Yes," Lydia answered, "but I don't—"

"Don't worry," he assured her. "You've made no mistake. Did we have an appointment? No matter. You're here. Please do stop standing beside the elevator. If word gets out that I let you go without interviewing you, I'll never hear the end of it." His head darted from the doorway, then reappeared. "Are you coming? Good." The head withdrew.

Lydia retrieved the listing from her pocket. Sweat from frequent fingerings had blurred the words into illegibility and fuzzed the paper's edges. She smoothed the scrap against her dress and folded it in half before returning it to her pocket. Then she followed the man in.

H. G. Cory's office was a small, cramped room whose walls were adorned with health advisory posters. Its single window was open to its limit, allowing a brisk breeze into the room. In spontaneous defense against the open window, the haphazard piles of paper concealing the desk had been secured by objects not originally intended as paperweights. A daunting metal medical instrument anchored one pile; a soda bottle topped another.

Mr. Cory was a frenetic man with shoulders that sloped as if also weighted by random objects. The gauze mask across his nose and mouth looked oversized on his small face.

"The office is a mess, I'm afraid, but don't let that scare you," he said. "There should be a chair here somewhere."

"Thank you," Lydia replied, "but I don't want to waste your time."

"You're confusing me, Miss—Miss—what is your name?"

"Wickett."

"First name?"

"Lydia."

"Miss Lydia Wickett. If you came about the Gallups Island position then you are most assuredly not wasting my time. You're a nurse, are you not?" Mr. Cory was bent over in his chair, opening and closing various drawers in search of something, the piles on his desk obscuring him from view.

"No," she answered.

"Well then, that's all—" He straightened in his chair, and was again visible from the shoulders up. She was reminded of a burrowing mole. "Did you say that you're not a nurse?"

Horace Gilbert Cory has no recollection of the young lady or of this interview. The epidemic survives within him as a frantic search for personnel, interrupted by fitful attempts at sleep and intervals of abject fear.

"That's right. I really am sorry. I'll just leave you to your—"

"You'll just—" He shook his head with quick, sharp movements. "No, please, not yet if you don't mind. You say you're not a nurse. Then what are you?"

"Pardon?"

Mr. Cory had produced a paper form from one of his drawers. "You must have experience, or else you wouldn't have come, yes?"

"Well, yes. I volunteered at Carney Hospital," she began, hungry to tell someone, even if only a stranger. "When I brought a neighbor's child there, it was already overcrowded, and then when I returned the next day there were so many ill that they'd been forced to put tents on the lawn—"

"So you're a nurse's aide then?" Cory asked as he wrote, once again obscured by the papers on his desk. "And how long have you been at Carney Hospital?"

"Just one day," she replied.

Cory stopped writing. "One day?"

At Carney masks had seemed appropriate, but here—inside an otherwise normal office—they gave the conversation the feel of a waking dream.

"Yes," she acknowledged. "You see, I oughtn't to have come. It's one thing to volunteer, but to seek a position, an official position—" She rose from her chair. "Good day, Mr. Cory."

"Please, Miss Wickett," Mr. Cory coaxed. "You would be doing me a great service if you allowed me to finish this interview." He held up his paper. "I've already begun to fill out the form, you see."

She sat.

"Age?"

"Twenty-three."

"Address?"

"28 D Street."

"Single?"

"Widowed."

"Oh." He looked up again. "My condolences."

The mask made it impossible to read his face. He returned his attention to his desk. His window looked out on the windows of other buildings. Without a view of the street, she could almost pretend the city was unchanged.

"It's really quite good of you to bear with me," Mr. Cory continued. "Just a few more questions and then we'll be done. Have you any children?"

"No, sir."

"Are you a drinking woman?"

"Certainly not!" she retorted.

"Good." He sighed gratefully. "Due to the extreme circumstance, some of the hospitals have begun accepting personnel with—handicaps of various sorts, but that won't do here," he explained. "We had one respondent, a lovely woman, but then she had some trouble and that scotched it. Oh dear, I believe I just made a pun." Cory paused and eyed the paperwork arrayed before him. "You'll have to forgive me, Mrs. Lydia Wickett. It has been a very long week. You don't have a fever, do you?"

"No, sir."

"Aches? Fatigue? Cough? Congestion?"

"No, sir."

"Excellent. It is likely to be a two-week study but it could go as long as a month. Influenza transmission, headed by Dr. Gold. We've got to sort out how people are catching this thing if we want to stop it and I'm sure I don't have to tell you that Dr. Gold—"

"Sir?"

"Well, exactly! Any other time and people would be clamoring to work with him. You will live and work on Gallups Island, where you will be expected to assist the nurses and doctors. Food and lodging will be provided. Salary is twenty dollars a week."

"Sir?" she replied. "You did hear all that I said?"

Mr. Cory consulted his paperwork. "Let's see. Your name is Lydia Wickett, you have limited hospital experience, you have no dependents, you are not a drunk, and you are not ill. Is that correct?"

"Yes, but—"

"Lydia Wickett, including yourself do you know how many candidates I currently have under consideration for this position?"

She shook her head.

"One. And while you are not ideal, you are infinitely better than no candidate at all. I don't need to tell you, Mrs. Wickett, that these are desperate times. Desperate times call for—measures. Would you like the position?"

Her hands were shaking. She had felt this way only once before, a lifetime ago, when she received Henry's first love letter.

"Mr. Cory," she answered slowly, measuring each word on her tongue. "I want to be—I am meant to be a nurse. I am as sure of this as I have ever been about anything."

"Well, Mrs. Wickett, I cannot think of a better time for you to have made such a discovery. Does that mean your answer is yes?"

Along one wall were several wooden cabinets labeled with the word PERSONNEL. From this day onward, there would be a file inside one of them bearing her name. She committed to memory the high ceiling, the smell of pipe tobacco, and the way the sun through the window framed Mr. Cory's figure in yellow light.

"Yes," she replied.

Cory clapped his hands. "Fabulous. The study begins Monday, so you really mustn't arrive any later than Sunday. There's a ferry departing Commonwealth Pier at Sunday noon. I shall reserve you a place. Did I mention it's to be headed by Dr. Gold? It's rather a rare—"

"Do you mean this Sunday, sir?"

"Of course," he answered.

"Isn't that a bit soon?" she stammered.

"Soon? But it couldn't possibly be any later. They were expecting someone last week." He paused and his eyes appraised her, as if it had only just occurred to him to do so. "You seem like a sensible girl," he concluded. "Do what the Head Nurse tells you and I'm sure you'll be fine."

She nodded. She stood and shook Mr. Cory's hand. Fifteen minutes after she had entered H. G. Cory's office she found herself outside it again, clutching a ticket for the Sunday ferry. Walking unsteadily toward the streetcar, her disbelief subsided just enough for her to realize that now she had to tell her family everything.

When she arrived home, James and John were racing to set the dinner table: their mother had deemed Thomas well enough to join them for supper. In the process of delivering a serving plate or a glass to the table, each boy's path curved to detour past the open bedroom door to catch a glimpse of Thomas, who lay propped up in bed. Lydia stood near the doorway and basked in the sight of the bedsheet rising and falling with his regular breathing. Thomas's flu had not given way to pneumonia. He would live.

Both John and James wanted to escort their brother to the table, but their mother still prohibited anyone else from entering the sickroom and fetched Thomas herself. Thomas looked as if he had been bed bound for weeks and not days. As he took his usual place at the table, he fixed his younger brother with a stare that shrunk James in his chair.

"Squealer," he muttered, causing James to pale, but then Thomas grinned. "I'm just kidding, Jamie. You did the right thing. If you hadn't fetched Ma that night I don't know what would have happened."

"I didn't want to do it," James countered. "It was only on account of you being so awfully sick that I knew I had to. I prayed so hard for you to get better, Tom. I never prayed harder for anything in my life!"

Jamie was so grateful that Tom was better and no wiser about the death wish he had made that for a few days he thought he might become an altar boy.

As if by previous agreement, they all waited for Thomas to lift his fork to his mouth before beginning to eat. Though their father grinned with every bite Thomas took, his smile did not reach his eyes. Their mother watched Thomas warily, either unable or unwilling to admit that he might no longer require her vigilance. Whenever Thomas coughed, James froze while John shook his head, as if vehement disagreement with the sound might convince it to leave his brother alone. Lydia waited for the right moment to speak, in the meantime striving to appear as if she had nothing on her mind. Each benign moment gained by her silence felt like a small gift. Then dinner was over. Soon Thomas would return to bed.

"I have something to tell you all," she said softly, regretting the tentative beginning. Her desire to go to Gallups had not diminished, but here its imperative was dampened by her knowledge of the grief it would cause. "I'm not the same as I was two days ago." She shook her head. That had to be wrong. It could not possibly have been only two days.

Her mother reached for her daughter's hand. "That's all right, Liddie," she soothed. "We're all different than we were."

Lydia shook her head. "That's not what I mean." She paused. "Perhaps it started with Henry. And then, when we received the news about Michael—" She had not meant to begin this way. "When Brian was at Carney, all I could do—all I did do—was *leave* him there. So when Thomas fell sick and I couldn't do anything for him either—" She looked to the faces of her parents and her brothers. "That was why I had to do it."

"Do what?" her father asked.

"Volunteer," she exhaled, loosing the word from her lungs. None of it was coming out the way she had hoped. "They had set up tents outside the hospital, and everyone wanted fresh blankets and water and there weren't nearly enough nurses. I might not have saved any lives, but no one should have to lie inside a tent, alone, away from their family—" Her breath failed.

There was a moment of bewildered silence.

"You helped at the hospital," her mother began.

Lydia nodded.

"You tended to the sick," her mother continued. "You brought them water and blankets and they were very ill, as ill as Brian and poor Alice. Not just one or two, but many, many people."

Lydia nodded again.

"And then you came back here without a word, to sleep in the same room with your brothers." Her mother was talking in a low voice that did not sound like her at all. "Do you mean to kill us all?"

"I took precautions—" Lydia began.

"Precautions?" her mother cried. "What sort of precautions? They don't know what it is or how to cure it or why it's killing so many." She looked around the table, as if taking stock of the family remaining to her. "Perhaps it is not very Christian of me," she resumed, "but I won't have you going back there."

Lydia looked toward her father and brothers, but their faces were unreadable.

"I won't go back there," she conceded.

"No," her mother quipped. "You won't."

John stood to clear the table, and that was how Lydia knew

that he was frightened, because he never voluntarily cleaned anything.

"I have found work somewhere else," she breathed.

To give herself strength she conjured Mr. Cory's personnel cabinets and the expression on his face when she had said yes, his smile so broad his mask had not impeded it. "There is to be a government study on Gallups Island in the harbor, and they want nurses—"

"But Liddie," her father protested. "You're not a nurse."

"I told him that," she assured him. "Mr. Cory, that is, but it is so hard to find nurses right now, and the work they are to be doing is so important that he said it didn't matter. He said that if it wasn't for me the project would be terribly shorthanded. They want to discover how people catch it, you see, so that they can—"

"Do you truly know what you're saying?" her father pleaded.

"There is risk," she affirmed, "but there's risk in what the soldiers are doing too, and this is an enemy that lives right here, not across an ocean, but right here, and it's killing people."

Her mother pushed herself back from the table. She rose to stand behind Michael's empty chair. "You can't bring him back," she said. "You can leave me like he did, and you can get sick like he did, and you can even die like he did, but none of that will change the fact that he is dead."

No one spoke.

"I know I can't bring him back," Lydia whispered. "I can't bring him back, or Henry, or Brian. But by going to Gallups I'll be helping to stop this from happening again. To you or Da, or Thomas or James or John."

Her mother shook her head. "No," she said. "You left me once, Liddie, and I forgave you. But now you're leaving me again, and you want me to believe that you're doing it for my sake? No. If you love us half as much as you loved him, you would not be throwing yourself into his grave."

The silence that followed was the same quiet that accompanies the witnessing of a red handprint surfacing on a slapped cheek.

"I leave Sunday," Lydia said.

. . .

> ## BRIDE IN GAS MASK AT UPTON WEDDING
>
> *Queerly Robed Party at Bedside of Stricken Soldier*
>
> CAMP UPTON, N.Y.—Sixty patients in the base hospital this afternoon bore witness of the fact that Love, which had hitherto laughed at locksmiths, was not to be baffled by Spanish influenza. There Private Walter J. McKenna wed Miss Lillian E. F. Anne, who traveled to the base yesterday from Westport, Conn.
>
> McKenna, lying ill from the malady complicated by pneumonia, is not expected to live. He had placed the facts before his family and that of the young woman. The arrangements were made for a wedding in the hospital, where masks were provided to prevent the possibility of contagion. When it was over the bride in the gas mask, whose wedding gown had been a hospital robe, left the hospital with the father of the man she had just married.

. . .

Congratulations! Not everyone has what it takes to be a QD Tour Guide (QDTG), but those who do will find it a memorable and rewarding experience. QDTGs are very important members of our extended QD Soda family. Visitors to QD Headquarters (QDHQ) come from all over the country as well as several foreign lands so it is important to think of yourself as QD Soda's ambassador to Boston as well as the world! The following guidelines will tell you everything you need to know to be the best QDTG you can be.

Please take the time to study this important list of QD Dos and Don'ts:

Do
- Wear the QD Tour Guide Uniform (QDTGU)
- Follow the approved tour script and guide route
- Create your own special puppet voice (SPV)
- Smile
- Stand up straight
- Speak clearly
- Behave respectfully toward QDHQ guests
- Have fun!!

Don't
- Wear sneakers, streetclothes, and/or conspicuous jewelry
- Improvise your tour
- Show disrespect for the puppet
- Allow others to operate the puppet
- Either directly or through the puppet express personal opinions about QD Soda or its operations
- Either directly or through the puppet solicit or accept tips
- Either directly or through the puppet flirt with QDHQ visitors
- Forget to have fun!!

The following script and accompanying instructions should be *memorized*. You are neither authorized nor qualified to change them in any way. Changes to the script or instructions are grounds for dismissal.

Please arrive at the tour departure point (TDP) ten minutes before your QD Tour (QDT) is scheduled to begin. Remember: you are responsible for your QDTGU. Your smock should be clean and wrinkle-free. Make sure you retrieve the QD Puppet (QDP) from its cubby and stow it in your QDTGU BEFORE arriving at the TDP. Don't be shy; promote your QDT! At three- to five-minute intervals leading up to the time of your QDT, say:

It's tour time, ladies and gentlemen! Don't delay, get your tickets right away! Learn about the exciting history of America's Most Beloved Soft Drink, QD Soda!

Direct anyone interested in the QDT to purchase a ticket from the gift shop. Every tour group participant (TGP) MUST have a ticket, *including* QDTG friends and family members.

When the time of the QDT arrives, say:

Hello! Thank you for visiting QD Soda Headquarters! My name is [your name], and I'll be your tour guide today!

Did you know that soft drinks are more popular than coffee, tea, and juice combined? Last year over 60 billion soft drinks were sold in this country! That means more than 53 gallons of soda for each and every American man, woman, and child, which averages out to more than one gallon per American per week!

You know, you're very lucky to have come to QDHQ today, because I've heard a rumor that we're going to be visited by someone very special. I have a feeling that you're going to get a chance to meet him really soon! In fact . . . [Pause and appear to be listening to something.] Ladies and gentlemen, do you hear something? [Look toward the door to Room 1.] I think I hear someone in there. I wonder if it could be our visitor. Oh, ladies and gentlemen, boys and girls, I think you're in for a very special treat! Follow me!

As you lead your TGPs into Room 1, put one hand inside the QDP and remove it from the pocket of your QDTGU, while hiding it from view of your TGPs. For the rest of the tour, even when the QDP isn't "talking," remember to keep the QDP upright and alert. Lines in italics should be spoken in your SPV. Don't forget to make the QDP's mouth move when he "speaks"! Once you have entered Room 1 and the QDP is securely on your hand, turn to face your TGPs. Say:

Why, ladies and gentlemen, it's Quentin Driscoll himself! Hello, Mr. Driscoll!

Hello there, [your name]*! Hello there everyone!*

You've arrived just in time, Mr. Driscoll. I was just about to tell everyone about how you invented QD Soda, but now that you're here, why don't you tell them yourself!

I'd love to! It all started when I was a young man of 22, just like this young lady here [point to an older woman in the group]*. In those days soft drinks were made at soda counters right before your very eyes! I was working at a soda counter when, one night, I had a dream. An Indian chief appeared before me holding four plants in his hand. The very next morning I went straight to the library. In a book about native plants and herbs, I found the exact pictures of the plants the Indian chief had shown me, and that was when I knew they were the ingredients I'd need to make a very special soda. And that, ladies and gentlemen, was how QD Soda was born!*

Open curtain using *non*-QDP hand. Say:

And this, ladies and gentlemen, boys and girls, is the result of Quentin Driscoll's efforts! This window looks directly into the QD Soda bottling facility, which was built in 1920 and which, to this day, produces delicious bottles of refreshing QD Soda. Mmm, just thinking of all those bottles makes me thirsty! It makes me wish I had my own glass of QD Soda right now! Well, lucky for us we'll get a chance to drink some very soon! Everyone, follow me!

Lead your TGPs into Room 2. Walk behind the counter. Say:

Well, Mr. Driscoll, does this place look familiar?

It sure does, [your name]*! Ladies and gentlemen, boys and* *girls, welcome to Quenty's, a genuine facsimile of the very soda counter where I was working when I dreamed up the recipe to QD Soda. Step right up for your complimentary soda sample!*

Using your *non*-QDP hand, give a cup of QD Soda to each TGP. Do not distribute more than one cup per TGP and do not give seconds.

NOTE: Some TGPs, especially younger children, may not enjoy their free sample. In the case of a dissatisfied child smile and say (using your SPV): *It's a very unique flavor, isn't it? Don't worry, you'll grow into it.* In the case of a dissatisfied adult, smile and say (using your SPV): *It's an acquired taste.*

Allow five minutes for your TGPs to drink their free samples. Then say:

Well everyone, we've got one more stop before Mr. Driscoll and I say our good-byes. Please deposit your cup in the trash receptacle to the left of the door as we exit.

Lead your TGPs into Room 3. Hand each TGP a song sheet as they enter. Say:

As you can see, this room is devoted to the "QD Follies" and the famous "QD Comedy Hour." There's so much in this room to look at and appreciate that Mr. Driscoll and I are going to let you see it on your own, but make sure to take a look at the dress worn by QD Cutie Cara Blaine, as well as a suit worn by Preston "Hewey" Hughes, the popular host of the "QD Comedy Hour." And save a little extra time for the special memorial devoted to the tragic fate of Quentin Driscoll's first wife, Sara Lampe Driscoll—and their young son Ralph. Several recordings of the show's classic radio broadcasts are available in our gift shop. Well everybody, it's been a real pleasure having you here today, hasn't it Mr. Driscoll?

Why it sure has, [your name]*!*

But before we say our good-byes, we thought it might be fun to sing a song! Songs were a very important part of the

"QD Comedy Hour," which featured celebrities from Milton Berle to Roy Rogers singing about how much they loved QD Soda. So before we go our separate ways, everybody take a look at your QD Soda song sheet and join me and Mr. Driscoll as we all pretend we're on the "QD Comedy Hour!"

Remember to sing loudly and clearly! If you'd like, sing using your SPV! Sing at least one of the following songs:

I Wanna Drink QD
(sung to "I Wanna Hold Your Hand")

My soda, it's really something.
Its taste makes history.
Be-cause, it is a soda
That's as unique as me!
I wanna drink QD!
Find me a cold QD.

Oh, I—I'll tell you something.
Your colas don't impress me.
They're nothing
Compared to drinking
A bottle of QD!
I wanna drink QD!
Give me a cold QD.

When I drink QD I feel special—inside.
Its taste gives me a feeling that—
I can't hide
I can't hide
I can't hide!

If I could name a soft drink
To be soda MVP

My choice of all the soft drinks
Would be the taste of QD!
I wanna drink QD!
Pass me a cold QD!

My Soda Is QD
(sung to "My Country 'Tis of Thee")

My soda is QD,
Its taste and history
Are quite unique.

It's the main beverage
Inside my kitchen fridge
Refreshment with a heritage
Have a cold QD!

At the end of the song/s, proceed to the gift shop. Retrieve a bottle of QD Soda from the display refrigerator and drink it slowly so that the exiting TGPs will see you enjoying the soda. The QDP should be looking at you as you drink. From time to time, use your SPV to express his envy with phrases such as: *Boy, does that look good!* and *It almost makes me wish I wasn't a puppet!* When the last TGP has exited Room 3, return the QDP to its cubby. If the QDP has become soiled or stained it is up to YOU to alert a manager to its condition. Remember: the QDP is YOUR responsibility. Treat it with the same respect you show yourself.

Cora would have gone along if Tom's health had permitted.

Tom recalls being well enough to look after himself. The minute Liddie left for the pier, Ma started on the kitchen floor with a bristle brush, which he had not seen her do since the time he got into Da's beer.

W hen Sunday arrived, Lydia's mother remained with Thomas—who was still too frail to leave the house—while the rest of them saw Lydia to the pier at Southie's northern edge. To those who called Southie home, the pier was only ever a place to earn a wage. Anyone who set foot on a boat there was helping to load it. As Lydia made her way to the ferry that awaited her, she wondered if in breaking yet another unwritten neighborhood covenant she had finally exhausted Southie's patience. Strange as it was to imagine her leave-taking, it was even more difficult to envision her eventual return.

The day's clarity recalled the blue sky that had marshaled the sailors in the Win-the-War-for-Freedom parade. Walking toward the pier, Lydia tried to recall whether those men had allowed their gazes to wander or whether they had stared ahead as they marched. Even without the distraction of onlookers, her eyes were drawn to either side. There was the doorstep where she waited for Margaret Kelly on the way to school. There was the curb where she and Michael found the one-legged pigeon. Here was where the hurdy-gurdy man had frightened her into believing that his monkey had once been a little girl. There was the building she used to think would have been better to live in because of its green-painted door. That door had a black wreath on it now.

She strode past shuttered corner groceries and apothecaries where masked pharmacists gazed wearily from behind wooden counters. She walked with her shoulders thrust back and her chin lifted. The benches in Commonwealth Park were empty of mothers. Its climbing trees and game fields wanted children. Though the specifics of her departure differed from that of the marching sailors, Lydia felt her mission was much the same: she too was leaving to fight a war. By looking toward the cobblestones, she erased the difference between a street edged with cheering crowds and the one that now sponsored her solitary parade.

Past the park, the street gave way to foundries and chemical plants and tanneries, their smells diminished only slightly by their Sunday sabbatical. Nearer to the pier the briny smell of the harbor took hold, and then she spied the small ferry tied off at the dock's end.

At the train station on the day of her brother's departure the air had been alive with shouted endearments, the calls of conductors, and the huff of locomotives. Here the air held only the sound of the water, the creaking of the ship, the occasional gull, and the groans of the planks beneath the two silent men who loaded sacks and crates onto the ferry's deck. In lieu of a duffel Lydia had her one suitcase, its West end dresses replaced with shirtwaists and the scant personal items she thought a few weeks away would require. Once they reached the pier, her father kept hold of the suitcase.

"It's not too late," he told her. "You could still come back with us. I'm sure that Cory fellow can find someone else." But his face anticipated her answer.

"Are you mad at me, Da?" she asked.

"No," he answered, "but I don't like it none. Better you stay here with us than go off where nobody knows you. There'll always be some place needing a nurse."

She eased the suitcase from his grip. "I'll only be gone a few weeks and then I'll be home again. Consider it a short enlistment."

John—who until now had preferred the safety of his older brother's shadow—shook his head. "It ain't the same as enlisting," he contended. "Girls don't get drafted. You're leaving because you want to."

"But doesn't that make me even more brave?" she asked. In her mind, John was still the shy kindergartner who had led her wedding procession and not the ten-year-old boy who stood scuffing his shoes against the dock.

John shook his head again. "Jamie says you're going because you're too sad to stay."

"I don't think that's the only reason," James amended, "but I wish you'd listen to Da and wait a little longer." To look at James was to see her mother's eyes staring out from a young man's face.

"Look after yourself," she urged. She wanted to say something they could take back to the flat as reassurance of some sort, but her search for the right words was cut short by a voice from the end of the pier.

"You the one to Gallups?"

Later, once the boat was under way, Seaman George Kurt asked the lady a different sort of question.

Though her thoughts and actions since first spotting the newspaper listing had been in the service of this moment, its arrival—even as she walked to the pier—had seemed distant. Now the men who had been loading cargo stood on the ferry's deck. The pier was empty save for Lydia and the family she was leaving behind.

Her father pressed her to him, his hand spanning the back of her head as though measuring it to remember its curve. "You come back," he pleaded in a hoarse whisper.

James grasped her shoulders. "If you get sick," he began,

then shook his head. "Don't get sick, Liddie. That's all there is to it."

"Let's none of us get sick," she said. "Not you, not me, not Ma and Da, and not John." Hugging him, she wondered when he had started wearing Michael's cologne.

John stood with his arms crossed, his eyes focused on the wood planks at his feet.

"Can I hug you good-bye?" she asked.

"If you're coming back," John answered, "then it ain't good-bye."

"Can I hug you good afternoon then?" she compromised.

John considered the proposition. "I guess that's all right," he shrugged, and allowed himself to be embraced.

After that, there was nothing left but to board the ferry. As she approached the boat, she recalled her brother's confidence on boarding the Devens-bound train, his body half turning to wave even as his legs had continued to stride forward. His fiercely proud expression was the last she ever saw of his face. Walking forward she dearly wished to turn and wave, but she could not bear to invoke her brother's ghost. Instead she waited until she had boarded the ferry and then leaned over the railing, her tears blurring the world as she waved, rendering her father's and brothers' figures indistinguishable from the diminishing shore.

It was startling how quickly all of Boston shrunk and then vanished as if it had never existed, the entire world nothing but water with vague shapes perforating its horizon. She wondered if her brother had been equally disconcerted by the sight of Boston unspooling into obscurity at the end of a lengthening strand of railroad ties. She decided this was one more experience they had in common.

"Liddie get your gun, get your gun, get your gun," she began. "Take it on the run, on the run, on the run," but her voice was thin and the sound of it made her lonelier.

Mick does not recall his feeling one way or the other. He was awfully hungover.

She had been placed at the front of the boat by the ship's mate, where she and her valise were lodged between a large burlap sack and several wooden crates. Gulls hovered off the bow before swooping away with disparaging shrieks. The wind was more unkind away from land, and she shivered. When she looked over the water, she was overcome by dizziness imagining the depth of the harbor. The mate stood with the captain inside a small compartment toward the boat's center, inside which she supposed she would not have comfortably fit even had she been invited. She would have liked to grip the rail with both hands, but could not bring herself to relinquish her suitcase and so instead spent the ride gripping both the rail and the suitcase handle so tightly that she lost feeling in both hands, tormented by images of her and it sliding off the deck and sinking to the harbor's bottom. She was ashamed of her faintheartedness: had her brother lived he would have been expected to endure not an hour-long journey, but a transatlantic passage.

Seaman Kurt recalls inviting the lady to do lots of things, joining him in the compass bridge being one of the less interesting.

To distract herself she focused on the horizon, willing her destination to come into view. As she scanned the skyline she thought of the hansom cab that in a previous lifetime had carried her and Henry, newly wed, from the church. She remembered her fear at the sight of her family disappearing behind her and her decision to focus on what was to come. The act of facing forward and reaching for Henry's hand had felt as significant as the vow sworn before the priest.

She gripped the boat's railing tighter and leaned into the wind. A few vague shapes in the distance were growing steadily larger—one of them had to be Gallups. The name Gallups Island conjured visions of a barren, rocky slice of land whose jagged and formidable shore was perpetually pounded by rough waves. As her departure neared, the romanticism of such an image had been replaced by foreboding—but when the ferry's heading became clear, the swath of land that rose into view was larger and more hospitable than her bleak fantasies.

Gallups was a place of sloping hills, the beach giving way to more trees than Lydia had ever seen. Southie's trees were a leafy variant of street pole, green utilities arranged according to a city plan. Gallups' trees clustered and spread according to arboreal precepts forever lost to their urban cousins. Save for a few crimson stalwarts resisting autumn's end, their leafless branches swayed with the wind against the blue backdrop of the sky. These myriad fingers beckoned Lydia toward an unspoiled piece of land that made Commonwealth Park seem like a window box. She knew at that moment how the first arrivals to the New World must have felt, the lushness of the coast hinting at its limitless potential. For a moment she forgot her difficult leave-taking and uncertain future: the island was beautiful.

The ferry met the dock with a lurch. She was tendered only slightly more consideration than the burlap sacks that preceded her disembarkation, the boathand's farewell the same grunt offered her at boarding. A nurse stood halfway down the dock observing the boat's landing with her head cocked to one side, as though trying to catch faint strains of music. The wind, which was constant, had dislodged a fine blond ribbon of hair from the woman's bun, but had made no progress with her white cap, which must have been anchored to the crown of her head with innumerable pins. Her spotless nurse's uniform seemed, on her, less like a uniform than like something fashionably up-to-the-moment that might be worn to one of the city's better theaters. Carney's nurses had never looked so elegant as this woman, who made even the simple act of waiting on a dock seem somehow expert and accomplished. Lydia felt a surge of excitement at the sight of her: she was the nurse Lydia meant to become.

"Nurse Foley?" she asked in a hopeful voice, this the name

Seaman Kurt is surprised the lady doesn't recall the pat he gave her backside as she debarked. She had a luscious ass for a prude.

supplied her by Mr. Cory. Though she had pinned her hair for the ferry crossing, the wind and sea spray had dismantled her efforts. She made a start of tucking stray strands back into place but stopped on realizing the hopelessness of the task.

The woman smiled and offered her hand. "Yes. And you are Nurse Wickett. I can't begin to tell you how happy I am that you've arrived, so I won't even try. You're a veritable angel for coming on such short notice. And please, call me Cynthia."

Cynthia had been born into the good diction Lydia had spent her Gilchrist career trying to emulate. Her hand was much softer than Lydia's, with long, tapered fingers Lydia could imagine playing a piano.

"I'm called Lydia, or sometimes just Liddie," she answered.

"I prefer Lydia," Cynthia answered. "Much more elegant, don't you think? Around here we need whatever elegance we can get. Doctors are so awfully plain. They live like bachelors, even the married ones. Of course, they haven't got time for the niceties that are second nature to a woman, especially not here, where there is so much to do." Cynthia paused. "Forgive me for babbling, but it's such a relief to have another nurse here. I'm afraid Mr. Cory didn't tell me much beyond your name and when to expect you. Are you Red Cross?"

"No—" Lydia began and then stopped.

"Of course you aren't," Cynthia agreed. "They never would have given you up. But the hospitals certainly aren't giving away nurses now either. I don't suppose you're Navy or Public Health . . ."

"No," Lydia hesitated, afraid her answer would countermand her warm welcome.

Cynthia tilted her head to one side as she had at the ferry's arrival, but now the gesture reminded Lydia of a cat in an unfamiliar room. "Well then," she asked with a thin smile, "what exactly are you?"

"Didn't Mr. Cory tell you?" Lydia prompted. She attempted a smile that would place her securely among the Cynthia Foleys of the world, but suspected she more closely resembled a shopgirl proffering a rain check.

"Apparently not," Cynthia answered.

"I was at Carney Hospital before this," Lydia began, "but as I explained to Mr. Cory I was more of a volunteer assistant."

Lydia turned to look behind her. She did not so much wish to reboard the ferry as assure herself that she still could, but the boat was far beyond the dock.

"You mean to tell me that you are not a nurse?" Cynthia asked. Her mouth had gathered in on itself as if cinched by a drawstring.

"It's only just what I told Mr. Cory," Lydia insisted. "When I read the listing—when I learned that you were looking for a way to prevent this epidemic from ever happening again—" Without warning she recalled her father's hand cradling the back of her head. "My brother died," she said. She forced back the taste of salt.

Cynthia stopped examining Lydia's face. "I'm sorry to hear that," she replied.

"Please forget I mentioned it," Lydia urged. "I prefer you to judge me on my own merits."

"But Miss Wickett," Nurse Foley exclaimed, "you have just led me to understand that you have none!"

Cynthia was at that moment trying desperately not to cry herself.

Lydia blushed. She could feel the hairpin at the back of her neck dangling uselessly against her collar. "It's only just what I told Mr. Cory. If you like, I can send word to the nurses at Carney. I'm sure they would vouch for me."

"Oh crumbs." Cynthia Foley sighed, staring past Lydia to the water. "It's pointless railing against you. You're here and I suppose you're all the help Mr. Cory was able to send." She turned and began walking toward the compound. "If you'll follow me we can get started," she said, sounding only distantly related to the woman who had extolled the elegance of Lydia over Liddie.

It was not a long walk from the dock. When they reached the summit of the small rise on which the compound rested, a flash of white crossed Lydia's path. She spun her head in time to see two long ears disappear into a meadow. She stood stunned as if she had just learned of the existence of fairies: she had only ever seen a rabbit on the tin of her father's hair oil.

"The island is infested with them," Nurse Foley called back. As Lydia continued forward her head remained turned. When the breeze parted the tall grass she spied a rabbit, frozen in place and staring at her with one round, dark eye.

For the fifty years preceding the war, Gallups Island had served as a quarantine station for newly arrived immigrants too ill to be permitted entry past Boston Harbor. Inside the station gate stood a flagpole displaying both an American flag and a white flag bearing a red cross. This, Lydia was informed, was in case of German invasion. War, unlike epidemic, honored certain protocols: anything designated a medical operation would remain unharmed. Gallups was not the most easterly island in the harbor but members of its staff nonetheless took shifts posting watch for the ominous rise of a periscope from beneath the surface of the waves.

The island housed a collection of utilitarian brick and wood buildings divided between barracks, mess halls, galleys, and a hospital. To the west of the complex stood a modest graveyard. The compound's squat, blocky construction was at odds with the sloping island and its graceful trees. Its structures might easily have been imposed, preassembled, onto the island's terrain. Fifty years of strong easterly winds had worn the buildings in the same uneven way, leaving their leeward sides the most pristine, as if each building had turned their best face toward Boston in hope of rescue.

We would like to think
We contributed at least
in part to this impres-

Lydia's introduction to the station began with her living quarters. When fully operational, the quarantine station maintained a larger staff, which permitted each current member of the flu study the luxury of a private room. As the only female medical personnel, Lydia and Cynthia would be neighbors, each inhabiting one room of a two-room barrack originally intended to sleep eight. Good manners required that Cynthia offer Lydia assistance unpacking. Lydia was not sure who was the more relieved when she said she would rejoin the nurse as soon as she was settled in.

Once alone in the strange, empty room, the tears Lydia had swallowed on the dock returned. She had not wept like this since the day she learned of Michael's death and it frightened her to cry like this now. The madness of the blind, determined thrust that had brought her to Gallups Island struck her with the force of a blow. Her family had been right. Of course it was too soon.

She opened her suitcase. In addition to her necessities, it contained her three favorite love letters from Henry, a button from one of Michael's shirts, her Communion Bible, a devotional card featuring the Sacred Heart, and a picture of Boston Common torn from a magazine. She pressed Michael's shirt button into her palm. Whether at Southie or Gallups, she was utterly unequipped to mourn her brother.

In Southie the question of how to grieve had been subverted by Thomas's sudden illness and her subsequent appetite for hospital work. But on Gallups, alone for the first time since Michael's death, the crux of Lydia's dilemma was revealed: she could not mourn her brother the way she had mourned her husband.

When Henry died, Lydia's grief had been an impulse as pervasive and persistent as hunger. She had submitted to its demands without thought or fear, as a child who has never suffered a fall will unhesitatingly climb a tall tree. But Lydia

sion. Among Us are several who whisper of purgatory in that drab place.

had overcome her grief knowing that she could not have done it alone. If Michael had not stewarded her return to the world, a large part of her would have remained buried with her husband. In the mechanism of her mourning, her brother had proven to be an intrinsic part. With Michael's death, this delicate instrument had been robbed of its counterbalance. As desperately as she needed to mourn her brother, she could not grieve him properly without him by her side. That impossibility had yielded this lopsided result.

Gallups' hospital was its largest building, having been built to house and treat every immigrant unlucky enough to be sent to the island. In the late afternoon its elongated shadow swallowed several of the barracks and dining halls. Its façade, however, was too spare to inspire fear. It was a simple rectangular prism with a door at its center, windows at regular intervals, and a slanted roof—a child's rendition of a building.

Georgio Maripone— who was diverted to Gallups on his arrival from Sicily in 1890— begs to differ. In all his life he had never seen a more frightening place.

The moment Lydia rejoined Cynthia she understood that any endeavor to emulate the nurse would fall short. At Carney, Lydia had not given any thought to her clothes, but now she was acutely aware of the ways her drab shirtwaist differed from Cynthia's proper nurse's uniform. She knew it was pointless to covet Foley's fitted dress or her handsome blue nurse's cape, but she hoped she might eventually be supplied with a cap.

If Cynthia was surprised at the sight of Lydia's shirtwaist, she kept it to herself. Her reticence extended to the hospital tour she provided, which placed special emphasis on all Lydia was unequipped to do. Lydia had never taken blood, nor procured a throat culture; she was unpracticed with medical charts and examination protocol. At first the nurse met each of Lydia's admissions of inexperience with downturned lips and a barely perceptible nod, but by the end of the tour even these expressions had seized up, as if the woman who had met Lydia at the dock had been replaced by a wooden decoy. Lydia wanted to grasp Cynthia's elegantly tapered fingers and plead to be given a chance to prove herself. Instead she assured Nurse Foley—whom it was probably best to forget even had a first name—that she would devote herself to improving her skills, a declaration that was received as mutely as the others.

The discouraging nature of Lydia's tour was offset by its brevity. The hospital's interior was no more complex than its exterior: it was a square divided into four equal quadrants by a cruciform hallway. During the hospital's tenure as an immigrant quarantine, the two rear quadrants had served as male and female wards. On Dr. Gold's watch, they would house the volunteers undergoing testing. The front right quadrant contained medical labs and offices that Nurse Foley made clear were off-limits save by express invitation of the senior medical staff; its neighbor housed the surgery and recovery rooms, the storage and utility closets, and the morgue.

Lydia offered to begin working at once, but Foley suggested instead that she take the time remaining before dinner to acquaint herself with the compound. The nurse then disappeared down the hallway that Lydia had been barred from entering without permission, leaving her alone in the empty ward.

Unused beds seemed indecent when the aisles at Carney were lined with makeshift cots. Walking among the crisply made beds of the quarantine ward, Lydia wondered if the study intended to cater to rich invalids. She had never seen such luxurious sickrooms. Each ward was easily large enough to hold twenty or even thirty beds, but contained only ten. The surplus space instead held several card tables, a writing desk, and a bookshelf. The patients at Carney had been too sick to

The rooms were larger than that. As she sweat her life away, Gala Theodopolus counted and recounted the beds in the women's ward and no matter how high her fever went they always numbered at least forty.

Yuri Turovic counted fifty beds in the men's ward, but he is not so certain of himself: the beds he tallied were usually occupied by dead ancestors.

Grygor Hansa thinks the lady does not have a good memory for rooms. He was two weeks in the rear barracks waiting for papers. There were fifty beds, almost always empty. Most people left the hospital inside a wood box.

enjoy such amenities, but she supposed that mild cases would be just as helpful as severe ones if the study's only concern was how flu was caught. This conclusion would make a fine topic for her first letter home, one that might put her family more at ease.

After quitting the hospital, she took the time that remained before dinner to make a cursory investigation of the compound. Near her own barrack were identical buildings that housed the other medical staff, but behind the hospital was a larger, longer barracks building—a single room that slept at least twenty. Catercorner from the hospital, the dining hall was at this hour the brightest object in the compound, its large windows casting elongated bars of light across the darkening ground. Like most of the island's facilities, the space was larger than the flu study required. When Lydia entered, she noticed that only two of the hall's ten tables were set for dinner. The remaining eight had their chairs stacked on top of them in the manner of a restaurant closed for the evening and awaiting the departure of its lingering guests. Nurse Foley's table was already full; and when Foley left her seat in order to present Lydia to the various staff, Lydia learned she was the only personnel member without some sort of medical title, leaving her feeling like a kid sister among the surgeons and acting assistant surgeons. The most senior staff member in the room was a gentleman not much younger than her parents, but the rest of her dining companions could have easily been Henry's classmates. It felt strange, years after the drastic revisions of her early marriage, to be among the very society to which she had once aspired—as if a genie had belatedly granted her abandoned wish. But if that were the case, Henry ought to have been sitting beside her.

Her awareness of being one of only two women on staff now struck her for the first time. She was usually at ease with the opposite sex, a trait she attributed to her Men's Department tenure and a flat full of brothers. But here, the seemingly commonplace experience of sitting at a table of young men was countered by the fact that, introductions aside, her dining companions looked past her as though she were an extraneous utensil. Lydia became an invisible party to a discussion peppered with erudite medical terms that struck her as deliberately opaque and which she vowed to remember long enough to copy down once she returned to her room; somewhere on the island there had to be a dictionary. But after a few fruitless moments of listening, she turned her attention to her meal. She abandoned her best table manners when she noticed they only singled her out further. Apparently her colleagues had left both conversational and dining etiquette on the mainland. Staring at her plate, she experienced her first wave of homesickness. At this hour her mother would have finished cleaning the supper dishes. Her father would be halfway through his nearsighted perusal of the daily paper, newsprint darkening the tip of his nose. John and James would have adjourned to the stoop and perhaps Thomas would have joined them, wearing a light jacket over his pajamas as a concession to maternal concern. Lydia gazed at her feet. The weeks ahead loomed like long, gray shadows.

When the door to the dining hall opened, she sensed the man striding to the front of the room before she saw him, and knew without being told that this was Dr. Joseph Gold. Conversations halted midsentence as people turned to witness the doctor's entrance. With his arrival, the mess hall no longer felt cavernous. She would not have thought one man capable of subverting the effect of eight empty tables, but at Dr. Gold's appearance the perceived boundaries of the room shrunk. Dr. Gold was a tall, imposing man of impressive build, with a neatly trimmed moustache and a regal nose, upon which

Rachel Gold assures Us her husband's stature was unremarkable.

rested a pair of gold spectacles. On a different face these would have lent an air of fragility, but on the doctor the delicate wire frames had the effect of strengthening his features.

"Gentlemen—and ladies," Dr. Gold commenced without preamble. "We come together today to embark upon a truly historic mission." His voice was simultaneously intimate and grandiloquent and caused the room to shrink even further, until it seemed to contain only the doctor and Lydia herself. Confidence radiated from Dr. Gold like captive sunlight. Previously she had witnessed such self-assuredness in ward politicians, but while they fly-cast their personalities outward, Dr. Gold's mien resulted from an intense interior focus that could not help but draw people toward him.

"Our task here is not new," Dr. Gold continued, his eyes flashing, his voice sonorous and crisp. "Just as yellow fever and typhus once demanded our vigilance, so too does influenza. Just as we conquered those blights, so shall we conquer this one. In league with the brave volunteers who have offered to aid in this quest, we shall penetrate the innermost mysteries of this affliction and, in piercing the veil, triumph over the ignorance which has allowed the epidemic to spread with such alarming speed. I am sure you have heard of the plight of our neighbors to the south: Philadelphia has suffered an even greater blow than Boston; New York and Washington, D.C., reel under the weight of their afflicted."

The doctor's voice was quiet and urgent now. Along with the rest of the room Lydia found herself leaning forward. No chair creaked and no toe tapped. No one dared risk missing a word.

"While our discoveries here will not bring the dead back to us or erase the suffering of the thousands now chained to influenza's yoke, we will prevent future deaths, future suffering. One day, our children will not know the word 'flu' and we will explain it is a disease long extinct. Through vigilance, sound

Though Rachel Gold was not among the Gallups Island faculty, she vouches for the tenor of his words. Her husband's bravura oratories were number-blind. To him, a single auditor was no different than an audience of one hundred.

method, and cooperation we will triumph. Remember: in our pursuit no task, no matter how seemingly trivial, is insignificant. Every observation, no matter how seemingly slight, may be the one to yield the crucial insight. Together we will function as one mind, striving with the noblest of purpose."

The doctor paused in order to sweep his eyes across the faces assembled before him. Lydia was certain he had, for a brief moment, looked at her. Having completed his circuit of the room, he cast his eyes downward before continuing, his voice now humble.

Dr. Gold would like to clarify that, in his case, the term "doctor" refers dually to his status as Ph.D. and M.D.

"The volunteers arrive tomorrow. I ask that you treat them with utmost respect. Fully apprised of the risks involved, they have selflessly given themselves to this cause and it is by this that they ought to be judged. Remember: we all make mistakes—mistakes in judgment, mistakes in action. At a time such as now, with our nation at war, these mistakes carry more weight than they might in peacetime. Whatever your politics away from Gallups, whatever feelings you might harbor toward these men, here on the island I ask you to keep them in check—for here, we serve a higher cause. Remember: no matter what their previous actions, these men by volunteering have professed their willingness to make the ultimate sacrifice in order to serve the greater good. And so, I thank you. For though it is the duty of those in the medical profession to ease malady at personal risk, the risk involved here is great and it is unambiguous. Many good doctors and nurses across the country and the world have already fallen to this epidemic, and I fear it is a sacrifice that will continue. I hope and pray we shall all be spared this ultimate sacrifice but I recognize and honor the willingness of every person in this room to place themselves directly in the epidemic's path. Our efforts will not go unnoticed nor will they go unrewarded. The future will be transformed by what we are about to do. Gentlemen—and ladies—that future begins tomorrow."

The room broke into applause. Dr. Gold shook hands with everyone in the room. His grip was firm, his palm cool—and when he looked at Lydia she did not perceive dismissal but avidity. Not until he departed the room did she realize she understood no more about the study than she had before.

. . .

OUR MAIL BAG

Enforce the Anti-Spitting Law

To the Editor of the *Herald:*

There is a law on the statute books of this state prohibiting spitting on sidewalks, subway stairs, and other public places, which, so far as I know, has never been repealed. Not so many months ago there was remarkable activity among the police in seeing that this law was enforced, and the morning papers reported many names of men brought into court and fined $3 for indulging in this disgusting and now extremely dangerous habit.

Why in the name of humanity cannot the police commissioner be induced to instill some enthusiasm among the patrolmen in trying anew to stop this spitting, which is done on the streets every day, apparently without fear of interruption from anyone, and the condoning of which, under the present conditions in the city, is nothing short of criminal?

HERMAN W. ABORN,
111 Devonshire Street

. . .

My Dear Boy—

Very late at night, it gets so quiet that I feel I am the only geezer left alive in this place. I have learned not to check the time. If I start looking at the clock, then I cannot stop. Before these dreams started their rotten habit of waking me up, I never saw a minute hand move. Now if I am not careful I end up watching the damn thing trace a full circle while my brain shows old home movies.

Remember when I took you to the boat show? Your mother wanted me to take you to the circus, but once you saw all those beautiful boats you quit bawling pretty quick. Do you remember what you did when I asked you which one you liked best? Without batting an eyelash, you pointed at the Chris Craft Triple and said, "That one, Father." And when we came home with it, the look on your mother's face was worth ten times the cash I had paid! God she loved that boat. That is why I know it must have been an accident. Because when it happened she was with the two things she loved most in the world.

I can always tell it is morning when I hear the medicine cart go rattling past my door. That sound means I can get out of bed and pretend I am just starting my day.

Your Loving Father

L ydia's first night on Gallups was interminable. Spurred by the unfamiliar room and her unaccustomed solitude, her mind reviewed in excruciating detail her actions since Michael's death. Her folly in leaving Southie struck with renewed force. Familiarity might have softened her self-judgment, but there was neither the deep, even rhythm of another's slow breathing nor an accustomed sight outside her window to counteract the night's innate dramatizing powers. Lying on a small, narrow mattress in a draughty room meant for four, Lydia's desire to prevent others from dying as her brother had died faded to gray insignificance beside the crime of deserting her family, a callous act that more than justified her current solitary confinement. The night seethed with strange sounds, amplified by the emptiness of her room. The wind rattled doors and moaned. The surf crashing on the beach sounded like the thrashings of a drowning woman, and every so often something somewhere screeched in such a way as to raise the hairs along the back of her neck. Twice she put her ear to the wall separating her room from Cynthia Foley's, straining to catch the sound of her neighbor, but the nurse was as self-contained asleep as she was awake.

As the night stretched longer, Lydia's thoughts turned to the island's anonymous graveyard. Though she considered herself neither morbid nor superstitious, insomnia's power to amplify vague notions allied lying on her back with Michael in his coffin and then with the forgotten tenants of Gallups' lonely graves. She wondered how many of Gallups' dead had left family behind, fatal illness condemning them to permanent isolation and exile. When exhaustion finally overpowered unease, she collapsed into a dead sleep for two hours before reveille. Bleary-eyed and lead-limbed, she began her first morning on Gallups.

The island air proved tonic. Southie's piers reeked of dead fish and rotting wood; Castle Point smelled of brine, doughnuts, and fried clams—but on Gallups the scents of human habitation had been winnowed by the air's passage over the ocean. It was the scent of new beginnings. As she left her barrack, the breeze combined with the morning sun and the memory of Dr. Gold's dinnertime speech to lessen the severity of the previous night's indictments.

The volunteers were expected later that morning. Lydia found Nurse Foley at the hospital, straightening pristine bed corners and recounting stacks of clean linens.

"Oh good, now we can begin," the nurse declared on Lydia's arrival. Foley was as meticulously dressed as she had been the day before—her uniform blindingly white, her cap pinned to her head with taxidermic precision. "Before the subjects arrive, I hope to show you how to make the daily log entries that I will expect you to maintain for the duration of the study. The rest you'll just have to learn as you go."

The medical logbook, with its various columns, was not much different than the Remedy accounts. In place of supplies and sales, Lydia would track temperatures and pulse rates. Pleased with her pupil's quick mastery, the nurse progressed to basic principles of patient care, but every few min-

This is Ismael Gorodo's only sign that his whispers among Us were overheard. Unable to send word of his debilitating Atlantic passage, he is tormented by the thought that his wife interpreted his earthly silence as his willful abandonment of her and the children.

utes Foley turned her head toward the windows that faced the water.

"The boat is on its way," she finally said, interrupting her own enumeration of the merits of thorough hand washing. From the ward window, Lydia saw a cluster of medical staff posting lookout from the compound's fence. A smudge was visible on the northeastern horizon. When the smudge resolved into a boat with a definite heading, the morning's lesson was abandoned. Along with the others, Lydia and Nurse Foley headed toward the dock.

Gallups was no less foreign than it had been yesterday—but as Lydia traced in reverse the path she had taken just the day before, her arrival felt much more distant. Trailing Foley, she passed the barracks and the flagpole with its two flags; she walked through the gate and past the rabbits' meadow. By the time she reached the dock, the boat was close enough to expose the barnacles stubbling its hull. The ferry was larger than yesterday's, with an enclosed cabin rather than an open deck. Lydia pictured a floating sick ward lined with rows of stretchers. She did not notice the bars bolted to the windows until the cabin door opened.

The sight of the volunteers was preceded by a metallic clanking sound Lydia associated with invalids and stretchers. But the men who emerged from the ship's cabin were not lying down: clad in rough, gray uniforms, they walked upright in synchronized, shuffling steps, their motion hampered by shackles at their wrists. Lydia's first thought was that the ferry had intercepted a German U-boat on its way to Gallups and that these were captured Germans. Then it occurred to her that the reverse might have happened, and that by some horrible twist of fate she had become a prisoner of war. But no one else betrayed alarm at the appearance of the shackled men, and now Dr. Gold was shaking the hand of a uniformed officer—the only one not in chains.

"Dr. Gold," the officer began. "Do you accept charge of these prisoners?"

"Officer Clancey, I accept these men into my care," Dr. Gold affirmed.

"I hereby grant transfer of custody to you." A cheer among the handcuffed men was squelched as the officer spun to face them.

"Under the terms previously presented, to which you have voluntarily submitted yourselves, I hereby declare you provisionally restored to service. You will be expected to conduct yourselves accordingly. Any infraction, however small, will be viewed as a dereliction of utmost gravity. There will be no second chances. Is that understood?"

"Yes sir!" thirty voices answered.

"Officers, release these men."

Only now did Lydia see the uniformed MPs standing at the end of each row. They went from man to man, freeing them from the heavy chain to which they were tethered.

Thirty handcuffs were unlocked. Thirty men appeared instantly taller.

"Excuse me," Lydia whispered to Nurse Foley. "Aren't these men supposed to be ill?"

The nurse raised one eyebrow, her expression suggesting Lydia had said something funny. "I should hope not!" She smiled, returning her attention to the recent arrivals. "You can't very well study transmission after the fact!"

Lydia reconsidered each word of Foley's response. "You mean to tell me that they're perfectly healthy?" she gasped, to which Foley, intent on watching the disembarkation, merely nodded.

The wind was fierce at the dock but Gallups' new arrivals gave no indication of the cold. Had Lydia not seen them chained moments before she would not have taken them for prisoners. They were all clean-shaven, with shorter, blunter

Captain Harold Clancey disapproved of this arrangement from the start. Had he been warden of Deer Island, he never would have approved the doctor's plan.

versions of crew cuts that drew attention to each head's weakest feature—a lumpy skull, a weak chin, a crooked nose. In handcuffs the men had seemed threatening; unbound, their appearance produced the opposite effect.

"Are they really criminals?" Lydia asked.

"Don't sound so impressed," Foley muttered. "They're cowards, mostly. Or at least they were until they met Dr. Gold."

The debarking men were close enough that Lydia could have brushed her hand against their passing sleeves. Until now she had only ever encountered convicts in the newspaper, in which case they were invariably escapees considered armed and dangerous. She was trying to reconcile her past associations with the present situation when one of the men turned toward her.

"I've died and gone to Heaven." He spoke in a Galway accent no different from the B Street greengrocer's. Lydia gasped. She would not have been more disconcerted if one of Gallups' gravestones had spoken her name.

"Mind your manners," Foley chastised—but the nurse was addressing the debarkee. The prisoner shrugged and continued forward, and soon Lydia lost sight of him.

"You'll have to excuse Patrick," offered another as he passed. He was too broad shouldered for his gray uniform. "It's been months since he's seen a lady and you really do look two parts angel." This man's voice was not Irish, but something in the way he carried himself struck Lydia as familiar.

"Ignore them," Foley counseled. In response, the broad-shouldered man doffed an invisible hat in Lydia's direction, inspiring several men after him to do the same. Once the arrivals had cleared the dock, the rest of the staff trailed behind them over the gravel path. Lydia was only vaguely aware of

Lydia Wickett's generally angelic appearance was helped along that day by the halo of sunlight in her hair. Frank Bentley was not the sort to speak to unknown women and his forwardness that day shocked him.

Maybe the clink changed him, but Seaman Ned Frommer remembers Frankie plenty ready her movements. She felt warm despite the wind and could feel her pulse in her neck.

"Nurse Foley," she entreated, "please tell me what is going to happen to these men."

The nurse turned toward her. "Didn't you hear Dr. Gold's speech?"

"Yes, and it was lovely, but he didn't really explain what we'd be doing."

Foley considered her for a moment. "Well, surely Mr. Cory provided you with some information."

"I wish I'd had sense enough to ask him!" Lydia exclaimed. She dug her fingernails into her palms. She absolutely would not cry.

"Lydia," Nurse Foley began. "I can see that you're upset, but to study the transmission of any disease requires healthy subjects, and Dr. Gold was quite deluged by prisoners wishing to take part. You ought to think of these men as lucky. For every one of them there are at least three prisoners wishing to be in their shoes. Perhaps you would feel better if you thought of their service here as penance."

If Lydia had ever doubted Cynthia Foley's religious affiliation, she could now be certain that the nurse was not a Catholic. No priest would ever prescribe a penance so cruel.

When Lydia reached the hospital, she learned that for the first five days the men would live in the rear barrack to confirm they had not brought flu with them to Gallups. Alone with Nurse Foley in the ward, Lydia's training resumed where it had left off before the boat's arrival, but now it was she who found it difficult to concentrate. Though her eyes attended her tutor, her thoughts inhabited the barrack behind the hospital.

When Lydia arrived at the dining hall that evening, the room's eight extra tables had been pushed together to form

to chat up the girls in Scollay Square the night that got him into all that trouble.

two long rectangles. She was cheered by the thought of the volunteers filling up those empty chairs—but when she asked one of her dining companions when the other men would be joining them, she was informed that meals were to be served in two shifts, the first being reserved for the medical staff. Her dining companions were Warner, Worth, Killington, and Vanderhuff, four junior medical officers who wore wire spectacles like Dr. Gold's and reminded Lydia of little boys clomping about in their fathers' shoes.

"If you ask me," Warner announced as he gestured with his fork, "it's indecent those jailbirds coming here after what they did. It steams me up just thinking about it! They hardly deserve what they're getting." Whenever Warner's speech became emphatic, his front forelock flopped back and forth like a horse's tail swatting flies.

"The flu isn't exactly a vacation," observed Killington, who was primarily distinguishable from Warner in that his forelock was blond.

Warner unleashed an eyebrow-raising technique similar to the one Foley had employed with Lydia earlier that morning. "If I was given the choice between the flu or a Rheims trench I'd take the flu in a New York instant," he cracked.

"Let's face it, boys," agreed Vanderhuff who, wanting to emphasize the special merit of what he was about to say, removed his spectacles and dangled them between thumb and forefinger. "The only difference between ourselves and those graybacks is that we're a hell of a lot smarter." The four men laughed.

"I'm sorry," Lydia demurred, "but I'm afraid I don't get the joke."

"You've got brothers?" Vanderhuff asked.

"Sure," she answered.

"Then you know as well as the rest of us!" Worth insisted.

"Once Wilson started this show anyone with half a brain either got himself an exemption or an assignment somewhere far from the action. Your brothers didn't wait like dumb bunnies to be drafted, now did they?"

Lydia felt as if she had been spoon-fed sand.

"Now you've done it," Warner admonished.

"What?" Worth protested. "What did I do?"

"You've gone and insulted her." Warner's voice thrummed dully beneath the blood that pounded in Lydia's ears. Though her feet felt unsteady, she pushed herself away from the table.

"Wickett," coaxed Killington, "don't go. Cecil's a dope. Whatever he said, he didn't mean it. Stay and finish dinner with us. Looking at you makes the food taste better."

"Excuse me," she whispered and turned toward the door.

"Cecil, you idiot," muttered one of them, indistinguishable from the others now that her back was turned. "Quick, apologize before she's gone."

"How can I apologize when I don't even know what I did?" Worth whined, but she did not hear the answer because by then she had closed the door behind her.

Cecil Worth found Wickett awfully uptight for an Irish girl. She would have been a lot happier on Gallups if she'd had a better sense of humor.

. . .

RAPID SPREAD OF DISEASE IN STATE

The death rate for the city was the largest yesterday of any of the days since the ailment became prevalent. Physicians who have been attending to influenza patients are puzzled as to the exact nature of the disease. They cannot follow its symptoms coherently enough to make an intelligent diagnosis of the cases which come under their notice. As a result two bacteriologists from Harvard University have been called upon to assist in studying the situation and make a report on their conclusion so that local physicians may know exactly what they are dealing with.

Watch Milk Stations

Believing that milk which is not up to the standard might in a measure be responsible for the present condition, the health commissioner had sworn in as his agents a number of the Fore River Shipbuilding Company's guards to stand watch over two milk stations which the authorities have under suspicion.

. . .

So this gob is milking a cow when a patriotic dame walks up and says: "Young man, why aren't you at the Front?" And then so the gob, he says—

Aw quit it, you told that one a million times.

I don't know that one, Georgie. What'd he say?

You do too know it! You was there with me the last time.

No I wasn't neither, or else I'd know it too.

Who's up for Acey Deucey?

Already? Those cards ain't lost their sea legs yet.

Count me in. I got a feeling the change in scenery changed my luck. What about you, Tommo?

Count me out.

He's still shaky from the boat ride. Ain't ya, Tommo?

Yeah, I s'pose so.

Aw look at him, he's still green around the gills!

I'll play, but not 'til Soapy tells the rest.

Have you got soup for brains? He told that one just the other day!

Not to me he didn't, Georgie.

And I'm telling you he did! You was standing right beside me in the yard!

Well then maybe it was too windy for me to hear.

You laughed, ya knucklehead!

Then it's somebody else you're thinking of 'cause I'm tellin' ya I ain't never heard it.

Yeah, you're right, it must of been that other gob I'm always stuck with in the yard.

Hey, when was they letting you in the yard and not me?

Chucklehead, you are so dim that when a doctor looks in your ear it's like looking through a peephole.

And so the gob, he says, "Because the milk is at this end, lady."

That one went right over his head.

Naw it didn't neither! It's one of them scientific jokes, ain't it? Cows don't even practic'ly exist over in France, am I right, Soapy?

Sure you're right, Chucklehead. Deal him in, Lucky.

. . .

February 11, 1924

Dear Mr. Driscoll,

It has been almost six years since you asked my permission to sell Wickett's Remedy. I always supposed you had no luck with Wickett's or, even worse, that you were killed in the war. Then, last week, I happened to try QD Soda for the first time. You can imagine my surprise when it tasted just like the Remedy, only with bubbles! After that it did not take me long to learn that the same young man I once met was now the president of QD Soda. I am glad for your success. When I met you I thought you were a person who would make his own way in the world.

Mr. Driscoll, I know that you would not have forgotten our agreement. Perhaps you sent me a letter that I never received, or perhaps you lost my address. It does not matter. Here is my present address and phone number. Please contact me however you like.

Sincerely,

Mrs. Henry Wickett (former)

Ralph Finnister
QD Soda Headquarters
162 B Street
Boston, MA 02127

June 7, 1993

The Honorable Mayor Raymond Flynn
Mayor's Office
1 City Hall Plaza
Boston, MA 02201

Dear Mayor Flynn:

On behalf of everyone at QD Soda, I would like to congratu-
late you. Your nomination by President Clinton to the
United States Ambassadorship to the Vatican brings pride to
every citizen of Boston. Although we are losing a mayor, it is
both humbling and soul-stirring to think that in some small
but tangible way we are all gaining a place in the house of
His Holiness!

I imagine the demands on your increasingly limited time are
impressive, but we at QD Soda sincerely hope that in the final days of your mayorship you will choose to honor us with
your presence at the QD Soda block-renaming ceremony,
which remains the cornerstone of our 75th Anniversary Jubilee celebration. If by the time of our festivities you have already been confirmed, we hope that you will attend in your
capacity as the United States Ambassador to the Vatican.

The Jubilee is honoring more than a soda—it is honoring a
man. Though Quentin Driscoll has not been one of Boston's

leading lights for many years, both he and the soda that car-
ries his name live on. Quentin Driscoll now abides in a South
Boston retirement home, where he has been largely forgotten
by the city to which he has given so much. It would mean a
great deal to me personally if you were to join him for the
Jubilee. He is three years shy of his hundredth birthday and
has, of late, become agitated. It is my heartfelt belief that it
would bring him great peace to be in the presence of a man
who will soon be in the presence of the Pope.

Thank you.

Very Sincerely,
Ralph Finnister

After marrying Henry, Lydia's new life had often left her feeling out of place, but at least the West end was still Boston: newspaper boys hawked the afternoon headlines, cobbles lay underfoot, streetcars screeched around corners, and the glow of streetlamps greeted the setting sun. On Gallups, the omission of such seemingly trivial aspects of life created gaping holes in her daily sense of order. The compound was too small. The path from living quarters to dining room and from dining room to hospital was uncomplicated by streetcars or drays, stray dogs or vendors. After a lifetime of zigzagging, walking in straight lines felt like going nowhere at all.

At first she was additionally haunted by a larger, more amorphous sense of loss as unplaceable as it was regular, as though she were inhabiting a photograph from which some crucial feature had been mysteriously blacked out. Four days passed before Lydia realized that Gallups lacked bells. Throughout Boston, church bells tolled the hours; and just as she took for granted the grumbling of her stomach to announce her appetite, she had relied all her life on the bells to divide her days into manageable portions. A day without bells was a lumbering parade, time bound into lead-lined shoes.

After the first day on the island she was not nearly so susceptible to bouts of weeping—but as though making up for its former disownment, the grief she had circumvented in Southie struck on Gallups without warning. She might be walking to the mess hall or receiving instructions from Nurse Foley when the world would dim. She would feel her brother's absence as keenly as if her chest had been opened. If she was walking when this occurred she would stumble. If someone was speaking to her, their lips would continue to move without sound.

Part of the difficulty lay in there being so little to do. Expecting to be put to immediate use fighting the epidemic, she instead found herself in the one place in Boston—perhaps all the east coast—where there was not a single influenza victim. It came as a grave disappointment to learn that aiding medical science was not the same thing as aiding medical practice. Lydia had abandoned her family and the ill at Carney to divide her time between receiving nursing instruction in an empty ward and recording the vital statistics of healthy men.

Once the study commenced, she would be responsible for the comfort and well-being of the men in quarantine. She would then serve more as nanny than nurse, bringing the men their meals and attending to whatever small requests were made. Nurse Foley's assurances that she would also be expected to assist in thrice-daily temperature taking and the monitoring of flu symptoms felt more symbolic than substantial, but this only made Lydia more determined to raise Nurse Foley's professional opinion of her before the study's end. She entertained more modest goals regarding Cynthia Foley's personal regard. Back in Southie Lydia would not have hesitated to call the nurse a snob, but on Gallups such an accusation would have been a lonely one. Cynthia Foley was simply a well-bred girl who had been to nursing school and could play bridge and had expected to be joined on Gallups by someone

Michael will never know if his whisperings sparked these episodes, but We derive solace from the thought that Our whisperings act as latent catalysts for countless private memorials.

with similar aptitudes. Lydia suspected that her nursing deficits might have been forgiven if she had exhibited a talent for bids, tricks, and trumps. Her first evenings on the island, she applied herself to Cynthia's tutelage at cards with the same diligence as her instruction in the hospital, but bridge was too complicated a pastime and there were too many abler partners among the medical staff. With the discontinuation of the bridge lessons, her treatment by Cynthia Foley became patient, courteous, and closed to the possibility of anything but the most superficial and polite of friendships.

During the preamble of days leading up to the test's official commencement, Lydia's realm was the nursing log. Twice daily she and Nurse Foley awaited the volunteers in the medical lab room, where the men submitted to the pokes and proddings of throat swabs, thermometers, and stethoscopes, their vital statistics monitored and recorded to ensure that Dr. Gold had procured viable specimens. The lab was a brightly lit, windowless space whose walls were covered in square white tiles identical to those at the bathhouse at City Point. The sight of the tiles triggered girlhood memories that were confounded and eventually dispersed by the smells of disinfectant and pipe tobacco, but Lydia could not enter the lab without first thinking of summer.

The volunteers were brought to the room in groups of ten by a blue-uniformed escort, who—once having delivered his charges to their destination—had even less to do than Lydia. While the ten men obligingly opened their mouths and unbuttoned their shirts, the escort leaned against the laboratory door lighting cigarettes and then picking his teeth and fingernails with each spent match. After she had recorded the volunteers' temperatures and pulse rates, Lydia's final responsibility was to rid the doorway of the evidence of the escort's boredom.

Standing behind a ledger now rather than a sales counter,

According to William "Kewpie" Gray, "escorts" was too nice a name. They were chosen from the same lunkheaded guards who bullied him at Deer Island.

she rehabilitated an old Gilchrist memory trick of alloying each volunteer's name with a unique personal feature. Patrick Shaughnessy's Galway accent would have been an obvious choice if the hospital confines had not turned him into a mute. She had looked forward to hearing that voice again, but when Shaughnessy opened his mouth in the lab, it was only to say "ah." Her disappointment at being denied such a reminder of Southie contended with her relief at being spared instant homesickness.

When the man who had called her part-angel arrived to the medical lab for the first time, she did not remember him by the sound of his voice but by the gray uniform that pinched at the shoulders. Though Frank Bentley did not doff an invisible hat when they met again in the lab room, he nodded in a way that affirmed he was the same man inside the hospital as he had been at the dock.

Among themselves, the volunteers called each other by the nicknames that numbered among their scant personal possessions. Frank Bentley was mostly called Frankie, but he was occasionally called "Guvnor," a title Lydia associated with the sort of Southie fellow who knew everyone and everything doing on his block. Frank Bentley cracked jokes and told stories Lydia knew she ought to have ignored, but when he told one about a fish, a priest, and a bottle of whiskey it was so like something she might have heard over dinner at home that she could not help but smile. Nurse Foley had cautioned her against selecting favorites from among her charges, but Frank was the first thing on Gallups to make Lydia think of home without also making her want to cry.

Without meaning any disrespect to Miss Wickett, Tommo Fells would like to point out that they called Frankie "Guvnor" on account of the statue he was found sleeping under when he didn't make it to his ship on time.

When they were not reporting to the lab, the volunteers were assigned light chores. Most preferred to spend their free time outdoors, where they reveled in the novelty of walking at any speed and in any direction they chose within the fenced perimeter. Several among the medical staff would have preferred more stringent restrictions, but Dr. Gold countered that of the over one hundred inmates who had wished to volunteer, he had chosen thirty whose infractions were so minor that they would have earned little more than a fine from a civilian court, an explanation that caused Lydia's tentative affinity for the volunteers to bloom into full-fledged affection.

Baseball was a popular pastime but only sporadically played. Once the volunteers had batted all three of the stained and battered balls belonging to the quarantine station beyond the compound confines, a willing retriever from among the medical staff was required to reclaim the balls from the opposite side of the fence. The medical officers talked of challenging the volunteers to a game but this remained only bluster due, in Lydia's opinion, to the likelihood that the volunteers would win.

Every third day a sack of incoming letters and packages replaced one of outgoing mail left on the dock for the ferry. Lydia posted a letter home at every opportunity, but writing amplified her homesickness; and being Henry's widow made her acutely aware of her epistolary shortcomings. Even more than reading his love letters, reading her own letters reminded her how much she missed him. Her naturally charmless prose was further hampered by circumspection. Not wanting to cause worry, she confined her letters to descriptions of the island and Foley's tutelage, subjects she could only sustain for a paragraph before her hand insisted on recording the litany of questions that kept her awake at night: *How is Tom? Is anyone else sick? Are things better or worse than before?* Writing these questions did not reduce their urgency—seeing them on paper only reminded her how little she knew. The knowledge that her letters would reach Southie mere hours after leaving the Gallups dock acted as a taunt rather than a comfort. It was un-

Billy Gray would like to point out that their "escorts" never once got a ball back for them.

Sergeant at Arms Matthew Price counters that the men under his watch were prisoners, not vacationers.

fair her words should be permitted such easy passage while Southie remained to her as distant and unattainable as Ireland.

Two mail deliveries passed before the first return letter came, written in her mother's careful hand. Though Tom was steadily improving, he was distraught at the news that the October draft had been canceled due to the epidemic. If rumors that the war would be over by year's end proved true, then Tom feared he would miss everything. Because Lydia could not help but wonder if her mother exercised the same dubious consideration in her letters to Gallups as she did in her letters home, neither the letters she sent nor the ones she received conferred consolation.

Instead, Lydia found solace in the island itself, making a habit of early evening walks beyond the compound confines and along the rocky beach that ran north of the dock, where she could say whatever she wanted and let the wind carry her words safely out to sea. Sometimes rather than return to the compound by the path, she would climb the grassy slope that rose up from the water where—if the sun had not yet set—she might come across the rabbits. Halfway up the hill, the compound would come into view, its buildings dark silhouettes against the sky. Walking along the periphery she would pass the illuminated windows of the volunteer barracks, where the word "bridge" had nothing to do with cards and where, if the windows were open, the sounds of the evening's poker game would be borne past her ears. Sometimes when she had difficulty sleeping, she would leave her window open to the sounds of the wind and the sea. Within a cocoon of surplus bedding scavenged from the room's three unoccupied beds, she would imagine the volunteers' voices being carried by the wind over the compound's fence and out to the water, where her words and their words could combine. Comforted, she would be lulled to sleep.

Cora admits to describing Tom through rose-colored glasses. The truth was that Tom was upset due to his high fever damaging the hearing in one ear badly enough to disqualify him for national service.

C'mere Lucky, you got some kinda bug sitting on your lip.

Leave it, that's my moustache!

Some moustache, Harris. Looks like a bug.

Give it time, I just got started on it.

You been trying to grow that thing for as long as Riley ain't been shaving an' he's practically got himself a beard.

Yeah, well, my hairs need more time to grow on account of that they're blond.

That so? Hey Lombardo! Lucky here says blond hairs takes longer than brown ones! That your professional opinion?

My professional opinion says that Lucky's all wet.

Oh yeah, what d'you know anyways? What's an Italian barber know from blond hair?

Who's up for baseball tomorrow? We got all three balls back.

What are you, cracked? They're starting tomorrow!

Sure, but they're only using ten at a time. The rest of us might as well enjoy ourselves, 'specially if it's nice weather.

I'm in.

Naw, I bet they take you, Frankie. I bet they start at the front of the alphabet.

You think that might get me out of here sooner?

I don't think nothing. Safer that way. Give it a try, Bentley. You gotta stop dwellin' on things you can't control.

. . .

UNDERTAKERS ARE RUSHED TO LIMIT

Decline Some Calls Owing to Lack of Help

Boston undertakers are seriously handicapped in handling the great number of cases that have resulted from the influenza epidemic, but several of them who were interviewed yesterday declared there is no foundation for the widely circulated rumor that undertakers are refusing to prepare for burial bodies of persons who have died of influenza.

It had been said that a number of the undertakers had declined cases because of fear of contagion. This is most emphatically denied.

A majority of the undertakers admitted, however, that they had been compelled, because of the extraordinary amount of deaths and the shortage of assistants and material necessary to their work, to decline to take charge of bodies in families not included in those with whom they had done undertaking work in the past and others not in their own district.

The undertakers pointed out that they had been working day and night, and that there had been such a heavy demand upon the casket makers that they had been unable to get the caskets as rapidly as desired. There was a shortage of other material also, such as branch candlesticks, not to mention the lack of hearses and undertakers' wagons.

. . .

Brothers and Sisters, a plague has befallen our fair city, a plague more deadly than that which was visited upon Pharaoh, for this plague does not afflict merely the first-born son, but every son and daughter that was ever born. Some have blamed this plague on the Germans but Brothers and Sisters, we all know where this epidemic was born: it was born in Sin.

Amen!

We have become complacent in our hearts. Because our brave soldiers are fighting the Hun across the ocean we have ceased to fight the war that never stops, the war against iniquity. The Devil has crept into this country and there is no mask that will keep him out, no pill or potion that will drive him out, no doctor who can flush him out. There is only one weapon, Brothers and Sisters, and that weapon is Prayer!

Hallelujah!

Every time we are envious, every time we are covetous, every time we speak in anger or with ill-will in our hearts, we open the door to the Devil a little wider. The Devil creeps into our chests and steals our very breath from us; doctors call this Influenza but, Brothers and Sisters, I call it Beelzebub!

Amen!

There is only one way to drive this epidemic from our chests and from our homes and from our city and that is to Pray it down! Not only on Sundays—

No!

Not only before bed—

No!

But every day of the week, every hour of the day! And Brothers and Sisters, we are going to start right now! I want everybody to stand up! If you are at all able, I want you to stand up! I know that some of you are in the grips of your own battle, perhaps it was difficult for you to get here today, perhaps it is difficult for you to stand, but stand if you can! Pray that Devil out of your chest! I see that some of you are not standing. Brothers and Sisters, if you find yourself next to someone unable to stand on their own, offer them your arm. And for those who cannot stand at all, we who can stand will Pray all the harder for you so that next time, when we come together, you will be standing right beside us! Let us now all join together and Pray—

On the morning of the study's commencement, Lydia woke earlier than usual. The disappearance of the last of Gallups' leaves had ushered in a cold autumn, but that day bore the portents of Indian summer. On D Street, her mother would be opening the windows to let in the last good air before winter. Lydia pictured the nurses at Carney untying tent flaps to allow their charges unlimited draughts of the warm, sweet breeze.

The inaugural assembly was to have been held inside the volunteer barracks, but in deference to the weather it was moved to the flag circle. On one side of the flagpole the medical staff stood in two white-clad rows of five; on the other, the gray-clad volunteers were arrayed in three rows of ten, each row punctuated by a blue-uniformed escort.

From her place in the second row Lydia could see only the swirl of hair along the nape of Nurse Foley's neck and the navy blue nurse's cape that fluttered about her shoulders like her own flag. Staring at that cape, Lydia was once again a little girl at the department store window, gawking at the objects on the other side of the glass. Her body assumed the posture years at Gilchrist's had taught her: she thrust back her shoul-

The day was too warm for her cape. Cynthia spent the assembly worrying about the widening perspiration stains under her arms.

ders and raised her chin; she held her arms at her sides and aligned her feet.

On the opposite side of the circle, the volunteers were variously stooped and erect, excited and anxious—but Frank Bentley stood patiently in the front row, second from the left, like he was waiting for a pal who was slightly late. Lydia found it difficult to maintain her regal stance: her toes wanted to tap; her arms wanted to cross. After days of endless preliminaries, she could barely contain the urge to yell, "Now! Now!" into the wind. Then Dr. Gold began to speak.

"It is beyond my power to express the pride and pleasure it gives me to be here with you today," he began.

He left the ranks of the medical staff and crossed the circle to present himself before the volunteers. As he approached, the men stood at attention. Dr. Gold was their captain, his words the ones they would take with them into battle.

"You are here because you have agreed to embark upon a noble and selfless journey of vital importance, as vital as fighting the war itself. For just as the Hun threatens tyranny, disease exerts its own tyranny. Our country has never known an epidemic the breadth of that which afflicts us today. Thousands have died, thousands more have fallen ill, and if influenza continues to blaze unchecked across our nation countless more will suffer and perish. It is my hope that with your invaluable help, this is a tragedy our country will never know again."

The doctor paused. The wind-gripped halyard was striking against the flagpole. This, Lydia realized, was Gallups' bell, its tolling a fitting accompaniment to Dr. Gold's words. Before that morning, history had never impressed Lydia as anything more than a dull litany of names and dates she was expected to memorize in school. But listening to Dr. Gold, the taxidermied specimen became a breathing creature. History was not the province of the dead; it was the daily result of people living their lives.

"It is no easy thing you will be doing," Gold resumed, his voice quieter but no less powerful. "The risks are clear. If any of you have developed reservations or doubts, now is the time to come forward. It is not too late to return to Deer Island, nor is there any shame in doing so. You will be free to resume your lives as before. Is there anyone here who wishes to reconsider? Speak now, as they say, or forever hold your peace."

Though this particular speech was not recorded, Dr. Gold would like to point out that an audiotape of his voice resides within the Library of Congress.

Lydia scanned the faces of the volunteers. The silence stretched tighter. Being free to return to a jail cell did not strike her as a particularly desirable freedom. Apparently the volunteers agreed.

"You are bringing honor to yourselves and to your country," the doctor declared. The entire assembly let out its breath. "Surgeon Bertram Peterson will now acquaint you with the protocols of the study."

Both Dr. Gold and Dr. Peterson were in their early fifties, but Gold's bearing gave the impression of a man still in his prime, while Peterson's paunch and thinning hair marked him as fully subscribed to middle age. When Peterson was excited or nervous he rubbed his hands together in a way that reminded Lydia of a squirrel, an impression that was aided by the doctor's angular face and slight overbite. He had the complexion of someone seldom outdoors and the brusque manner of a man more accustomed to associating with petri dishes than people. According to Lydia's dining companions, Peterson's brilliance lay in a methodical mind paired with limitless patience.

Peterson plodded across the flag circle to join Gold and in a dry, professorial voice described what would be expected of the volunteers and what they should, in turn, expect: each test would last a week, during which the test subjects would be quarantined with brief opportunities for outdoor exercise. Test subjects were expected to cooperate fully with the administration of each procedure and with the daily monitoring of their condition.

When Dr. Peterson asked if the men had any questions, some shifted from foot to foot and peered at the ground. Others gazed at the sky, while still others stared blankly at the assembled medical staff. Finally from somewhere behind the first row of gray uniforms came an anonymous query—quiet and worried and impossible to trace.

"What happens when we get sick?"

As if the word "sick" carried its own smell, there was a palpable shift in the group. Though the volunteers remained quiet, they were no longer still. Hands clenched and unclenched, stances shifted. The word loomed over them, freighting the air.

Even with his back to her, Lydia could tell Dr. Peterson was rubbing his hands.

"I will personally attend any man who manifests symptoms," Dr. Gold interceded. "I will do everything in my power to return him to full health. Because we will be monitoring each of you quite closely, we can commence treatment at the very earliest signs of onset. We will spare nothing in the care we administer—every treatment, every medication will be at your disposal. If Surgeon General Rupert Blue himself were to fall ill he could not expect better care than that which you will receive at our hands."

Dr. Gold's words evinced murmurs and nods from the assembled men. Shoulders and stances relaxed, but Lydia felt her heart quicken. A door through which the volunteers might have retreated had been shut. Having apparently been waiting for this moment, Acting Assistant Surgeon Percival Cole left his place in the front row to join the two doctors. Cole was Dr. Gold's protégé and the only junior medical officer who dined at the senior officers' table. He was the dispositional opposite of his mentor: quiet and unassuming, he was easy to overlook, but inside the hospital his efficiency and encyclopedic memory made him indispensable. He shared Peterson's affinity for the lab, his methodicalness expressing itself in every aspect of his person—from the latitudinally precise part that separated his hair to a personal bearing that eschewed wasted movement. Lydia suspected that Percival Cole never used his napkin when he ate, and that he was constitutionally incapable of lodging even a stray crumb among the hairs of his neat moustache. She admired Cole's propensity for work and his disinterest in the medical staff's nightly bridge games.

Once Cole reached the volunteers, he consulted his notebook. "The following men should collect their belongings and report at once to the hospital," he announced. "Able, Bentley, Cataldo, Cohen, Denson, Evert, Fells, Gray, Harris, Kipling." This had been the first group to report to the lab room each morning, the first names Lydia had memorized.

Harold Able and George Denson had the broad backs of icemen. Before realizing that Able was far too fastidious for a naval career of dirty fingernails, Lydia had imagined him and Denson stoking furnaces in the bellies of ships, their faces dark with soot. Theodore Evert was their physical opposite. Slender and compact, he seemed meant for a navy of tall-masted ships, whose smaller crewmen still perched in crow's nests above massive white sails. The remainder of the ten fell somewhere between these physical poles, men with whom Lydia had, since their arrival five days before, grown familiar. Ralph Cataldo did not go anywhere without a comb, his immaculate grooming coaxing charm from otherwise ordinary features. William Gray was distinguished by ropy arms that would have required custom tailoring for a truly smart suit. John

Being tidy had nothing to do with it. Neither he nor Georgie would have been caught dead belowdecks shoveling coal—that was Negro work.

Kipling rolled his eyes before having his temperature taken, as if this were just the next in a series of injustices that characterized his life. Joe Cohen was an inveterate whistler; Tommy Fells liked to chew gum; Sam Harris always carried a deck of cards in his breast pocket. And then, of course, there was Frank Bentley, who walked like a man who had never been lost a day in his life.

Though the assembly had ended, staff and volunteer alike remained in place, silently watching the leave-taking. Finally the silence was broken:

"Show your stuff, Sammy!"

"Hang in there, Joe."

"Lucky, stay strong!"

"Show 'em Frankie!"

The calls tumbled one over the other, some loud, some soft, an uneven chorus of encouragement tinged with relief. The five-day countdown had ended.

Lydia and Nurse Foley preceded the ten men to the hospital's east ward with Peterson—who had yet to acknowledge Lydia's presence—and Cole—who had been polite enough to wish her a good morning. Lydia tempered her nervousness by imagining Peterson gnawing a giant acorn. The previous day, she had felt silly standing behind her supply cart while she and Nurse Foley enacted a procedural dry run on a cast of invisible patients. Today, she was grateful for that dress rehearsal. If she paid close attention, there was a chance she could anticipate each request with the object about to be requested. Perhaps by the next test, Foley would entrust her to do more than handle equipment.

On hearing the volunteers' approach, Lydia placed herself behind her wheeled cart with its culture dishes, tubes, cotton swabs, and syringes. Between leaving the flag circle and arriving to the quarantine, Cole had collected from the lab a bottle filled with milky liquid. He added this to her cart as though he were restoring a baby bird to its nest. There was a gentleness to his face that Dr. Peterson's lacked and that seemed wasted on the sterile confines of a laboratory.

At the sound of approaching footsteps, Lydia looked over the ward. A wave of anticipatory excitement passed through her, a ghost from Gilchrist mornings when she had stood behind her counter in the moments before the store opened. Beside each of ten perfectly made beds rested a footlocker onto which she had affixed a name the night before.

Dr. Gold was the first to step through the door, ushering the volunteers into the room with a grand sweep of his hand. Each man arrived carrying whatever scant personal belongings he had managed to acquire while at Deer Island: a deck of cards, a pair of dice, a few envelopes worn from frequent handling, a photograph, a page torn from a magazine. The men could just as easily have been recent immigrants, the bulk of their earthly possessions given away in exchange for passage to the New World.

Lydia had anticipated that she would feel at ease inside quarantine once the volunteers appeared, but their presence made the room seem even less like a hospital. The men were too healthy, their faces ruddy from time spent outdoors. They moved with none of the deliberation displayed by hospital patients and visitors. Footlockers creaked, feet stomped, and bedsprings squeaked as mattresses were tested. Voices called out in normal tones and not in the hushed whispers reserved for sickrooms. A stranger peering through the window might have thought he was watching a traveling baseball team. Inside the ward, Lydia found the invigorating effect of Dr. Gold's speech counteracted by the fact she was about to help make flu victims of healthy men.

Once the ten beds had been claimed, there was some confusion as to the proper bearing of a person who was expected to fall ill but was not yet sick. Joe Cohen and Harold Able stood

When Tommy Fells saw how much nicer this joint was than the cages at Deer Island, he knew he had done right volunteering.

When Teddy Evert saw how nice the place was, he was sure that they were in for something terrible.

at attention beside their beds as if being inspected. George Denson tested his mattress by rolling on it. Sam Harris and Frank Bentley moved toward the tables and chairs, while Ralph Cataldo investigated the washroom at the ward's front left corner. Teddy Evert removed his shoes and lay down in anticipation of what was to come.

Dr. Gold explained the procedure: he and Dr. Peterson would look into each man's nose and throat, then a blood sample would be taken and an inoculation applied. The men would be expected to remain lying down for a few moments to allow the inoculation to sink in, but afterward they would be free to go about their business so long as they remained in the room.

Cole opened a notebook and began writing. Nurse Foley gestured to Lydia, who approached the first bed with her cart. The cart squeaked when she pushed it, causing Dr. Peterson to glare as if she had made the noise herself. At the sound, ten gazes converged on the cart's contents.

"Able, is it?" Peterson asked, referring to Cole's notebook.

"Yes sir," Harry Able replied, still staring at the cart, his hands gripping and releasing as if he was squeezing an invisible railing. Harry was older than the other men by a few years, with a face that appeared both kind and disappointed—the latter quality perhaps the result of the former not having done him much good. He had what Lydia's mother would have called a tippler's nose, burst capillaries alluding to the path that had led him to his gray uniform.

Harry took a drink now and again, but he wasn't half the boozehound his father was. As he recalls, he was thrown in the brig for sleeping on duty after he had finished drinking for the night, and not for the drinking itself.

"We will now examine the nasopharynx of Subject One," Peterson dictated while Cole duly scribbled. Having forced his eyes away from the cart Harry now stared intently at the door through which he had entered as if he might, through the power of his gaze, compel himself to the other side.

"All right, Able," Gold continued, "we'll need you to open your mouth and say ah."

Harry opened his mouth but his eyes remained fixed on the door. He had ceased squeezing his palms and instead stroked one trembling hand with the fingers of the other as if the former was a small, nervous kitten.

Harry was not nervous. Sometimes his hands just shook on their own.

The room was silent save for Harry and the sound of Cole writing. The eyes of the other nine men focused on Harry with an intensity Lydia could practically feel on her skin.

"Tonsils are slightly enlarged, with minimal congestion of the pharynx," Peterson dictated to Cole. Peterson swabbed Harry's nose and throat with such casual efficiency that they might have been furnishings from which Peterson was removing dust. The doctor then handed the swab to Nurse Foley, who smeared it across the interior surface of a culture dish. Gold took Peterson's place, gazing into Harry's mouth a little longer, his expression pensive.

"Very good," Gold remarked, as though Harry had performed a clever trick. "Nasopharyngeal examination and culture complete," he announced to the accompaniment of Cole's assiduous note taking. "And now for the blood sample. If you would be so kind, Able, as to expose your inner arm."

"I don't much care for shots," Harry protested in a gravelly voice while he pushed up his sleeve, his eyes fixed on the cart from which Lydia handed Nurse Foley a syringe. The skin of his arm was pale and soft and seemed too vulnerable to belong to a man with such a rough voice.

"Don't worry, Able," Gold assured him. "Cynthia is a veritable angel with a needle, isn't that so, Nurse?"

Foley nodded. "You're not even getting a shot," she cooed as she swabbed a small patch of Harry Able's flesh just above the crook in his elbow in a manner that again reminded Lydia of housecleaning.

"A shot's when you have something put into you and I'm—" She slid the needle into the skin with one deft, seamless motion. Harry did not even flinch. "—taking something out." The nurse drew the stopper steadily up, the space it revealed filling with red. The syringe was replaced with a wad of cotton gauze and the forearm bent upward to hold it in place.

"Blood sample obtained. We will now proceed to the inoculation," Peterson continued, his eagerness leaving a sour taste in Lydia's mouth. "Able, please lie on your back and open your mouth while keeping your face as relaxed as possible."

"What're you putting in me, Doc?" Harry asked, remaining upright. His eyes darted from the doctor's face to the glass dropper Peterson now held in his hand.

"Quit mewling," muttered George Denson. "This ain't dancing school."

Harry blushed. "I'm gonna do everything the doc here says," he mumbled. "I just wanna know."

"It's an enhanced dextrose solution," Peterson explained. Harry looked at him blankly. "In other words, sugar water. Now lie down, open your mouth, and hold still."

Slowly, as though he were afraid he might come down on something sharp, Harry lowered himself down, nine wary gazes following his progress, the room silent save for the creaking of his bed. Once Harry was supine, Peterson administered drops to his subject's nostrils and mouth. Harry began to cough. "Try not to do that," Peterson instructed. He dictated, "We are now administering one point five ccs of Mather's coccus solution via both nose and throat."

"What the Jesus, Joseph, and Mary did you just say?" Harry demanded, bolting upright.

"Able!" Peterson squawked. The dropper fell to the floor. "Now look what you made me do!" Peterson's face flushed red. The glass dropper lay in several pieces at his feet. Lydia offered a fresh dropper to Nurse Foley. She expected Dr. Peterson would not so much mind now about her squeaky cart.

"Now lie back down or I'll have to readminister the inoculation."

Harry shook his head. "I don't care if there are ladies present. Hell, I wouldn't care if it was Mabel Normand herself." He blew his nose and wiped his mouth with his sleeve. "I wanna know: who's this Mather bastard?"

"Well, Able," Peterson sniffed, "you've just wiped inoculation all over your sleeve. Now I'll certainly have to repeat the procedure. Mather, if you must know, is the individual who isolated this particular bacterial sample. Hence, Mather's coccus."

The room gave a sigh. Several men snickered. Harry Able's face turned the color of his nose.

"What is so amusing?" Peterson stammered. Oblivious, Cole continued to write in his notebook. Nurse Foley's face, rather than blushing, lost all color, lending her the appearance of a blanched almond. Finally a bemused Dr. Gold leaned toward Peterson and whispered in his ear.

"Oh!" Peterson exclaimed, grinning weakly. "Oh dear, now I understand. No, no, Able, it's nothing like that! Oh dear. Mather's coccus. I suppose it does sound rather—awkward, doesn't it?"

Harry lay down again. "Yeah, Doc," he replied. "It sure does."

After Harry had been reinoculated, the rest of the men made a show of complying as nonchalantly as possible to Gold's and Peterson's requests, making a point of smiling at Harry all the while.

"Mm, tastes good!" murmured Cohen.

"I can't believe you was afraid of a little sugar water," Gray teased.

"I think you oughta give Harry more of that coccus," suggested Kipling. "I think he secretly likes it."

"Aw, you're all wet," Harry scoffed. "Go ahead and talk."

"Hey Doc," Frank Bentley asked once all ten inoculations had been administered. "How long you want us lying down?"

Peterson explained they would soon be permitted to sit up, at which point they could do anything they liked so long as they remained inside the room, which would be locked from the outside to prevent against accidental exposure. Throughout the period of quarantine, their temperatures would be monitored three times daily and regular blood and throat samples would be taken. Dr. Gold encouraged the men to relax and to enjoy themselves, and to remember that they were doing a great service for their country.

Lydia did not understand how anyone could be expected to enjoy himself inside a locked room where he was waiting to fall ill, but if anyone else found the suggestion inappropriate, he did not show it. She darted covert glances at the volunteers as she cleaned up the shattered dropper and tidied her cart. Having been released from his bed, Frank was setting up a game of checkers, while John Kipling and Sam Harris gathered at the card table. Tommy Fells and Joe Cohen pulled up chairs to look through magazines. Nothing about the scene hinted at the strange procedure that had preceded it. It was far easier to believe nothing out of the ordinary had happened at all.

Gold and Peterson left the room with Cole, who clutched his notebook tightly under his arm. Foley indicated to Lydia that they were to follow. Lydia took one last look at the men before trailing the procession with her cart. As the last one to exit she realized unhappily that she would be expected to act as jailor, a role that had not crossed her mind when she was first provided a key to the ward. She swallowed the urge to apologize. She wondered if the click of the bolt falling into place caused the men to shiver as she did or if their time on

Deer Island had inured them to the sound. The door secured, she pushed her cart down the reverberant hallway, its squeaky wheel reminding her of an alarm.

Sammy Harris never got used to the sound of a door being locked behind him. For years afterward he never locked anything he was inside at the time, not even the bathroom.

. . .

How come it's luck if I win and science if you do?

If you gotta ask I sure ain't telling. You want in or not?

Go ahead and deal.

Hey Evert, howya feeling?

All right, I s'pose.

Stop asking him, wouldya Harry? You're making it worse. Who wants checkers? How 'bout you, Joe?

Can't you see I'm busy?

How many does that make, Cohen?

Four.

You write the same thing to all of 'em?

Sure.

That's smart, Joe. Saves brain waves. I oughta do that myself.

Go on, Barber, I'm sure there's a million dames out there who wanna read what you write to yer crusty old ma.

Can it, Tommo. At least I know how to use a pencil.

I'll play checkers with you, Barber.

Thank you, Frankie.

How're *you* feeling, Frankie?

Harry, if you and Soapy're so worried, go take each other's temperatures and leave me and Ralph to play checkers in peace.

We were chumps to sign up for this.

What're you talking about, Soapy? Do you know how many gobs back at the Island would kill to be here right now?

I only had a few months to go.

Sure, but then you'd be out with a yellow ticket. Who's

gonna give you a job with a yellow ticket? You wanna be a grayback for life? A chance like this, Soapy, you did the right thing to jump on it. What'll you do when you get out?

I dunno.

That's what you oughta be thinking on. Making plans. Your life's just been handed back to you on a big fat greasy platter. You know how old I would've been before I saw another woman if I hadn't volunteered for this hayride? Sixty.

A sixty-year-old virgin.

That's Soapy for you, always talking about his father.

Yeah, yeah. Very funny.

King me.

Aw Frankie, that was a lucky move.

Nothing lucky to it, Ralph. Checkers ain't Acey Deucey.

. . .

NEW SERUM BARS PNEUMONIA

Federal Doctors Declare It as Efficacious as Other Vaccines

Congress Grants Million for Fight

Vaccination with a recently discovered serum, which has been found to be an almost positive preventative of contraction of pneumonia, will be used to combat the current epidemic of Spanish influenza.

Use of the vaccine will be widely extended, Congress today having appropriated a million dollars to be used by the public health service in fighting Spanish influenza. The serum is designed primarily to prevent pneumonia, which often follows attacks of influenza, and which is the cause of practically all the deaths attributed to influenza.

One treatment with the vaccine only is needed. Though medical authorities connected with the public health service declined to venture a prediction as to its effectiveness, they said confidently that it will prove as valuable as the vaccines being used against other diseases.

. . .

October 10, 1924

Dear Mr. Driscoll,

I thought I would have received word from you by now,
but there has been nothing. Mr. Driscoll, do not worry, I do
not expect you to honor our contract as it was. Maybe you
wanted to buy the recipe from me years ago but you could
not find me. I am not a money-grubber, I only want what is
fair.

Sincerely,

Mrs. Henry Wickett (former)

. . .

FAX

DATE: 8/17/93

TO: Mr. Thomas M. Menino

FROM: Ralph Finnister

SUBJECT: Ambassador Flynn/QD Soda Jubilee

Mr. Menino:

For several months I corresponded with The Honorable
Mayor Flynn regarding next week's QD Soda 75th Jubilee
Celebration—in specific to the Jubilee's street-renaming ceremony, over which he has been invited to preside. Until recently I had reason to believe he would be attending.
However, with the Jubilee just days away I have yet to receive confirmation.

To be blunt, I fear that the events surrounding The Honorable Mayor Flynn's Ambassadorship confirmation may have
precluded provisions being made for the QD Soda Jubilee. If

that is not the case, then please accept my gratitude and kindly disregard this correspondence.

Mr. Menino: the inventor and founder of QD Soda, Quentin Driscoll, is an aged man. As of late, his golden years have not rested lightly on his shoulders. He has become troubled by the false notion that his professional life was not the exemplary model the rest of us know it to be. It is a tragedy that such a man, who devoted himself so fully and selflessly to the soda that bears his name, should be troubled in his twilight years by such thoughts. I cannot overstate the potential good—at the ceremony designed to honor his lifetime of service—of the presence of a man soon to be in the presence of the Pontiff. If there remains any chance that you could, in your capacity as sitting mayor, prevail upon Ambassador Flynn to attend the Jubilee street renaming—I would consider it a personal favor that would not go unrewarded in the fall when, as I understand, you will be seeking to win a less temporary appointment to the mayor's office. If you are unable to effect the Ambassador's attendance, I hope it will not prevent you from attending the street-renaming ceremony in his stead and reading a statement on his behalf.

Enjoy the accompanying case of QD Soda with my compliments.

Sincerely,
Ralph Finnister
President and CEO
QD Soda

That night Lydia was haunted by visions of Dr. Peterson looming over each volunteer, his dropper releasing not a fine, clear liquid but something with the ominous viscosity of mustard gas. The war was transposed onto the bodies of ten quarantined men: on ten corporeal maps she pictured yellow markers clustered at noses and throats. Then the volunteers' physiognomies shifted until Michael or Henry occupied each of the ten quarantine beds, an image that startled her awake.

She would never grow accustomed to sleeping alone. The silence of her dark room amplified her unease. The instinct to flee outpaced her ability to reason, the impulse driving her from the barrack before she could think to don slippers or a robe. The moon was half full and draped in clouds, with a smattering of stars visible across an overcast sky. The roughness of the ground and the brisk air on her skin encouraged her to breathe normally again. In Southie she would have known whether it was closer to midnight or sunrise by the disposition of the streets, but on Gallups the night lacked familiar markings. Such anonymity was unexpectedly comforting: the blank night sapped the power of the vision that had sent her running.

In the weeks following Henry's death she had seen him

everywhere—striding past the D Street flat, boarding a street-car, driving a hansom cab, and drinking a pint on the corner. The smallest resemblance between a stranger and her dead husband could spark the transformation. Here on Gallups, Lydia had not yet managed to dispel the notion that she might, at any moment, spy her brother among the volunteers. Observing a group from a distance or hearing their laughter caused her heart to beat with such fierceness that her chest ached. An easy way of walking, a head held at a particular angle, or a broad-shouldered silhouette would combine with her mourning to achieve a fleeting alchemy: for a moment Michael would be standing before her or walking just ahead. Then the moment would pass and the figure in the gray uniform would revert. Only in the margins of her letters home, in invisible ink, did she dare imagine writing: *Do you see him too? On the street, in the house, created from a stranger or from no one at all?* According to her mother, D Street was slowly regaining its balance. Tom was venturing outdoors each day and walking a little further down the block, Malachy had returned to work and Lydia's mother was helping to look after his girls in the daytime. Not wanting to sully her mother's reports of cautious recovery with the taint of her own ghosts, Lydia kept her visions of Michael to herself.

Though she longed for the comforts of home—a kitchen that smelled of gravy and biscuits; the sound of her father snoring; the small bedroom window through which she could watch pigeons circling as they returned to a rooftop coop, their breasts reflecting the pink light of the setting sun—the sight of the empty compound limned with moonlight bestowed its own comfort. As she stood barefoot, the coolness of the ground seeping into her toes, she realized she only disliked the night from inside her barrack. D Street's night was punctuated by the barking dog, the hoofstep and rattle of the late-night livery driver, and the homeward

Henry is especially pleased with this last vision: he had aspired to one day stroll into a Southie pub as if he were a local.

Cora did not care to mention she was looking after Meagan and Patty because their grandmother was not up to the task. Jennie Feeney was never quite the same after Alice's death.

stumble of the mumbling drunk. On Gallups the constancy of water and wind replaced the sounds of dogs, horses, and men. Soothed, she returned to bed.

She dragged herself awake the following morning to a fluttering in her stomach, as if her body encaged a small, nervous bird. Its imagined plumage was the same murky yellow as the sickness she had envisioned inhabiting the men. Only a visit to quarantine would placate her unease, but deferment postponed the greater torment that awaited her if the men truly had fallen ill overnight. Lydia preferred apprehension to the complaints of chills or aches or fatigue that would precede more profound debilitation, the men's wan smiles foreshadowing the creatures she feared they would become: enervated forms too weak to raise their heads, muddy-chested creatures who struggled for breath.

And yet, the very sense of mission that had drawn her to Gallups was dependent on the volunteers falling ill. Once influenza had struck the quarantine she would no longer have time for homesickness or mourning: each day would wring her dry. Each night she would collapse into her bed, asleep the moment she closed her eyes, too exhausted to dream. She had come to Gallups in pursuit of oblivion. Now she dreaded her wish's fulfillment.

Clear morning light poured through the ward's wide windows, spilling across the wood-planked floor and onto the beds. The room was stuffy despite its size, but she refrained from opening the windows, uncertain whether outside air was permitted under the strictures of quarantine. The men were evenly divided between late sleepers and early risers. George Denson was the most impressive of the former: he lay splayed on his back, his arms dangling off either side of his bed as if he had been tossed there by a receding tide.

"He snores," complained John Kipling at her arrival. "Kept me up pract'ally all night."

"You ain't no sleeping beauty yourself," Billy Gray countered. "You was sawing plenty of your own wood."

In the corner by the far window, Frank Bentley was engaged in calisthenics.

Billy noticed that Frankie saved his exercising for after the quarantine door was opened.

"Good morning!" he called out. "Is that breakfast?"

The cart, which yesterday held the accoutrements of disease, today held ten covered trays. "It's breakfast," she confirmed. "There's coffee as well. If any of you weren't warm enough last night I can bring extra blankets."

At the sound of Lydia's voice the remainder of the men began to stir. She watched for signs of listlessness among the late risers, for any indication that the seeds sown the day before had taken root. Instead the men stretched and yawned like this was any other morning. Their sleep-tousled hair reminded her of her brothers, who at that moment would be seated before bowls of oatmeal and mugs of tea, kicking at each other beneath the kitchen table.

"This is the life, eh fellas?" bellowed George, his voice breaking her reverie. "The boys on the Island would blow their lids if they knew how good we was getting it here, pretty ladies bringing us our grub."

"How are you feeling this morning?" she asked, unable to gaze past the floor.

The men grew quiet. They scanned one another's faces, their eyes wary.

"I don't know about the rest of you," Frank ventured, "but I feel just fine."

"So do I," George confirmed.

"Me too," added Teddy Evert who, at twenty-one, was the youngest of the ten. The rest of the men broke into relieved grins.

"You see," George explained, "Teddy here's the smallest so we figure if anyone's going to catch it he's the one. He's our canary in the coal mine."

"It's been less than twenty-four hours since the inoculation," came a voice at the door. Lydia had not heard Nurse Foley enter and now she felt as if she had been caught out in something. The nurse had arrived holding a vial of thermometers for the day's first temperature readings. Their tips glinted silver in the morning light like a strange, sterile bouquet.

"If you boys were already unwell I would worry the test had been compromised." Foley smiled. "The inoculation needs time to take effect. It's unlikely you'll feel anything before tomorrow."

The men nodded, though whether in agreement or resignation was uncertain. Lydia trailed behind the nurse as she had always done, recording thermometer readings. True to Foley's prediction, there was no hint of fever among the men.

With a brief nod, Nurse Foley collected the medical log and exited the room, leaving Lydia—with her cart of breakfast trays—feeling like a maid whom the lady of the house, in passing, had deigned to greet.

"Whatcha got for us?" Billy asked once the nurse's footsteps could no longer be heard.

"Whaddya think, Kewpie? It's eggs," George retorted. "Ever since we got here it's always been eggs."

"Y'never know, Georgie," Billy replied. "It could be something different now we're quarantiners."

George Denson shook his head. "Kewpie here thinks he's still on the Island. The eats was always extra in sick bay."

"I don't, neither," Billy protested. "I know exactly where we is. All I'm saying is maybe it's something else. There's no law saying otherwise, ain't that right, Nursie Lydia?"

"It's eggs," she confirmed.

"Good," Billy nodded. "I like eggs."

Her progress around the room was uneventful until she offered Joe Cohen his tray.

Ralphie Cataldo would have agreed with anything Nurse Foley said. She had the nicest bubbies he had ever seen.

Joe Cohen liked blondes as much as the next guy, but that Nurse Foley was a prig, with a skimpy ass besides.

Tommo agrees with Ralphie: the nurse had the juiciest tits he had ever seen on a classy dame.

"Do me a favor and take that off for me," he said, pointing to a slice of meat. "It's ham, ain't it?"

"I think so," she concurred.

"Bring that over here," Harry Able advised. "Joe don't eat ham but I like it fine."

"Pork is Yid poison," Joe explained.

"Oh dear!" she exclaimed, almost dropping the rashers on the floor in her rush to remove them from Joe's plate.

"Don't worry over it none," Joe assured her, accepting his tray with a grin. "Being a Mick there's no way you could know. You don't eat meat Fridays, Yids don't eat pig Fridays or any other day neither."

"Never?" she asked, shuddering at the thought.

"Never," Joe confirmed.

She nodded, making a mental note to request in the future a plate with extra eggs instead of ham. As she headed toward the door with her empty cart, the sight of ten men with healthy appetites stilled her apprehension enough to allow her to realize she had skipped her own breakfast. If what Cynthia Foley had said was true, she had at least a day, maybe even two, before her fears would manifest.

For the rest of her time on Gallups, she became attuned to the timing of temperature readings. She tended to skip lunch because temperatures were read directly afterward. Instead she ate during the hour-long grace period between the completion of one temperature reading and her body's inexorable windup in anticipation of the next. Though her physical unease would diminish over the course of the study, it never disappeared. By the end of the study she would lose enough weight that shirtwaists she had once hand-tailored to fit would come to look like hand-me-downs.

At the study's outset Lydia was careful not to linger in the ward, but Nurse Foley was so often in the laboratory wing—assisting with a report or in conference with Dr. Gold—that

Lydia soon became adept at multiplying the number of quarantine visits her duties required, until bringing fresh towels or linens, distributing trays, and delivering and collecting mail required as many as seven separate forays. She discovered she enjoyed supplying meals and mail, blankets and news. In the east ward she did not feel scrutinized or judged. Among the quarantiners her feelings of homesickness and loneliness diminished. Afternoons with the men reminded her of rainy Sundays on D Street taken up with cards and checkers.

Sometimes Tommy Fells would ask her to write a letter for him. Though he claimed his handwriting was illegible, she suspected he could neither read nor write. Likewise when a letter arrived for Tommy he asked Lydia to read it aloud, explaining he preferred the sound of a woman's voice reading the words. Soon Lydia found herself reciting the words of mothers and sisters from Missouri to Illinois, Idaho to Virginia, though she refused to be the voice of girlfriends on moral grounds, which exempted Joe Cohen's letters from her talents.

When on the third morning every temperature reading, throat swab, and blood sample from quarantine continued to indicate that the men remained healthy, she felt something inside herself loosen. Though Peterson and Cole continued to monitor the men's blood and sputum, even they seemed less intent on their task. Foley must have shared their growing ease because she finally allowed Lydia to insert a thermometer between a volunteer's lips.

That afternoon Dr. Gold announced the inauguration of a second test in the west ward involving ten more volunteers. In an empty room in all other respects identical to the one in which ten men were celebrating their enduring health with homemade cookies sent by Teddy Evert's mother, Lydia affixed ten new names to ten footlockers. The tentative sense of well-being that had stolen over her in recent days diminished

Harry won't argue that Foley had the best bubbies, but as far as he is concerned Nursie Lydia had the best all-around goods.

Nursie Lydia had one of the sweetest figures that Joe ever saw on a Mick.

Tommo insists he just enjoyed having his own secretary.

with each additional name, until by the tenth footlocker she felt as ill at ease as on the first morning. In the afterglow of the east ward's daily defiance of sickness she had forgotten that those ten men represented a beginning and not an end.

The next morning she once again found herself behind an equipment-laden cart that included a bottle filled with milky liquid. The familiarity of these objects was consoling. Having observed their harmlessness once, she had reason to believe they might again prove benign. Apprised of their predecessors' good fortune, the second group seemed less cowed by the doctors, and her cart received fewer apprehensive glances. This time Peterson explained the inoculation would taste salty, and he avoided terms like Mather's coccus.

Trailing Foley from bed to bed, Lydia found herself comparing each bed's occupant with his counterpart in the east ward. Paul Louden was similar in build to Harry Able but lacked the affability of his precedent. Lawrence Matthews seemed a pale imitation of Ralph Cataldo. Ronald Nestor was as young as Teddy Evert but had close-set eyes that aroused Lydia's suspicion. None of the men had the easy bearing of Frank Bentley. As she continued from bed to bed she tried to banish such comparisons from her thoughts. Had these men been her first patients, she would surely be holding Joe Cohen and John Kipling up to standards set by Fred Paley and Leonard Osterman rather than the other way around—but despite this intention, the men of the east ward remained at the forefront of her mind as Dr. Peterson traveled from bed to bed inoculating compliant noses and throats.

Perhaps because she had one such test behind her, the second round of inoculations seemed to elapse more quickly. Soon Percival Cole was heading toward the laboratory and Nurse Foley was returning to the east ward for the second temperature reading of the day, an event whose results were so consistent that the men had taken to predicting their temper-

Larry resents that none of them had a ghost of a chance with Nursie Lydia. From the first day it was obvious that she'd already picked her favorite.

atures beforehand. Because Cole tended to read or write as he walked, he was quickly outpaced by Peterson and Foley and it was easier than Lydia thought to find herself alone with him in the hospital corridor.

"Cole," she began, keeping her voice low. "Dr. Peterson told the volunteers that the inoculation would taste salty this time. What was different about it?"

The manner in which Cole responded reminded her why she had sought him out: he answered without talking down to her, as if she were a fellow medical officer and not a nursing assistant.

"It's a different isolate this time," he explained while continuing to write in his notebook. "Dextrose bouillon was the growth medium for the cocci, but this time we used crude secretions from three acute cases. Which are naturally saline, of course, hence the saline suspension."

"What's a crude secretion?" she asked, for once not feeling she ought to apologize for not knowing.

"Just what you'd expect," he answered to his notes. "Mouth, nasal, and pharyngeal washings, also bronchial sputum."

"Of course," she concurred, her mind racing to make sense of the words. Decoding medical terminology was pleasantly reminiscent of Sunday School Latin. But once she had deciphered the meaning of "crude secretions," her enjoyment vanished. When she stopped in her tracks, Cole continued down the hallway, unaware he was no longer accompanied.

"Cole," she called. She was grateful Foley and Peterson were by this time out of sight and hopefully beyond earshot. Cole froze and, for the first time, looked up from his notebook.

"Yes, Wickett?" he answered.

"Doesn't it—" she began, but stumbled. The courage her question required vanished with Cole's gaze. She wished he was still walking—it would have been easier to address his retreating back. "They are healthy men—to give them *secretions*—" She was trembling, but she knew this would be her only chance.

"Do you hate them?" she asked, the words practically bursting from her after their long confinement. "Do you hate them for what they did—for their crimes? Is that why you can do this like it's nothing at all?"

Cole cocked his head to one side as if to allow the words a more direct route into his ear. "Their crimes," he repeated pensively. "You mean because they're graybacks?"

She nodded, her heart pounding.

He paused for a few moments more before answering. Whenever he spoke he gave the impression of having carefully considered every word, checking and cross-checking for alternate meanings before offering each up for conversation.

"I don't hate them," he answered. "If anything I would say I sympathize with them. I would have made a terrible soldier," he shrugged. "It's not in my nature."

She sought some sign that this was an elaborate joke, but they were alone in the hallway and Cole was not known for his sense of humor. He looked toward her now with the same patient, reasonable expression that distinguished all his conversations.

"But if that's really how you feel," she said, her voice echoing up and down the corridor, "how can you have done what you just did?"

He gazed at her with incomprehension. "But Wickett, the stated purpose of this study is the transmission of influenza! I know that, the volunteers know that, you know that—"

"I didn't know that we'd be helping to kill people," she blurted. She swiped contemptuously at the tear that had appeared on her cheek.

"Oh dear!" Cole cried, closing the distance between them. Without preamble, he removed his white lab coat and placed

Before she stopped him in the hall, Percival Cole had not differentiated Lydia Wickett from Cynthia Foley.

The expressiveness of that gesture stamped itself on Percival Cole's heart. He will forever remember that single tear, trembling at the swell of Lydia Wickett's cheek and the arc of her hand as she brushed it away.

it on the floor, then gestured for her to sit. She was too surprised by the gesture not to comply. He knelt beside her. He smelled comfortingly antiseptic, as though his skin were made of soap. She had never seen Percival Cole without his lab coat. He wore it even in the dining room. He was surprisingly solid.

"Is that how you've been thinking of our work?" he asked, his voice solicitous. "That's not at all descriptive, you know. While it's true that this is a particularly virulent strain of influenza, the mortality rate is still only ten percent." His voice had grown so soothing that his words, no matter how academic, could not help sounding like a lullaby.

Cole nodded with small, quick jerks of his chin, his cerebral machinery practically made visible. "Considering the level of care they are receiving," he continued, "I would submit that the chance of one of our volunteers succumbing is really quite lower than that. Yes. Quite lower." A final, decisive nod. "Which still poses a risk, of course, but man's greatest accomplishments have always involved a modicum of risk."

In that moment she became certain he had younger siblings, and that as an older brother he was adored. She was on the verge of asking him this when he abruptly stood and gestured for her to do the same, whisking his coat out from under her as she did. Once the coat had again disguised his frame, the previous moment was so thoroughly effaced that it seemed possible that she had invented it.

"The chance to make history rarely comes even once in a lifetime, Wickett," he said, reverting to the tone he employed to explain laboratory procedures. "I, for one, feel lucky to have been given that chance and I suspect the volunteers do as well, or else they wouldn't be here."

To her shock, he placed his hand on her shoulder. It was the first time since arriving at Gallups that she had been touched and she feared for a moment she might have to sit down again.

Though he had not previously regarded Lydia in anything but a strictly professional context, her distress at the moment filled him with the urge to stroke her head.

Lydia most certainly did not imagine this exchange; it remains one of Percival's most treasured memories.

Percival was unaccustomed to touching a member of the opposite sex outside a professional or familial context. As troubled as he remains by his motivations at that moment, he has no regrets.

"Please don't upset yourself," he urged, the disarming warmth of his voice having briefly returned. "You do yourself and this study a disservice."

"Oh," she stammered. Footsteps sounded from around the corner. Cole removed his hand.

"Good day," he offered quietly before hurrying away.

. . .

It's a matter of viability—it's common sense, really. The samples from the acute cases were extracted between thirty and seventy hours after onset, correct?

Sure.

For the purpose of discussion let us assume that is early enough in the disease cycle to obtain infectious material, though I have my doubts. But for the sake of argument, let us say they begin as viable, infectious samples. How long does it take these samples to reach Gallups? Almost *two hours.*

Outside a human host.

Exactly! Outside a human host. And how are they transported? In an uninsulated glass bottle inside an assistant surgeon's pocket, for the love of Pete! A damn lot of good that'll do when it's practically winter! I tell you those cultures were dead before they docked.

Then explain the presence of *Streptococcus viridans,* explain the presence of *B. influenzae!* These organisms were produced in the control cultures. You saw them yourself. They were *not* dead cultures.

Maybe they were dead for influenza.

Are you deaf? *B. influenzae!*

Well, then maybe *B. influenzae* doesn't cause influenza.

Come on! Go tell that to the Surgeon General. "Excuse me, Rupert? You know that flu vaccine your boys are cranking out? I'm sorry to tell you, but you're wasting your time. *B. in-*

fluenzae is useless." Next you'll be saying that influenza isn't even bacterial!

Okay, Cecil. You win. But we've got to be doing something wrong if all we're getting out of these graybacks is a few sore throats.

Fine, Dick, but I'm telling you the fault lies with the transfer medium, not the organism. I think *B. influenzae* loses potency in suspension—there's no evidence that the samples grown in the control culture are as powerful as the organisms extracted from the nasopharynx.

Is your theory.

Of course it's a theory! Krikey, Dick, if someone knew the answer none of us would even be on this rotten island!

At the very least they could have gotten us more nurses.

From where? Wickett isn't Public Health Service. Hell, she isn't even a nurse! The nurses are too busy taking care of sick people. We'd have better luck getting dancing girls.

There's an idea.

Foley's got the legs for it, don't you think?

Forget it, Cecil. She won't even give you the time of day.

What about Wickett then?

The girl doesn't know how to play bridge. She eats bacon like it's filet mignon. She washes her clothes by hand rather than send them to the laundry. Perhaps you haven't noticed, Cecil, but she's strung a clothesline behind her quarters. And that accent!

What accent?

She works hard to cover it up; perhaps the poor thing even took diction lessons, but if you listen closely you can hear it.

You ever been to South Boston?

You couldn't pay me to go.

It's not so bad. When I was a boy we had a maid from South Boston who had the most delicious fanny.

As tasty as Wickett's?

I'll be happy to let you know should the opportunity for comparison arise.

Opportunity indeed. Half the so-called gentlemen of this world are merely cowards.

Does that make you a coward then?

I, for one, would rather be a living coward than a dead soldier.

. . .

OUR MAIL BAG

An Excess of Clothing Promotes Disease

To the Editor of the *Herald*:

It is my belief influenza is caused chiefly by excessive clothing on an animal by nature naked. The skin is a true breathing organ; its millions of blood vessels are forever gasping for air under even the lightest of drapery, while under the ordinary garb of many folds of clothing it is practically smothered and the blood is deprived of needed oxygen. Blood, thus depleted, loses its vitality and becomes a medium for diseases of all sorts. Proof of this is provided by the observation that while the people of Boston are languishing under the current epidemic of grippe, Boston's animal population—such as its many dray horses—seem to have been entirely spared from this affliction.

Citizens of Boston, while in the privacy of your own homes, please consider the foregoing of clothes or—if modesty demands it—retaining only the loosest of undergarments. These measures will repay you hundredfold in sustained health in these challenging times.

MERVIN K. LANGERHORN,
16 Summer Street

. . .

Sir, you've got to return to your bed.

Where is she?

You ought to be in the men's ward.

Nelly, it's Poppa!

Please! You're upsetting the others. You must get back—

I won't. I'm fetching my Nell.

Sir, you are very ill. And you're upsetting the children. If you'll just come—

Don't touch me, you bastard. Nell, where are you?

Oh! Help! Doctor! Come quickly!

Nell, we got to get out. There was a fellow beside me, and he just—we been tricked. We ought never to have come. Hey! What the—

It's going to be all right, sir.

Get off me! Nelly, run!

We're going to return you to your bed now.

Where's my little girl?

Please, sir.

Her name is Nelly Grace Dearborn.

If you'll just return to your ward—

I won't! You can't make me! I'm a free man!

Sir, please come along.

Please, mister, just tell me true. Is she gone?

James, quick, fetch the ether.

Where is my little Nell? Where is my—

Easy boy, easy. You get his feet. Let's get him back before he wakes up.

. . .

WHOLE COUNTRY IN GRIP'S GRASP

Epidemic Spreads to Middle West and on to the Pacific States

Spanish influenza has now spread to practically every part of the country. Reports today to the public health service showed the disease is epidemic in many western and Pacific coast states as well as in almost all regions east of the Mississippi river.

Influenza now is epidemic at three places in Arizona, in Maryland, in many parts of Arkansas, in Louisiana, Missouri, Mississippi, Nebraska, North Carolina, North Dakota, Ohio, Pennsylvania, South Dakota, Tennessee, Texas, Vermont, Washington, West Virginia, and many other states. The disease is reported from many parts of California. In the District of Columbia the malady is spreading rapidly. The disease is epidemic throughout New England, where it first made its appearance, and officials in that section are considering drastic steps to curb its spread, including the prevention of public gatherings.

. . .

My Dear Boy—

I used to say that any successful businessman was the equal of any headshrinker when it comes to knowing how people tick, but now I am not so sure. Wasn't it one of them who talked about our dreams coming from someplace outside of ourselves? I am thinking there might be something to that theory.

It always goes the same way: A dead man lies on a table but his face is blocked by the doctors standing all around him. I do not know who this man is and I suppose I never will. All I know is that he is dead. I expect if I had fought in the war a dead man would not be such a shocking sight, but I did not fight in the war and so it hits me upside the head every time. Especially when a doctor cuts into the dead man's chest. He carves a Y that starts below the shoulders and ends below the belly button. Once the cutting is done, it looks less like a man's chest than a brisket butchered all wrong.

When the dream changes *I* become the one lying on the table—except that it is not me. It is the widow. She is older than when I met her, but I still recognize her. And in the dream I am *her,* looking through *her* eyes as she lies on a bed. She has been lying there for a long time and I can feel that there is something wrong. When I wake up, that wrong feeling follows me into waking. Which is when I scream just like you used to scream when you had your nightmares. It turns out that my scream and your scream sound exactly the same.

Your Loving Father

Winter arrived to Gallups. The island's denuded tree branches were nubbed with migrating birds, Gallups a comma punctuating their southward journey. The disappearance of the season that had greeted Lydia's arrival—in combination with the foreshortened days—made it seem like months rather than weeks had passed. The fear that haunted Southie, the emptiness of Boston's streetcars and the desolation of its shuttered shops, all blurred in her memory, their intensity diminished. Sometimes entire days passed before she thought of Carney. Her amnesia was aided by letters from home—which lately avoided all talk of the epidemic—and by the newspapers—which were subject to the same frustrating delay as the mail—forcing Gallups' inhabitants to traffic in old news, war and epidemic unfolding in three-day intervals. News of Boston had come to feel as remote as news from Europe. When she took her nightly walk along Gallups' shoreline, both places were equally invisible, confirming the notion she was impossibly far from everything and everyone she had ever known.

Every Sunday a Protestant chaplain was brought in by ferry

to lead a nondenominational service in the dining hall. Though the chaplain's aim was to satisfy Christians of all creeds, his service was familiar to no one and sparsely attended. She would have preferred a priest empowered to hear her confession, but the chaplain was always happy to talk with her after the service. Had he been Catholic she would have told him of her immoderate affection for the men in the east wing, but such a topic felt indecorous outside the confines of the confessional. Instead she related her anxieties regarding the volunteers' health and her ambivalence toward her role in the study's mission. The chaplain's kindness girded her for the week ahead.

Chaplain John Grimes remembers Lydia well. When she stopped attending services he worried that she had fallen ill.

By the end of their second day, the men inhabiting the west ward remained as stubbornly healthy as their counterparts across the hall. Disquiet began to spread among the medical staff. During the days following the first inoculation, wisecracks about the volunteers' contrarian constitutions had been commonplace—but when the second group of ten also defied infection, the jokes disappeared. Talk among the junior medical staff avoided the topic of failure, which remained foremost in everyone's minds. The resultant dinner conversations about Europe and bridge made Lydia feel as if she had been deposited into a drawing room occupied by vacationing pensioners.

The senior medical table fared the worst. Forty-eight hours following the second inoculation, Dr. Gold began dining in his office, enabling Percival Cole—whom Lydia suspected found communal dining an unwelcome distraction—to take his meals in the lab. This reduced poor Cynthia Foley to sitting with Bertram Peterson. The junior table could have accommodated one extra diner but not two and the circular tables did not lend themselves to being pushed together—though Lydia suspected that even had the tables' geometries been more accommodating, pride would have prevented their merger. The sight of Nurse Foley soldiering through meals with the doctor left Lydia feeling that, for once, she might possess the more enviable position.

Even filled with healthy men, two quarantine rooms required constant maintenance. Whatever time was not taken up by the logistics of meals and temperature readings was spent assisting with throat cultures and blood samples, leaving less time in which Lydia was tempted to visit the east ward, where she continued to spend far more time than she knew was proper. She doubted Foley was blind to her habits, but so long as the nurse did not see fit to mention it, Lydia was content to pretend she was the embodiment of the impartial professional. For their part, Harry, George, and the rest were careful to refrain from calling her "Nursie Lydia" in the presence of Foley or the medical officers.

Then, on the fifth afternoon of the east ward's confinement, Lydia arrived to ten empty beds. This had happened once before: on hearing her approaching footsteps, the east warders had hidden beneath their beds or inside the bathroom. If Harry Able had not attempted to fit under his bed, the deserted ward would have come as more of a shock. Instead, Lydia had distributed meals to the empty beds with barely a hitch in her stride, a reaction that profited those in the ward who had wagered on her sangfroid.

"Olly olly oxen free!" Lydia called into the ward on finding it deserted a second time. But the men did not appear. It was not mealtime and the next temperature reading was ninety minutes away. The excuse for her visit was a fresh towel that no one had expressly requested—in truth she wanted to see who was ahead in the perennial checkers match between Frank and Ralph. Though she never placed any actual bets with Billy, the ward's unofficial bookie, she had privately predicted she would find Frank up by three games.

"Frank?" she called. "Georgie?" The nightstands beside

the vacant beds were bare and the few pictures that had been affixed to the walls had been removed. Then she heard Nurse Foley's footsteps behind her.

"Where are they?" Lydia demanded.

"The first study ended just before lunch," the nurse replied. "Assuming they're not still at the mess hall, the men are most likely in the barracks."

"It's just that I was surprised to find the room empty," Lydia stammered. "I expected I would be asked to help when the time came."

"It happened rather suddenly," Foley explained. "Joseph had been in communication with the Chelsea Naval Base for days trying to get the necessary transfer permissions and when they came through this morning there was no time to waste. He left on a special ferry just before lunch. Even Bert is rather excited about the whole thing."

"Are we getting more volunteers?" Lydia asked. Though Nurse Foley seemed to be avoiding any sort of direct chastisement, her presence turned each empty bed into a rebuke.

"Heavens no," the nurse replied, "though there are more than a few people around here who would be thrilled to trade ours in for new ones. The Chelsea Naval Base patients will be enabling the direct transmission study. Joseph has high hopes. According to him, our first two tests here were pro forma; this is the test that will yield the real results. I'll need your help now, of course, in preparing the room for the next group."

She turned to go but stopped before she reached the door.

"You know, Lydia," she added, "your dedication is admirable but you mustn't become too attached. I think perhaps it was for the best that Joseph and I supervised the men's return to their barracks while you were at breakfast."

She was on the verge of asking who Joseph was when she realized Nurse Foley was referring to Dr. Gold.

"Now that both wings are to be continually occupied,"

Nurse Foley offered, "I suspect that you'll find it easier to manage your time. If what Joseph says has any bearing on things, we're going to be rather busy from here on out."

Mechanically, Lydia stripped the beds and made them up with fresh sheets. She removed ten names from ten footlockers and threw the labels in the rubbish bin. She opened the room's windows and rid the room of the smell of men until, finally, there was nothing left.

Just as they had at the volunteers' arrival, the entire staff was on hand to meet the ferry that docked the next morning. The first person to emerge from the ship's cabin was Dr. Gold. Lydia thought they all could have benefited from a rousing speech but without preamble Dr. Gold enlisted the aid of the junior officers and Dr. Peterson in carrying four stretchers from the boat, leaving as passive spectators only Lydia and Nurse Foley. On each stretcher lay a man, his head emerging from a cocoon of bedding. Three lay with their eyes closed; whatever curiosity they might have had about their new surroundings was trumped by illness. The last was either too weak or too tired to raise his neck and saw only as much as the placement of his head on the stretcher would allow. Only the color of the uniforms beneath the bedding identified them as naval recruits who had fallen ill before shipping out.

The path leading to the compound was unpaved and ran uphill, precluding the use of wheeled gurneys. As the stretchers got under way Nurse Foley assumed the head of the slow procession, walking beside the stretcher carried by Peterson and Gold. Watching the nurse from her own place at the rear, Lydia tried to recall the sense of limitless possibility that had struck her on first spying Gallups from the bow of her own incoming ferry, but that feeling seemed to have belonged to someone hopelessly young.

At the hospital entrance, the four new arrivals were transferred to wheeled gurneys and brought to the recovery room, which lay along the same hallway that housed the surgery and examination rooms. The recovery room was the twin of the lab where the volunteers had reported for preliminary tests, but here beds took the place of counters, lessening the power of the white tiles to evoke memories of City Point. The beds were arranged in two rows of four separated by a wide aisle. The curtains that had been pulled around the sailors' four beds reminded Lydia of Carney.

"We are joined today by four seamen from the Chelsea Naval Base, who have generously agreed to aid us in our study," Dr. Gold explained once the last sailor had been bedded down. "I met and interviewed several seamen at Chelsea who were eager to help our efforts, but these four represent our most ideal donors." The doctor walked to the bed at the far end of the room.

"This is Seaman Pruett. An early but acute case, he claims to have experienced the first symptoms this very morning. He arrived at Chelsea just as I did and immediately expressed his heartfelt willingness to help in any way he could. The other three arrived at Chelsea the previous night but represent candidates almost as impeccable."

Dr. Gold turned to face the bed behind him. "Son, you've done your country a great service by agreeing to come here."

"Sure, Doc," rasped an unfamiliar voice from behind the partition.

"We're going to take good care of you, sailor, even better care than you would have received at Chelsea. You're in excellent hands."

"Thanks, Doc. I'm awfully grateful."

As Gold proceeded to the next curtained bed, Cole and an escort led ten volunteers into the room. These men represented the last of the thirty, whom Lydia had not seen since the interim days preceding the study's commencement. She could only vaguely recall their names, but on seeing her several

When Davey Pruett got to Chelsea, it was so crammed with flu patients that just the smell of them would have made him agree to practically anything the doc wanted.

smiled and cried out, "Nursie Lydia!" their faces lighting up in recognition.

The men's faces quickly changed at the sight of the four curtained beds.

"What's happened?" she was asked by a tall, narrow-necked volunteer with a prominent Adam's apple and a thatch of straw-colored hair. "Have the west ward boys gotten a dose after all?"

"Your friends are fine," Lydia assured him.

As if he had been waiting for her cue, Dr. Gold approached.

"Good morning!" he began, either unaware or unconcerned that he only received wary nods in reply. "Boys, today we will be inaugurating the next phase of our tests, which is called the 'direct phase.' Behind these curtains are four enlisted men who, unlike the fellows we've been working with here, *have* managed to catch the flu." The doctor's chuckle, emerging from behind the white blind of his mask, elicited uneasy smiles.

"We'll be employing two techniques today, split evenly between you," he continued. "The first couldn't be simpler: all it involves is talking to these fellows and allowing them to breathe and cough on you a bit. For the second you don't have to be nearly so sociable, we'll just be asking to swab your noses and throats with a bit of donated material. Are there any questions? Good. When Dr. Peterson calls your name please proceed to the indicated bed and await further instructions."

Gold spoke so assuredly and with such speed that by the time Peterson had divided the men into two groups of five, Lydia suspected they still had not grasped the meaning of his words. While Foley assisted Peterson, Cole motioned for Lydia, the two of them leading their five to the bed nearest the door.

She had not been within the confines of a curtained bed

Rudy Unger wishes his name fell at the beginning of the alphabet. From what he hears, Nursie Lydia would have had no trouble remembering him if it had.

Cole wished he had been given more opportunities to work with Wickett. Her dedication to the volunteers provided him valuable lessons in bedside manner.

since her time at Carney and, for a moment, she felt like she had been transported back across the harbor. She had a sudden flash of Brian O'Toole struggling to raise his head from his pillow as he begged her not to leave, but this vision was dispelled by the sight of the naval recruit and the nervous silence on the other side of the curtain.

The sailor opened his eyes as she entered. He was not nearly as ill as some of the patients she had helped at Carney. Though feverish, he was alert and his breathing was unimpaired. In a kind voice, Cole described the procedure. The recruit lay perfectly still as Cole circled a swab inside his nostril until the soft white of the swab's tip had been obscured by a layer of yellow-green mucus. Then, handling the glistening swab with the care a jeweler might lavish on a rare gem, Cole rushed from the bed to the other side of the curtain, where he spread the contents of the swab inside the nostrils of a volunteer, stroking back and forth within the nostril as though applying a thin, fast-drying coat of paint.

The only reason Oscar Irvine stayed quiet was so as not to spew all over the nice nurse. He had never heard of anything more disgusting than what that doc was up to.

For the sake of the volunteers Lydia was happy for the obstructed view—the swabs, once they emerged from behind the curtain, were wielded quickly enough that the volunteers did not have time to dwell on their appearance. The unwieldy tubes, however, required a greater degree of collaboration. Under Cole's instruction, the naval recruit cleared his throat and expectorated thick, yellow-streaked spittle into one.

When Cole emerged holding the vial, the first volunteer paled. "You're not serious?" he asked.

"Just tip back your head and open your mouth and you'll barely feel a thing," Cole assured him.

"Gimme a minute, Doc," the volunteer said, turning away. When he turned back his eyes were closed. "All right," he resumed. "Go ahead and do me."

"Try not to cough or spit," Cole advised, "or I might have

to repeat the procedure." He was so quick and gentle the fellow did not even gag.

When it was done the young man opened his eyes and grinned. "No problem, Doc. That wasn't nearly so bad as I thought. It's like swallowing oysters."

The next volunteer stared at his tube like it had challenged him to a drinking match. "I'm good for more than that, Doc," he boasted. "Whatever you can give, I can take."

"You tell 'em, Dukey!" called one of the men from the other group. "If Riordan could see you now his head would near about fall off."

"He'd be a helluva lot better looking that way," Dukey replied, rubbing a scar that lay across his left cheek like a stray piece of embroidery thread.

Eventually Lydia stopped watching, focusing instead on the recruit, but even as she made polite conversation and adjusted bedding, it was impossible to close her ears to each struggle to permit Cole's fingers to accomplish Dr. Gold's bidding.

When Cole was finished, she led the group to the empty east ward. In silence the men found their beds. In silence, Lydia locked the door behind them.

. . .

How're you feeling?

Not so great. S'good t' be here though. You wouldn't believe the crush at the pier.

You coming or going?

Going. My company prob'ly shipped today. I tell ya it's awful lousy getting left behind.

Don't I know it. Say, you think it's true about the Gerries?

Sure. They started running outta gas soon as Wilson took us in . . . ya know it's funny them dressing you in gray—if I didn't know better I'd take ya for a jailbird.

Yeah, s'funny all right. They got a real sense of humor around here.

Okay Thompson, that's good enough. Now lean toward Seaman Riley's face. Closer. Good. Seaman Riley, if you would, please exhale deeply five times. Then, if you'd be so kind as to cough.

Sure thing, Doc. Feels a little funny doing this, though.

Don't worry about it, sailor. A little closer, Thompson. All right, Riley. Go ahead.

You gettin' any good flickers?

Last week at the Pier they showed a Keystone caper that was pretty first rate. But I'd ruther a Norma Talmadge pic any daya the week. Even when the picture's lousy she's aces.

I'd give my right nut to see Theda Bara.

I heard they was sendin' a bunch of Hollywood dolls over t'France. I tell ya, I'm missing all the best parts of this war.

Where're you from anyway? You sound like Detroit.

South end, born an' bred.

You're kiddin' me! You know Pauley's?

Do I know it? Chum, if I could have one thing right now it'd be one of Pauley's roast beef sandwiches, extra mustard, extra horseradish.

Gee that's funny, two Detroit fellas like us meeting in a place like this. How'd you land this duty anyways? Seems like a bum steer.

Believe me, it was better than where I was before.

Remember me to the 45th when you get there.

If I get there. At the rate things're going it'll be all wrapped up by the time I'm ready to ship. Anyone in particular you want to be remembered to?

Anyone but Greenaway. We never got along too good.

I'll try to remember. Besides this Greenaway fella they're mostly good guys, am I right?

They're tops. I miss 'em like brothers. But steer clear of Greenaway. He'll land you in all sorts of hot water.

Thanks fella.

That's good enough, boys.

. . .

BODY LEFT FIVE DAYS ON SHELF

Shocking evidences of apparent neglect by undertakers in the failure to bury the bodies of three children, victims of the grip, were brought to the attention of the board of health last night, and a far-reaching investigation of undertakers' methods where reports warrant inquiry at this time will be started today by Dr. William C. Woodward, Boston commissioner of health.

Discovery of yesterday's cases followed description in the *Herald* last Friday and Saturday of deplorable conditions in the North end. In one case of an unburied child, disclosed yesterday, the body of the infant was found "on a shelf, covered with a rubber cloth, with rubbish on top of it." The body had lain in the undertaker's shop since it had been removed there from an East Boston home on Thursday morning last. "It was decomposed and in bad condition, with offensive odors therefrom," according to a report filed in the health department last night by Police Officer Roger Flynn.

. . .

I don't think we ought to do it.

And I'm tellin' you you're wrong.

It's a sin, is what it is. It's deserating the dead.

It ain't deseration; the body don't know the difference. It's the livin' you gotta worry about. How'd you like bein' told there ain't no coffins fer your loved one, he'll have to go straight into the ground?

But ain't that exactly what we're doin'?

Sure, but only after his people already saw him. It won't hurt nobody to take him out now. Don't you want to let another family get their loved one buried proper?

But ain't this coffin paid for?

That ain't none of our business. Doncha want to earn a little extra?

Sure, but—

And don't it say in the Bible "dust to dust"?

Yeah, but—

Well, we're just helpin' that along, see?

But we can't just—

It's a unique situation. If we do it like Mr. K wants then everyone's happy: me, you, Mr. K, the families, everybody.

What about Jesus?

What's he gotta do with anything?

If it's a sin I gotta know so I can confess it.

Jesus wasn't even buried in a box. He was wrapped up in a sheet!

Gee, I never thought about that.

Well don't feel like you gotta start now.

But I think I ought to confess it anyway, just to be sure.

I don't care what you tell the priest so long as right now you give me a hand.

Aw, jeez—

Look, you're so bothered by it, turn your head. Good. Now, wait—just—a minute. All right, now help me put the dirt back in.

But—

Just shovel, all right? We got another one waiting.

. . .

My Beautiful Darling—

Our house is much smaller than it used to be and I do not recognize anything. Today I opened our front door and some rascal had switched our front lawn, our driveway, and even our Packard for an ugly brown hallway lined with ugly brown doors. Where are you? I have looked everywhere. Are you at your mother's?

Darling, I have a confession to make—I never wrote to the widow. Perhaps you guessed as much. I wish there had been someone like you to give me advice at the very beginning, before I had a family to consider! Please believe me when I tell you that I did not act as I did out of cruelty. I am a coward, not a villain. But I guess you already knew that too.

What do you hate most, my cowardice or my weakness? It does not matter because soon I am to be done with both. I know I was a terrible old goat, but I have been faithful to you for so many years that when I see another woman the thought does not even cross my mind. And now I plan to make a clean break of the business with the widow. It is something I ought to have done long, long ago.

Always,

Your Loving Husband

That night was strangely quiet, the breeze and ocean still. Lydia occupied a different room—one with pale wallpaper adorned with cornflowers, a Queen Anne dresser made of dark wood, and a tall wardrobe with brass fittings. The sickness inside her was an undulating creature with arms that clamped across her chest and up her spine and into her skull. Her insubstantial body was covered by a sheet from which one skinny leg protruded, sheathed in striped pajamas. When she heard movement she turned to see herself enter the bedroom carrying a bowl of chicken broth. She watched her image claim a chair beside the bed and lift a spoon to the lips of the invalid she had become. The broth was almost impossible to choke down, but she managed to swallow. She was overcome with gratitude for the broth and especially for the steady, patient hand holding the spoon. She wished to speak. She could feel love welling up within her, a physical presence antipodal to her illness.

"Thank you," wheezed a thin voice that jolted her awake.

Lydia stared in confusion at the dark window and at the three vacant beds as the sound so unattuned to the curve of her throat echoed in the empty room. In the grip of that sound she

We regard this as a triumph for Henry Wickett. His whispers among Us most often concern the unexpressed feelings he had for his wife during their last living hours together.

could assign herself neither name nor place. She bolted from bed. Her pounding heart pushed her from her room, down the hallway, and outside the barrack. She stood motionless, her face flushed as the dream faded and her body once again became her own. She began to walk.

It was late. The lower portion of the diminishing moon was draped in gauzy clouds, as if even it were wearing a mask, but enough remained unobscured to illumine her steps as she traced the compound's edge. She crept forward on the balls of her feet, not wanting to stir even the wind with her trespass. Then the quality of the island's silence changed. She thought she heard a footstep. She told herself it was her imagination, or perhaps a rabbit, though she had never seen a rabbit at night.

She strained her eyes toward the fence. A figure appeared to be standing frozen just outside the compound's perimeter, but in the moon's dim illumination its outline was vague. She was not prepared for what she did next.

"Henry?" she whispered.

The shadow—or what she took for a shadow—did not move. The longer she gazed the more it seemed to approximate a human figure, but moonlight could be deceptive. She moved closer. As she neared, she thought she saw the shadow shift slightly, as though deciding whether to flee; but instead it remained, more broad shouldered and sturdy than Henry had ever been.

"Michael?" she gasped. She stilled the urge to run forward and instead gazed at the figure as if her eyes had grown fingers. Slowly the figure began to move. Like part of the wind itself, it entered the compound through a hole in the fence and made its way toward her. Warmth welled from within her as though her body had grown, in its longing, a second heart. Then her lips formed her brother's name again. The figure was too close to deny. The fence was behind it now and it approached faster than before. If she could be held one last time in her brother's arms she would memorize everything: the press of each muscle into her torso; the places on her body where Michael's palms and fingers fell; the smell of him; the confidence contained in his limbs.

She wobbled on her feet. She rushed toward the figure and gave in to the broadness of its chest and its encircling arms, her head pressing into the space just beneath the neck.

"Liddie?"

The voice was familiar. When she gazed upward she recognized the broad nose, the full mouth. These features did not belong to her brother. She pushed away from the chest with such force that she lost her balance. Gravel pressed into her palms and knees, but the coldness of the ground did not erase the lingering warmth beneath her skin.

"Careful," Frank Bentley's voice whispered. "I didn't mean to give you a fright." He held out a hand to help her up.

Slowly she stood. She felt like a part of her had been emptied onto the gravel beneath her and was now indistinguishable from the dust.

"You all right?" he whispered. "If I thought you hadn't seen me I would have stayed put, believe me."

"You're not supposed to be outside," she warned. "You're supposed to be in the barracks." She looked around, expecting to see someone running toward them. "If they catch you they'll send you back."

On the contrary, once Frank saw it was Lydia he felt driven, past all common sense, to be seen by her.

"On nights when I can't stand it anymore," he whispered as though he had not heard her, "I crawl out the barracks window. If any of the other boys see me they keep it to themselves."

There was no more than a foot of space between them. He smelled of brine and wet sand. "Usually I just walk along the beach but sometimes I go in up to my knees." He smiled. "I can't swim, you know. Most gobs can't. Throw us in the drink and we'd drown like a bunch of rats."

"When I first saw you I thought I was dreaming," she whispered. "I thought—" She stopped. She was no longer certain what she had been thinking.

"You're cold," he said.

She was wearing only a nightgown and ought to have been embarrassed. She could smell the ocean on him.

"Don't ever do this again," she cautioned. "You'll be sent back for sure."

Frank remembers Lydia inviting him to dance.

"Dance with me," he whispered.

She meant to speak, surely she meant to protest, but then came his hand at the small of her back, the warmth of it running along the length of her spine. They stepped as if to a waltz. She could hear pebbles shifting beneath her feet.

"Aren't you frightened?" she whispered, but he shook his head. She watched the tendons of his neck rise to the surface of his skin and then resubmerge.

They were no longer dancing. They were standing frozen, the way dancers do while waiting for the next song to begin. She knew she ought to remove her hands from his shoulders. She ought to turn away and return to her room.

He lowered his head. She could feel the warmth of his cheek and the slight stubble there. She could smell soap and salt and the clean, pure scent of skin.

"Thank you, Liddie," he whispered.

There was the fleeting press of his lips against her cheek, and then he was gone.

. . .

You all right, Percy? You're looking peaked.

I'm okay. A little tired perhaps.

You work too hard. You ought to play a rubber with me

and Chaz; forget the lab for an evening and give us a chance to win your hard-earned wages.

Thanks, but I think I'll pass. I'll probably make an early night of it.

Don't be such a grampus. The way you're going you'll run yourself into the ground before things even get interesting—at least wait until the graybacks get sick before you start making the rest of us look bad.

It's nothing personal, Cecil. Maybe another time when I'm not feeling so worn out.

You think you're coming down with something?

I don't know, Cecil. I guess I'll see how I feel in the morning.

. . .

UNDER CITY ORDINANCE
ALL PUBLIC MEETINGS BANNED

The following is an order issued by the Board of Health last night at a special assembly to consider the Spanish influenza epidemic:

Whereas, The city of Boston and the State of Massachusetts are currently in the grips of an epidemic of Spanish influenza of the virulent type; and,

Whereas, The daily increasing number of cases reported by physicians indicates a very serious situation which can only be met by the most stringent measures; therefore,

It is moved, seconded, and carried that the Board of Health of Boston hereby directs the health officer to carry out the following measures for the protection of health and in order to assure a timely control of the present influenza epidemic; closing

All places of amusement, including theaters, moving picture houses, concert halls, and dance halls.

All lodge and fraternal meetings and gatherings.

All penny arcades, merry-go-rounds, and other or similar types of public amusement places.

All private dances, balls, club gatherings, and social gatherings of whatsoever nature and kind.

And further:

That all Sunday School classes, church services, and socials be discontinued.

That community singing be discontinued.

That all public and private schools and kindergartens be closed until further notice.

. . .

THE QDISPATCH

VOLUME 11, ISSUE 5   AUTUMN 1993

Boston or Bust

Well, QDevotees, we came, we saw, and we celebrated. QD Soda is now officially seventy-five! Talk about aging well—the birthday girl didn't look a day over twenty! I don't know why I've always thought of the soda as a lady, perhaps it's those cute bottles she comes in. But enough about me. The rest of this issue will be devoted to the main event: the QD Soda 75th Jubilee Celebration.

A Happy Arrival

In addition to those of us who live in the QD capital, a few of us from out of town were able to attend the festivities. Audrey Mantz and I both came in by bus Friday afternoon and Harold Lozenge drove down from Hartford. I think our most long distance ar-rival was Selma Kupik, who took the train all the way from Chicago. All of us out-of-town-ers stayed at the Best Western. Even though most of us stayed up past our bedtimes talking, it was still hard to fall asleep that first night. I for one didn't get to sleep until long after mid-night, and then I spent the whole time dreaming about the Jubilee.

A Promising Beginning

Saturday morning we met on Washington Street to take the walking tour. Many of us had taken it before, but it was still a real treat. For me, one of the most bittersweet parts is seeing what little is left of the neighborhoods where the *QD Follies* used to be and where Quentin Driscoll grew up. It re-ally steams me to see how much

QD history has been erased, but I suppose that's the price of progress.

When we arrived at QD Soda Headquarters we were met by the QD President, Mr. Ralph Finnister himself, which was a big thrill. It turns out he is a real gentleman in addition to being a "great Sodaman" and a fine writer! He gave us complimentary bottles of soda as well as free tickets for the tour. Most of us remembered the original tour from when we were kids and it wasn't the same, of course, but it's a really cute tour and perfect for all ages. There was even a puppet!

We spent the rest of the afternoon in the museum, which proves the saying: good things come in small packages. It is always a pleasure to while away the hours among the museum's beautiful mint-condition collection of signs and magazine advertisements, not to mention their complete line of bottle caps and bottles, all of which were in beautiful shape, including the elusive 22-jag cork cap. Though of course I'd love to have a 22-jag of my own, it does my heart good to know there is one in a place where everyone, young and old, can come to enjoy it.

Reliving History

That night, we convened at the hotel to reminisce. To honor the Jubilee year, everyone agreed to share their first memories of QD Soda. Ken Gerard gave a touching description of his neighborhood soda counter, which left us wishing those places hadn't gone the way of the dodo bird. Judy Niggles kept us laughing with her story of being a very, very little girl when she was fed her first QD Soda in a bottle—with a nipple attached! As usual we stayed up far too late catching up on each other's lives, but for those of us who attended the Coin-Op show this year, there was a little less ground to cover as we had enjoyed the pleasure of each other's company just a few months before.

A New Name for an Old Street

The next afternoon, we headed back to 162 B Street for the Jubilee's main event. While it's true I would have attended QD Soda's seventy-fifth birthday party whether or not Quentin Driscoll was going to be there, I am not alone when I say that meeting the inventor of the best soda in the world was something I had dreamed of since I was a little girl. I even sewed a special dress to wear to the occasion! Now before you QDevotees get too excited let me tell you I had no designs on Mr. Driscoll—after all I *am* a happily married woman and he *is* old enough to be my grandfather. I just wanted the day to be special, as it isn't every day you get to fix your eyes on your girlhood hero.

The weather was nice, and it was good to see so many neighborhood children in attendance. There were free balloons and free cups of soda. Recordings from the *QD Radio Comedy Hour* "Best of" collection were played, which was a real hoot.

We hadn't been there long before Ralph Finnister arrived with Quentin Driscoll. The two of them were absolutely adorable in their matching QD Soda ties. But Quentin Driscoll was so old! I know that's a silly thing to say considering that unless Quentin Driscoll had his famous dream while he was still in the womb he would have to be even older than his soda, but I've always thought of him as eternally in his prime—sort of a Sodaman version of Cary Grant in *His Girl Friday.*

Knowing how thrilled we were to meet Mr. Driscoll, Ralph Finnister led him right over to us to shake our hands and take pictures. I haven't developed the film yet but I'm sure my smile is a mile long.

We were a little disappointed not to see the Mayor in attendance, but I suppose it's hard to be everywhere when you're in charge of a whole city, and he was kind enough to send a representative who presented QD Soda with a lovely signed citation. Mr. Finnister spoke next, and as you might expect from having read his fine writing in past issues, his speech was quite inspirational. The way he talked about the soda over the years brought tears to my eyes!

Then came the moment we'd been waiting for, which is to say it was Quentin Driscoll's turn at the microphone. He didn't speak at first, which I took for his being overwhelmed by the emotions of the moment. Then he smiled at the crowd and raised his cup of soda as if he was about to begin a toast— and I'll be durned if he didn't surprise us all! That man might be in his golden years, but he has some spunk in him yet. If he hadn't made it in the soda business, I bet he would have gone far in show business. He stood on that stage and with a completely straight face said that he was not the actual inventor of QD Soda! It was hard to hear what he said after that because of all the laughs, but it was something about the soda's true inventor being a woman he had known back when he was a young man. Then he suggested that the block of B Street be named after her instead! We thought that was a real hoot and gave him a big round of applause, though Mr. Finnister looked none too pleased as he led Mr. Driscoll off the stage. I only hope that when I'm that old I have as good a sense of humor!

Fond Farewells

Once the ceremony was over it was time to say our good-byes. After a grand time sharing old memories and making new ones, we went our separate ways feeling new bonds with our old soda friends. To Quentin Driscoll, whose appearance made our trip so special, I offer on behalf of all of us QDevotees the following words from a certain inspiring memoir: Sir, you have filled my little bottle with everything that you have, and I am all the richer for it.

In This Issue

. . .

LAWNVIEW SENIOR COMPLEX

"Right in the Thick of It!!"™

9/2/93

Dear __Mr. Finnister__ :

Greetings from Lawnview Senior Complex! Please call us at __ext. 62__ regarding __Mr. Quentin Driscoll__ . A representative will be available to take your call Monday through Friday, from 10 a.m. to 4 p.m. We look forward to talking with you soon!

Lydia awoke feeling as though she had already drunk her morning coffee. Usually it was a struggle to leave the warmth of her blankets but today she was spared the usual foggy preamble to alertness and went immediately to her window. It was a clear, cool morning and the breeze flirted with her skin. If she had seen a person or even a rabbit or a bird, she would have bid that creature hello. She wondered if she was becoming ill and felt her forehead to see if it was warm, but everything was as it should be—from her bare feet on the floor to the way her vertebrae sat stacked one atop the other to the air that ebbed and flowed from her lungs. That several moments passed before she identified this condition as happiness was a testament to how long the feeling had eluded her. The last time she had been happy—but she could not remember when that had been. Not on Gallups, certainly, or during the weeks leading up to her arrival. At Carney she had felt satisfaction, but that was not the same thing. It shocked her that she had not noticed the duration and degree of happiness's banishment. She needed to remember this was how she was meant to feel. This was the essential state to which life—after necessary digressions and detours—ought to return her.

She was grateful that her feet were dirty and that the hem of her nightdress was soiled: this proved that she was not basking in the afterglow of a particularly potent dream. She could recall with delicious precision the press of Frank's hand on her back, the briny smell that had enveloped her as they danced, and the fleeting warmth of his breath gracing her skin.

She looked at her clock: she had woken early. She lay back down and closed her eyes to enjoy the novel feeling of being awake without needing to be anywhere. At the sound of footsteps in the hallway she almost got up again—she found the notion of surprising Cynthia in the hallway to wish her a good morning oddly appealing—but when the door to the barracks opened and closed she did not really mind having missed her chance.

Cynthia is profoundly grateful Lydia did not choose that morning to become an early riser. She could not have borne the consequences had Lydia seen who was truly leaving their barracks at that hour.

When she next opened her eyes it was to the sound of reveille. Her earlier, first awakening had the distant and slightly embarrassing feeling of an impassioned midnight conversation whose fervency, by day, seems due less to its substance than to the lateness of the hour. As she dressed she thought of the east ward. She dreaded entering that room. Her anticipation of that moment muted her happiness, but it did not vanquish it entirely. As she made her way across the compound, her memory of the previous night lodged warm and solid in her chest, a small blue candle.

No one in the east ward was asleep when she arrived, but it was difficult to discern whether the men's wan expressions were the product of encroaching sickness or fatigue. Some lay propped against their pillows. Others sat rigid at the edge of their beds. The room's stagnant air held a sour, sweaty odor. She did not mind the smell of a room where men had been working, but this smell—sharper and more pungent—was different.

"What's going on?" accused Roland Thompson as soon as Lydia had closed the door behind her.

"What do you mean?" she stammered. Until now she had forestalled—from one moment to the next—considering the larger implications of last night's encounter. Though reason assured her that Roland's question had nothing to do with Frank, her imagination conjured less comforting possibilities. After last night, fear of discovery would dog her for as long as she remained on Gallups.

"I mean all that running back and forth, and the voices, and us pounding on our door fairly begging them to tell us the trouble, and them acting like we was invisible," Roland fumed. "It ain't right. After all the hullabaloo last night we oughta be told."

"Rollie thinks it was one of ours from the west ward," chimed Arthur Sealey from Evert's bed, "but I say it's one of them gobs that breathed and coughed all over us."

"If you ask me, they oughta've told us last night, 'stead of making us wait like this," protested Leonard Veeson from across the aisle, where Cataldo had once been. "Like Rollie says, we gotta right to know."

"The way they was actin', it could've been a fire," Francis Maddox accused from Denson's bed in the far corner. "For all we knew the hospital was burnin' down."

"I'm so sorry," she apologized. "I'm afraid I don't know what you're talking about."

Several of the men scowled; a few muttered under their breath. She was divided between alarm that something had happened and relief that it did not involve her and Frank.

"I haven't talked to anyone yet this morning," she explained. She wondered if news of whatever had happened in the hospital had reached the volunteer barracks. "As soon as I learn anything I promise to tell you straightaway."

She distributed the breakfast trays. The men accepted them grudgingly, most placing them beside their beds uneaten.

"You wouldn't hold out on us, would you?" Roland asked,

eyeing her. "Thinking it was for our own good? 'Cause I don't know about these fellas, but I'd rather have it straight."

"Rollie, drop it," Arthur Sealey groaned. "She don't know and neither do you. And even if she did there's nothing anyone could do either way. If we're goners, we're goners. If we ain't, we ain't. Maybe it was a gob got sicker, maybe not. I don't know why some fellows think that knowing a situation is a good thing, when usually knowing just makes it worse."

"If something has happened, it's only right that you be told," she confirmed. "I promise that if there's anything to know, I'll tell you as soon as I can."

Roland nodded glumly and turned his attention to his breakfast, the rest of the room following his lead. Since arriving on the island, Lydia had become accustomed to being a source of disappointment, but not in the wards.

"Hey, Nursie!" Max Stein complained after she completed her breakfast duties and was wheeling her empty cart toward the door. "I got a bum plate. There ain't no bacon on it."

"I told the cook to give you extra eggs instead," she replied.

"Aw, whaddya do that for?" Max groaned. "How am I s'posed to keep my strength if I don't get meat? Now I'm a goner for sure."

"But it was bacon!" she explained. "When Joe Cohen was in here—"

"Do me a favor, honey," Max interrupted. "Keep Joe out of it. I don't go in for none of that dietary mumbo jumbo. Be a doll and fetch me some bacon before they run out and I gotta cut a slice off the Mad Ox over there."

"Let's see you try," warned Francis Maddox from his bed.

"Hey I'm just kidding, Ox," Max chuckled. "I was just providing the lady an example."

The west ward still wanted breakfast, but she did not want to appear there without answers to the questions she knew would be waiting for her. She tried to imagine which of the four seamen might have deteriorated, but their features had merged into an amalgam of all the young men she had seen inhabiting hospital beds. She left her cart in the hallway and ventured to the forward portion of the hospital. Nurse Foley, Dr. Gold, and a good portion of the medical staff were already in the recovery room, anxiously gathered outside a fifth curtained bed opposite the aisle from yesterday's four arrivals.

"Who?" she asked to the air, her mind reeling off names as she fixed on the curtain, as though it might tell her which of the volunteers it concealed.

As she neared the bed, Dr. Gold gestured for Peterson and Foley to follow him to the bedside. Lydia positioned herself to catch a glimpse of the patient's face when the curtain was parted, but so many medical staff followed the three past the curtain that there was no need for her to hang back.

At first she thought the new patient was a stranger: the invalid's sleeping features did not match any of the faces she had braced herself to see. Her relief evaporated when Percy Cole opened his eyes.

"How are you feeling, Percival?" Dr. Gold asked.

Cole held out a bandaged arm. "Do you need any more, Doctor?"

"No, son," Gold assured him. "You've given us quite enough."

"You can take more if you'd like. I would hate for the opportunity—" Cole's words were truncated by violent coughs.

"Your dedication will not be forgotten," the doctor assured him. "You have a bright future with the Health Service, son. I can promise you that."

"But first you've got to get better," Nurse Foley chided. "You really ought to have reported to the infirmary earlier. Flu can't be given any leeway."

"But I wanted to make absolutely certain first," Percy whispered, his breath gone. "I assure you I kept out of quarantine and kept my mask on even outside the hospital."

Foley stroked Percy's head. "That's fine but I wish you'd shown as much concern for yourself."

"You must conserve your strength," Gold instructed. "Bed rest is a potent medicine."

"Yes sir," Percy replied, closing his eyes.

The group followed Gold from the bedside but Lydia lingered, placing a tentative hand on Percy's shoulder.

Percy opened his eyes. "Wickett," he murmured and smiled. Until he held out the notebook he had been clutching, she did not realize how strange such an object should have seemed in the possession of a bedridden man. Percy always carried a notebook; it was as natural to him as a hand.

From his supine position, Percy Cole had the pleasure of observing Lydia's nostrils, which were dainty and well formed, Cole considering himself a particular connoisseur of female nostrility. This was additionally the first and only time Lydia touched him.

"I think you'll find this of interest. I started keeping it yesterday," he whispered, "when the aches started. In the event it wasn't just overwork."

The notebook contained an immaculate ledger. Percival Cole's entries had begun at noon the day before, with hourly notations charting appetite, temperature, respiration, heart rate, and overall condition until he had been confined to bed, after which the entries became more erratic as he awoke and returned to sleep. Even when he was sick, Percy Cole's handwriting remained immaculate, the chart of his continuing illness a paragon of organization. It was of momentary comfort to Lydia to suppose the order Percy had imposed upon his symptoms would somehow make sense of his disease.

"It's beautiful," she said, returning it to his hand.

"Lydia?" came Foley's voice from the other side of the curtain.

"Get better," she whispered before slipping out.

"You ought not to be in there," the nurse admonished. "Dr. Gold has given explicit orders that Cole is not to be unnecessarily disturbed."

"I'm sorry," Lydia said, "but Percy is a friend." She could feel her pulse in her neck and the heat of her flushed cheeks. In the split second before the curtain opened, she had tendered an urgent prayer that the bed's tenant be anyone save for a particular volunteer. It was a child's impulse; and her knowing that it had been an empty, impotent plea had little bearing on her guilt that the wish had been granted.

Nurse Foley looked toward Dr. Gold. When she returned her gaze to Lydia her face had softened. "Then you mustn't visit him too often," Cynthia Foley advised, her voice unexpectedly kinder. "And make sure no one else is nearby when you do. Now I need you to report to the west ward and prepare ten fresh beds."

"But what happened to the ten who were already in the west ward quarantine?" Lydia asked. "I've got their breakfasts." Too much was changing too quickly. Time seemed to have accelerated with no concern for her ability to keep pace.

"Save those for the new men," Foley answered. "The others are back in the volunteer barracks. Now hurry. Dr. Gold will be needing your assistance." The kindness in her voice had not yet faded and Lydia would have liked to linger.

"Yes, ma'am," she answered instead and returned to the quarantine hallway.

Frank had thought of Lydia in her nightdress so often since the previous night that when he at first saw her in the ward, he did not recognize her.

She was making up the last of ten new beds when the door to the west ward opened. On seeing Frank standing with Dr. Gold in the doorway, the blood rushed from her head and she wavered on her feet. She wondered if a special ferry would be sent or if she would be kept on Gallups until the next mail delivery, if she would be permitted to eat with the medical officers until her departure or if she would be confined to her room. She looked over the ward she had just prepared. At least she could be satisfied with the last duty she had performed. She turned toward Dr. Gold, determined not to avert her gaze.

"I'm sorry," she confessed. "I know I ought to have said something, but I just couldn't." She could feel her beating heart. "I couldn't bring myself to do it."

The moment stretched. She looked from Dr. Gold to Frank. She thought she saw him shake his head.

When she turned back toward the doctor, he offered her a puzzled smile. "No apologies necessary, Wickett. I'm sure you got these beds together as soon as you could. Is the room ready?"

Only now did she see nine other men standing behind the first two, their scant possessions clutched in their hands.

"Oh yes, Dr. Gold, of course," she replied in a rush. "The room is perfectly ready. Everything's fine."

She fought the desire to put as many words between herself and near catastrophe as possible. Even a misplaced breath might revoke her tenuous reprieve. The men filed into the room, in the absence of name cards assigning themselves the same beds they had occupied in the east wing. For a moment she allowed herself to enjoy the notion that time had reversed. Then Nurse Foley appeared at the group's flank with a cart containing syringes and a tray of blood-filled test tubes.

"Good morning, gentlemen," Dr. Gold began. "As you may have heard, Acting Assistant Surgeon Percival Cole has contracted influenza. It is through his dedication to the study that we are able to perform this test, which will involve a small, subcutaneous injection of blood. It is not at all a painful procedure; in fact, it's less intrusive than the blood samples you boys have grown so accustomed to giving. It will leave a raised bump underneath your skin a lot like a mosquito bite; and like a mosquito bite it may itch, but try to leave it be. Are there any questions?"

There was a pause. Lydia recalled the happiness that had attended her earlier that morning. She would have preferred never to see Frank again than to see him in this room. She

Even on the day he got sent to the brig, Frank did not feel more cheated than when it looked like the doc might be onto him and Liddie.

Bertram Peterson deliberately absented himself from this test, which Joseph implemented in direct contravention of the protocols they had cowritten.

Dr. Gold is afraid Bert has overinflated his role at Gallups.

Bertram holds Joseph's inflated ego largely responsible for his failure to progress within the Washington medical establishment.

looked toward him briefly—she could not help herself—and was relieved to find he had not been looking at her. A shared gaze could indict them both.

"How sick is he?" asked George.

"He's got a rough case, but he's receiving the best possible care," Gold assured him. "Anything else?"

Teddy spoke, shocking everyone, his quiet voice filling the otherwise silent room. "How long is this testing business going to keep up?" he ventured. "Are we stuck here until one of us gets it?"

A small muscle below Gold's left eye pulsed three times and was still. Dr. Gold walked toward Teddy and placed one hand on the boy's shoulder. Dr. Gold's hand was large and broad and into Lydia's mind unbidden came the image of Gold's other hand encircling Teddy's neck.

Dr. Gold smiled as he spoke, his words navigating his frozen grin. "You agreed to a month-long study, and Washington lacks the resources to extend our time together. In fact I did not expect I would be calling on you twice, but due to the extraordinary circumstances—let me assure you that the test we are about to conduct will be our last."

The liquid filling the test tubes was a beautiful poppy red. She remembered the pride with which Percy had offered Dr. Gold his bandaged arm. She wondered when the blood had been taken and whose idea it had been.

Nurse Foley approached Dr. Gold with the notebook that in previous tests had been Percy's sole dominion. To her dismay Lydia realized that with Nurse Foley filling Percy's shoes, she was for the first time expected to play an active role in a procedure. Dr. Gold was deft with the syringe and the men—by now accustomed to needles—compliant. When she reached Frank she focused first on the scissors as she cut a bit of tape and then on the raised bump she was to cover on his forearm. She focused on the arm with such single-mindedness that she was able to separate the hand filling her vision from the one that had pressed into her back. Then Frank said "thank you" and she nearly collapsed.

"You're welcome," she quickly replied, and hurried to the next man. Within minutes the deed was done, the test tubes spent. Dr. Gold and Nurse Foley departed, leaving Lydia to deliver the men's breakfasts. She removed the bacon from Joe's plate and wrapped it in a napkin to bring to Max. The men accepted their trays without a word, for which she was grateful, as she felt incapable of speech.

Frank was never all that religious, but right then he was praying that these wouldn't be the last words they would ever say to each other.

Even with her back to the men she could sense his exact location. She did not turn toward him one last time. She put one foot in front of the other until she exited the room. And then, feeling as if her hand had been replaced by cinders, she locked the ward door.

The anticipation that gripped the compound that day was a malevolent cousin to that which had set the staff scanning the horizon for an approaching ferry almost one month before, only now lookout had been posted for several portents, none of which was as simple as a ship's outline against the sky. The junior medical officers were in agreement that in the course of that day or the next the volunteers in the east ward would manifest symptoms. It was only fair play that the quarantiners fall ill now that Cole was sick. Over lunch, they spoke of this event with the dogged certainty of war generals. After having stared at ten raised bumps left behind by ten injections of infected blood, Lydia was inclined to believe them.

The junior officers were unabashedly relieved at the prospect of a positive outcome. Dr. Gold had promised individualized letters of reference, but the value of such a letter would be compromised if associated with a study that had yielded no results. All agreed that by falling ill Cole had guaranteed himself, at the very least, a prominent assistantship. The assurance of their words was undercut by the fear that inhabited their voices, reminding Lydia that white coats and elaborate titles disguised students for whom Percy Cole represented their first encounter with genuine sickness. She felt unexpected compassion at the realization she was better prepared than they for what was happening.

It was a day of empty gestures performed to hasten the intervals that stretched between the taking of new samples from quarantine or the invention of a pretext to visit the recovery room, which continued to be called the recovery room even though no one thought of it that way anymore: it was Percy's room now. Dr. Gold and Nurse Foley became the room's custodians, controlling all access to Percy's bedside. Dr. Gold went so far as to have his desk transported there from his office so that he could conduct his work within earshot of his patient. Lydia despaired at ever seeing Percy again, but to her surprise Nurse Foley charged her with attending Percy whenever she and Dr. Gold collected quarantine samples, a duty from which Lydia was happy to be recused. She could not think of Frank without her hands shaking. They shook violently whenever she delivered meals to the west ward, and she shuddered at the prospect of handling thermometers.

Though she had been instructed not to approach Percy's bedside without due cause, she permitted herself one visit each of the four times she posted watch. All four times he was asleep, though once—having noticed that his notebook had fallen to the floor—she permitted herself to approach his bed in order to replace the book at his side. Her desire to remain with him vanished at the terrifying, irrational notion she would see Henry's eyes staring out of his face should he awaken.

Percy Cole was not asleep on this particular occasion. Having heard Lydia on the far side of the curtain he deliberately dropped his notebook. Though he felt too ill to speak once she appeared, her brief presence was a balm.

By dinner, word spread among the staff that Percy's chest had become fully involved. The news was never more than whispered, as though giving the words more substance would somehow make things worse. Neither Dr. Gold nor Nurse Foley was present at the mess hall that evening. They were taking their meals in Percy's room now, leaving Dr. Peterson to eat his dinner stubbornly alone.

There was not much talk, and what there was pertained directly to the tests, to quarantine, or to Percy. Having been granted four audiences at Percy's bedside, Lydia was imbued with rare authority, her dining companions plying her for particulars. But throughout the day Percy had steadily deteriorated and she did not want to describe his pallor, his fever, or the swampy sound his chest made when he coughed. Such details might have been novelties to the likes of Worth and Warner, but she had seen them too many times before.

That night she returned to the spot at the compound's periphery where she and Frank had stood a lifetime ago, before Percy's illness. Then she passed through the hole in the fence through which Frank had come to her. At the beach, she walked into the surf up to her waist. On returning to her room, she did not change out of her wet clothes, but instead stood shivering at the room's center, attempting to retain for as long as possible the feel of wet fabric against her legs and the smell of the ocean.

. . .

Explain to me how a doctor gets it and we don't.

Is Cole the quiet one with the notebook?

That's the one.

Then there's your answer. A fella like him ain't exactly durable.

Sure, but he was always wearing those masks.

If those masks was half as important as the doctors make out, one of us woulda caught a dose long ago.

I heard he got worse and now it's pneumonia.

Naw, it's flu.

It started out that way but now it's flu and pneumonia both.

Can you get both at the same time?

Sure you can. Double whammy.

Does that mean we've got pneumatical blood in us?

I hope not. That's serious.

Is yours still red Sammy?

A little. Yours?

Yeah. But it's not a lump anymore. It flattened out.

I don't like it.

Don't like what, Sammy?

Having that sorta thing inside me. I can feel it traveling round my body. There's this little lump of sickness traveling all around.

Aw, that ain't how it works, Sammy. It don't stay lumped together. It's like putting whiskey in your coffee. The whiskey don't stay in one place, it spreads itself out.

Why didja tell me that? That's worse than having a traveling lump.

You feel all right though, don't you?

Yeah, 'cept when I think about that sick blood moving around inside me.

But it oughta make you feel better—you got the blood of a doctor in your veins.

I wish it was a nurse instead.

You can say that again. It's been so long I'd take anything, even blood.

Can you do that? Mix a lady's blood with a man's?

Sure. It's a modern age.

I'd rather be doing the injecting. A special injection just for Nursie Lydia.

Watch it.

What?

I don't wanna hear you talking like that.

What's it to you, Frankie?

Nothing. Just keep your trap shut.

What's with you, Bentley? You been acting strange ever since we got back to the ward.

It's nothing, Joe. I just want this whole mess over with.

. . .

GAMES FOR STAY-AT-HOME CHILDREN

The closing of the Boston schools on account of the influenza epidemic and the advice of the health authorities to avoid as much as possible promiscuous association of all kinds have thrown thousands of boys and girls back upon the resources of the home for things to do during the long hours of otherwise unoccupied days. The *Herald,* appreciating the problem this presents to many parents, will publish daily for the next ten days a game suitable for the front-step, backyard, or indoor use by groups of from two to five children. These games have been selected and adapted for this purpose by Gilbert H. Boehrig, city-wide and community boys' work secretary of the Boston Young Men's Christian Association. Today's game is:

"Buzz"

Children sit on step in row. First child says, "one," next "two," and so on until they reach "seven." Instead of saying "seven," he must say "buzz." "Buzz" is said for every multiple of seven and for every number in which seven occurs.

For example—"Fifty-seven" would be "Fifty-buzz." "Fifty-six" would also be "buzz." "Seventy-seven" would also be "buzz-buzz." "Seventy-four" would be "buzz four."

A person who makes a mistake may either pay a forfeit or drop out of the game. The object is to stay in as long as possible.

. . .

January 7, 1925

Dear Mr. Driscoll,

This Christmas we visited my youngest brother in South Boston and decided to visit you at the famous QD Soda Factory. We arrived in the morning but you were not in so we took the guided tour.

Mr. Driscoll, you are not telling the truth! The tour does not even mention Wickett's Remedy and then there is that whole business with the dream about the Indian! If you had bought the recipe from me I suppose you could do whatever you wanted, but Mr. Driscoll, you never did! And when I went back to your office your secretary said that you would not be in for the rest of the day!

Mr. Driscoll, I believe that you are an honest man at heart. Even honest men make mistakes sometimes. You do not need to feel embarrassed, but now the time has come to do what is only fair and right! It would mean a lot to me and my husband.

Sincerely,
Your Disregarded Business Partner

. . .

Lawnview Senior Complex
14 Telegraph Hill
South Boston, MA

Mr. Ralph Finnister
162 B Street
Boston, MA 02127

September 10, 1993

Dear Mr. Finnister:
We at Lawnview Senior Complex have made repeated at-

tempts via both telephone and mail to contact you regarding Lawnview community member Mr. Quentin Driscoll, but our phone messages and letters have gone unanswered. It has become of *vital importance* that we discuss with you our changed living strategies for Mr. Driscoll either by telephone or in person, as he has recently progressed to requiring new levels of care currently unaccommodated by the present terms of his residency. For his comfort and yours we urge you to contact us *as soon as possible.* A representative will be available to take your call Monday through Friday, from 10 a.m. to 4 p.m. We look forward to talking with you very soon!

    Sincerely,
Lawnview Senior Complex
Community Care™ Department
Ext. 62

The next morning, Lydia awoke to the same smell that had accosted her when she visited the east ward. Neither her morning ablutions nor a fresh shirtwaist made any difference. Dread had taken up residence beneath her skin.

Percy's condition had deteriorated overnight and the recovery room was barred to everyone save Dr. Gold, Dr. Peterson, and Nurse Foley. The junior medical officers were hungry to know more, but Lydia could picture all too well the dull cast of Percy's skin, the grayness of his lips, and the sounds he would make as he breathed. She was only partly grateful that there was no word of the men in quarantine; the absence of news increased the chance that she would be the messenger of bad tidings. She dawdled over her food and made idle talk with the cook as she collected the breakfast trays in an attempt to postpone the inevitable, but soon enough she was headed toward quarantine. She would visit the west ward first because she had no choice in the matter: Frank was there. Percy had once comforted her in this hallway with talk of making history. If this was what history making required, then Lydia was content to remain outside history's reach: a nameless clerk in a department store, a childless woman who would be forgotten after her death.

When she entered, she was careful to glance at two other fellows before turning toward Frank, and then she only gazed long enough to determine he looked no worse than the rest.

When Lydia wouldn't look at him that morning, Frank was afraid she had forced herself to forget their encounter.

"Hey Nursie," Joe asked in lieu of good morning, "is it true that Cole fellow has caught pneumonia on top of the flu?"

He deflated at the sight of her nod.

"Then here's the thing we gotta know," Sam interceded. "Did he catch it before or after we got his blood?"

She could feel the men's eyes on her. "I'm not sure," she answered. "Perhaps Dr. Gold or Dr. Peterson would know; they're the ones who have been treating him . . ." Her voice ebbed.

Sam slammed his fist against his bed frame. "Are they tryin' to make us crazy as well as sick? You gotta tell us, Nursie. You're the only one we trust."

She longed to tell them she was not really a nurse, that she understood as little as they did, that every day she awoke feeling like more of an impostor.

"I'm sorry," she faltered, "but it's really quite complicated. I've barely seen Percy Cole since he fell ill."

Sam shook his head. "Even if they do know something, you can bet the docs won't tell us. They oughta try lyin' here all night long, with some sort of injection spreading all through them and them not knowing what it is."

"Would you shut up about it already?" George growled. "There ain't nothing we can do about it so what's the use? We asked for this mess. You think they would've called on gray-backs if it was gonna be fun and games? We ain't worth nothing—that's why we're here. And the sooner you get that into your skull the better off you'll be!"

There was a knock on the quarantine door. "Is there a problem in there?" came the voice of an escort.

"Everything's fine," she tried to assure him.

"If those fellows are giving you a hard time—" the escort began.

"No, no," she insisted. "We were just having a conversation."

"Don't make me come in there," the voice threatened before footsteps were heard walking away.

"How are you boys feeling today?" she asked. She wanted to apologize for everything: for the gaps in her knowledge, for the escort's rough voice, for the locked door and the closed windows and the helplessness that inhabited quarantine with them. She wanted to give each man a pair of proper trousers and a decent shirt. She wanted to stand them all for a pint at O'Reilly's. She wanted to dance with Frank again, somewhere no one would give them a second glance.

"We're all right," Frank answered, their eyes briefly meeting. "At least for now, anyway. Ain't that right, fellas?"

As far as Lydia could tell, Frank's assessment was correct. No one appeared feverish, which meant she needed only to serve breakfast to consider her responsibilities met. "You're all really quite brave," she said, the private thought coming to her lips.

"We ain't brave," George said quietly. "Just desperate."

She distributed ten trays and without another word left the room.

She treated the rest of the day as a complex mechanical contrivance in which she was a smallish cog. She filled her mind with the clicks of a cog; she moved with the steadiness of a cog, traveling her designated circuit in Dr. Gold's machine. She did not attempt to visit Percy. She did not want to see him now. This shamed her, but the truth of it kept her speeding past the recovery room whenever she entered or exited the hospital. Percy had become Henry; he had become Brian O'Toole; he had become Michael and every Carney patient she had visited for whom a glass of water was a token gesture, good only for filling the time that remained before the bed was vacant again.

Lydia was eating dinner when Dr. Peterson entered the dining hall and did not take his seat. Every head in the room turned as though attached to a single string held in Peterson's hand. Everyone knew what he was there to say.

"I have some sad news," he began, and the room exhaled. The doctor gave details but Lydia did not listen. The details did not matter. She stared at her plate, shocked by the anger that had bloomed inside her. For all his confidence, Dr. Gold was no better equipped than she to battle the flu. Their presence on Gallups was absurd. They ought never to have come. When she looked up from her plate, Dr. Peterson had finished speaking and was walking toward her table. Killington and Warner turned toward him, certain his approach was meant for them, but she knew, somehow, that he had come for her.

"Hello, Wickett," Dr. Peterson said.

"He went quickly," she replied.

"He was an incredibly promising young man. His death is a terrible blow." There was a pause, during which the doctor stared at her as though trying to peer under her skin. "Even in the depths of sickness," he resumed, "Percival's thoughts were of research and the advancement of knowledge." He paused again. "To that end," he finally continued, "he wished to invite you to his autopsy."

Lydia stared at Peterson incredulously. To her further surprise she found him blushing.

"I am extending this invitation solely out of respect for

Bertram is outraged that after commandeering Percival Cole's care, Joe left it to him to inform the others of the young man's death.

Percival Cole's wishes," he blustered. "I ought to tell you I don't think this at all appropriate." He shook his head. "Some sights were not meant for—"

"I'll come," she said.

Peterson's voice was firm. "I'd be happy to provide you a chance to see him one last time under—better circumstances."

"Thank you, Doctor," Lydia answered. "I would like to come regardless."

"I assure you," Peterson tried one last time. "You will not cheapen Percival's invitation by choosing differently."

"When is the autopsy to take place?" she persisted, her mouth dry. She had seen corpses before. More importantly, Percy thought she could do it. After weeks of foundering, she would leave Gallups with a bit of real medical knowledge, something concrete and incontrovertibly true.

"An hour from now, in the lab."

"Thank you, Dr. Peterson."

"You're making a mistake," he pronounced, his voice gentle. "You will likely find you prefer to remember Percy differently."

Only after Peterson's exit did Lydia appreciate the table's silence. Warner looked like he might speak, but she left the dining hall before he had the chance.

Lydia had been inside the morgue only once before, during Nurse Foley's cursory tour of the hospital. It was a cramped, windowless room lined with black counters. Percy's draped form lay on a marble slab at the room's center. Dr. Gold and Dr. Peterson stood beside the body, attired in surgical caps, gowns, and gloves. The rest of the medical officers ranged in a semicircle just beyond arm's reach. The room was too small for so many people. Only once she joined the periphery of the semicircle did Lydia realize she was the only woman. Cynthia Foley's absence felt both like a victory and a warning.

"If any of you should begin feeling uncomfortable," Dr.

Though not quite the sort of overture he had imagined proffering before his illness turned grave, Percy Cole is pleased to have eventually learned, among Us, of Lydia's acceptance of his invitation.

Dr. Peterson points out that Nurse Wickett's recall of the morgue has been affected by her subsequent traumatization there. The morgue was quite large, with several modest windows and deep green counters.

[300]

Peterson cautioned as if addressing the group, though looking only at Lydia, "I ask that you leave quickly and quietly by the door so as not to disrupt these proceedings. I now defer to Dr. Gold."

Towering over the draped figure, Dr. Gold resembled an Old Testament Abraham who had heeded too late God's call to spare his son. "Percival Cole was a friend and colleague," he began in a subdued voice. "His desire that his death not be in vain is shared by us all. We are honored and grateful to have this opportunity to so honor his wishes. *Hic locus et in hora mortis nostrae.*"

"*Hic locus et in hora mortis nostrae,*" a few of the interns repeated. For a strange moment Lydia felt like she was witnessing a funeral mass.

"In the necropsy of Acting Assistant Surgeon Percival Cole," Gold continued, "I, Surgeon Joseph Gold, Ph.D., will serve as prosector and Surgeon Bertram Peterson shall be my diener."

The silence that filled the room had the sanctity and weight of the nave. The covered marble slab at the room's center had become its own pulpit, the half dozen medical personnel its congregation, and Dr. Gold their surpliced cleric. That Lydia felt more intruder than member of this uncommon sacrarium was due to the glances sent her way by the rest of the flock.

The instruments on the tray between Gold and Peterson glinted silver under the electric lights. A pair of scissors, a large pair of tweezers, and what looked like a long, sharp bread knife with a narrow blade were frighteningly banal: it seemed profane to employ such everyday objects for such a grim purpose. The others—like the handsaw and what resembled a large pair of clawed pliers for pulling a tooth from a mouth of terrible proportions—were disturbingly singular.

Lydia's attention was diverted from the tools by the rustle of

Dr. Gold thinks it only proper to secularize Lydia's ecclesiastical Latin. He and the interns pronounced the words: *Hic locus est ubi mors gaudet succurrere vitae*—This is the place where death rejoices to teach those who live.

Cecil Worth, for one, was quite unhappy to see Lydia in attendance: he had wagered a modest sum that she would lack the nerve to come.

cloth as Dr. Gold pulled the sheet away from the slab. Percival Cole's body had not been permitted to lie flat. An object had been placed beneath his torso, so that his chest protruded upward while his neck and arms fell back in a morbid swan dive. The body had lost its natural color to become a waxy blue-gray; someone had fashioned a loincloth from a towel, a gesture of modesty for which Lydia was thankful.

Corpses, in Lydia's previous experience, had been clothed in pajamas or hospital gowns. This, in her mind, was their natural state. Clothed, a body still pretended at belonging to the world it had abandoned. Until viewing Percy, Lydia had not realized the degree to which the hospital gowns of Carney's corpses had softened the bluntness of death. A corpse was a dead animal. They were all nothing more than animals, bloated by vanity into wearing clothes and ascribing lofty purposes to their actions, when in reality they all died the same dumb death that awaited any overworked nag—limbs stiff, features frozen in a rictus of shock and pain. Percy did not look like he was sleeping. His mouth gaped; his eyes bulged. Lydia did not imagine he might raise himself from that marble slab to reassure her once again with a gentle hand on her shoulder. His corpse resembled a deft but rote facsimile of a man, crafted by the industrious but uninspired apprentice of a dead master, whose gifts lay buried with him.

"External examination reveals the body to be tinged a shade of heliotrope consistent with cyanosis. There are several raised purple blisters ranging in diameter from one-sixteenth to one-eighth of an inch about the chest and neck."

As Gold spoke, the interns took notes while Peterson stood ready, the instruments waiting beside him. Lydia began to wish she had not come.

"We will now proceed to the opening of the trunk," Gold pronounced with a confusing mixture of solemnity and detachment, making it difficult to determine whether he viewed the corpse before him as a former colleague, or a specimen, or something impossibly in between. Dr. Peterson reached for a large scalpel with a flat, wide blade and—before Lydia fully realized what was happening—sliced into Percy's chest. The sight launched a gut-level alarm through her body, but she did not want to be seen turning away. Instead she stared just below the level of the slab, though that did not erase what she had already seen. Peterson had cut a deep, Y-shaped incision through Percy Cole with only slightly more effort than was required to slice through a roast pig. The arms of the Y started at the shoulders and met at the breastbone. The tail of the Y ran down past the navel. She had expected greater resistance to the blade and more blood. The absence of both disturbed her as much as the sight of Percy's torso divided into three unequal portions.

The room took on the faint butchery smell she associated with the meat market on Dorchester, a smell previously linked to Sunday dinner. She kept her gaze averted. She had not noticed before that Percy wore a ring, but there it was—a silver band encircling his dangling pinky finger. Then came a liquid plash as a thin stream of pinkish water drained from a hole in the slab to a bucket below. She heard the clink of metal; Peterson had obtained a new instrument from the tray. Next came a crunch, similar to that of a tree bough breaking but moister and duller. Then it came again. Another clink of metal, then a pause, and then the scalpel hit the floor with a purely musical sound, like a triangle being struck from an orchestra's back row. Several people gasped. Somewhere to her left, a low voice beside her murmured, "My God."

"With the removal of the chest plate," came Dr. Gold's voice, now slow and strained, as if hands gripped his windpipe, "we can observe the lungs, which are extraordinarily swollen and discolored." The silence of the room had electrified. "In thirty years in this profession I have never seen anything like this." She stared at her feet; she would die staring at her feet if that was what it took to avoid seeing what had made Dr. Gold sound like a frightened old man.

"Percy never had a chance," someone near her groaned. "The poor fellow drowned inside his own skin." Her throat constricted and the air around her felt warm.

Another instrument was removed from the tray. The air smelled more strongly of meat now and she thought of the dinner she had just eaten. Sour saliva filled her mouth. She forced the sour taste back down. Her feet had become fixed to the floor.

"The left lung is uncharacteristically heavy," Dr. Gold murmured. She watched Gold's legs move as if underwater from the slab to a nearby counter. In the silence of the room it was possible to hear him placing something on the metal tray of a scale. Then, speaking almost to himself, Gold said, "That can't be." His voice wavered. "Seven hundred grams. It's all fluid." There was another pause before Gold's voice returned, as small as a child's. "This must be some new kind of infection—" He paused again. "—or plague."

Something solid hit the floor with a heavy thunk and she shrieked with a sound that did not seem born of her throat. Though she knew the body on the slab had not moved, in her mind's eye Percy was now standing, his chest dangling open, a dark space where his left lung had been.

"Get some ammonia from the cabinet," a voice commanded.

"He's coming to," said another.

"You all right, Cecil?" asked a third.

As she turned her head toward the voices she caught a glimpse of Percy's dangling hand. In place of fingers she now saw five test tubes filled with red fluid, one of which was encircled by a silver ring.

"Excuse me," she whispered. Her feet, now uprooted, carried her toward the door—and past the slab and the doctors and the medical student on the floor. She kept moving until she was through the hole in the fence and heading toward the beach and only then, out of view, did she allow herself to retch, silently and repeatedly, onto the sand.

. . .

Joe?

Who is it?

I waited in my room but you didn't come.

It's useless.

You did everything you could. I know it, the men know it, and Percy knew it.

You didn't see him. You didn't see his lungs.

I'm so sorry, Joe.

I was going to give him so much.

It's a loss.

It's a goddamn travesty. To think what he could have become.

We're doing important work, Joe.

No one thought I would find enough volunteers, but I did. And I was honest with them. They knew what they were getting into.

We all knew the risks.

And at Harvard—the kids were falling over each other to work with me. Dr. Joseph Gold, defeater of yellow fever and typhus. Dr. Joseph Gold, who can't transmit flu to a single goddamn Navy deserter but kills off his best assistant surgeon.

Shh. Let's go to bed. You'll feel better in the morning.

Don't touch me.

It's all right, Joe. I know you're upset.

You don't get it, do you? Every study I do, I can find someone like you. But not someone like Percy.

Joe—

Get out of my room.

Joe, please—

Get out of my goddamn room.

. . .

FAILS TO FIND INFLUENZA CURE

Joint Board Endorses None of the Vaccines at Present in Use

A joint board of medical scientists and statisticians appointed by the state board of health to inquire into the prophylactic and therapeutic qualities of several vaccines which have been made to fight the so-called Spanish influenza germ has submitted the following report, which does not make a definite finding as to any one vaccine, but generalizes in its conclusion:

"1—The evidence at hand affords no trustworthy basis for regarding prophylactic vaccination against influenza as of value in preventing the spread of the disease or of reducing its severity.

"2—The evidence at hand convinces the board that the vaccines we have considered have no specific value in the treatment of influenza.

"3—There is evidence that no unfavorable results have followed the use of the vaccines."

. . .

Hello? Ladies Relief Society. I'm leaving soup and bread by your door. Are you well enough to retrieve it?

Are you a nurse?

I'm afraid not.

We're five of us, all ill. Can't you fetch us a nurse?

A member of the Red Cross Motor Corps will be coming when she can. In the meantime, keep your windows open and drink lots of water. Have you any—has anyone gone to their final rest?

My youngest.

Is she—still with you?

Yes. Yes she is. It's been two days now but the undertaker hasn't come.

If you can manage it, you ought to try to bring her to the street tomorrow morning. There will be a wagon—

Can't you help us? If you can't get a nurse, can you get us a proper coffin?

I'm very sorry. The Red Cross should be here any day now. There's a good bit of bread and soup here. Are you well enough to fetch it?

My son, he can't breathe so good.

You could take him to the hospital.

I hear they're no good anymore. And someone's got to stay with Mary. Please, miss. What's your name?

My name is Miss Perkins.

Well Miss Perkins, can't you do something?

I'm so sorry. I've brought you—there's bread and soup here.

Will you pray for us?

I will. Of course I will.

Hello? Ladies Relief Society. I'm leaving soup and bread by your door. Are you well enough to retrieve it?

Come in, come in.

I'm afraid I mustn't do that. Are there many of you ill?

Come in, come in.

I really can't. You see, I'm not a nurse and the risk of infection—I'm bringing soup and bread to all the families on this street.

Come in, come in.

Please, if you'll just—

It's the bird.

What? Oh my goodness, you startled me. Does your mother know where you are? Oughtn't you to be with her?

Ma says it's better for me to play outside. It's Miss Constance's bird, ma'am.

Come in, come in.

Excuse me?

Who you're talking to. It's her bird. She don't come to her door no more.

Is she very unwell?

Come in, come in.

Can I have that bread?

. . .

May 18, 1925

Dear Mr. Driscoll,

Mr. Driscoll, I tried to call you every week since my last letter, but your secretary will not let me speak to you. I suppose it was silly to think that you would talk to me when you are not answering my letters. Frank got so angry about the whole thing that he wanted to go back to the soda factory himself but I convinced him that this was between you and me.

I went to a lawyer but lawyers cost money and we don't have any. I have looked for the contract you signed with Henry, but if I ever had it I do not have it anymore. I am telling you this so that you know the only way for you to do the right thing is to decide to do it. I cannot make you. Quentin, this is the last letter I will write. It is not too late for you to make up for the wrong you have done. I am a Christian woman. I believe in repentance and in forgiving those who seek forgiveness.

Sincerely,
Lydia

. . .

My Beautiful Darling—

I am afraid our dear boy is really angry with me this time. I suppose I ought to have warned him about what I planned to do, but I wanted it to be a surprise. You always loved surprises. I will never forget the look on your face when I brought home the boat.

It was quite daunting stepping up to that podium knowing what I planned to do. Can you imagine the weight of a duty that has been deferred for seventy-five years? The first time I tried to stand, my legs gave out! It was a struggle, but I made it to the microphone. And then, my darling, I said aloud what I only ever said that once in a whisper to you. I could tell from the first that our dear boy did not take it well, but he tried to hide his disappointment for the sake of the party. I did not stay long after that—I was so very tired—but everyone was quite kind. Soon I was in a car heading home and the horribly wrong feeling that had been haunting me was finally, finally gone.

I wish our dear boy would talk to me. He used to visit every Sunday and sometimes on Wednesday as well, but now he does not visit at all. I have tried to telephone but he does not answer. I even called the police. I told them I thought our dear boy had been kidnapped or maybe even murdered, but when the police came to my door they did not do anything and then that girl took away my phone. Now I have to ask every time I want to make a call and most of the time she says no. I take consolation in the sleep that has finally returned to me, but when I wake up at each dreamless night's end I am still alone.

Will you ask our dear boy to forgive his old dad? If you ask him, I am sure he will. Once you and Ralph return we will all leave here together. Now that I am retired we can do anything, darling, and I have all the time in the world to give to you and our son.

I am Yours Everlasting,
Your Devoted Husband

Lawnview Senior Complex
14 Telegraph Hill
South Boston, MA

Mr. Ralph Finnister
162 B Street
Boston, MA 02127

September 27, 1993

Mr. Finnister:

We at Lawnview Senior Complex take great pride in our community, which provides independence and security to seniors and is based on communication and responsiveness to their evolving wellness. As sponsor of Mr. Quentin Driscoll's membership at Lawnview you are a crucial part of this community.

It is our goal at Lawnview Senior Complex to provide a restraint-free environment for seniors that maximizes their physical and emotional wellness levels. When a senior's lifestyle cannot be maintained or improved at one level of care, our Ongoing Wellness Program™ evolves to address their changing life situation. When you signed our Comfort Contract™, you agreed to provide for this inevitable evolution. You consented to respond in a timely manner according to our professional, qualified assessment of Mr. Driscoll's changing life situation.

We have contacted you repeatedly regarding just such an assessment, but you have been unresponsive to our phone messages and letters. This certified letter will be considered as legally binding notification of Mr. Driscoll's condition. We refuse to be held liable for any failure on your part to respond to this formal, legal notification of our recommendations regarding Mr. Driscoll.

Mr. Driscoll joined Lawnview at Community Care™

Level 1. This is the level of living accorded to our most independent seniors, who require a minimum of supervision and health care as they conduct their daily lives. Four weeks ago Mr. Driscoll's residential adviser noticed that he had become withdrawn, choosing not to eat in the dining hall and foregoing several of his regular group activities. He then displayed inappropriate telephone behavior, resulting in his private telephone being removed. At his wellness interview on 9/1/93, Mr. Driscoll expressed distress over an incident that reportedly occurred during an out-of-center trip with you. As Mr. Driscoll remarked and our guest book confirms, you have not visited him since that out-of-center trip. Mr. Driscoll commented that you have not answered or returned his phone calls, inaction that apparently precipitated the inappropriate telephone behavior. This occasioned the first of our phone calls and letters to you, which went unanswered.

At his next wellness interview, on 9/8/93, Mr. Driscoll appeared unkempt and had difficulty engaging with his residential adviser. An apartment visit revealed that he had been subsisting on substandard pre-prepared foods that lay half-eaten and strewn about the apartment, attracting bugs. The residential adviser scheduled an extra Sunshine Cleaning Call™ (see attached invoice #102346) and advised Mr. Driscoll to resume his prepaid meal program in our communal dining room, but her recommendation was ignored. When the adviser made an extra Courtesy Visit™ (see attached invoice #102389), she ascertained that Mr. Driscoll was living under several misconceptions regarding his first wife, who we understand has been dead for over fifty years. Though previously a tidy man who took pride in his personal appearance, Mr. Driscoll was unkempt and exhibited an unwashed odor. A Happy Home Aide™ was dispatched (see attached invoice #102405) to administer a sponge bath.

Once-daily delivery of meals from the dining room to Mr. Driscoll's apartment was commenced.

Mr. Finnister, at each of these junctures we attempted to reach you via phone and mail to secure approval for these extra care measures but were stymied by your lack of response. As the Comfort Contract™ stipulates a margin of discretional care on our part, we implemented the aforementioned additional care measures, but the outer fiscal limit of this discretional care stipulation has been reached. Until you pay the combined amount indicated on the attached invoices *we can take no further steps to accommodate Mr. Driscoll's evolving wellness needs.* We *strongly* recommend that you upgrade Mr. Driscoll's residential status to Community Care™ Level 3, which includes daily visits from a residential adviser/home health aide and twice-daily meal delivery. Should Mr. Driscoll's wellness needs continue to evolve, you may wish to consider relocating him to The Glade™, which provides special care for special seniors in a group setting within the Health Center.

Mr. Finnister, you can see for yourself the urgency with which a response from you is required. We pride ourselves on maintaining the dignity of our community members. Failure to respond to this letter within seven days will result in a formal neglect complaint being filed against you and the commencement of proceedings to transfer Mr. Driscoll to a state facility.

Sincerely,
Yolanda Bogart
Department Manager
Lawnview Senior Complex Community Care™

A memorial service for Percy Cole was to be held that Sunday, when the chaplain would be on Gallups, but Cole's body was scheduled to leave the island by special ferry the morning following the autopsy. When Lydia again awoke earlier than usual, the happiness she had felt the morning before had turned into a pincer. As she stood by the window, the day no less clear and cool than its predecessor, her thoughts were metered by the flexions of this small, painful claw. To think of quarantine or Cole was to feel its pinch. She would not permit herself to think of Frank, a useless prohibition since the wind whispered his name.

She was thankful it had not been her job, at the autopsy's conclusion, to prepare the body for its departure. The ferry was scheduled to arrive before breakfast. She did not want to wait on the dock, where she would miss its progress from the compound, but neither did she wish to wait in the hospital or remain in her room. On leaving her barrack, she saw people at the flagpole. Ten men in gray uniforms stood at attention just outside the flag circle. She was puzzled by their placement until she realized they had positioned themselves within sight of the west ward windows. She knew if she glanced toward the hospital she would see the west warders standing at those windows. Within an instant she would be able to discern Frank's presence or absence among them. She was spared the decision to turn or not to turn by the appearance of Percy's corpse.

The draped stretcher, carried by Dr. Gold and Dr. Peterson, formed the head of a funerary procession composed of Nurse Foley and the four surviving junior medical officers. As the cortege crossed the flag circle, the volunteers fell into line behind Lydia. The west ward's sight lines fell short of this procession. Though Lydia had not turned toward the men at the windows, she could picture perfectly what they would see: ten men disappearing from view until all that remained was an empty compound. When the procession passed through the compound gates, the volunteers remained at its threshold, their arms raised in salute. This was as far as they were permitted to go. As long as the path toward the dock permitted the view, Lydia alternated between facing forward and turning to view their diminishing silhouettes.

She thought Dr. Gold might speak once the cortege gained the dock but he did not. In silence, Gold and Peterson carried the draped stretcher into the ferry's cabin and in silence they reemerged with empty hands. The mate untied the mooring lines and the ferry set off. They all stood on the dock until the boat was no longer visible and then, in silence, returned to the compound. By the time of their return, Percy Cole's honor guard was gone.

The meat served with that morning's breakfast reminded Lydia of dangling fingers. She gazed at her plate to avoid the sight of mouths chewing and swallowing. Beneath the white lab coats of her dining companions she could picture the broad, Y-shaped incisions that would divide their chests into three unequal portions.

Her eagerness to ascertain the health of the men in the west ward was equaled by her dread of discovering illness. She would arrive to the ward at exactly the time she had always arrived. She would distribute breakfast, she would look for signs of illness, and then she would leave. And she would accomplish these feats without once thinking of Percy.

The silence in the ward was not the natural quiet of morning but that of ten men holding their breaths.

"Nursie, is it true about the doctor?" Harry asked, but she did not look at him because his bed neighbored Frank's and she was not ready to look at Frank.

"Don't spare us the truth," George cautioned, " 'cause we already know he's gone."

"It coulda been one of the gobs," Sam insisted.

"But it wasn't no gob," George avowed. "Was it, Nursie?"

Images of the autopsy filled her mind. She tried to transform Cole into a man asleep; when that did not banish the image of his trisected chest, she pictured a field of flowers. "It wasn't a sailor," she confirmed once she was sure she could control her voice.

None of the men recall Nursie Lydia speaking. Her hair was untidy and her dress was creased and she stood completely still and quiet until Harry mentioned Frankie.

"And he's the one, ain't he?" Harry asked softly. "The one whose blood is in our veins?"

"Under our skin," Joe corrected. "If they'd put it in our veins we'd be dead already—no one can take a dead man's blood to the heart—but now we got dead man's blood under our skin and that's the undeniable truth."

"Can't they take it out?" Teddy asked. "Let them run a different test if they like, but this one's no good."

"I don't think something can be taken out once it's been put in," she whispered. To forestall further questions she directed her attention to the breakfast trays. She would have preferred to start at the row of beds headed by Teddy, but she had always begun with Harry. When she approached he leaned toward her.

"Frankie's sick," he said softly.

She heard a low buzzing in her ears. "What do you mean?" she asked, unsure how loudly or softly she had spoken.

Nursie Lydia's voice raised the hairs along Harry's arms and made him wish, for the first time, that Nurse Foley was handing out breakfast instead.

"See for yourself." Harry shrugged. "He was tossing and turning all night. He didn't want me to say nothing but I keep something like that to myself and it's on my conscience."

Lydia left the cart and crossed to Frank's bed. He was curled on one side, his eyes closed, but she could tell he was awake.

"Bentley," she said as evenly as possible, "Able tells me you're not feeling well."

He opened his eyes. "I'm fine," he said. His face was pale and gray circles ringed his eyes. She fought the urge to stroke his cheek. "I just didn't sleep too good last night."

According to all the men, Lydia was crying.

"He ain't been sleeping good for a few days now," Harry reported.

"I'm fine," he insisted. "I've had a lot on my mind is all. You promised not to tell," he accused in a voice that tripled Lydia's heart rate until she realized he was speaking to Harry. "I tell you it's nothing a walk outside won't fix, but in here I just stay all wound up."

"I know it, Frankie," Harry apologized, "but if it turns out it's something more serious I wouldn't be able to live with myself for keeping quiet."

"It's all right, Harry." He sighed. "I know you mean well."

"I'm taking your temperature," she announced. Her hand shook as she removed the thermometer from its case. She blocked her hand with her body to prevent anyone from witnessing, but Frank saw it all.

Frank took the thermometer and inserted it himself. Her hand was shaking so much he was afraid she would break it.

As she brought the thermometer to his mouth she set her eyes on the stretch of skin just below his lower lip. There was stubble there, just as there had been the night his chin had glanced her cheek. The thermometer would need to be in his mouth five minutes before she would know. She began delivering the trays, but now she could not hold them steady and she almost spilled Ralph's breakfast. She finished the first row of beds and started on the second. If everyone acted as they were supposed to, she might survive the minute that remained before she would have to read the thermometer. She returned to Frank's bed, silently counting her steps as she went: one, two, three, four, five, six, seven. The numbers crowded out her other thoughts and that was why she clung to them. She continued her silent counting once she reached him, now counting the small blunt hairs emerging from the soft stretch of skin below the swell of his mouth. She had barely begun before the thermometer was no longer between his lips. She held the thermometer, still moist from his mouth, in her shaking hand. She would allow herself one moment before looking at the mercury. She would allow herself one more.

"You have a slight fever," she quavered, her voice carving a Y-shaped incision through the silence. "I'm going to call for the doctor."

"You don't have to do that," he said, his voice low and steady. Perhaps he was trying to hypnotize her.

"Of course I do!" she exclaimed.

"It's nothing," he persisted. "I always get like this when I don't get a good night's sleep."

Other voices might have spoken then; she was not sure. It was all she could do to discern his words from the buzzing in her ears.

"Don't move," she commanded, sounding like she was underwater. She pointed at him the way a teacher points out an errant student. She knew she could not so much as brush her hand against his shoulder. She walked toward the door.

"Liddie, don't." The name pinned her in place. "Liddie," he called.

"Please don't call me that," she whispered, her mouth gone dry. "Please don't call me that here."

Frank was speaking as much for her sake as for his. When she announced he had a fever she sounded like a crazy woman.

The door was quite close now. She would reach it in three steps. The thought of having to hold her hand steady enough to unlock the door with her key was almost enough to make her shriek, but then she fit the key in the lock. The lock turned.

She was a small cog in a large machine. She filled her mind with the clicks of a cog as she completed her designated circuit. She found a doctor; she said the requisite words, and trailing him, she returned to quarantine. Somewhere along the way she was joined by the other doctors and an escort with a wheeled gurney. Each doctor was trying to be the first to reach the quarantine door without it looking like that was what he was doing. She could barely hear for the buzzing in her ears but she could read the doctors' intentions perfectly. The doctor who won the race was Dr. Peterson, with his squirrel's face and his clever fingers that did not tremble as they opened locks.

Frank had straightened his pajamas and started his breakfast, but he was pale.

"There's nothing wrong with me, Doc," he insisted, shuttling food to his mouth. No one else was eating.

"Nurse Wickett reports you have a fever," one of the doctors said.

"Aw, she's just upset over all that's been going on." He shrugged. She prayed he would not look at her but when her prayer was answered, she did not feel grateful.

"It's probably nothing," one of the doctors lied, "but just in case, you wouldn't want to get your buddies sick, would you?"

"But isn't that the whole point?" Frank said. "You want me and my buddies sick, but we ain't been obliging you and that makes you look bad, especially now that Dr. Percy—"

She shook her head. It was bad to say that name here.

"I think you'd better do what the doc here says," the escort cautioned, moving toward the bed.

Frank raised his hands. His fork gleamed in the light coming through the windows. "Where're we going, Doc?" He sighed. "To the gobs' room?"

"That's right, Bentley," one of them said.

"That the room where Dr. Percy was?" he asked, looking toward her, but she could do nothing. There was nothing she could do at all.

"Don't worry," one replied. "You're going to be just fine."

"Dr. Percy wasn't fine," he said, "and I've got his blood."

None of the other men spoke. As terrible as this moment was, she would have done anything to freeze it in place, barring the arrival of something worse.

"Cole died of complications due to pneumonia," one of them explained slowly, as though speaking to a child. "You've no need to worry on that score. Pneumonia is not hematogenous."

"That's a nice ten-dollar word, Doc," he replied. "But answer me this: if you don't even know how people get the flu, how do you expect me to believe you know how they catch pneumonia?"

"I don't like the way you're holding that fork, Bentley," the escort warned and moved toward the gurney. "I think you'd better calm down."

Frank dropped the fork soundlessly on the bed. "I'm calm," he replied. "I'm talking nice and calm—ain't I, Sammy?"

"You're calm as a clam, Frankie," Sam assured him.

He nodded. "You see? Don't worry, Doc, I ain't gonna be any trouble. I'm going now."

The escort held the gurney steady while Frank climbed onto it. On the gurney he looked inert, as if his body had been replaced with clay.

"We're with ya, Frankie!"

"Don't let 'em getcha!"

All the voices were calling out at once. She did not know how he could possibly keep them straight.

"Don't anyone else get sick," he answered. "You've done your part. Now you can all go home."

"You too, Frankie! You're going home too!"

"I know I am," he replied. "All I need's a good night's sleep, and away from Georgie's snoring I'll be sure to get it, so don't give away my bed."

"We won't, Frankie. It'll be here waiting," the voices called as he was wheeled out the door.

For the rest of the day, the world existed on the other side of a gray curtain. She performed her duties; she avoided the sailors' room; she ate at the expected times. In the dining hall the talk was of the future. Some wanted to be done with Gallups while others hoped their efforts might be salvaged after all. Even looking at the moving mouths she could not attach the streams of words to names or faces. She was thankful no one spoke to her. She was not sure what would happen if she tried to talk.

Cecil tried to speak to Lydia several times, but she was in some sort of fog that made him wonder if the rumors about her and the graybacks were true.

The sun set. She told herself she was tired. She donned her nightclothes and buried herself under the blankets even though it was only seven. She closed her eyes and repeated the word "sleep" to herself so many times the word lost all meaning and became only the sound of her mind struggling against itself. And then at some point, sleep came.

When she startled awake the moon shone brightly through her window. Someone was crying. She put her hand to her mouth, but it was not her—the sound was coming from Cynthia Foley's bedroom. In the hallway the noise was louder. The bedroom door was thinner than their shared wall. She knocked, softly at first and then with more force.

"Joe?" came Cynthia's voice from the other side of the door.

Lydia heard the creak of a mattress, followed by footsteps, but she disappeared before the footsteps could reach the door.

Outside it was cold but she did not mind. Nor did she mind the small, sharp pebbles as she crossed the compound. She did not worry about being seen. She did not worry about anything except how fast she could reach Frank's room.

She had never been in the hospital so late at night. In the silence of the building she found it difficult to believe anyone save herself was inside. She fought the urge to yell his name as she neared the door. She turned the knob. There was his bed, the only curtained bed in the far row. She trembled as she crept toward the curtain. It was not too late to turn back. She could hear his exhalations, slow and regular, from inside the curtain. She could return in the morning. But even as she took a step backward, her hand reached toward the curtain and slowly, quietly, eased it aside.

He slept on his back, one arm at his side, the other thrown above his head, the bedsheet rising and falling with his untroubled breath. His color had returned. She knew his forehead would not feel warm if she touched it.

As she closed the curtain she heard him whisper.

"Liddie?"

He opened his eyes.

"I knew it was you," he said.

"I'm sorry," she whispered. "You ought to go back to sleep."

"Don't go," he answered. "I'm wide awake. I slept all afternoon. If we whisper I'm sure we won't wake anyone."

"I should go."

"Don't," he countered. "Not yet."

"Are you truly feeling better?" she asked.

"Feel my forehead."

"I don't need to," she answered. "I can tell you don't have a fever."

"So can I."

More than ten years later, after she had died, Frank returned to this memory of his wife to comfort him. What woke him up at that moment was not the sound but the smell of her, a clean smell that made him think of sunlight on skin which he took for perfume but which proved to be her own simple scent.

"You don't have the flu," she whispered.

"I don't have the flu," he echoed.

"Frank," she said.

One of the sailors shifted in his sleep. The room was filled with the interwoven rhythms of breath. She had missed that sound, the simple confirmation that she was not alone.

"Stay with me," he urged. "Just for a little while."

She took a step away from the bed and then toward it. She reached her hand toward the edge of the mattress and slowly, quietly, eased herself down. She thought she had never seen his face so clearly, or in such soft light.

· · ·

OUR MAIL BAG

Positive Outlook Is the Best Medicine

To the Editor of the *Herald:*

I am writing to remind your readers not to give in to fear. Fear is more than just a feeling: it disorders the thoughts, heightens the pulse, and weakens judgment. In such a state it is no wonder influenza is getting the best of us, for a fearful body is an open door for disease. As long as we cower inside our homes, wondering whom influenza will strike next, we will remain in sway to this terrible fiend. Fight back! Greet the morning with a song and a smile on your face! Do not tender influenza the honor of speaking its name, for in doing so you increase the fear inside your person. If the disease must be spoken of at all, give it some other name, preferably a playful term that weakens its power on the imagination. With my children I have begun to call influenza "that dirty dog" and I cannot tell you what a difference it has made! It is difficult not to smile when speaking such a funny name and, as we all know, a smile is the antidote to fear. I think it is precisely this attitude that has spared my family from serious illness.

MRS. HOWARD VEERS,
38 Hereford Street

Darling Sara—

To think that I will soon be able to hold you again! I have
tried so hard to become the man you wanted me to be. The
years have been lonely, but with you back again they will all
have been worth it. Once you return I know that our dear
boy will come back too. He could never stand to be away
from his mama.

I will keep this letter short because I have a feeling we will
be seeing each other very soon. In fact I think I hear your
footsteps coming down the hall! Ha!

. . .

April 15, 1931

Dear Quentin Driscoll,

Many years ago I sent you a letter that I said would be the
last. I will make this short. I am very ill. Please send the
money that is rightfully mine.

Lydia

Author's Note

The 1918 influenza epidemic—whose cause is still a matter of debate—killed more Americans in ten months than died in all twentieth-century wars combined, and killed well over 20 million people worldwide. The epidemic is generally thought to have originated in the United States and to have shipped overseas with American soldiers en route to the final battles of World War One.

Gallups Island (now known as Gallops Island), in Boston Harbor, was in November and December of 1918 the site of a United States Public Health Service study designed to determine the cause and mode of spread of influenza. The subjects—inmate volunteers taken from the Deer Island Naval Prison—were subjected to the tests described in this book's later chapters. The only person to catch the flu was a junior medical officer, who died.

Most of the newspaper articles in this book are taken from period newspapers.

A slew of nonfiction works contributed to the writing of this book, but I am particularly indebted to *America's Forgotten Pandemic* by Alfred Crosby and *The Plague of the Spanish Lady* by Richard Collier for their insight into the 1918 epidemic; and to *South Boston, My Home Town* by Thomas O'Connor and *I Remember Southie* by Leo Dauwer for their portraits of life in early twentieth-century South Boston. Dr. Ed Uthman kindly shared his knowledge of period autopsies.

Thanks to the New York and Boston Public Libraries and the Library of Congress for their lovely reference librarians, their beautiful reading rooms, and their smorgasbord of reference materials.

Thanks to Wendy Schmalz, agent extraordinaire; and Bill Thomas, ready editor. Thanks to Maria Carella, Christine Pride, Shauna Toh, and Alice van Straalen.

Thanks to Stefan Economou and Ruth Murray for hosting my Boston expeditions.

Thanks to Mark, Ellen, and Saryn Goldberg for unflagging love and support.

In the five years it took to write this book I relied on the honesty, intelligence, and advice of Julie Ashley, Oliver Broudy, David Gassaway, Megan Kelso, Jason Little, Chloe Mills, Lisa Rosenthal, and Michael Wilde to help keep this book from foundering or veering terribly off-course. I am honored to call each of them reader, editor, and friend.